The Chronicles of Trevel:
Dragon Tears

By Gregga J. Johnn

Copyright © 2015 Gregga J. Johnn & Story-in-the-Wings.

All rights reserved.

No part of this book may be reproduced or transmitted in any form or by any means, graphic, electronic, or mechanical, including photocopying, recording, taping, or by any information storage retrieval system, without the permission, in writing, of the publisher.

For more information, send a letter to:

Email: greggajjohnn@gmail.com

Story-in-the-Wings at Springhill Farm

1446 Arrowhead Rd

Cedar Rapids, Ia. 52314

For information about special discounts for bulk purchases, please contact Gregga J. Johnn, at

greggajjohnn@gmail.com

ISBN: 978-1515306122

SECOND EDITION

(A special thanks to **Aubree Pinckney** for her eager assistance. The Power of the Universe bless the Dragon Prince born of thee.)

Dedication

This tale is dedicated to my sons:

Shiloh, Andy, and Luke

In memory of a cousin whose light, though extinguished, still manages to get through the cracks:

Kristian Anderson, 1975–2012

Life, Love, and Liberty are what you make of them, so continue, continue, continue . . .

Table of Contents

Title   *page*

Preface and Introduction   9
Geography   10
Nine Energies of the Trevel Universe   11

Prologue
    Mystic Vision   13
    Introduction   13

Chapter 1
    The Boy   16
    The Mines   18
    The Cities   20
    Royalty   22
    Close Call   24
    Boom!   26
    Thunderstorm   28

Chapter 2
    Little Girls   31
    "Wattle-Gum" No More   34
    Cheers!   35
    Foster Home   38
    Blue Castle   40
    Tears.   41

Chapter 3
    The Healer   45
    A Mountain Life   48
    The Party   51
    Finances and Farewell   54

Chapter 4
    Family   59
    Miss Taylor   62
    Goodbye Song   65

ANL Binay	67
The Caravan	70
Pirates	72
Gash Again	74

Chapter 5

Dragon Mist	77
Royal Surprise	80
Years Ago	82
Local School Boy	84
Rio	88
The Proposal	90
Sights	94

Chapter 6

The Game Is On	99
Trips and Tickles	104
Curious	107
Emergency!	111
The Connection	114

Chapter 7

An Invitation	119
Royal Court	122
Welcome Indeed	124
Private Escort	129

Chapter 8

First Class Attention	135
The Morning After	141
Scholarship Particulars	145
Apology Arranged	148

Chapter 9

Marina	152
Fare Thee Well	154
Registration	159

Relative Freedom	167
Great Expectations	173

Chapter 10

Captain's Assistant	180
Aboard	184
Scholarship Perks	186
Janeiroan Brat Pack	193
A Horrifying Discovery	194

Chapter 11

Falk's Landing	201
A Rush	206
The Stilwells	213
The Luau	218
Two Tutors	222

Chapter 12

A Letter	233
Sydney Port of Call	239
Science Expedition	246
Return to Snowy Mountain	251

Chapter 13

The Tube Takes Time	257
The Port of Hanain	264
New Management	266
Lord Deagan	279

Chapter 14

Torres Entrance	290
Dating Games	294
Parting	301
Lemuria	307
The Garden and the Gardener	313

Chapter 15

The First Night's Ball	321

No Chance	332
Gash Arabol	336
Poolside	341
Laray	346
Hadigan in Motion	349

Chapter 16

Shocking News	352
Marina's Orders	355
Lemuria	356
Hadigan's Silvertongue	361
Laboratory Discoveries	368
Physiochemical Recognition	378
Last Night before School	383

Chapter 17

The Stables	395
Bonjour!	401
Marina's Match	406
Bowra House	410
Settling In	417

Chapter 18

Lord Deagan Revealed	422
Mail Call	424
Courtesan Court Case	429
Engineering vs. Mutation	434
A Shock	438
The Defense Secretary's Secret	441

Chapter 19

Mitch's Appointment	446
Lord Deagan at ANA	454
The NLL Arrives	461
Fur and Metal	464

    Tanya Touched   471

Chapter 20
    Colonah's Offering   478
    Parental Protection   481
    A Strong Fulcrum   484
    Championship Lineup   490
    A Key Assignment   496

Chapter 21
    Cupid's Contract   502
    A Clean Discovery   505
    The Big Game   508
    Halftime   514
    Who's the Rogue Now?   519

Chapter 22
    Out of Sight   522
    Face-Off   525
    Unlikely Rescue   529
    Marina Breaks Trust   531

Chapter 23
    Hanain Refuge   538
    Funeral for the Ages   540
    Psyche   543
    The Unraveling   546

Epilogue
    The Pact Continues   550
    Marina's Return   551

Dragon Song Lullaby   555

Review Request   556

About the Author   557

End Notes / Book Lists   558

Preface and Introduction

The *Trevel Universe* is a place where fantasy and reality collide; where truth breeds her lies in shadow and the dark is the brightest place to shine.

All human legend, fairy tales, and stories of super human and mutant, or alien powers originate in the history of the Trevel.

To be Trevel is to be "at one with the power of the universe." To be Bacht is to be "powerless, or human."

But, these definitions are strictly from the Trevel who despise the Bacht for consistently refusing to bow to them as gods.

The Bacht (humans) don't even know they are the Bacht.

Geography

The Trevel have lived upon the Earth since before any can remember and at one time walked among the Uplanders as gods. However, the humans (or Bacht), have a disease of spirit. They consistently refuse to be ruled and choose rather to rebel against their divine guides.

A great migration of the Trevel civilization was orchestrated at the sinking of Atlantis, which granted the Bacht their desire to be left alone.

Further transfers of civilization occurred throughout the latter years and now over 80% of Trevel live in caverns within the continental shelves hundreds of feet below sea level. Some still hide their true identities and share the Upland with the Bacht, but only out of necessary co-existence.

Human history is littered with the interruption, interference and sometimes, the intercession of the Trevel.

The Nine Energies of the Trevel Universe:

1} Illumination

2} Air

3} Electricity

4} Fire

5} Water

6} Fauna (animal)

7} Flora (plant)

8} Earth (& mineral)

9} Metal (& ore)

The Trevel have the ability to bend and manipulate Energy in manifestations of defense, attack, or simple daily convenience.

Most Trevel have one major and one minor in Energy, yet some double up in either a major or minor manifestation. Some even have a triple blend in minors, however, as rare as only in myth and legend is the Chameleon Energist who has access to all nine.

Prologue

The nature of the Deeper Evil is appealing, attentive, accommodating, and patient.

Mystic Vision

The image was clear and vivid.

In her sleep, Colonah saw two women: one surrounded by family in a tree-cliff house, encompassed by Blue Mountains, the other alone in a rocky, underground blue castle. Both women were in pain. Both women were giving birth.

Colonah watched the agony continue until finally a son was born to family and a daughter was born to solitude. Fire sprayed as Colonah sneezed out of sleep. The five-foot red dragon called to her flock. She would share the vision with the dragon colony so they could seek out the time of the boy and the girl.

Introduction

Below the Great Barrier Reef, off the coast of Queensland, Australia is the most magnificent sight hidden from the eyes of the entire Bacht population. That is,

"The 'human' factor," Franc Belle snorted these words as a curse whenever anyone even thought of the Bacht in his presence.

Although his buildings and design company, Belle's Architecture, had been accused of reflecting Bacht elements, he insisted that they were influenced by him, not the other way around.

The term Bacht is the name given to any of the powerless, namely the current Upland inhabitants of the planet Earth.

The Trevel are not of their kind.

Thousands of years have brought about a mixing of the races. There is little difference between the pure Trevel families and the mixed ones; it is only that the mixed families do not know if their offspring will be powerful Trevel or powerless Bacht. It is rumored that some pure marriages have produced the rare powerless Bacht, but they are just rumors.

Mystery surrounds the origin of the Trevel. Some say it was celestial, some say it was beneath the earth. It is even said that they are images of a higher mind. It is only known that in ancient days, they came to seek dominance over the Bacht.

At first, the goal was to blend the two races and create a divine breed. They would live in the skies in a great tower that rose above the clouds. Only a sudden disaster of linguistic complication divided the Bacht races, causing them to abandon the project and disperse to the ends of the Earth.

"Any unification and true dominance on our Trevel part is now a completely unrealistic option." Nimrod, the strongest of all the Trevel kings, shattered the table at which he sat, horrified to think that perhaps he must resign himself to a quiet leadership rather than ultimate dominance.

"We can't control the Bacht." The table crunched under his pacing. "Their frames maybe ridiculously fragile, but we cannot contain their spirit."

Later, in continued efforts of domination, individual Trevel set themselves up over the larger civilizations, seeking a supernatural status in the Bacht society. Surprisingly, the Bacht continued to revolt, sometimes subconsciously as they simply ceased to believe in the existence of the Trevel.

When the manipulation of natural energy was mastered and engineered, the Trevel, to save their lifestyle from the growing number of Bacht, took the opportunity to vanish beneath the waters. Thus, as a civilization, they were gone.

Some remnant Trevel still strove for dominance, and others chose to live in harmony with the Bacht. Thus began the mixing of the races, and the secret lives of the Trevel began to weave in and out of Bacht history.

Today, about twenty percent of the Trevel population lives happily in the human world, and the humans don't even know they are the Bacht.

The Boy
The Mines
The Cities
Royalty
Close Call
Boom!
Thunderstorm

Chapter 1

The Boy

Wattle-Gum Gecko Mitchell was three years old when he first saw anyone outside the Commune. The "Community" of Nimbin, Australia, was a happy, hot place to live. Everyone shared; everyone cared. Sometimes he quite forgot which of the uncles and aunties he played with were actually Daddy and Mummy.

Today, when the commune truck arrived, carrying town supplies and mail, Wattle-Gum was chasing a blue-tongued lizard. His shoulder-length, white-blond curls were tied up in a pretty ponytail, and his girlish features deceived any who didn't already know him.

A special letter arrived that day from his gamma and papa in Brazil; airline tickets!

It didn't take long to pack up their few belongings and hitch a ride to Lismore, another hot and lovely town in northern New South Wales. From there, they took a bus to Brisbane, then flew south to Sydney.

Wattle-Gum had never seen so many people dressed so strangely. All the people were shiny clean and wore clothes that covered all of their bodies. He also noticed that, for some reason, people called him a "pretty little girl."

Too many people and too much noise all ended when he slept soundly for the first time in days on the big plane that would take them across the ocean to his Brazilian family.

Mummy and Daddy argued about how long they would stay in Brazil. Mummy had been born in Brazil and had not seen her family in years. But Daddy didn't think Mummy's family liked him, and Mummy was sure they didn't.

Brazil was hot, too. There were still too many people but, everyone was nice and they stayed for half a year. Well, Daddy went home after three weeks.

Wattle-Gum forgot his name for a while. They called him Nino now or Gummo. Mummy cried a lot, and Grandpapa went away on a trip with someone called Angel.

Gamma was strong, so everyone kept saying. Wattle-Gum just thought she looked scary.

Mummy and Wattle-Gum finally went home after he was just about as confused as he could get. Where did he live? Where was he now? When would Daddy come home? But he liked the medicine Mummy gave him, and he woke up feeling much better, suddenly in Lismore.

They visited home: the commune, which was suddenly no longer home.

Now, in Lismore, Wattle-Gum learned his school lessons above the café that Mummy ran. Daddy still did not come home. Wattle-Gum forgot what Daddy looked like. He even forgot he'd had his hair cut in Brazil. It was long again and always in a ponytail at his neck.

Other kids laughed at him, but he had the last laugh. They went to school while he had lessons at home, and he could read any book he liked.

By eight years of age, Wattle-Gum had read many of the books on plants, animals, and alternative living in the local bookshop.

He wondered why anyone would want to live in a house. He was above a shop; everyone knew him and he played in the street.

Why would anyone want to stay inside? There was too much sun, wind, and rain to experience. And above all, why would anyone want to be quiet?

He cried to the wind, squealed in the rain, and chattered nonstop to anyone who passed in the lovely hot sunshine, for summer was best of all.

The Mines

Beneath the Great Barrier Reef, the water, the coral, and the ocean floor are caverns full of power—some might even say magic. Magic it is, if magic is found in the forces that hold the universe together.

Trevel minds are wider and can reach further into the air we breathe and touch the energies that flow through all things. "Magic" is in the redirection of Energy, and the redirection of Energy is in the hand of the one whose mind can draw from it and bend it.

It is the magic in the Mines of Hanain that causes the beauty of the Great Reef above. The essence of the power-force from processing the mined jewels feeds and enriches the Barrier, a glory enjoyed by all.

These mines contain an expansive yet concentrated measure of jewels and precious metals, twisted and distorted in a dizzying dance like that of an addict in delirium.

As riches buy power, the mines also contain a rustic gathering of peoples from all over the Trevel civilization. They come for the glory dipped in grime, then leave with the stench of their own greed.

"Those towns, my Prince, are not for you." The Senate Minister always warned, "They are full of dark people."

He insisted on restricting the movements of the boy, Prince Hadigan.

"Stay in the City Clusters. They are full of more light."

Those Clusters, so full of light, were many, and they were the focus of the young royal's curious imaginings. He memorized the facts of each flourishing development down to the smallest outpost.

A complete understanding of his father's, King Darsaldain's, entire empire was the desire of the boy, who was destined to become the Prince-in-One and heir to the throne of Lemuria, Atlantis, and the entire Trevel expansion.

The Cities

Atlantis is the center of trade and commerce. It exists today, 300 feet below the ocean in caverns, built into the oceanic continental shelves, coated in Trevel technology.

There is a force, HDP (hydro-plano) that can hold back the waters like a window holds out the rain. The cavern entrances are built with a double HDP wall that flows and sucks water and oxygen in and out with the tide.

Connections are made where the HDP touches the ocean and the ocean touches the air above. Everything is connected by the forces of energy that flow through them.

Through this flow, complete and complex climates are imitated to recreate what occurs above. Thus, one sunny day, Upland is enjoyed also by the Trevel nation's Underland.

Bacht can and do survive in these surroundings. Even the transports of the Bacht, with a little HDP mechanics, drive, sail, and fly into the docks of the great city Clusters.

The busy White Circle City of Atlantis is set in the depths among great arches, columns, and supports. There it thrives with businesses and many a townhouse, or second home away from the deeper Underland country estates, for a large, growing aristocracy.

But the wealthy Trevel aren't the only inhabitants of the circle cities. All manner of peoples and creatures populate these energized and magical places.

In the middle of the city, at the top, are the places of centralized defense and tradition that trickle into high set living. Further around the spiral are comfortable middle class sets, and then on, down to the most ragamuffin of street urchins in the lowest levels.

There are enough characters living out their daily grind here to fill the largest of imaginations.

The military is also welcomed with open arms. To the Trevel, they are called the Strategist, or Strategic Defense Force. They fully support the current royal family, led by King Darsaldain.

The king does not reside in Atlantis, however.

The Royal White Circle City of Lemuria is the second largest nation city cluster. It is the center of all society and government. Here, Trevel royalty rights are not passed down strictly by birth.

A king has every right to elect his successor from wherever he wishes, but only as long as the Senate vote agrees with his choice.

Royalty

King Darsaldain has one son, Prince Hadigan. The Senate would have the king choose someone other than Hadigan to succeed him, for, from an early age, Hadigan exhibited distasteful choices. Yet the king has dreams of glory for his son and hangs on in life to see if he can prove the boy fit to be king.

"I will not die," Darsaldain whispered from behind the bed curtains.

The Senate Minister rolled his eyes at the Trade Minister, the Strategist Director, and a number of other government heads in the quiet room.

They had all been here before. It was best to count the number of times the king's health had failed by the age of his son.

Hadigan had been two weeks old the first time. The queen had died due to an illness from the birthing process, and the king lost interest in life without his wife. The next few times, Hadigan was six, nine, ten, and twelve.

Each time, the boy was hustled into the Poseidon Memorial Parthenon, ready to be crowned at a moment's notice.

Five times Hadigan was expected to ready himself to take the throne. What does that do to a young boy? If he were close to his father, he would be glad not to be king. However, if he were ambitious and kept away from his father due to the business of royal life, the result might be less favorable.

"Let us hope this visit is also wasted," said the Senate Secretary, chilled by the night air as he watched through the massive arched doors of the Poseidon Memorial Parthenon. The Senate Minister would arrive, maybe soon, and tell them if the boy, now fourteen, could go free or stay to take on the crown.

"I hope he doesn't die. I'm not ready, yet."

The Secretary nodded meaningfully and patted the young teen's shoulder.

Hadigan Andrew Hades Darsaldain, the handsome prince, desirable to all the young girls of society, turned as if to wipe tears and snorted through a slender, strong nose over pinched and furious lips. He was not ready, not ready to make his move in a revolt.

Hadigan's plans required many years yet. He fully intended to be king, but he knew the Senate would never allow him access to the power that would make him the greatest leader the Trevel nations had ever known, even above Poseidon, Zeus, or Hades, after whom he'd been named.

He must first complete his higher-level school training, preferably taking every course the school offered so as to not miss a thing. Then, power required money. Yes, his family was on a significant salary, but it was never enough.

Hadigan was a born businessman, and he believed that the key to it all was in the Mines. The Mines of Hanain were the centerpiece for his round table of power.

His chin-length hair was black and curly. It served as a good veil to cover his determined, ambitious eyes and complimented the compelling, handsome figure.

"I will have the Mines," he murmured, and smiled as the Senate Minister waved heartily at the Hall entrance to say that the king was well that morning.

"But," Hadigan smiled, genuinely relieved, "what of Latoona?"

Close Call

Some years later, Hadigan had the chance to visit the growing resort village of Latoona located in the Upland jungles of the Amazon, but not without consequence.

The marketplace rocked under the fire and smoke. Even the thousands of jungle birds, squawking and screaming and shooting into the sky, could not be heard over the explosions.

It began by the chemistry potions booth, the most fire prone of all the booths. There was a chain reaction that made it impossible to tell if there were further bombs or just fire spreading.

Hadigan hit the floor with three Strategist Agents on top of him. This was a blatant attack on the royal family! Everyone ran everywhere, and it was impossible to make a head count.

A camouflage Hummer showered the Agent pile with cool, wet dirt, and there was barely a break in time before they were all inside, pawing at the prince trying to confirm that he had sustained no royal injuries.

Hadigan looked dazed, but his personal Agent could not tell if it was from shock about the attempt on his life or a high form of excitement; if he was enjoying the experience.

Hadigan had always been a thrill seeker.

Last year, Hadigan had been kidnapped, and the terrorists demanded such an exorbitant amount of money that it drained the family's charity budget for the year. Hadigan had been found, tied to the cavern roof, only inches from the incoming tide of the entrance walls. His manic laughter was naturally a reaction to the trauma he'd experienced, but watching the boy recover that night as he pushed his muscles beyond his usual strength work, his personal Agent began to suspect that the boy liked all the drama.

As the vehicle drove on, unseen by the jungle, the Agents buzzed and hustled around Hadigan, reporting the horror to their superiors by hydrotel.

Hadigan's personal agent crushed an HDP bead in his hand and it opened up as water falling in a circle, hovering above his palm. The stern face of his commanding director answered through the center of the water,

"Report."

"There has been an assassination attempt, sir. All are accounted for and the seal is intact with no physical injuries appearing," the agent responded.

The commanding director listened to the personnel with him and ordered,

"Get to the extraction point; co-ordinates to follow."

A series of latitude and longitude points followed and the agent squeezed his fist around the HDP bead again. It closed and was returned to a small shoulder pocket

As they drove off, Hadigan could not keep his eyes off the fire that licked around the village of Latoona. The reflection flickered hungrily in his eyes.

Boom!

Salla Dijex walked past the double cradle quietly and smiled over the sleeping heads. Baby Tanya curled around tiny baby Holly, and they slept in perfect peace. Tanya was just over a year old; Holly was a newborn.

They were cradle mates with different memas.

Beth and Salla, best friends from school, took turns watching each other's daughter while the other went to work in the famous Latoona Village Market.

The sudden jolt of the cradle startled both babies awake, and they screamed in protest. Salla did not move to quiet them. The cradle swung up forcefully, and Salla stepped backward against the heat wall that surged through the house.

The door was open to admit the cool summer breeze, but now it only let in the horrific vision of flames crawling ten feet into the air.

The babies screamed again, and the neighbor girl ran over, frightened, seeking comfort.

"Watch the girls. You'll be fine," Salla told her, and ran to the fire.

The entire market, as well as the new resort construction site, was entwined in smoke. A partially invisible Hummer nearly ran Salla over as it careened out of the chaos.

In the next hours, injuries were catalogued and assigned healers in order of urgency. Salla worked frantically for fear that she wouldn't see her husband in the line of the injured. Finally, he came. A quick bandage on his arm was all it took for them to break the silence before she asked about Beth and Dan.

"They will never hurt again." A streak of clean slipped down Hal's cheek, and Salla joined him in his grief.

"We can't separate them." Salla and Hal sat in the kitchen rocking Holly and Tanya to sleep.

"We won't," Hal reassured his wife. "We will keep them both and raise them as sisters."

"I think we should keep the secret about which one of them lost her mema and deda today," Salla concluded thoughtfully.

"I agree. They'll both be equally ours."

The girls were laid back down in their double cradle as the village quieted itself with the soft hiss of an extinguished tragedy.

Thunderstorm

The rain was so thick that the other side of the road was lost to the waterfall. Wattle-Gum watched through the window over the café. Still eight years old, he was proud that Mummy thought he was old enough to be left at home alone for a little bit while she ran down to the bank.

A long time had gone by, although he knew it always seemed longer than it really was. But then, he heard the music for their favorite TV show. He and Mummy watched it together every night; she would never miss that. It must be nearly an hour by now.

Wattle-Gum dialed the triple "0" on the phone to call the police because he knew that Officer Terry was working tonight.

"Police, what's your emergency?"

"Hi, Linda, it's me, Wattle-Gum."

"Hey, hon, what's up?" Linda couldn't bring herself to call him by his name. "Tell your mum not to bring her pie down tonight; the road's all washed up."

Wattle-Gum was silent for a bit.

"My mum's not there?"

"No kiddo, I haven't seen her tonight."

The bank was right by the police station, and Mummy liked to drop off pies and pastries for the night shift when she was down there.

"She's been gone nearly an hour and our favorite TV show has started. She'd never miss that."

"Hang on…" Linda called through to the other room, "Terry, Rachael's been gone an hour and is supposed to have come down here. Have you seen her?"

"Is that Mitchell on the phone?" Terry switched Wattle-Gum's first name for his last.

Linda nodded.

"Tell him I'll come get him." Officer Terry grabbed his slicker and keys on the way out the station door.

When Terry arrived at the little apartment above the café, he grabbed a few things and took the boy down to the police station to watch the telly there.

Terry said he would tell Mummy where they were. Bruce, the other officer on duty, had gone out driving in the pelting rain, checking things out around town. Terry was called out to join him, and Wattle-Gum was left with Linda. He fell asleep on Terry's cot in the locker room.

Donuts were waiting for Wattle-Gum's breakfast, and he learned that Mummy had been in a car accident and was in the hospital in Brisbane.

Officer Terry took Wattle-Gum on the two-hour drive to go and see her.

She didn't talk when they got there. Wattle-Gum was allowed to go in and see her while she slept. He would not believe what the doctor said: that she wouldn't wake up.

There was a lovely lady with long, curly hair, just like his. She took him to a hotel. They stayed there for two very quiet days until Wattle-Gum's favorite toys and clothes arrived.

That afternoon, he stood in the cemetery and was expected to say goodbye. Such a ridiculous request made Wattle-Gum very angry, but he didn't feel like telling anyone.

He and Danny, the lady, then drove south to Sydney. It was an eighteen-hour drive, all toilet stops included, and finally Wattle-Gum was allowed to go to bed in a tall, red brick building.

> Little Girls
> "Wattle-Gum" No More
> Cheers!
> Foster Home
> Blue Castle
> Tears

Chapter 2

Little Girls

> *"A dragon tear for you,*
>
> *A dragon tear for me,*
>
> *Will you ever see-*
>
> *Dragons come to tea?*
>
> *The song will rise above*
>
> *The new song down below;*
>
> *See the dragon come,*
>
> *See the dragon go."*

A group of little girls skipped around in a circle tossing flower petals into the air. The light-hearted singing rose above them in the summer breeze.

"If you're not careful, the dragons will answer your calling," an old man sitting in the shade warned them with a smile and a wink.

The girls giggled and, throwing the petal-less flowers at him, ran off to the river fountain.

"While you're there, Tanya, Holly, get me a jarful."

The two girls ran back to their mema, Salla Dijex, to fetch the pretty jar she held out. Other memas called the same, and each of the girls left carrying a jar up the hillside to the fresh spring outlet.

The river itself was a simple water source, but at the top by the spring, some of the water slid through a little tunnel and bounced into a good-sized well. This was where the girls headed.

The tunnel was the key. It was full of mineral deposits that supplied the drinking water with such nourishment that it could refresh the heaviest heart or spirit. It was nicknamed, "dragon tears" by the locals, in honor of their very real and rather secret dragon neighbors.

On special occasions, the Latoona villagers would bottle up their mineral water and give it as a precious gift to an honored guest. This practice is what brought fame to the little jungle outpost. Bottled Dragon Tears were a rare and precious commodity.

The group of little girls chatted as they took turns drawing from the well.

"I've seen a dragon," Tanya whispered to her friends.

"You have not."

"When?"

"One sang over me when I was born, sang over Holly, too," Tanya insisted.

"Did not."

"Anyway, how could you remember that? You were just a baby."

Both Tanya and Holly leaned in close. They chanted fearfully:

"Once you've seen a dragon,

You never forget their song.

Once you've seen a dragon,

Your life will never go wrong."

The other girls joined in, giggling.

"Once you've seen a dragon,

Your heart will always be strong."

They got a little louder.

"Once you've seen a dragon . . ."

They shouted to the sky,

"Your tales will always be long!"

Laughter spilled water all around, and the pack of giggles floated back down to the village.

On the other side of the river, hidden by the jungle, was a large crater, the only remnant of the market explosion from seven years ago.

On the far side of that, a five-foot red "something" sank down and slithered on four feet back through the trees, humming the happy song.

"Wattle-Gum" No More

Six months after Wattle-Gum arrived at the red brick orphanage, he was in the top of his class for all his subjects except physical education.

It seemed he'd lost his desire to move about. Any effort to encourage physical activity resulted in his flopping to the ground and sitting, immoveable, right where he was.

In all academia, however, none could come close to his scores. The orphanage director began throwing "genius" around and was sure he would be placed in foster care quickly.

Unfortunately, at nine years of age, exercising his mind was crushing his possibilities of making any friends.

Wattle-Gum was alone, scared, and picked on constantly by both the boys and girls in the orphanage. It wasn't hard to find something to laugh at; long, curly, blond hair and the name Wattle-Gum Gecko Mitchell provided much ammunition.

But, a free spirit can only take so much.

One morning, Wattle-Gum woke up with his hair slathered in black, sticky, smelly vegemite. He carefully combed it through as if it were hair gel and went to breakfast. Even the teachers grimaced at the stench.

When he was strongly encouraged to go shower, he glowered at his laughing peers and quietly requested to visit the barber on their field trip to the shopping center that day.

By the time his classmates had exhausted their financial freedoms at the shops and were ready to return to the orphanage, the boy known as Wattle-Gum Gecko Mitchell arrived at the bus with his washed, white blond hair cropped just under his ears, the natural curls expressing a rough, movie-star look. The girls stopped laughing and took extra notice.

Chester stood up to him.

"I hope you don't think a little haircut is going to change anything, Bottle-Lizard."

The short-haired boy stood his ground and said,

"No, but I will."

Chester landed flat on his back with a bloody nose.

"And, by the way, my name is Mitch."

Mitch spent the night smiling in solitary confinement.

Cheers!

"Come in, Gash." Prince Hadigan, aged twenty-one years, welcomed his eighteen-year-old friend.

The two sat on a private balcony overlooking the great columned Poseidon Memorial Parthenon.

"Remarkable feat that, don't you think? Drink?" Hadigan motioned to a large selection of crystal bottles and decanters.

"N-no, no th-thank you." Gash wrung his cap in his hand and peeked out over the balcony. "Ooh." He stepped back again, not enjoying the height.

"That is the greatest memorial to the greatest king of our entire history. Cheers!" He raised his glass.

Gash wavered back from the edge and stuttered.

"M-m-m-maybe I will have a d-drink, j-j-just what you're h-having."

Hadigan looked to a tiny wrinkled man in the corner, who moved remarkably fast for his age and had an odd, long snout.

It took Gash a minute to realize what it was. He, being poor, had never seen one before and stared blatantly at the little figure pouring the drink.

The Kobolds — or box brownie, for that was what it was — are bad-tempered lizard-ish creatures. Their service is given, grudgingly, only to those who can afford it.

They come in boxes that are kept by their masters, who also keep many other boxes lying around to hide the real one. If someone other than the master opens the Kobold's home box, setting it free, the Kobold will run riot in an impish raid of mischief.

The extra boxes have frightful carvings on them and ugly surprises in them that jump out at you should you open the lid. This fact usually deters any from meddling with the boxes.

Hadigan snorted the air with vigor.

"I love this spot. When I was younger, I would climb up the side here and go all the way to the roof. Do you know what it feels like to be on top of the world? I do."

"This is s-s-soft d-drink?" Gash looked at the tumbler in his hand, at the Kobold by the bar, and then at Hadigan in disbelief.

"Spirits will cloud your mind, my friend. Didn't you pay attention in Mind Powers class at school?"

The prince jumped up onto the balcony railing. An Agent in a suit the color of seaweed quickly rushed out and reached for him. Hadigan kicked him in the chest, jumped and spun in a straight layout over the Agent's head, and landed walking straight back at him.

"I keep telling you people, I am NOT going to die! Just like my father, great leader that he is, says every time he tries to cheat death. I, however, will not, barely hang onto life. I WILL LIVE IT!"

Hadigan hissed at the Agent, who retreated to his quiet place trying to breathe out the kick in his chest.

"Gash, my friend, I tell you, we are the ones who will live. We will make our names so great that no memorial will be big enough to house us."

He stepped over to his nervous friend and drew him right to the edge of the balcony. Leaning the both of them over it, he whispered,

"Stay my friend, Gash, and you will see more in life than anyone in this gilded cage could imagine possible."

Gash threw up over the edge.

"I have just the place for you. A young scientific genius, with no family, wants a quiet place to work, right?"

To steady himself, Gash grabbed at the table set for tea.

The prince was mysteriously quiet.

"I will set you up in my hidden castle beneath the river. You will work your little potion-secrets in peace, and I will sell them for what they are worth. The Trade Minister has a son who offered his help, and we will be a happy little family. Now, go home and shower, you stink. I will call for you to leave tomorrow. Be ready. Cheers!"

Gash left with a green but greedy smile. His gift with chemistry was one he was as desperate to explore as Hadigan was to exploit.

Foster Home

Despite further roughhousing difficulties, enhanced by a sudden renewed love for athletic opportunities, the Orphanage Director was not exactly timely in assuming that Mitch would be soon placed in foster care. The boy lived at the orphanage for eleven months before his dream came true.

Tom and Helen Jaack always kept their eyes open for unique children. They looked for strong boys to train up on their horse and cattle homestead in the Snowy Mountains. They were drawn to Mitch not only by his healthy physique but also by his uncanny mathematical skills and already feisty attitude.

"I'm looking for a kid strong enough to control his own will. You think you can find that strength on the lonely mountains in the south?"

Tom Jaack squared his shoulders and examined Mitch.

"I'd do anything s'long as ya just get me out of the city and this scum house."

Tom laughed heartily.

"I've got to agree with you there, about the city. C'mon, kid, your number's up."

Mitch liked his new home, a lovely open farmhouse in the Snowy Mountains. Even if the constant temperature was considerably colder than his northern home, it was perfect. How Mitch was so lucky he would never know.

He wrote his Gamma in Brazil:

"The whole house is wood, not just shop wood either, Mr. Jaack and his four sons built everything by hand. They all work their own businesses and Mr. Jaack Sr., my foster dad, runs a small stock horse farm so they're hugely rich. It's just like a movie here.

Mum would have loved it, but she would have frozen. Apparently, it snows here too.

I'm to be home-schooled, again, by one of the son's wives, Becky. She is teaching me the basics. Her husband, Craig, is teaching me martial arts. I was woken up at 5:30 am for my first lesson. They tell me that that is the schedule every morning, rain, snow, or shine. They are really tough, especially Tom, my foster dad. If he weren't so kindhearted, he'd be an ogre.

I like it here.

Oh, yeah, I'm to learn how to use a computer too. I played some games these last days and they say I'm pretty good, but that's just the way they talk. They say everyone is good at anything, if you practice hard enough.

Maybe I'll see you again, someday, Gamma. Bye."

Blue Castle

Gash was tired but excited when he entered his new home. There was a calm, almost clear blue glow all around him.

The castle was the most beautiful place he had ever been in. He didn't think it was beautiful for the majesty of the carved walls, the delicate balance of jungle courtyard and manicured gardens, or the clear river roof that ran overhead. No, Gash was enamored by the quiet Underland solitude.

There were only the two Kobolds to keep him company, and they wouldn't talk often. This is the place where Gash would have his peace.

The aged Kobold spoke in a rusty voice,

"There is a rich market in Latoona, only ten miles straight shot from here, and if you like, the dragons are helpful if you respect them." Both Kobolds then bowed and left.

Dragon compounds could be useful in chemistry, Gash knew. Their potency was beyond any other known source and had not been explored much.

Truly, did the creatures still live, or was the liquid called dragon tears simply a rich mineral water?

"Many hours, many minutes, all will be told when time will tell."

Gash began to set up his laboratory. There would be time to see the rest of the place later.

Tears

Who could resist either of the Dijex sisters? The whole village loved Tanya and Holly.

There was a faithful agreement between Salla, Hal, and the villagers: they all chose to forget which of the girls had lost her parents in the bombing.

Now, seven years later, here was Holly with her rich brown hair shining as bright as her dark eyes. She had begun questioning everything when she was three years of age and never stopped.

Yet today, something was not quite right.

"I tell you that chemistry is a fine art, little one." Karenina, the primary teacher for the village, tapped Holly's head, reminding her to pay attention on this field trip to the Main Street Market. "It would do you well to attend to your studies."

"But I want to go to that pagoda and see the garden." Holly pulled at her teacher's arm.

"It is not like you, Holly, to fuss like this. Now, stop and listen to the Potions Master."

Holly dropped her head and peaked out from under her hair at Tanya.

Her sister was standing right up against the counter behind the Potions Master. He scooted her away as soon as he realized how close she was to his wares. But was too distracted by all the eager young students to observe her too closely.

The sisters exchanged a serious nod.

When school was let out, the girls ran home to play.

"Can we take our tea set out, Mema?"

"Just be home for early dinner," Salla instructed. "I want to get to the memorial service on time."

Tonight was the anniversary of the Market bombing, and a service was to be held at the top of the crater to pay respects to those lost. The cause of the bombing would also be discussed. No one knew the answer, but all the rumors would come out again.

The villagers spent too much time on the horrors of the past. There was still so much fear surrounding the attack that no recovery plan had been set in action.

Occasionally, a youngster would suggest they rebuild the resort and restart the plan for a Trevel vacation venue in the heart of the Amazon Jungle. But the elders would ominously warn them all that a royal life had nearly been taken, so the royal family would set a curse upon any who tried to rebuild over that sacred spot.

Holly gathered the teapot and two teacups from their play set while Tanya tugged at a blanket in the closet. They hugged each other solemnly and walked out the back door.

It took a lot of slithering and sliding to reach the bottom of the crater, but once they did, the ground was solid. Surprisingly, no water gathered here, even after the recent rains. It was dry, cracked, and hot.

The girls set up their blanket and tea set right in the center. Tanya pulled a small, red crystal bottle from her pocket and set it next to the teapot. It was delicately labeled,

"Liquide Compound: Tears, of the Dragon."

She whispered conspiratorially,

"I've never stolen anything before."

"I know. I've felt sick all afternoon." Holly rubbed her tummy.

"Let's just do this." Tanya poured the clear, thick liquid into the pot.

"Let me stir the dragon tears; you sing." Holly swirled the teapot around and around.

Tanya sang gently,

"A dragon tear for you,

A dragon tear for me,

Will you ever see-

Dragons come to tea?

The song will rise above

The new song down below,

See the dragon come,

See the dragon go."

The girls paused a moment to let the atmosphere build, then Holly poured into Tanya's bright little sunflower teacup, then Tanya poured into Holly's. Together they raised the cups high and chanted,

"As much as the parents who live are ours, so also the parents who died are ours, and together we vow to destroy the one that took their life from us."

They drank.

As the friend-sisters lie there unconscious, overwhelmed by the potency of the liquid that passed through their young bodies, a rumor was whispered above them.

Some said the Market bomb wasn't just an attempt to kill Prince Hadigan. They said it was also a plot to destroy the vacation resort that was being built. Someone didn't want Latoona to benefit from the money it would bring. Someone wanted to divert that money elsewhere.

Some also believed that the prince had laughed at the tragedy.

The Healer

A Mountain Life

The Party

Finances and Farewell

Chapter 3

The Healer

The memorial service didn't take place that night. When Salla couldn't find her daughters, the alarm went out.

It took several hours of searching through the jungle and scouring the river before someone heard a scream over the crater. The girls were discovered quickly under a hot wind beating down on the place from a red cloud above.

An accurate guess as to the reason for their unconsciousness was made, and the girls were immediately taken to the Potions Master, Master Su.

"My friends," Master Su addressed the anxious crowd at his doorstep after the girls were brought to him. "It is good you have brought them to me. I know exactly what must be done. Do not fear; Hal, Salla, and I will see to it that they are well again. Return to your homes and rest well."

The door was forcefully closed, and the three healers took the girls to the cool basement to keep their temperatures down.

"You say a scream led you to them and some saw a red cloud?" Master Su reassured the parents. "It is Colonah. All will be well, then."

"What is Colonah?" Hal interrogated the master while he wiped the crater dust off the girls' faces.

"Who? She is the one who led the chorus when these little ones were born. I heard it clearly on the wind, and I know you did. I saw both of your faces."

"Do you mean to tell me, my daughters summoned a dragon?" Salla brushed their hair. "They're so young. Is that possible?"

"Dragons come to help those who call them, especially if it is someone that they are already watching. I don't know what kind of tea party these two were having, but if it was with Colonah, it was serious."

"Who is this Colonah?" Hal was frustrated by his inability to fix the situation. "If my daughters are calling to dragons, I want to know what kind."

The Potions Master snuggled the girls under soft, leathery blankets and motioned for their parents to leave the room. By the firelight in the living room, he finished explaining.

"Very few dragons today are intent on evil. They are not the demons most think they are. They are ministers of help that watch over those chosen before they are born. You'll only see the small beasts now, as the larger ones were all killed by Bacht knights. They have always had an awkward relationship with the Bacht, based on fear."

"I heard they like Trevels." Salla was hopeful.

The healing Master nodded and encouraged,

"If you respect a dragon's power, he—or she, in this case—will respect yours."

"So," Hal pressed on, "what kind of beast is this Colonah?"

"Colonah is the Mother." Su informed them, "The dragons' social setting is a lot like the society of elephants. One mother matriarch cares for the colony. The males are loners and come back only for rituals and mating."

Salla pondered,

"So, Colonah is the leader? What has she to do with my girls?"

"The question, Salla, is what do your girls have to do with her? They must have called out with a serious need. What great trouble haunts Holly and Tanya that they should call on Mother Colonah?"

They all fell silent and pretended to listen for any stirring in the other room.

Hal changed the topic.

"You said you knew exactly what to do." He paced, desperate to do something. "What is it?"

"I do know." Master Su tried to dismiss his concerns, "We let them sleep. That is all there is to do."

But, Hal would not be so easily pacified and demanded,

"Sleep for how long?"

"Depends on how much they drank. It could be a few hours, or it could be a few days."

A Mountain Life

Wattle-Gum Gecko Mitchell—forever, now, just Mitch—soon developed a passion for the martial arts lessons he was subjected to in the early hours of the morning. Jaack, as everyone called his foster dad, kept a close eye on his development.

As Mitch practiced his katas, Jaack would often remind him,

"The only time you ever use attack is to protect the ones you love."

So once, when the boy was watching the wild horses that roam over the mountain, he spied some older youths with rifles, shooting over the creature's heads for sport.

Mitch loved the horses; therefore, he thought he should step in and protect them despite their ability to take care of themselves, as they had done for hundreds of years already. Still, Mitch prepared to put into practice all he had learned.

He rode his horse down the hill to where the shooters had parked their Jeep.

"I don't think you should be here," he warned from his horse's back, looking down on the surprised group.

"I don't think you should be talking to us. Get lost." A black-haired teen rested his rifle on his hip, the tip pointing over Mitch's head.

"You're lucky the stallion doesn't attack you." Mitch nodded to a great brown horse watching suspiciously from the hill. "He's pretty viscous if you're too close."

"If he gets too close, I'll shoot him."

The snarly teen fired his rifle barely over Mitch's head, who gripped the saddle with his knees as his horse reared, screaming. Mitch slid to the ground and calmed his mare, quietly feeding her carrot chunks.

There was no telling if the stallion's intent was to protect his friend or to claim his carrots. Mitch always brought a bag of carrots at this time of day, and the great brown leader of the pack was beginning to expect them.

The youths scattered as the violent stallion stormed them and tromped a couple of rifles. Mitch joined the fray, and between horse and boy, much damage was done. The Jeep suffered also.

Interestingly, there was no mention of a twelve-year-old boy when the report was made at the hospital that evening. Only the nurse on duty questioned some of the injuries the older teens had acquired.

She called her friend Becky Jaack and just happened to mention some of the patients brought into the ER that night, and wondered out loud how such injuries would have occurred on a lonely mountaintop.

At breakfast the next morning, Jaack changed Mitch's work duties.

"I need extra help feeding the cattle in the bottom field. I'll meet you there in an hour."

Mitch tried to work well, but he couldn't help wincing and groaning as his aching muscles and bruises from yesterday's battle surfaced. Jaack kept pushing and pushing him to work faster and harder.

From tossing bales of hay all around the bottom paddock, he was then required to help refit the corral fence, digging the holes and planting the poles. Then Mitch was called on to carry all the massive feed sacks from one end of the barn to the other.

At lunch, he could barely life his vegemite sandwich to his mouth. Jaack was nowhere to be found, and no one else would tell him why he was on such hard duty.

He spent the afternoon until dinner hauling trees, chopping them down, and stacking firewood. The evening of the week before his first teen birthday, Mitch dragged his aching body straight to the shower.

He heard Jaack walk down the hall, laughing with his wife after they had gone to town to see a movie, something they had never before done without him. He let the shower's hot water rush down his back as the even hotter tears ran down his cheeks.

Despite the smell of store-bought fried chicken, Mitch pulled the covers over his head and was nearly sleeping in more tears when Jaack spoke in the darkness.

"Next time you attack anyone, older or not, if they end up in hospital, you'll join them after fetching feed bags and chopping wood all night long."

The tears and self-pity stopped. Mitch smiled and snuggled deeper under the covers.

If this had all been about discipline for his mountain fight, then that was okay. He slept very well that night.

The Party

The teen girl stood nervously on stage in the Latoona Village Gathering Hall.

"I've only been there three years, but I've found that if you work hard…"

"Like they have any choice about that?" Tomey lifted his glass of mineral water as he interrupted Katiel's advisory speech. She smiled nervously and continued to read from her shaky script.

"…If you work hard, and keep out of everyone else's business, you can have a really nice time."

She stepped down and the audience applauded her shy efforts.

"There you have it, girls." Chancellor Stonewall Tanker stepped forward. "Tomey says, 'Get used to walking,' Candice says, 'Choose your friends wisely,' and Katiel says, 'Work hard and you can have a really nice time.'"

He then motioned Tanya and Holly to the stage.

"Now, it is your turn to tell us what you are looking for in your first year of higher-level learning at the Academy."

Tanya spoke first.

"I intend to blast the socks off every boy on campus."

The whole village burst into laughter.

Each year that young high-school students from the village of Latoona left home to begin attending the prestigious and expensive private school, "Atlantis National Academy," a village-wide celebration was held.

Attendance at ANA was voluntary, but acceptance into the program was based on energy skills and required a higher level of achievement than the average Trevel population possessed. Thus the hall was especially full of party guests today, as the new seventh-grade students starting this year were the village darlings, Tanya and Holly Dijex.

"I also," continued Tanya, "want to learn how to better smell metal ores so I don't always have to touch the dirty rocks to find them."

There was applause, and Tanya took her seat next to her parents, Salla and Hal.

Holly approached the podium slowly, still trying to think of a response.

"Tanya had her speech prepared a week ago, but I still can't think of anything to say… I guess I plan to spend most of my time cleaning up all the broken hearts Tanya leaves behind."

Uproarious laughter, and a few stood to cheer.

There was a distinct lack of young men in Latoona, so Tanya worked hard to draw the attentions of those who visited the market. She had many admirers from miles around. Her attraction was a lovely innocence and confidence.

Holly, just as lovely and as confident, preferred to quietly watched amused and sarcastic.

"I'll also grow at least one new species of plant each month, to discover what new energies I can draw from and bend with them."

Holly sat between her parents and they hugged her. Tanya added a smart whap to the back of her sister's head.

With the pleasantries over, the gathering filtered down to the main families, who gravitated toward each other. Chancellor Tanker, Tomey's father, vigorously rubbed his son's shoulder, nearly knocking him off his feet.

"So, Tomey, as a twelfth-year student, you'll be keeping an eye on these young ladies, now, won't you?"

"Yeah, Dad."

"You've never taken any notice of us before, why start now?" Holly casually snubbed the offer as she served herself another drink of guava juice mixed with the local mineral water.

"Well, I assure you," he tried to stand tall under his father's heavy arm, "my socks won't be blown off by either of you."

"That, Tomey dear, is because you don't wear socks."

Tanya jabbed him in the ribs with her fingers.

"Even so, girls," the Chancellor continued, "it is good to have a man around."

The three students weakly nodded and the village leader left.

"If you need me at school, I'll be in the art studios."

"Tomey, what is the Academy really like?" Holly looked him straight in the eye.

"Your small time jungle fame won't carry you there. Wait till we're on the ship. Candice and I will tell you then."

The party continued only a short time longer as everyone understood the students' need to pack.

Finances and Farewell

Mitch was amazed by how much money could come to one person in one year. He did the math and understood how it worked, but that it should happen to him was truly, he thought,

"Excellent!"

The whole Jaack family had joined together for Mitch's thirteenth birthday to pay for his gift. Mum Jaack had told him that the extension off his room was an extra closet. Becky said they could use it to do lessons in.

"We could put a desk in there and you'd have a nice, quiet place to study."

"I have a quiet place to study." Mitch threw a "yeah, right" look at her. "I have a quiet mountain place to study."

"Uh huh," was all Becky had as a reply.

The project only took two days to complete. Everyone helped but Mitch. There was always something else to work on or practice, until Jaack offered to take him to town, just the two of them.

"A birthday treat; you and me."

"Being alone with you is supposed to be a present?" Mitch screwed up his nose at his foster dad, who g up the gently shoved him in the back of the head just hard enough to unbalance him.

The boy laughed and gave his foster father an affectionate shoulder punch.

They had a good time eating hot, fat, greasy chips and hamburgers "with the lot," a term that meant that, along with the half pound of beef and cheese, there was also an entire garden of ingredients on the burger, from beetroot and fried egg to pineapple and alfalfa sprouts, as well as the basics of lettuce, cooked onion, and tomato: delicious.

The two then checked out the feed stores and hardware stores in town before they headed over to see the latest action film. It was almost dark when the truck rolled into the yard.

As usual, the house was lit up and open. Everyone was inside, and Mitch smiled in anticipation of the birthday dinner. Meat pies, sausage rolls, fresh fruit salad and cream, scones, homemade jam, and éclairs filled the table. There were also skinned baked potatoes, peas, carrot sticks, and celery flowers with Mum Jaack's famous veggie dip.

All in all, it was perfect for a first-time-a-teenager's birthday. When the lime spider drinks (lime cordial and a carbonated soda with ice-cream) were brought out, Mitch actually gave a whoop, he was so happy.

The boy's sharp eyes did notice the lack of wrapped gifts, but no one said anything, so he didn't either. When there was no dessert, or cake, Mitch couldn't help jokingly asking where it was.

Jaack scolded him,

"You think that after making this huge meal, your mother has time to bake a cake, too? Everything here was made from scratch. Are you so ungrateful? I know you're not."

The last statement seemed more of a threat than an affirmation and the big man continued,

"Go to your room."

"What?" Mitch had been sent to his room before, but it was usually to study or think over a bad move. It was his birthday; this couldn't be real.

"I think it's time you went to your room." Even Mum Jaack sent him.

But Mitch's confusion turned to anticipation when the rest of the family, uncles, aunts, and cousins, all began chanting,

"Go to your room. Go to your room. Go to your room."

Jiggling the table and spilling the drinks, Mitch clambered out of his chair and ran to his room.

The only thing that was different was the back wall. Instead of a flat brick wall, double doors shone shiny brand-new. How much could a kid get without exploding in thankfulness?

It was a computer room.

Large-screen monitors and all the basics, as well as a synthesizer keyboard, guitar, and complete surround-sound speakers stood before him. The walls were covered in egg-crate foam for sound proofing, and the sunroof had blinds to close out the sun when necessary.

"Of course, if we want to use it, you'll be gracious enough to allow that." Craig, the oldest son, couldn't keep his eyes off the equipment.

"Yeah… sure..." Mitch would have said that to anything. He was so engrossed in playing with it all, he didn't eat the cake that Mum laid next to him. She returned to retrieve the cake at 2:00 a.m. and told him to shut down.

From then on, Mitch's mornings were spent working out and doing chores, but the afternoons were his to play.

It was Christmas holiday time, and there were no lessons for six weeks. Over and over, Mitch tested and worked on a special project. He wouldn't tell anyone what he was doing, and after checking to make sure it was age appropriate, the Jaacks left him to it, questioning him only on his progress and achievement.

It took him three weeks to build, but he spent the next six months adding, adjusting, debugging, and tweaking it. Finally, at breakfast one morning, Mitch handed everyone a computer disk.

"When you have a chance, have a go," was all he said.

Two months later he signed a contract with a major computer gaming company. Mitch thought he had all the money in the world when the payment came through, but then the residual checks began rolling in.

Not only were there home console versions of his game available, but there had been allowances for arcade games to pick it up also.

The boy began playing with another secret project while the contract offers piled up on the front veranda. Over and over, he walked the mountaintop with his laptop. He searched the skies and mapped the property, where every detail was entered into his plan. Paper maps were checked against computer maps, and sometimes he wasn't sure if all his research took him to legally open access sites.

Finally, when he was fifteen and a half, he presented Mum and Dad Jaack with his gift of "thank you for all you have done."

It was a computer program that connected satellite mapping abilities and scanned the whole Snowy Mountain region. It pinpointed cattle and horses through GPS, infrared tracking, and ear tagging.

From full mountain view to a six-foot-by-six-foot close-up view, the Jaack Corporation would be able to track its animals, family, staff, and trespassers over the entire property, from any computer, anywhere in the world.

Soon, every property manager throughout the Mountain Region wanted his or her own version of the program. Then word began to spread to the outback, and more requests for individual property mapping came pouring in. Mitch had to contract with a government computing firm to cover the vast need.

In his newest project, one month before his sixteenth birthday, Mitch began searching other sites and making plans that no one expected— but unforeseen circumstances suddenly made it vital for him to quickly follow through with them.

Family

Miss. Taylor

Goodbye Song

ANL Binay

The Caravan

Pirates

Gash Again

Chapter 4

Family

Two years before the farewell party in Latoona, Mitch enjoyed his new computer programming fortune under the financial mentorship of his already wealthy foster family. At sixteen, he learned how to balance and invest a sizeable cash flow. The Jaacks never considered using any of Mitch's wealth for their own benefit and were excited for the boy's success.

"You'll have nothing to worry about when you turn eighteen." Jaack sat on the veranda with Mitch, watching the sunset. "Not many foster kids start adulthood like you will. Remember them, and don't forget your beginnings and blessings."

"I never knew anyone to be so lucky. Why me?"

"Don't question a blessing. There is always only one thing to do with it."

"I know. You pass it on." Mitch smiled as he repeated yet another philosophy that had been drilled into him these last seven years.

Jaack began to look awkward, so Mitch knew he was about to get personal.

"What is it?" Mitch broke through Jaack's discomfort.

"Ah. I thought you might like to know why we never adopted you."

Shrugging off the nagging insecurity, Mitch flatly commented,

"I figured you had enough kids."

"Well, yeah, that's right, but… I wanted you to never begin relying on the money we already had for your future. Although we will always be there if you need anything."

"I don't expect any more from you. You've given me enough already."

Jaack jumped off the veranda edge and turned to look Mitch right in the eye.

"You should expect a lot more from us. We're your family. You belong to us and we love you." He turned his back again.

"I wanted to teach you how to take your life and make it your own, not hide in us."

"Like your sons?"

"They've all made their own choices and are traveling their own journeys. That's not for you to question. But I will say they have all achieved their own dreams without hiding anywhere."

"Sorry. I just never saw why anyone would want to stay home, or even in one place, all his life."

Mitch considered revealing his latest plan.

"It's good for some, not for others. I have a feeling you will be one of the others. There's been travel in your life already, and it's a hard bug to get rid of."

"I was thinking of taking a trip to see my Gamma in Brazil."

"You've got it all planned out, haven't you? Down to the last date and meal ticket, I guess?"

Mitch's stomach lurched. How did Jaack always know what he was doing?

"Aw, kid." Jaack wrapped his viselike arm around the boy's head and rubbed his hair with his knuckles. "Seven years is a long time to get to know someone." Jaack bent over in a wrestler's challenge. "And I've enjoyed every minute."

The challenge was accepted, and the two laughed through the whole match.

Unfortunately, as coincidence would have it, when a grey van pulled into the yard, both males were dusty and grass stained. Mitch also had acquired a bloody nose from banging his face accidentally on Jaack's head.

Miss Taylor was not impressed.

Miss Taylor

"Miss Taylor?" Jaack wiped himself up and Mitch tried to stop his nose from gushing blood everywhere. "We weren't expecting you till next week."

"Obviously not." She stalked past Jaack and went to Mitch's aid.

"That looks awful, you poor thing. Don't worry; I'll take care of this for you."

"Ids nodd'n, ids append before. Ids wad I ged for wrestling de big guy." Mitch was not yet aware of the precarious situation.

"Let me take you inside and get you cleaned up."

Even when she tried really hard, Miss Taylor's nurturing spirit was dead cold.

Inside, the blood was all washed away and Miss Taylor began her planned interrogation, encouraged by the bloody nose.

"It has come to our attention that these arrangements may not be in the best interest of the boy."

"What?" Mitch sputtered.

Mum Jaack calmed Mitch when she whispered,

"We expected this."

Miss Taylor continued steadily.

"The Children's Welfare intends, now that the boy is receiving a private income, to ensure that his money is being applied in the right places and not into your family pocket."

"I assure you, Miss Taylor," Jaack said as he offered her a chair, "Mitch's money is completely his and completely accounted for, down to the penny."

"I'm sure it is, Mr. Jaack." She sat rigid at the big country table. "But the child is still under the protection of the Australian Children's Welfare system, and as such, we are the ones who need to guide the child in his finances."

"The 'child's' name is Mitch, and I'm not a child." Mitch leaned over the table but maintained his control.

"I had intended to inform you that Wattle-Gum..."

"It's MITCH!" the forenamed enforced.

She smiled, sort of.

"Master Mitchell needs to return with me to the orphanage at the end of the week."

Gasps and shouts arose from the usually calm family. Miss Taylor spoke loudly over their objections.

"However, after what I have seen tonight... is your nose okay, Mitch? Perhaps I should take him now."

Mum Jaack quieted everyone.

"That won't be necessary. We will take care of him. I am sure that after all the visits you've had with us before, you know he is safe here."

Mitch, over everyone's head, silently nodded outside to Miss Taylor. It had the desired effect.

"You're right, Mrs. Jaack. I will see you in one week."

She stepped outside, but instead of heading to the van, she slipped over to the barn.

The family was trying to make sense of the surprise announcement, but Mitch stood quietly.

"Go on, don't stop talking." He winked. "I have a 'secret' appointment in the barn."

"Watch yourself, son," Jaack warned him.

"It's okay. I don't intend on spending tomorrow shifting hay bales and feed sacks all day."

In the barn, Miss Taylor tried to begin, but Mitch interrupted and took control of the conversation.

"Miss Taylor, I thank you for your concern. You and I both know that this is just some ruse to get money from me to fill your own pockets. I will reward your stupidity by making my usual donation to the orphanage, for the benefit of the kids."

She tried to interrupt again.

"You will not find me here next week. You will not find me here tomorrow. The only thing you have achieved here is a shorter good bye to my family." He nodded and turned away.

"You won't get away from me." She stood her ground

Mitch slowly walked back to her and stood very, very close.

"But, Miss Taylor, remember, I am a troubled foster child." With one hand he closed the barn door. It quietly creaked closed.

"Perhaps I won't let you get away from me?"

She faltered a little.

"I could have you tried as an adult if you even touch me."

"An adult? Then I shouldn't need the Australian Children's Welfare assistance."

She tripped backward. "If this is what they teach you here, I'll have you back in the orphanage tomorrow."

"I learned discipline and compassion here. You are the one who taught me to be troubled at your precious orphanage. Thanks for reminding me."

Miss Taylor sneered and stalked back to her van rather quickly.

Goodbye Song

The Dijex family — Hal, Salla, Tanya, and Holly — lay in bed early the night before they left for Rio, yet none of them were able to sleep.

In the morning, they would join the caravan of travelers to Rio de Janeiro and from there, Underland to the Trevel port town of Janeiro, where the girls would register and shop in preparation for the voyage to high school at the Atlantis National Academy.

TSNS Atlantis (Trevel Strategic Naval Service) was the ship that would take them to school, and school was to be their home for the most part of the next six years. There was a lot of shopping to be done.

Sunrise pushed its way through the jungle trees and over the crater. The girls were at the bottom already with hydro lights and their old tea set.

"The teapot hasn't been washed since the last time we had it here."

Tanya sniffed the sunflower clay.

"I didn't want to get any more tears in case we slept too long."

"I suppose the well water will pull the tears off the sides?" Holly poured the heavy mineral water into the pot and Tanya swirled it around.

"They said her name was Colonah."

Holly nodded looking into the red sky. "I can't tell if that's a warning sunrise or Colonah wishing us well."

Tanya gazed upward too. "Shall we say goodbye, then?"

They chanted:

"A dragon tear for you;

A dragon tear for me,

We've come to say, 'goodbye,'

With our dragon tea.

Our song will rise above

To a song from long ago,

That we may see a dragon come

Before we have to go."

They sang again, and again.

All was quiet, but for a soft echo. Holly saw it first and hit Tanya's arm.

A section of the crater wall sort of wiggled as if it were holding something invisible. The wiggly bit wound around the crater and circled them completely. The sunrise sky became a deep, deep red directly above, and water splashed down upon them from an unseen cloud.

When the sisters entered the house, Salla looked up from the breakfast table she was setting.

"Gracious! Did you swim in the river fully clothed?"

"Something like that." The girls sloshed up to their rooms to dry and change their clothes.

ANL Binay

Forty-four days at sea on a cargo ship had shown Mitch the entire southern and western coasts of Australia. Now he was looking into the harbor of Hong Kong.

The night of Miss Taylor's visit, Mitch's already-laid plans were put into early action: switching the dates was easy.

All had gone smoothly after the not-so-social worker left. Everyone was prepared for the goodbye, sad though it was, and within an hour, everything was packed—food, clothes, and the laptop.

Mitch had already spread his money out in various bank accounts all over the world and could move it around without his location being discovered too quickly. In fact, he was already supporting his Gamma in Brazil with a steady, more-than-comfortable income. That was where he was headed.

He chose cargo ship transport because it was the least likely to be watched for his escape. That and, for a sixteen-year-old, it was also the most exciting route.

Leaving the mountain was fairly easy. A friend who owned a helicopter was recruited to "search for the missing boy" by air. He picked Mitch up from a high mountain ridge and flew him off to a distant bus station.

Oddly enough, Children's Welfare never did find out that Mitch disappeared despite the wide search orchestrated by Miss Taylor.

The orphanage did not record the search at all. They were delighted with the generous support offered by the young Wattle-Gum and believed all was well with Master Mitchell.

The first month on board the ANL Binay was rough. Mitch was tired by the trip that took him from the Snowy Mountains to the city of Melbourne, Victoria. Then he had to find his sea legs.

Storms took him all the way to Adelaide, in South Australia, and then a horrid summer heat wave saw him to Perth on the very western tip of Australia. The weather was supposedly nice from there, but waves were still new to the mountain boy. He ate very little.

Sailing up across the north coast of Australia and on through to Hong Kong was hot and rainy, but now Mitch spent most of his time at the prow of the great ship, watching the dolphins play in the surf before the boat and breathing gallons of fresh salt air.

The spirit that had once been crushed and contained, then renewed and disciplined, was now set free. The wild boy spirit that had threatened Miss Taylor was intoxicating and as the sailors on board encouraged open expression, the discipline learned at the Jaack's was laid aside. The basic understanding of morals still ruled, but there is little a sixteen-year-old can do to maintain "good manners" when there was so much fun to be had.

Hong Kong was spectacular! Mitch discovered the power of money, and most importantly, the power of anonymity. The men of the Binay were pleased to show Mitch where all the fun was, though he stayed away from the more desperate passions they delved into. As long as the boy paid, though, everyone was a friend.

On the second day in port, they took on a passenger, another gentleman of youth and wealth, called Hui. He also carried a laptop, and from their ship's cabin, the two teens hacked into all the ship logs in the harbor just to find out what they were carrying, diverting the occasional package to themselves.

Mitch still rehearsed his martial arts exercises and surprised his shipmates with his determination to not drink too much alcohol or smoke anything. Mitch told them,

"In a world where no one knows you, your physical abilities are all you have. I won't trade any strength or focus for artificial thrills."

After two weeks, he said goodbye to Hui and changed ships to leave Hong Kong on the Ville de Blanc, headed for open sea.

As they crossed the Pacific, one of the sailors who loved marlin fishing showed Mitch how to respect the ocean creatures, using them only for necessary food, and how to get a live one on board without losing an arm. The fish supplied good meals for three days. Thus, it was a quiet cruise until they were a day off the Panama coast and Mitch had the need to exercise his computer networking skills.

The Caravan

Generally, students from Latoona made their own way from Upland Latoona (located in the Amazon Jungle) to Underland Atlantis (located beneath eastern Indonesia). But a surprise package arrived at Chancellor Stonewall's, from an anonymous donor, which included free hotel reservations in Rio de Janeiro, for all the students and their families. Everyone was more than excited about using their saved money to shop in the bigger city.

The vehicles slithered out of the village in a full-color parade. Waterworks exploded everywhere, leaving brilliant trails of red, green, and orange shimmering and dripping in the air.

The Dijex family van was the first in line and followed the motor skis carefully as they wove their way through the trees that bowed out of the way. The family, all smiles and laughter, were not taking their first trip to Janeiro, but this was definitely the biggest farewell they'd had.

"Look back, girls," said Hal. "You won't see that village for a long time."

A number of small, soft objects were tossed at him.

"Hush, Dad. I'm not thinking about that yet." Tanya watched the glorious jungle plants wave to and fro, moving around the cars, then magically returning to their previous planting spots unharmed.

"It really is something to be able to bend so much foliage at once." Tanya swayed with the rhythm. "How long does it take to become a jungle guide?"

"Ask your sister," said Salla. "How long would it take you to be able to bend that much plant energy at once, Holly?"

Holly watched the guides on their bikes ahead of them. The riders steered the single-seat jungle skis, or motorbikes, with their feet and waved their arms carefully in time to the organic rhythm and wind.

Each tree, bush, and flower — and even the dead plants — wavered, slid, or walked out of the way so that the caravan procession could drive by unhindered.

"I guess it would only take a couple of months' simple focus to build the mental memories in order to do that much on demand."

Tanya stared at her sister.

"So you can do that now?"

"Uhh…" Holly suddenly realized that once again, her simple gifts, as she saw them, were not that simple.

Pirates

An old coast guard ship approached the Ville de Blanc and fired a warning flare over the prow. The captain of the cargo ship, noting the lack of radio salutation, avoided it.

Mitch joined the captain at the helm as the pirates made efforts to board. Some gunshots were fired, and armed men clambered onto the Blanc.

Mitch studied the aerials on the pirate ship and began working with the communications systems. The captain watched him.

"I hope you can attack them with a keyboard."

"Okay," affirmed Mitch.

"You can?"

"Don't interrupt."

The crew was silent as his fingers tap-tapped on. Hitting the "enter" key smartly, Mitch turned to his shipmates and said, "In a couple of seconds, that ship will receive an order from a British submarine demanding they stand down because they are committing an act of war."

"Committing an act of war? Where'd you get that one, kid?"

"I've been reading spy novels. There now, see?"

Stepping up to the window, they saw another flare fly, and the pirates already on board dropped what they were stealing: a couple of boxes from one specific crate they had targeted. One of them tried to carry a box back over, but it weighed down his jump and he landed in the water.

The phony coast guard ship sailed hastily away, leaving the man behind in the waves.

The captain laughed a little and spoke into the microphone.

"Man overboard." Turning to walk down onto the deck, he continued, "Let's see what they wanted so badly."

Dinner that evening was silent. No one looked at anyone, and Mitch noticed how agitated the crew was. The captain spoke in casual tones.

"I wonder if the people receiving that crate know exactly how many diamonds to expect?"

No one said a word. He munched on his sausage and continued,

"I think I should take them all into safe storage, now that everyone knows they are there. That way, if any of the diamonds fell out and were found by any of us, we can return them all without any complicated questions once we reach dock."

"I reckon you're right, Captain," said Mitch with a sigh. "I bet those diamond smugglers know exactly how many pieces are in the shipment.

I'll keep an eye out, in case any were dropped."

"That's it, son," confirmed the Captain. "We don't want any trouble."

Random diamonds were returned throughout the rest of the day, so all was well received when they reached the port at the Panama Canal.

Mitch spent much of his time with the Captain, learning about sailing. By the time they reached the Everglades in Florida, he was given a certificate of achievement for passing a couple levels of seamanship.

The goodbyes were brief, and Mitch left the Blanc feeling lonely. He stayed in a hotel overnight, then rented a car (with a forged license) and drove across the peninsula to Miami.

There he took some down time and rested on solid ground for a week. He found Miami Beach quite a trip. When he finally boarded his new home on the cargo ship, the Mical, Mitch had been hit on by someone of every type of population in the world. He was quite flattered.

Gash Again

"I'm very excited, your Highness." Gash rushed around his lab in the Blue Castle, dabbling in various pots and beakers. "The properties of their tears are amazing, but their blood is what will earn the most money."

"I think I would prefer 'My Lord' to 'Your Highness.'" Prince Hadigan watched the birds and small jungle creatures jitter about in the garden under the river. To them, the blue water above was their sky and the hydro lights in the Skyling were their sun.

It truly was a marvel to see the castle cut into the rock in elaborate balconies, windows, and arches. The bright Skyling imitated the sun perfectly as it followed the course of daylight above, cutting through the river water ceiling, flaring across the open courtyard, and edging every carving in a blue shimmer.

"Pardon, Sire?"

"I think 'Highness' sounds... soft."

"But, about the blood, My Lord?"

"Now, that, I like." Prince Hadigan smiled and turned his attention to the scientist. "What is this disgusting goop you're playing in?"

"Blood, Sire."

The prince glared at him.

"I-I mean, My Lord."

The prince smiled and nodded.

"As I was saying," continued a confident and passionate Gash, "it's the dragon blood, or you can think of it as red cash."

The prince sniffed it. "Pungent, but sweet. How did you get it?"

"They will respect you quite obligingly if you respect them."

Hadigan turned and stared, surprised.

"I am learning to speak their language, slowly. It's quite difficult, yet simple. I know that sounds off, but... I managed to tell them I was a chemist looking for substances with healing properties. As soon as I said that, this little orange one, like an oversized dog, cut her arm with her claw and dripped out a beaker for me."

"I'd like to meet your dragons."

"Ah, well, I haven't seen any since. But I did manage to pull out the DNA and I'm working on duplicating it. Synthetic dragon blood, not nearly as potent, but enough to make you as wealthy as you want." Gash finished all puffed up and proud of his plan.

"That's all I need to hear." The prince casually studied the carvings on the ceiling. "What do you know of the Dijex sisters from Latoona?"

"I've seen them. They are what inspired me to extensively study dragon elements. Pretty little girls, scary in their own ability to truly use their power, but they'll be off to school soon, I guess."

"What do these girls like?" the prince inquired.

"One of them loves boys. The other, well she is the special one. I think you should keep an eye on her."

"And her name would be?"

"Holly. Caught my eye in a freaky way; she is, after all, only twelve."

"Thank you, Gash. I won't be in touch for a while. Just keep my traders supplied and we'll be fine."

As he left, the prince ran his fingers along the walls. "I think I'm ready for a quiet institutional life."

Dragon Mist
Royal Surprise
Years Ago
Local School Boy
Rio
The Proposal
Sights

Chapter 5

Dragon Mist

The cargo ship, The Mical, was delayed a couple of days, and that put the captain in a bad mood, although the crew assured Mitch that this was normal.

"Unless he is at least two miles off the coast line, Captain is in a bad mood, but once we're out to sea a ways, it's dancing all night long."

"How far out do we sail following the coast to Rio?"

"As far out as time will allow." Rico, a native Brazilian sailor, winked at Mitch, and it was hard to tell if he was serious or not. Mitch changed the subject.

"I thought ships were named after women, not men?"

"That same question comes up with all the unchurched." Again, was he serious, or not? "If you'll notice, it's spelled M-I-C-A-L, not M-I-CH-A-E-L. Mical was King Saul's daughter and King David's first wife.

Y'know David and Goliath... the giant... the stone... the dead hit in the middle of the head?"

Mitch pretended he knew nothing. "Is he the one that built the ark?"

But then Mitch couldn't hold back the smirk, and they both laughed. "I didn't know about Mical. I only remember Bathsheba."

Rico whistled,

"Who could forget her?"

Mitch enjoyed the bantering conversations with Rico all the way through the Caribbean and on down the east coast of Brazil. On their way past the quiet jungle shoreline, Rico came alongside Mitch again.

"I call that the Dragon Mist Mountain Range. It sits in the middle of the Amazon Jungle and holds the greatest," here the Brazilian whispered, "secret wonder of the world."

Mitch looked out through the haze.

Rico whispered right into his ear.

"My great grandfather says he saw it himself, in an open clearing inside one of the valleys. He was carried there by 'he-knew-not-what,' and woke up, healed of a broken leg, hearing a seductive song trickle through the trees."

Mitch allowed himself to be enchanted.

"After two days and two nights of laying on the mountainside, with fresh food and revitalizing mineral water laid beside him daily by 'he knew-not-what,' he began to make his way to the valley floor. Each morning, when he woke, again there was fresh fruit, cooked fish, and that revitalizing mineral water set beside him by…"

Mitch joined him, smiling.

"He-knew-not-what."

"Until," continued Rico, "on the third day, just before he reached a tiny village, he saw a rush in the jungle and a green and orange dragon flew over the trees and back up the mountain."

He paused for effect, and Mitch stayed silent.

"Great-grandfather said it was the size of a wild dog, long and quick. It circled around him once, and crazy as the old man was, he said it smiled at him."

Rico stepped back and shook off the misty mood.

"So, what do ya think about that, boy?"

"I'd say that as crazy as you are, it'd still be awesome if your great grandpa was telling the truth."

The captain approached with a sarcastic look on his face. "Let me guess," he slapped Rico on the back, "dreamer here has been telling you about the dragon tales of his crazy grandfather?"

Rico shrugged.

"Believe or not, doesn't make it not true."

"True or not doesn't mean you can pester my passengers with your crazy stories. The only truth the boy needs to worry about is the fact that tomorrow, we reach Rio."

Royal Surprise

It had been arranged quietly, and considering the last visit, it was probably the best idea. Prince Hadigan arrived in Latoona the evening after the Atlantis Academy caravan had left.

Defense forces suddenly surrounded the village. He just walked in. Chancellor Stonewall Tanker blustered out of his house, pulling robes and state chains over his head.

"Your Highness, we welcome you to our village again. May the Powers hold that this visit is full of great prosperity for you."

A secretary, or someone of import, spoke in the prince's place.

"Thank you for your welcome. We apologize for the inconvenience of such a sudden appearance."

"As you would have it, Sire. All is yours to enjoy." The chancellor nodded curtly. "To what end are we honored by such a visit?"

No one answered. The prince continued his examination of the marketplace; each stall and shopkeeper in turn bowed courteously and silently.

The prince turned with a brilliant smile and spoke.

"I understand there are some remarkable young ladies here. I wish to meet them."

There was no need to explain which ladies he meant. Others had come before him to question and stare at Tanya and Holly.

"Forgive me, Sire, the Dijex family is not here." The chancellor involuntarily stepped backward.

The prince continued studying the objects for sale on the nearest table.

"Really? Where are they?"

"Well, Sire, Your Highness... ahh... Tanya and Holly Dijex are even now on their way to Janeiro to catch the ship to Atlantis National

Academy. It is their first year in attendance there."

"Tanya and Holly Dijex are sisters?" Mr. Secretary queried.

"Well, not biologically. They were simply raised as sisters."

"And why were they raised as sisters? Are they orphans?"

"Forgive Mr. Secretary's curt tones." The prince threw his arm chummily around the chancellor's shoulders, matching his height inch for inch. "There is nothing to fear in me. I am merely a curious tourist."

Leading him away from the others, Prince Hadigan continued,

"Tell me about these sisters."

The chancellor swallowed hard and began to speak but could not. He cleared his throat and stuttered.

The prince interrupted,

"Perhaps we can just sit on the fountain here and talk. Is there any place to buy a drink?"

A lady rushed over from a chirpy village café. "What would you like, sire?"

"I hear the water here is excellent." His Royal Highness nodded to a Defense aide in green, who handed a handful of colorful bills to the waitress.

"Indeed, Your Highness, as you will."

Sitting in the cool evening, sipping the bubbly mineral water, Chancellor Stonewall began again.

"Well, Sire," he cleared his throat once more, "One of the girls lost her parents in the..." he paused, and Prince Hadigan suddenly turned directly attentive, "...in the Market Explosion of twelve years ago."

The prince answered, "Indeed." Suddenly losing all politeness, he growled, "I choose to not dwell on that day."

Without any further words, the entire Defense team melted into the jungle, and Prince Hadigan stepped into his transport and was gone.

Years Ago

It had taken one week for the seven-year-old girls to awaken from their dragon tear trance. They rose up from their beds healthier and stronger than they had ever been, with a maturity not previously present, and they frightened most of the villagers.

Reverence and mystery always surrounded the dragons and, of course, their tears. Outsiders would argue that they didn't exist, but the people of Latoona knew where they lived. They didn't go there, not out of fear of the dragons, but out of fear of themselves.

You see, when a Trevel is touched by a dragon, he or she is transformed beyond recognition. Dragon power fuels whatever the strongest desire is within the heart; many fear their strongest desires.

When the newly woken girls walked out of the Potion Master's house, they had not gone more than eight steps before they were suddenly swept off the ground by their parents and rushed home.

Master Su immediately began tending a new flower garden to the left of his front door, and a rock garden to the right that had sprung up under the girls' feet.

In secrecy, the girls were tutored on the far side of the river-well hilltop. There, they worked in a sheltered cleft that could not be seen from above, and anyone approaching would be heard long before they came into view.

Tanya brought her favorite rock collection to the very first lesson, and Holly brought her potted pansies. As an Earth Energist, Tanya began to sense various smells coming from the different rocks and soon developed the ability to smell what ores and minerals were hidden within.

Holly's Flora Energies reached into the essence of each plant, and she was able to amplify such energy, thus appearing to grow and reproduce seeds from nothing.

Each girl manifested levels of intensity far beyond any seen in other children or even other adults. Master Su took on the responsibility of teaching them to bend their powers away from destruction and toward construction and productivity.

Master Su also secretly noted that not only were their Energy powers beyond their years, but that in fact their years, their very chronology, seemed further advanced as they no longer behaved as little girls, but instead, emanated a more womanly essence. Master Su was deeply concerned about what affect this might have on socializing outside the small protection of Latoona's village.

For the first few months they were left alone, all alone. The other children were not allowed to play with them. The girls kept their amplified gifts secret, as if ashamed of them.

But when Chancellor Stonewall's son, Tomey, arrived home for school break, he explored the jungle for painting subjects and discovered the natural laboratory, with hundreds of bonsai specimens as well as shelves full of precious metals and gems drawn out of the various rocks lying around.

The girls were no longer feared, but revered as they and the Latoona Market benefited.

Local School Boy

Mitch was sixteen and still had two years of schooling to complete. His Gamma, of course, arranged for him to attend a fancy private school, but he refused. In fact, he refused to do most of what his Gamma wanted.

He wasn't necessarily rebellious; he did all the jobs and chores that needed to be done. He just didn't take part in the lifestyle his grandmother had accustomed herself to since she had begun receiving her income from Mitch.

When Mitch sent the retirement fund to her, she instantly took up the life she had always wanted. In eight months, she was president of three charities and on the board of directors for two more. She didn't pursue these positions out of a desire to help the underprivileged, but rather out of a desire to control and have power. She was a masterfully strong woman, as Mitch had heard her called so many years ago.

But Mitch no longer found her scary. He thought her rather pathetic. Everything depended on her apparent affluence, and she refused to admit that her money came from her grandson. She told everyone that one of her "investments" had finally come through.

Mitch went along with the game and played the part of a misfit grandson who, because of his genius, was rather antisocial.

Yes, Gamma loved to boast about Mitch's computer industry success, but she strategically omitted the fact that it was due to computer games. Instead, she made it appear as though she had gotten him started in business — after her investments came through — and no one bothered to check the details.

So, while Gamma waltzed around the rich and famous, Mitch played.

The first thing he did was set himself up as a computer securities investigator. It was not long before companies all over Rio de Janeiro and up and down the coast were begging him to work out the bugs and fire-proof their business systems.

The biggest advantage of this was that he did all his work from his own computer at home. No one noticed that it was a teenager hacking into and reprogramming office securities for large amounts of money and gaining an important professional reputation as one of the best.

Mitch registered himself at the public school and joined the Computer Science Club, whose president was a girl named Vanga, short for Evangeline. She was the perfect combination of pretty and geeky.

"You completed the entry project quickly." Vanga stood over Mitch's desk scanning his flow chart.

"Does that make me a suck-up?" Mitch continued staring at the desk.

"No, it makes you a member, if you can afford the fees. If you can't, there are scholarships, but it takes longer to receive the membership pin and magazine subscription."

He pulled out an acceptably full wallet.

"How much do you want?"

She balked but regained her cool quickly.

"The sign-up sheets are in the folder on the front desk."

Mitch calmly stood, fetched the folder, and began filling out the form.

"If I pay in cash, will you go out to dinner with me tonight? Not that I'm suggesting I need to pay for your company... I... It was just a line."

Vanga smirked.

"Pay me for the full year's fees, and you can have the pleasure of buying me dinner every night this week."

Despite the apparent rip-off, it was a done deal.

Vanga recommended a popular fun spot for dinner, the Trey, Vale, & Bacht Corporate Complex.

The ground floors were all jungle foliage with streams, mists, and jungle sounds creating a tranquil place for conversation and meditation. The two ate burgers on the second floor looking over the balcony, watching all the people come through the front doors.

"Busy place," Mitch mumbled through a mouthful of fries.

"Always is, don't know why. The public areas are never full. I guess the hotel is always packed, though," Vanga explained. "The two lower floors are entry and food courts; then there are five floors at the top for restaurants, shopping, and entertainment. The rest, in between, are offices and hotel rooms."

Mitch was intrigued.

"I'd like to stay over one night, just for kicks."

"It's a private hotel. You can only stay here on the invitation of the owner."

"How do I get that?"

"Don't know anyone who ever has." She shrugged, and they spent the rest of the evening wandering the shopping floors and enjoying a couple of indoor rides.

Without letting Vanga notice, Mitch kept an eye on the security system and grew more curious the longer they were there.

He delivered Vanga back to her home at a reasonable hour but was so distracted by his thoughts on hotel security that he didn't notice his missed opportunity for a goodnight kiss.

Vanga noticed the offense with contempt.

Immediately after a distracted goodbye, the sound of the car door slamming still ringing unnoticed in his ears, Mitch staked out the Complex. He walked around until the open areas closed, then sat in his car watching the many people from the private hotel come and go all night long.

Rio

Miles before the Atlantis Academy Jungle Caravan from Latoona approached any Bacht settlements, it lifted off the jungle floor and soared over the landscape, invisible and swift.

Flying was the best way to travel when avoiding Bacht. Their technology, although much improved, still could not track the water-based camouflage and wind-based mechanics.

There was no real hurry to get to Rio de Janeiro, the Bacht Brazilian carnival city, and the students' families had those free tickets for two days in the Trevel Upland hotel to enjoy the city's beauty.

Right in the middle of busy Rio stood a modern, glassy building that was both an office complex and luxury hotel: the Trey, Vale, and Bacht Office Complex.

The landscape around it was lush and full of foliage with running water. This theme continued into the lobby, which imitated a jungle clearing. Fountains and waterfalls, runoffs and pools lapped though flowers and ferns singing songs of distilled peace.

On entering, even Bacht chose to simply sit and enjoy.

Brazilian Trevel are much like the Bacht in their love of life. Thus, there were no racial barriers in the open floors. The floor overlooking the lobby was an eatery that offered fast food, and the top five floors offered fabulous mall shopping, an indoor amusement area, and sky-level restaurants, sports bars, and dance clubs.

A couple of floors between the dinning and hotel levels were finance, trading, and legal offices. They worked only specific cases in which Trevel interests mingled with Bacht interests. In the basement was a post office that also carried specified interracial mail.

The whole building was jovial and encouraged the secret mixing of Upland and Underland livelihoods.

The backside of the building was a large parking and landing port. It looked simple enough but for one side being open to the air for three floors, with a large gaping hole that was disguised as a large gaping hole. With a building that luxurious, you can get away with any kind of eccentricity.

On approaching the city, Tanya cried out,

"There it is, Holly, that shopping venue we read about!" The excited teen smeared her face across the window in an effort to study it as they flew over.

"I think you had better stay inside our hotel, girls. There are shopping floors there."

"You say that every time, Deda."

"And he is right!" Salla turned to look at the two headstrong girls.

"You cannot continue your independence here. There are too many opportunities to get lost."

Tanya snorted,

"Hello? Earth Energist tuned into the magnetics of the earth−−does not get lost!"

"Bacht technology is not like ours. It can do things to Trevel without any warning. You stay in the hotel unless you have a guide, okay?"

In unison, the girls sighed, "Yes, Deda."

The caravan maneuvered into the gaping hole and materialized on the landing track.

The Proposal

Mitch was confused by Vanga's standoffish attitude the next school day. He was completely clueless, and it took a detailed explanation via Vanga's intimate friends to have him realize the offense he had unwittingly committed.

"It's not that I didn't want to kiss her, I just… well, I got a little distracted by something."

"She should be the only thing you're distracted by when you're dropping her off after a date."

"Girls are weird." Mitch stalked off, now completely distracted by how he should get back into Vanga's good graces again. He settled on a direct approach.

That afternoon, at the onset of the Computer Science Club meeting, Mitch entered the room and, without a word to anyone else, immediately advanced upon Vanga, interrupting her current conversation by gently but firmly placing his hand on her neck and pulling her close in a deep kiss. At first, she pulled back, then soon melted into the moment.

Mitch pulled back, looked her directly in the eyes, and asked, "We good now?"

"Uh-huh," was all the girl could muster up to respond with, her mouth still open.

"Good."

Mitch then plopped down at his computer keyboard and immersed himself in completing the afternoon's project.

Mitch and Vanga dated on and off for the next two years in a turbulent relationship. The problem was no more complicated than the fact that Mitch considered many other things more important than the pretty girl he liked to have around. Vanga would have been done with him soon after the first-date fiasco, but he took on such interesting projects that she kept herself in a position to be a part of all he did.

His latest and longest-running investigative project was nearly ready for her to partner in.

"Want to go to dinner tonight?" Mitch surprised Vanga in the school hallway.

"Not if we go to the Complex again. I'm sick of that food."

"Okay. See you round, then, but I thought you wanted to get on board with my latest 'exploration.'" He quoted the last word with his fingers.

Vanga jumped at the offer.

"What time will I meet you?"

"No, no." Mitch smiled secretively. "I'll come by and pick you up at six. Wear something formal."

"What?"

"There's still one last restaurant we haven't tried yet."

"The Lemuria Banquet Hall?" It was a preposterous suggestion. A meal there was three times more expensive than any other meal in the whole building, probably combined.

"Yeah, I hear it's pretty."

Mitch swaggered off to class and Vanga spent her next free hour asking as many friends as possible if they had a formal gown she could borrow.

"You don't think he's going to propose, do you?" one romantic friend suddenly suggested.

"I thought you were a career girl?" Her independent friend stared in horror.

Vanga hadn't even considered such a ridiculous proposal… ah… idea. She just laughed and tossed an,

"I have no freaky idea" at them as she disappeared home early.

All was amazing: the beautiful sleek rental car that Mitch drove, the gracious attentions of the restaurant staff, and of course the meal itself.

They began the tasty feast with coxinha, a breaded appetizer of chicken-styled croquettes. Vanga then chose the vatapa, a prawn curry, and Mitch chose the traditional feijoada, an assorted meat stew. After, they shared delicious pudim custard.

Delightfully full of excellent traditional food, Vanga thought. Nothing could be more romantic.

Over espresso at the end of the evening, on the high glassy balcony, Mitch put his hand in his pocket and said,

"The reason I brought you here tonight is to ask if you will join me on the biggest project of my life."

Vanga's heart leaped into her throat. It was way too early to be thinking of such long-term commitments. What was he thinking?!

He pulled out a small notebook.

"I'm going to hack into the security system in this building and figure out how to get onto the guest list for the hotel."

Vanga emitted a loud, short, "Ha" and stared, unbelieving. "You are the dorkiest, geekiest, most shortsighted, self-absorbed, incoherent, death-wishing boy in the whole world."

Undeterred, Mitch replied,

"I'm also richer than you could possibly imagine, and I'm asking you to partner with me."

She shook her head and smiled at his all-too-familiar nonchalant jokes.

"I stayed this far…?"

"I'll get us both off school this week to work as interns for a local, high-level security business."

"But its graduation parties all this week! And how are you going to swing a legitimate cover for that?"

"I own that business." He winked, rose to his feet, and extended his hand to her. "Shall we dance?"

Sights

Three Kobolds hauled the luggage off the bus and sorted through it all. They truly were the house laborers of only the rich and wealthy, with no respect for anyone else. Tanya and Holly watched, fascinated, and the creatures each in turn made rude faces at the girls.

All four of the Latoona families were staying together on the same floor, so they walked to the lifts as a group. There was a wonderful gut-rushing feeling as the lifts shot up to the right floor and everyone walked into the hall, giggling.

The Dijex family suite was designed to look like a beachfront cottage, except that instead of a sandy ocean, the glass doors opened onto a spectacular view of downtown Rio.

They settled in well as the maids unpacked everything for them, and they dressed quickly and arrived early for their dinner reservations. During dessert, the hotel owner found them.

"Welcome, my jungle friends. I am pleased to see you are satisfied." He did not allow anyone to respond; even if they were not satisfied, he would never know. "This is my son, Andros."

A perfect sixteen-year-old in a white shirt, red tie, and blue cardigan stepped up with a perfect smile and a perfect handshake.

"Tomorrow he will take your young girls around town to see the sights, if that is to your liking." It wasn't a question. "You will join me for lunch. I always eat with the parents of new students."

Again, a fact, not a request.

"You will have your invitation in your room, tonight. Andros!"

The whirlwind departed with the superficial teen in tow.

"Bacht or Trevel?" Hal stared after the man and son.

"I didn't get a good look. It is as if he wouldn't let you." Salla shrugged and returned to her mango-sticky rice dessert. "Mysterious Rio."

They had no idea how he knew where they were, but Andros turned up as soon as they finished lunch the next day.

"What do you want to see?" Andros looked at his nails as he talked.

"I think it best that they stay near here." Hal stared meaningfully at his daughters. "Their energies are temperamental in Bacht surroundings."

"Dad!" Tanya was quite embarrassed.

"I don't recall having problems before." Holly looked suspiciously at her father.

"You've never been alone in Bacht society before." Salla was strangely cautious also. "Master Su suggested we be careful."

"Whyyy?" Tanya elongated the word in disbelief.

"One: you haven't even started seventh grade at school yet, and, two: I'm your father. You know you can trust me, right? Do you trust me?"

The girls sighed in frustration but admitted that they did indeed trust him. With that, Andros led them to the lifts, down to the lobby, and out to his flashy truck.

"We can start by driving around and we'll see what you want."

Andros skidded out to the parking lot and whipped through traffic.

"Can we go over there?" Tanya looked, with eyes closed, to the side and pointed over Holly.

"Why there?" Andros' perfect face turned into a disgusted sneer.

"I don't know. I just feel drawn to something."

"What's over there?" Holly strained to look around the buildings.

"Botafogo beach; there is great shopping over there."

There was a guilty silence.

Andros baited them,

"Plenty of Trevel go there."

"Well then, it should be okay." Tanya nodded, her mind made up.

The touristy shops came into view and Holly's eyes got a little glassy as she tried a quick count of the multicolored windows,

"Yeah, perfectly okay."

Andros parked as close as he could and waited for them. They jumped out and dodged through the street.

People were everywhere, and Holly was jostled through the crowd, but she deeply breathed the leafy air of the tree lined entrance.

Tanya ran her fingers across the cement wall along the street. They both shivered in delight.

"I thought we'd catch a movie." Andros tossed his hair in the direction of the cinema.

Holly didn't take her eyes off the doors. "I don't want to waste my time sitting watching someone else's imaginings. There's too much to see and fill my own mind with."

"No. I'm going to see a movie." Andros was bored with them.

Tanya balked. "Aren't you supposed to be our guide?"

"Well, if you need a babysitter, fine, but you seem mature enough to me."

"I don't need a babysitter. I just don't know if we can find our way around in there, it's pretty big." Holly tried to be controlled and calm, but it wasn't working.

"There are maps everywhere. You can read a map, can't you?"

Tanya was getting mad also. "I don't need a map. I can tap into the earth's magnetic field and find my way anywhere."

"Sensitive to magnetic fields, huh? Then I don't suggest you go in."

Holly stood right up to his face.

"With, or without you, we are going in."

For the first time, Holly saw Andros's eyes and gasped. He pushed her away.

"You're Bacht!"

He cursed at them and stormed off.

> The Game Is On
> Trips and Tickles
> Curious
> Emergency!
> The Connection

Chapter 6

The Game Is On

"So? Did anything happen last night?"

That same romantic friend who had suggested the possibility of a proposal interrupted a perfectly calm planning session between Mitch and Vanga.

Vanga dismissed Mitch's awkward questioning eyes as she coldly responded,

"Yes. We were treated like royalty and danced, but nothing else too exciting."

Mitch, a little perturbed, replied,

"If last night wasn't exciting for you, then you're impossible to please."

Is it possible for a romantic seventeen-year-old girl to notice anything and keep her mouth shut? Vanga wished it were so, but she was not that lucky.

"I don't see a ring. Did you chicken out at the last minute, Mitch?"

Such a comment could not possibly register in Mitch's indifferent brain waves, but he questioned the furious look that Vanga bored into her friend's head.

"My dear friend." There was nothing dear about Vanga's tone. "We enjoyed a beautiful car ride, a delicious meal, pleasant conversation, and romantic dancing. That is all."

Mitch picked up on the last sentence.

Vanga continued,

"Now, we are busy working on an outsource project for a top computer securities company in town, and I insist that you go away and don't distract us."

The hurt and downhearted romantic slumped out of the room. The couple studied their work until Mitch asked with a teasing grin,

"How do you suggest we get into the basement, my dear fiancé?"

Vanga calmly swiped a book across Mitch's head and answered,

"Why don't we just walk in?"

And that was the end of the awkwardness.

On the afternoon of the infiltration, Mitch met Vanga in their usual spot by the misty waterfall. The lobby of the Trey, Vale, & Bacht Corporate Complex was just as busy as always, and the two joined the crowd walking to the elevators.

Instead of stopping in the public waiting room, however, they casually walked through the steel doors with another couple about the age of Vanga's parents.

Although the temptation was strong, they did not stop and stare at the lavish design and luxurious setting of the Hotel's private guests' waiting room but, instead, followed the couple to the private elevator shafts.

They could not help over hearing the conversation of the obviously worried parents.

"Hal, I just don't trust Andros. He drove off with such carelessness. I think we should go and find the girls."

"Salla, let them go. They have to learn their lessons on their own."

The husband hugged his wife and she whispered,

"But what lesson will they have to learn?"

"They will come home tonight, very late. They'll be sick and weak and know, first hand, that Bacht society is really dangerous if you aren't careful."

"I don't want them to be sick. Do you think they will go shopping?"

Hal turned to Mitch, casually nodding at the elevator door.

"Can you get that?" Turning back to his wife, he said, "That is the direction they drove off in, and with all the magnetic security doors in each of the shops, Tanya will not be able to help being drawn to it."

Mitch stepped up to the elevator door and looked for a button to push, but there was none. Vanga moved in and pointed slightly to a long panel of glass down the side of the door. It looked like an aquarium, but there was nothing inside. Mitch touched it gingerly with his fingers. The glass undulated and rolled as if it were thin plastic.

"Will they know what to do? Oh, I know, they're fine, I just want to run and rescue them. Can I do that?" Salla noticed the two and stopped suspiciously. "Are you okay?"

Vanga smiled and coolly responded,

"No, actually, I was just at the Mall myself and I feel quite woozy."

Mitch casually wound his arm around her waist and touched his head as if he had a bad headache.

"I'm sorry." Mitch turned slightly, squinting, with his eyes to the ground. "One of the security magnets activated right when I was walking through it. Could you get the door?"

Salla swiftly moved to Vanga's side and helped hold her, as she was swaying quite a bit.

"Of course, honey, get that? Oh, you look awful." Mitch watched as Hal placed his palm over the plastic and it began to glow and the door dinged open.

The four walked, or staggered, into the glass elevator. It was completely surrounded by a bubbling aquarium, this time with fish and plant life swimming around them.

"Where are you headed?"

Mitch breathed deep and smiled at Hal.

"The basement, please."

Hal nodded.

"Yes, you'll get good attention down there."

When the elevator stopped, Hal shook hands with Mitch and looked him square in the eye.

"You look after that lovely lady of yours."

"I will definitely look after my lovely." Mitch tenderly squeezed Vanga's hand and pulled her to go. Salla pulled back and hugged the girl then held her shoulders and smiled right into her eyes.

"You'll feel better in a little while, just rest now."

"I will thank you. You're so kind."

The doors of the elevator closed and the young couple sighed together and walked to the door they believed was the securities antechamber.

The couple in the elevator raised their eyebrows to each other. Hal reached for the hydrophone and Salla acknowledged,

"They're quick and very clever, I'll give them that. Poor Bacht who stray too far in, I wonder how far they'll get."

Hal spoke to the circling waterfall that had activated at eye level by the door. "There are two Bacht teenagers in the basement. They just left the elevator now."

Through the spinning water, a voice spoke back, "We can see them. Thank you for reporting. I'll take care they don't do anything stupid."

Trips and Tickles

"What a farce he is." Holly lost all respect for Andros and his pretend sophistication. "I thought he was too perfect. Tanya?"

But Tanya was already walking in through the front entrance of the shopping center.

"Wait up!" The two walked through the brilliant entrance one behind the other.

"Sorry, I just couldn't help it. I just had this urge to get in here."

The first few clothing stores they saw, as they began to wander, sold clothes something like their mother would take them to.

"I have to go in there."

"We'll go to plenty of stores like that down in Janeiro. Let's go somewhere else." Holly dragged Tanya over to the map. "Look." She coughed. "There's a specialty place a couple of stores down."

Holly didn't pay too much attention to her sister's inability to walk past any of the stores' entrances. She just dragged her along focused on her own mission.

"Please, I've got to get inside somewhere." Tanya wandered from side to side of the walkway, trying to enter any of the doorways she saw.

"Tanya, stop it! Here, this is not what Mema would want us to wear to school. Isn't it perfect?" Holly pointed out the massive wall pictures beneath the swirly sign.

Girls in beachwear, many-layered and scanty, laughed, silent and frozen, in the perfect joy of the perfect fun offered inside, all because they wore the right clothes.

Tanya giggled,

"Me first."

They giggled their way to the door and paused briefly, knowing that neither Salla nor Hal would want them to buy from here, but still, it was culture to be explored.

Tanya tripped over something in the doorway and fell loudly, grabbing a table of neatly folded T-shirts. Every one of them tumbled to the floor, burying the disoriented girl.

"They are on sale, but we usually limit them to a hundred per customer."

A strong, dark hand reached around Tanya's shoulders to lift and steady her. If she hadn't been so dizzy, she would have been dead of embarrassment.

Holly didn't move to help her sister, as she was frozen to the rack of leather jackets, coughing.

"I'm so sorry, I… ah…" Tanya blinked at her feet.

"Grab a chair, Nina. Are you okay?" The native sun god who stood over the young teen lifted her chin to check her pupils.

Tanya registered her rescuer. She became frozen like her sister.

"I reckon you'll live, but you should buy something. It'll make you feel better." The gorgeous boy assured her.

Tanya held up the t-shirt she still unwittingly clutched. Without even glancing at it, she said,

"I'll take this one."

"Darling, as joking."

"Thank you, Reynaldo. I will take it from here."

The massive form of rippling delectation moved off to help someone else. "Drink this, darling. What is your name?"

"Tanya." She tasted the cool water.

"I'm Holly, her sister," came another small but persistent cough.

"Sorry about the disturbance."

"Yeah, we'll go now."

"There is no need, wait till you are steady again." The saleswoman led the two girls to a couple of cushy armchairs by the dressing rooms. "I'll be back in just a moment."

Nina nodded the delectable hunk toward the back room.

"What just happened?" Holly, truly worried, coughed and held her sister's hand tenderly.

"I think I've been struck by lighting and woken by a god." Her gaze was fixed on the curtains behind which Reynaldo had disappeared in search of espressos.

"Mmm, exceptionally delicious, but you fell before you saw him."

"Did I? What was in the doorway that I tripped on?"

"Nothing."

"Here we are, ladies." Reynaldo came up with a handful of light, lovely outfits. "While you were resting, I took the liberty of finding something luscious just for you."

On cue, they both stood and reached out to the offerings.

"I thought dresses would work best." He helped each girl hold one up against her body as they studied their reflections.

"They bring out the womanly innocence you hold in your eyes."

"Oh?" they smiled. It was like a bad soap opera with a happy ending for commission-bound Reynaldo.

On the way out, with two purchases each, Tanya tripped again, but without falling this time. Reynaldo snorted a contemptuous "Ha" behind the cashiers' counter.

"I need something to wet my throat." Holly had a little coughing fit.

"What's with all the hacking?"

"I don't know. Something's tickling my throat. Where can I get some mineral water?"

"I could use something to eat, too." Tanya pointed out the map.

"Let's find the food hall."

Curious

The securities antechamber was just what they expected. The room was cool and quiet, calm and efficient. A couple of couches surrounded the coffee table, which caught Vanga's attention.

The table had a glass top and one thick, glass tube for the leg support. Inside the tube, visible from all angles but best viewed from the top, was a swirling mass of cloud. It was like a Tesla ball that you touch and lightning from the center reaches out to your finger, only it was the clouds that swirled in stormy tornadoes. There was lightning, too, but it flashed on its own without any tactile assistance.

The rest of the room was open but for a couple of work booths with outlets for all types of facilities, even some Mitch didn't recognize.

"Look at this, Vanga. It's the same as the elevator." Mitch touched the glowing circle in the wall right next to the cable outlet. It undulated but didn't glow.

"There's another one here by the inner door." Vanga laid her hand against the glass panel by a great strong door, obviously for Personnel Only, but nothing happened. "What did that guy do to make it glow?"

Mitch sat in a booth next to a large aquarium set into the wall.

"I have no idea. Keep trying." He opened his computer and began connecting himself to the Complex's main operating system. Feeling a little as if someone was watching him, he glanced at the fish swimming next to him.

"What's with the fish fetish?"

"Let's just locate the cameras and be professional." Vanga gave up on the open panel to join Mitch in the nearest booth and pulled out her own laptop.

The fish continued to swim indifferently, but through the water, others watched in rapt attention.

The Defense Strategists, hidden on the other side of the fish tank, observed the young Bacht in readiness.

Primer Stacey Tanner flipped her hair behind her shoulders with one hand and flicked a fire ball, the size of a pea, at the glass screen in front of her and growled,

"Imbecile, I'd like to fire a shot or two at them."

"Stand tall." A secondary officer by the back door announced the arrival of Champion Tambeaux.

"Take allay, strategists." The militia in the room relaxed a little.

"What is all the excitement about, Primer Tanner?"

"Two Bacht teenagers were reported in the basement ten minutes ago, sir. They have made their way into the entry room and are attempting to log into our system."

Primer Tanner, equal to one of the Bacht military lower-level soldiers, stood at ease, or at allay in Trevel terms, and relayed her observations, anticipating an exciting encounter. This was why she had signed up for service and dedicated her life to Defense. Living among the filthy, powerless Bacht was not her idea of a productive existence.

Everyone waited for Champion Tambeaux, a leader of excellence with family connections all the way to the Prince-in-One himself. The air was taut with readiness.

"Who is it? Someone we know?"

Secondary Officer Martin stepped forward.

"It's the Bacht Mitchell, sir."

"Indeed, I see it is." Ch. Tambeaux tapped the screen and enlarged the image of the two deep in conversation. He changed the angle of view and spied on Mitch's progress online.

"Persistence: a worthy trait. How many times has he been here, spying?"

S.O. Martin searched a nearby screen using a water-type keyboard.

"In the last two years, sir, he has visited the Complex 416 times. That's approximately four times a week."

"I'd say that's quite an obsession. Let's give him some headway and see what he does with it. Primer?"

"Yes, sir." Pr. Tanner tapped her own water keyboard.

Watching the enlarged image of Mitch's own screen, she took him through corridor access just far enough to frustrate him, then changed direction.

"Keep that up for thirty minutes. Call me if something changes."

Ch. Tambeaux left the room, and Pr. Tanner watched through the water maliciously. She was going to have fun with this Bacht boy.

Emergency!

The girls made their way up to the food court. Tanya was still unsteady on her feet and began going down the stairs.

"Tanya, the food court is up over there."

"It is?" She slowly moved her head from side to side as if listening closely for some quiet sound. She almost tipped over.

An elderly couple scowled at them and whispered to themselves,

"Stragglers, drunken children, where are their parents?"

"I'm not drunk," Tanya defended herself, but in turning quickly, she nearly hit the ground again. Holly caught her and spied a security guard looking at them.

"Come on, let's just find a seat and eat," she wheezed, and Tanya swayed all the way up the stairs.

The burger and fries revived them, and they glowed as they inspected their whimsical dresses. Holly leaned back, nearly disappearing into a fern in the planter behind her. She came out coughing.

Tanya beat her on the back and noticed the plastic veins of the fern.

"It's weird." Holly cleared her throat yet again. "It's as if I can't breathe the air in here. It smells bad. I think it's the Bacht air circulation. It's recycled so many times the freshness is flat."

"Maybe we should find a flower shop and stick a rose up your nose."

"Ha. Ha. Maybe you should stop tripping over your own feet."

"You clam up. I know there was some kind of blockage in the doorway. You would have fallen too if you'd gone before me."

"Well, next time, I will. Let's go. That guard keeps looking at me strangely."

Tanya gave the young man a "What are you staring at?" glare, and he adjusted his eyes with all the authority of a siren-defeated sailor and turned his attentions to a party of Bacht mall rats.

Feeling a little creeped out, Tanya took the lead.

"No. You tripped last time. My turn," said Holly, pushing forward.

"So go already." Tanya's impatience was clear in her response.

Noses in the air, they silently stalked through the field of tables and chairs. They re-entered the busy walkway and maneuvered through the crowd. Holly coughed again, and Tanya accidentally bumped into a passing group of shoppers.

Tanya steadied herself and walked to the nearest trashcan. Her face was a pale shade of green.

Holly's eyes widened.

"You look awful..." a suffocating cough exploded from within and would not cease.

Tanya heaved her barely digested lunch into the trash, loudly and continuously.

Both girls continued for half a minute till they passed out.

The pure oxygen and electromagnetic shock treatments they both received right where they landed, brought life back to their squeezed lungs.

The paramedics whisked them into the ambulance and an elderly doctor, in the emergency room, stabilized their systems enough so they could talk.

"That's quite a trip you two took. Has this ever happened to you before?"

The two shook their heads "no" in unison.

Dr. Chapman studied their eyes with his flashlight and asked,

"Illumination, Electricity, Air, Water, Fire, Fauna, Flora, Earth, or Metal?"

Tanya hiccupped in disbelief,

"Earth… and Metal, sir, thank you."

Holly dropped her head in shame.

"Flora, sir."

Dr. Chapman pulled a hidden medical briefcase from under the counter and prepared a syringe of green fluid; he also pulled a large magnetic-weighted blanket from the heating station and draped it over Tanya.

"Why do I get the needle?" Holly winced.

"You're just lucky, I suppose." Tanya sighed, quietly lying in the comfort of the heaviness around her.

"I'll arrange for the ambulance to return you to the hotel basement. There you will receive extended care."

Rubbing the back of her neck where the needle had entered, Holly asked, "Does this happen a lot?"

The doctor grinned. "Only this time every year, when the new seventh-graders are in town."

The girl blushed and then looked at her sister in disgust. Tanya lay catlike, curled up under the comforting magnetic rocks sewn into the blanket.

The Connection

Mitch swore loudly and threw himself out of the booth, stalking around the antechamber.

"It's as if someone is playing with me. Every time I get close enough, the walls close up and I end up behind myself again."

"Just cool it, Mitch. This place gives me the creeps." Vanga walked along the length of the aquarium and turned to watch the table swirl.

There was also a constant fire burning in a large lantern and a rock garden in sand. In the far corner was a small jungle of potent-smelling plants inside a fence of weird flashing lights.

"Have you even noticed how weird the decorations are?" Vanga pointed out the various objects.

Mitch wasn't too interested, at first. "Water, fire…" He suspiciously noted the elements. "…earth, air?"

"Those rocks aren't simple, either, look." Vanga picked one up and turned it over. It was full of golden veins.

"That's metal."

Mitch looked at the jungle corner.

"There's vegetation, too." He walked over and brushed his hand against the leaves.

Suddenly there was a rush and a vicious barking sound. They both jumped, and in the split second of terror, Mitch thought he heard laughter.

In the security booth, S.O. Marten commented,

"There you have it folks, the boy has discovered Dawn. Careful, little girl, you almost wet yourself." The Strategists cackled together, spinning in their chairs.

A large prairie dog growled at the visitors from beneath the foliage.

Vanga whimpered from on top of the desk. Mitch took a deep breath.

"That would be animal. Anything else?"

"L… Light, and electricity," the poor girl stuttered, pointing to the lamps that illuminated the jungle, an alternating choice of pulsing solar lamps and sizzling Tesla balls.

"Animal, vegetable, metal, light, electricity, earth, wind, fire, and water: think about it, these elements are all over this building."

Mitch looked at Vanga, and they played through their minds all the images they remembered from their visits over the past two years. Yes, this theme touched everything, everywhere in the Complex.

Further contemplation on the subject was impossible as the door opened and two lovely native Brazilian girls walked in.

Everyone in the Securities room sat up.

"We have a situation. Primer Tanner, go fetch Champion Tambeaux."

S.O. Marten advanced the view and audio on the room behind the aquarium.

"Nobody else goes anywhere or touches anything."

On the screen, Tanya sauntered into the antechamber with her blanket robed beautifully around her lithe body. Holly entered with the grace of a fairy queen.

"Oh!" Holly stopped, suddenly ashamed of her situation, and addressed Vanga. "I didn't think anyone would be in here."

"Neither did I... ah... I'm Vanga."

"I'm Holly, and this is my sister, Tanya."

Tanya noticed Mitch and addressed him.

"Hello." There was much pleasure in her voice. "What's your name?"

"Mitch."

Tanya flirted as usual.

"Well I've never seen such blond curls before. I know I'm just a backward jungle girl, but you are beautiful."

Mitch picked up easily,

"I've never met a backward jungle girl. Are they all as gorgeous as you two?"

Vanga snorted, but no one paid attention to her.

"No, they aren't. I stand out above all the others. It's a known fact. Ask my sister."

Holly nodded and rolled her eyes.

"Men and boys come to see her from miles around."

Mitch casually, and with great charm, leaned up against the great security door.

"Don't underestimate yourself, Holly, is it? Together, the two of you bring out the man in any boy."

Tanya promenaded through the room with a sly smile.

"Well, if you're such a man, why don't you get the door for us?"

There was the catch.

During the conversation, Champion Tambeaux returned.

"I see, the situation has heated somewhat. What shall we do with you, Mr. Mitchell?"

Mitch, too, was trying to figure out what he would do with himself. A moment of hesitation melted away in oozing charm.

"I don't know what to do. I am paralyzed by your presence."

Tanya giggled, but Holly glided over to the handsome young man.

She lifted her face as if to kiss him but tilted her head down and pouted at him from under her eyelashes. She smiled knowingly at him.

"You don't know how to open the door do you?"

"Holly?" Tanya stared at Vanga, then at Mitch, and noticed their lack of Trevel energy marking. "How did you get in here?"

It was Vanga's turn to be haughty.

"We walked right in. Why don't *you* open the door?"

Holly grinned and placed her hand on the glass panel. It glowed and the door slowly swung open.

"How did you do that?" Mitch was exasperated. He grabbed Holly's hand and placed it back on the panel.

"Make it glow."

"No, you."

A figure came through the black rubber curtain that covered the inside of the door.

"Lady Tanya, Lady Holly, welcome. Dr. Chapman called and the healers are waiting for you."

> An Invitation
> Royal Court
> Welcome Indeed
> Private Escort

Chapter 7

An Invitation

Champion Tambeaux stood tall and saluted the girls with his left index finger straight and angled across his left check just under the corner of his left eye. This is, the Trevel salute based on the idea of, "I'm watching you, looking out for you." With this, the Trevel military, strategists, swear to serve and protect the Trevel Nations and citizens.

"Lady?" Mitch tried to play off the awkwardness. "Are you some kind of royalty?"

Tambeaux chatted back as casually as Mitch.

"They are Atlantis National Academy students, first years. That makes them as good as royalty."

Vanga slid back into a corner. All she saw was a towering military figure with brown hair braided half way down his back. His uniform, unlike any she'd ever seen, had deep black dress pants, and a black buttoned coat that was tailored all the way down to his knees accented by navy blue ribbon.

Around his waist was a simple black belt slung down his left side holding what looked like a red dagger hilt, only there was no blade.

"No need to hide, Vanga, we've been watching you two for a while, now." Tambeaux bowed to her slightly.

"Ladies, I think it best that you see the healers now. Your parents will be expecting you for dinner."

Holly grimaced. "Do they know we're here?"

The Champion said,

"We leave such news to the discretion of the individual student."

"Well then, good." Holly made her way to the curtain.

Tanya hesitated. Turning to Mitch, she said,

"Come in, won't you?"

"Absolutely. Coming, Vanga?"

Vanga didn't trust the whole, "we've been watching you" idea.

"I don't think so." She pulled Mitch aside. "This is a bit weird, don't you think?"

"It's even more 'weird' than you think, my dear." Ch. Tambeaux pulled out the bladeless dagger, and a clear, icy stump appeared, rather like a policeman's nightstick.

"The invitation is for Mr. Mitchell only. You are not ready for such a jump in your life."

Now Vanga was suddenly on the defense.

"I beg your pardon? I assure you, I am ready for anything that Mitch is ready for."

WHAM!

The rounded end of the nightstick suddenly shot out from the Officer's hand and tapped Vanga on the forehead just hard enough to knock her out. The stump then whipped around and held the girl by the shoulders.

Vanga lay limp in the stick-whip's grasp.

"Hush now, Evangeline. You will wake in a little while, forgetting all you've done on this exciting day."

A couple of plain clothed aides took her out of the room to deposit her on one of the comfy couches in the lobby.

Mitch considered protesting, but he was so enthralled with the weapon being closed up and put to rest back on the belt of the Officer, that he made no objection.

"So, Wattle-Gum Gecko Mitchell, would you like to enter Wonderland?"

Mitch actually wasn't too surprised to hear his full name. After all, he had been wrestling with the most brilliant computer system he'd ever come across. Naturally, they would know all about him.

"It's just Mitch." He stepped forward to enter the door, but Tambeaux shot his arm across the entrance and warned him,

"Once you're in, there's no leaving for at least five years."

"I have nothing here to hold me back."

"So be it."

Mitch stepped through the rubber curtain, only to find himself instantly thrown to the floor, tied up, blind folded, and dragged to somewhere quiet, very quiet.

Royal Court

King Darsaldain sat snacking on fruits and cheeses in his casual entertaining room when a uniformed aide approached with some private news. He whispered into the king's ear and awaited his response, which was immediate.

"Come, come, everyone." Darsaldain stood and clapped everyone's attention to himself. "Our son has returned and awaits our welcome."

The fairly large yet intimate crowd of family and friends bustled with boredom into a preordained arrangement.

The older gentlemen stood on the steps leading up to the dais where the king sat with three advisors and the latest young face of the year. She was older than the others had been, but still just as beautiful.

The remaining married women, uncles, aunts, and cousins decorated the edges of the Hall, and, of course, the eligible women lined the aisle, the most beautiful and ambitious ladies in front.

Trumpets called out from above, and the red gilded doors opened together as His Royal Highness, Prince Hadigan Andrew Hades Darsaldain, was announced.

Under his breath and beneath his winning smile, the twenty-six year old prince whispered to himself,

"Someday soon, I will be announced as the Prince-in-One, Heir to the Throne."

He bowed before the dais and, aloud, greeted his father. "May the Powers allow that you are in strong health throughout the year, my father?"

"You find us well, and we welcome you, our son."

The formalities aside, a gaggle of ladies boldly stepped forward to engage the handsome and eligible royal in hopeful conversation.

Hadigan flirted and gave more confidence than there was to at least four women and one young girl. The four giggled and the one froze, only to be awakened by her delighted mother.

Hadigan was eventually able to pry himself free of his admirers and gallantly strode up the steps to sit on his father's right. He ignored the lovely on the king's left side, as was appropriate for a son still mourning his mother's death from years ago.

He sat in silence, knowing this would heighten his father's curiosity.

"We are informed, Hadigan that this latest trip of yours took you back to Latoona: a memorial visit?"

"Something of the sort."

The king's lady, disgusted by the son and his disinterest in her, caught back her man in some captivating jest, and the two giggled together for some time.

"Son, we must ask you," the king returned his attentions, "have you given any further thought to our last conversation?"

Hadigan wiped the fruit juices from his chin. "Remind me of it, Father."

The napkin was thrown to the table and the king burst out,

"You know exactly that conversation of which we speak."

The entire Hall hushed and listened.

"It is quite time for you to marry. Up till now, you tell us you have 'never even thought of such a thing.' We tell you, it is time you did."

Hadigan stood and gracefully wiped his mouth before toasting a glass to his father.

"And since that conversation," he paused for a drink,

"I promise you, father, I did just that. I considered it."

He drank again, bowed to the gathering and exited via the private door. The four women he had flattered flushed and fanned their faces rapidly, while the young girl squealed and her mother swooned.

King Darsaldain, Ruler of the Nation Cities of Atlantis, residing in the ancient palace of Lemuria, sat down in shock and held his heart.

Welcome Indeed

The room was carpeted with something luxurious. Mitch knew this because they had taken off his shoes. Somehow he was tied to a chair, but as he could move his arms freely, he felt no fear and, as his eyes were still covered, his other senses kicked in.

The area smelled fresh and clean without the help of chemicals, and there was a movement in the air similar to the ocean tide. Back and forth, back and forth; Mitch was nearly rocked to sleep. It was all so peaceful.

A door opened and the blindfold was removed.

"Welcome. I'm Champion Marin Tambeaux of the Trevel Strategic Defense Force. In your world, that would be somewhat equal to a military major. But you are not in your world any more. So from now on, most of what you know is irrelevant."

Mitch stayed silent and attentive.

"I will begin with some history for you." Tambeaux sat in a comfy chair opposite Mitch. "The myths and legends you have grown up with are mostly true. The gods, supernatural beings, enhanced human abilities, they all happen to hold some degree of truth, leaving room for historical and artistic embellishments. All of them were Trevel. You are Bacht, one with no power.

"We, the Trevel, are not human, yet we are of the same makeup. The difference is, our senses are more active and in touch with our surroundings than yours. For example, you cannot use any of the enter pads by the doors because you do not possess the ability to focus your energies and use them as an extended hand, so to speak, although, with your expert abilities in technology, I have some questions as to your ancestry. That is why, against regular policy, I granted you access."

Mitch interrupted,

"Will you get into trouble?"

"As a Champion of the Strategic Defense Force, I am the trouble. I am required to register you, though."

"I get the impression that registering is going to hurt?"

"Yes, but only for five years."

"Oh, well that's all right, then!"

Tambeaux chuckled.

"It will be."

The champion stood and, with his hand stretched out, sent a thin stream of blue from his ring finger to the bonds around Mitch. They fell off him, melting to the floor. The young man gingerly stood and smiled.

"Cool, let's do it."

Through the door was a laboratory of sorts. A gentleman with fuzzy grey hair waved Mitch over to him.

"So the little one wishes to join us? Then join us you will."

Mitch turned to Tambeaux with a mock look of fear.

The champion laughed.

"I'll leave you to it. Do everything he says. I'll see you on the other side."

Mitch nodded then watched the "doctor" sink his hand into a hot, soapy dish with a thin layer of plastic coating it. His hand sank right through into the hot water. When he pulled it out, the plastic top layer dragged across his skin, drying it perfectly.

"What is that stuff?"

"Hydro-plano or HDP. When the Bacht figure out how to make and use it, I'll open my arms to them. Until then, boy, get used to being spat on. I, and many others like me, don't like your kind. You are the reason we went under. Not that that's a bad thing. We live much better here, but it is still ridiculously grating that the Bacht" he spat the world like an angry camel "can dictate our movements without even knowing about it, much less knowing they – you- are inferior to us."

"Okay?"

"Give me your hand."

Mitch withdrew from the man's reach. "Why don't you run through what's about to happen first?"

"Won't make any difference. You made your choice, it's not an option anymore."

"I know, but I like to be an informed consumer."

The old man looked the young man over, thoughtfully sizing him up.

"If Tambeaux brought you in, then there must be something to you." The doctor wiped his hands on his coat, walked to a drawer, and pulled out a shiny new booklet. "Why don't you read this? You'll be as informed as I am, then."

"Doesn't look like it's been used much." Mitch ran his fingers over the slick cover.

The doctor said,

"Never had to use it before. Bacht living here, like you, are few and far between. Let me give you a brief synopsis."

The doctor explained:

"If a Bacht accidentally enters Trevellia, then his or her choices are limited to memory correction, as was performed on your young female friend, or the Bacht is sent to a Bacht mental institution with memory damage or stays in Trevellia with the application of an Open Market servant tattoo and remains in slavery for ten years at the Trevel Nations disposal."

The doctor made himself more comfortable in his chair and continued.

"If, however, a Bacht is legally sponsored into Trevellia, as you were, then the responsibility for the Bacht rests on the Trevel sponsor, and the sponsor's family crest is tattooed on the mid-section of the inner left index finger and the Bacht remains in slavery for five years.

There is an added five-year bond-servant option for those who enter accidentally, but have been sponsored within twenty-four hours, and the sponsor family tattoo is marked on the left cheek bone beneath the outer corner of the eye, and the Bacht remains in custody with his or her sponsor family."

The doctor cleared his throat trying to recall where he was in the explanation.

"But, back to you. For each successive year after the first year in Trevellia, you will receive an annual tattoo on the inner end section of your left index finger, and at the end of the first five years, if the bond servant option is not taken, you may receive a freedom point tattoo and will then be free to move and live as you please in the Upland or Underland world."

The doctor took a huge breathing sigh.

"The difference between a Bacht servant and an L1 Bacht citizen is seen in the family crest tattoo as a small circle indicating the added freedoms of an L1 citizen. Any questions?"

Mitch thought he understood and, for the first time, began to realize the weightiness of the decision he had just jumped into, but recognized that this understanding had come too late.

He just held out his left hand and said,

"Okay, then, let's do it."

The symbol on the far right is the freedom point received at the conclusion of five years. The central figure is the Tambeaux family tattoo with the added black circle to indicate the L1 citizenship. The final four moon figures are for each year after the first full year of service. Thus, this tattoo is the complete mark that Mitch, now Tambeaux Mitchell, will receive after five years of restricted life in the Trevel Nations.

Private Escort

The elevator chirped as the door opened. A rosy-faced, cheery Tanya and Holly joined Tambeaux Mitchell on his journey from the basement back to the lobby.

"Mitch? Did you say your name was?" Tanya naturally opened the conversation.

"Yeah, was. Apparently now it is Tambeaux Mitchell."

"You ought to realize how lucky you are." Holly smiled. "The Tambeaux are an exclusive family."

"Uh huh," Tanya agreed, "and Champion Marin Tambeaux, your sponsor, is the greatest of them all." She gingerly lifted Mitchell's hand and investigated the water bandage on his left index finger. "Does it hurt?"

"Stings like… all get out."

The clear watery film over the tattoo was bloody, but dry.

"I'm supposed to clean it in an hour and put another bandage on. I have no idea how to do that, but I presume someone will help me."

Tanya was quick to volunteer.

"I can do that for you."

"Tanya, darling sister, I'm sure you won't ever see Mitchell again, once we exit this elevator. You'd best get all your drooling in now."

Tanya's glare fizzled the silver earrings Holly was wearing.

"Hey. You know how much I love these!" Holly objected.

"Then you shouldn't say such hurtful things."

"You'd better fix them."

"You know I will, as soon as I'm ready."

Holly growled.

"I'm sorry." Mitch interrupted their spat. "Forgive my Baahk ignorance, but, how did you do that?"

Tanya was sweetness all over again.

"That's B-A-C-H-T. You pronounce it B-ah-k-t. And I do it simply with my energy powers."

She gloated over him, and Holly took over.

"The Trevel," she pointed to herself and Tanya, "are able to connect with the energies around us and use them to channel and manipulate our surroundings."

Tanya made a yapping gesture with her hand behind Holly's head, but Mitchell was too intrigued by his first lesson to notice, so she gave up.

"Each one of us is gifted with certain abilities and strengths in the Earth's energies. Tanya is gifted with Earth and Metals. She can, as you saw, melt solid silver with a simple glare. It's quite annoying, really."

Tanya stood for no more hogging of attention from Holly.

"Holly, my dear sister," Tanya's voice dripped with sarcasm, "is a vegetable." Holly mimicked disgusted laughter. "She can grow and change anything that has living, growing cells, but is not animal, bird, fish, etc. You get my drift?"

"No, I'm sorry. What can you do?" Mitch tried to grasp the new concept.

By this time, the elevator opened into the lobby, where Hal and Salla were waiting for them.

"My babies!" Salla was all mema. "Do you feel all right now?"

In the midst of all her squeezes, Holly feigned innocence,

"What do you mean?"

"How was the mall?" Hal ruffled the girls' hair and hugged them, too. Mitchell disappeared into the corner.

"Oh, Deda, it was wonderful and horrible all at once." Tanya was a little teary.

"Don't look so confused, Holly." Hal took her into his arms for an extra squeeze. "I know you two. I know that with a place that held so many magnetic security doors and indoor plants like that, it would be impossible for you to resist."

"Then why did you tell us not to go?" Holly complained.

"Because I would not willingly put my daughters though all that you have just experienced."

"But, Deda," Tanya cocked her head sideways, "why didn't you just tell us what would happen?"

"Would that have kept you out of there? No, I didn't think it would. You're ANA students now. It is time to learn some things on your own."

"Oh!" Holly glanced around and waved Mitchell out of the corner.

"Mema, Deda, this is Tambeaux Mitchell, a brand-new Level One Citizen."

"Ah, we've already met." Mitch was embarrassed by the attention.

Salla smiled with a surprised look on her face and Hal shook his hand again.

"Welcome. Tambeaux, did you say? Well, so great an association, so early. You will do well here."

Salla agreed, and a deep voice behind them all spoke. "That was my first impression of him."

Everyone turned to greet the champion himself.

"Champion Tambeaux," Hal gave a slight bow, "we are honored."

"Nonsense, it is I who am honored to meet you and your daughters."

Hal introduced them all. "My wife, Salla, and my daughters, Tanya and Holly."

"Let me guess," Tambeaux studied the girls' appearances. "You, Tanya, are the Earth and Metal lady, and you, Holly, are the Flora lady?"

Tanya giggled slyly, as she just couldn't help herself around grand and handsome males, even if they were much older.

"You knew already?"

"Actually, no I didn't. But it wasn't hard to guess." He leaned in closely to Holly and reached behind her ear. Holly gulped and blushed.

She was not blind to the fabulous figure and presence of this Defense officer.

Tambeaux gently picked three flowers from the garden planter behind them and bowed, giving one to each of the ladies.

"There were no flowers behind you, Miss Holly, when I walked in. They all bloomed as you were introduced, and, Miss Tanya, the same goes for the stone pavement you're standing on." Everyone looked down. "It began bleeding orichulum on your introduction."

Tanya moved her feet. The red, sticky ore clung to her shoes. She wiped it off with her hands and rolled it all into a thin snake. Then, she pulled the strand thinner into a chain, laid it on her palm, and watched it slither into the stunning figure of a flying horse.

"I always liked these. One day I hope to see one." She handed the ornament to Mitchell. "Here is a welcome pin to say that all your fantastic imaginings just might come true, now that you're here with us."

She pinned it to his coat pocket.

"Thanks. I don't even know how to react to all this." Mitch ran his fingers through his sun-streaked hair.

"There'll be plenty of time for that. But now I would like to extend an invitation." Ch. Tambeaux turned to Hal. "Please honor me with your presence on my private cruiser, the *Hera*. I would like to escort you all to Janeiro myself."

> First Class Attention
>
> The Morning After
>
> Scholarship Particulars
>
> Apology Arranged

Chapter 8

First Class Attention

It had been delightful to watch the jealous faces of their Latoona companions as they drove off in a military escort to the Tambeaux family's private cruiser. Even Andros and his father looked red with rage at the importance given to one of their guests but denied them.

There were trumpets and flags, flashing swords and shooting rifles as they boarded the boat. Even the Bacht around them joined in the cheering.

The overnight trip out to sea was cool and pleasing. They ate dinner in the shiny modern dining room fitted with platinum and ebony highlights.

"You need more color in here, Champion," Holly advised Tambeaux when she arrived before anyone else.

"You're aboard my private vessel, Lady Holly. Call me Marin."

Holly was shocked. It was almost like the prince asking her to call him Hadigan. Such an intimate honor was beyond the village girl's imagining.

Marin turned to look at her reflection in the mirror.

"And I have all the color I need while you're here."

He saluted her and turned to discuss something with the butler.

Holly sputtered a quick laugh, closed her eyes and shook her head.

What freaky world was she putting herself into? He is just being flirty to make me feel good about myself. She scolded her imaginings,

"The day a man as grand as that ever talks to me again, much less makes me fantasize about being with him, is the day I grow flowers out of the air."

Dinner was delicious and the conversation delightful. It wasn't all sophisticated like she and Tanya thought it would be. Even Mitchell relaxed and acted at home with everyone.

"Marin and Mitchell really get along well with each other," said Holly as she and Tanya wandered up onto the deck. "They're like brothers already."

"He's not the only one Marin apparently gets along with." Tanya jabbed her sister's ribs. "Since when do you start calling a champion by his first name? Mema and Deda were shocked. They're pretty angry with you."

"He asked us to call him Marin. Don't you remember?"

"I don't remember any such request. And I know Mema and Deda don't. Even Mitchell avoided calling him anything at all. Do you need to tell me something?"

"Tanya, don't be ridiculous. That jealous tone doesn't work with me." Holly tried to throw off an uncomfortable feeling of foreboding.

"Marin seems to have found a tone that works with you."

"You're sick. He's twice as old as me. He's just being nice to a little girl."

Tanya spied the champion lurking in the darkness but pretended she didn't see him.

"Since when have you ever called yourself a little girl? You told me that the dragon tears matured us early and that we were really young women. 'Little girl?' Not in your personal world."

"I know who I am," Holly defended herself, "but he doesn't, so he's just being nice to a little girl, in his understanding."

"You know, I had a sister who once told me to never put words or thoughts into another person's head. They will always be wrong." Tanya displayed her best Holly impression.

"The word always is a blanket statement and shouldn't be used."

"Shut up." Tanya turned to leave. "Be quiet when you come to bed,

I'm going to sleep."

"Remember, I have the bottom bunk."

"Not if I'm there first you don't."

Holly watched Tanya flaunt off down stairs, desperate not to allow any inkling of what Tanya hinted at to be taken to heart, but then there was that deep voice again.

"This sister of Tanya's sounds pretty wise."

Holly jumped and screamed. Marin had walked up so quietly behind her, and his voice was just so… so… close!

"That's a reception I've not had before." He offered Holly a soft drink. "Stars should be enjoyed with a cold drink. It makes you feel closer to them."

"That's the crappiest pickup line I've ever heard. What are you doing?"

Marin stepped back and laughed quietly. "I am flirting with a girl who chronologically is half my age, but puts out more energy than most of my female peers."

"I am a first-year Atlantis student."

"Who is on a pretty hefty scholarship; someone is expecting a lot from you."

"No I'm not."

"Yes, you are. I'm to inform you parents tomorrow."

"How do you know?"

"Because, I am Champion Tambeaux of the Tambeaux family line of Strategic Defense Officers; I know a lot of things."

"Like what?"

"Like, I really want to ask Hal if I can court you."

"I'm a first-year Atlantis student."

"You've already said that."

"What are you thinking? I'm only… I'm only…."

"Twelve. Yes, and I'm twenty-four," Marin admitted. "When you put it like that, it does sound sick."

"I wouldn't say sick," Holly was quick to object.

"The problem is that anyone who knows you, or knows about 'Holly Dijex.' doesn't think of you that way. I know a lot of guys, boys and men, who want to have a chance with you and Tanya."

"So this is a competition with you? You want to be the first to kiss me or something?"

"If that were the case, I'd have already done it."

"You would not!"

"Would you have stopped me? No, I didn't think so."

"You are so sure of yourself." Holly wasn't sure if this was a good thing or a bad thing.

"Sorry. It's a habit. When you have thousands of people following your orders, you have to sound confident, even if you're not."

"Thousands? Really?"

"The crazy thing is," Marin leaned back on the rail, "I've been leading bands of men since I was just a boy. For my ninth birthday, my father bought me a commission on a Royal Strategic Defense ship. I spent four years there learning how to be a Naval Officer with at least thirty men under my leadership and responsibility."

"I drank dragon tears when I was seven."

"And while you were learning to control your energies, I was learning to control my men."

The black, silver-lit ocean waves caught their attention for a moment.

"You don't know me. Why do you want to court me?"

"I like what I know."

Holly challenged him, "Where will you be for the next six years?"

"Around. I expect a promotion to Mentor soon. That's more money and a more important social status."

"Good for you. I'm not even discussing this. It's too bizarre."

"As a Mentor in the Defense Force, I am expected to have an excellent wife. I thought you would be just that."

"You're looking for an excellent wife? I just want to be an excellent student. I want to be a teenager. I want to grow up!"

Marin stared at Holly for a moment. He looked nothing like a Defense Champion; he looked like a boy, deflated and rejected.

He took a deep breath and raised his glass to her and said,

Then, may the Powers see to it that my family will love and protect your family, for as long as the Tambeaux bloodline holds true."

He stood tall, saluted, and abruptly walked back into the cabin.

The Morning After

"What a glorious sight." Tanya gazed at the beautiful sunrise, then giggled as Holly staggered up to join them on the breakfast deck.

"Had a late one last night, sister dear? I didn't hear you come in."

"What were you doing up so late?" Salla tried to pick up on her daughter's emotions. "You knew we were sinking just after sunrise."

"So why did I have to be awake for it?" Holly mumbled groggily.

Hal suspiciously reached out to steady Holly as she bumped her way to the table. "Why so grumpy this morning?"

The champion and the boat's captain appeared. Tanya was quick to her mischief. "Does it have anything to do with your secret rendezvous last night?"

Holly sat next to Hal and held her head and her stomach to keep back the nausea. Hal sniffed her. "Are you drunk?"

"Not anymore."

"Good waves, Holly, are you hung over?!" Salla reached over and touch her daughter's forehead.

She tried to nod, but it hurt too much.

"What on earth! You know... Where did you get it?"

"This isn't like you, Hol! What's going on?" Hal drew his girl under his arm and Salla ran a cool napkin across her brow.

"YOU!" Tanya stood and pointed to the champion. "You got my sister drunk. What did you two do last night?"

"Tanya, what has gotten into you two?" Salla began apologizing to Tambeaux.

"No need to apologize, Mrs. Dijex. Tanya's accusation is understandable. I was the secret rendezvous last night."

"You got my daughter drunk?" Hal's question was not as angry as it was confused.

"Absolutely not, I was serving soft drinks."

Salla put her arm around Holly and said, "Why were you serving my daughter anything privately? Did you tell her she could call you Marin?"

"If I may express myself, please, my intentions for Holly last night were only to ask her if I could court her. I then planned to approach you this morning, but things didn't turn out as I hoped. Your daughter rejected me in favor of growing up."

Hal jumped up from the table, crashing the glasses over, and dove at the champion. He grabbed the soldier by the coat and threw him against the railing.

Surprisingly, the Defense Champion, who could have killed Hal in a moment, took the attack and allowed the angry father to have his say.

"What kind of pervert are you? I trusted you with my family and you disrespect me by going behind my back and seducing my twelve-year-old daughter?"

"Forgive me, sir. I meant no disrespect. There are obviously still some major cultural differences between

Uplanders and Underlanders. In Atlantis and definitely Lemuria, it is not uncommon to betroth girls at fourteen, or at forty."

Still in his face, Hal yelled, "Holly is only twelve!"

"Champion?" A call to attention echoed behind them. "We are ready to descend, sir."

"Just a moment, Captain."

"No." Hal stepped back with power. "We are done here. The sooner we get off this boat, the better."

But Hal suddenly stopped. "That still doesn't account for Holly being drunk."

All eyes turned to the hung over-girl.

Holly shrugged her shoulders. "I was in shock, and the aloe Vera makes a nice wine when it's heated just right."

"You made wine out of my houseplants?" The champion shook his head in disbelief. "You're going to have to keep tight reins on your girls,

Mr. Dijex. I know for a fact that I am not the only man that wants to meet and greet these two powerful Trevels, first years or not."

The champion and his captain left the breakfast deck, but the captain returned immediately.

"These orders are for you, sir." He handed over the black and gold leather-bound package. "Please enter the main cabin, sir, we'll be sinking momentarily."

Hal took the package and gestured for his family to follow him inside.

To Holly, he said,

"And you, young lady — seeing as you feel so inclined to turn your hands to home remedies — you will spend every night for the rest of this trip working with your mother and me to concoct healing potions from as many plants as we come across. You will then go with your mother to work in healing stations for the whole weekend instead of shopping."

Holly wailed in objection, "But Deda!"

Hal was firm. "No Holly. I will give you one afternoon with Tanya, but the rest of your time here will be spent working off your drunkenness. Now sit and be quiet."

The family gathered inside. They recognized the Atlantis National Academy Symbol pressed in gold on the front cover of the package.

The black leather glistened silkily, and they immediately recognized it as dragon skin. Hal unloosed the latch and opened the folder. It was a planner that laid out everything they would need to know as they prepared for their trip to school.

The first section was sealed and titled, "Scholarship Particulars."

Salla reached over, just as excited as the girls, and flicked the edge of the seal. It fell open perfectly, as if it had never been sealed.

"I hope none of the Lemurian Senators find out you can do that."

Hal winked at his wife and began reading.

Scholarship Particulars

From: Atlantis National Academy Board of Directors.

To: The Parents of First-Year attendees Tanya Dijex and Holly Dijex.

"Dear Mr. and Mrs. Dijex,

The following information outlines what level of scholarship has been awarded to

Tanya and Holly Dijex

Our records show that you requested a Basic Scholarship, which was awarded immediately.

However, when your particular case was studied and the unique gifts and talents of your daughters were understood, we, the Academy Board, took the liberty of upgrading your scholarship level by two points to Regulated Scholarship.

This scholarship allows the recipient access to all higher-level products based solely on their expected excellence. An added plain uniform allowance is granted to allow the recipient to keep herself in casual attire appropriate for a higher-level student who is placed in the society of the Main Circle of the cities' social Clusters.

However, there has been another change of plans as of last week, an anonymous sponsor has requested adoption privileges. With an Adoption Sponsor, your benefits have been upgraded again to the Sponsor's requested level. In this case, your point level was raised another three times, based entirely on the excellence of your expected success.

You are now approved for a Prince's Scholarship.

This scholarship has only ever been awarded to members of the royal family, or those with close connections to them. There are duties to fulfill under this privilege:

1. You are required to attend all major royal functions in both Atlantis and Lemuria. On such occasions when these interfere with regularly scheduled School duties, a private tutor will be assigned to you.

2. You will be required to be present on the school senate's dais at all ANA functions.

3. You will be required to take defense arts every school afternoon for each year you attend ANA.

4. Your presence will be required at all Powers seminars and ANA banquets.

5. You have now entered into a public life and all who see you will monitor your behavior. Please adjust your lifestyles accordingly.

6. Your Sponsor has granted this scholarship to you and has every right to cancel or continue this privilege at his/her own will.

7. Your sponsor will remain anonymous at his/her own will. Upon registration in Janeiro, you will be assigned two card keys, one for each student. They will give access to all the necessary products available to you free of charge at the stores outlined

in your planner under the heading Janeiro stores. These also apply to the stores on board your travel ship, the TSNS Atlantis.

On a more personal note, I look forward to welcoming Tanya and Holly myself upon their arrival. If you have any questions, feel free to contact me directly at Atlantis National Academy.

May the Powers prosper you,

Sincerely,

Principal Verity Zane

The mood of the Dijex family sank in accord with the *Hera* as they read the restrictive expectations placed on the girls. None of them noticed the champagne bubbles slither passed the window like rainbows. No one saw the fish in the depths bump curiously into the HDP barrier, wondering,

"Who is this new creature of the ocean?"

There was no one to sit in the bay window and relax as the coral and rocky hills of the bottom of the sea saluted the passersby.

The *Hera* turned about in the sea depths and headed back to the under-sea shelf of Rio de Janeiro. By nightfall, she would pull into the Underland docks of the Trevel city Cluster Janeiro.

But for the remaining undersea trip, Tanya and Holly stayed in their family suite, and Champion Marin Tambeaux sulked in his. Mitchell, on L1 house arrest, could care less about his restriction. The porthole in his room was all the freedom he cared to have.

Apology Arranged

"Today is a tight one, girls." Salla stepped onto the large balcony of their townhouse. Tanya and Holly were dressed in loose white pants and T-shirts, practicing the basic moves in the Beginning Defense Strategy textbook they had found their room.

Around suppertime last night, they had arrived at the lovely townhouse assigned to them on behalf of the Academy and their Prince's Scholarship (which the girls quickly dubbed the P.S.).

It was a large four-story home nestled among the other townhomes in the circle that reminded Holly of a Bacht book she had read that took place in the 1800s of Upland London, England.

The first floor was for receiving with parlors, formal and family, as well as dining rooms and a games room for billiards and Trevel darts.

The second floor held a private writing room, library, and the master suite. The back of the third floor hid smaller rooms for the Kobolds (two came with the place) and other staff, but the front contained grand guest rooms.

Holly and Tanya were originally settled in these front rooms until they explored and found the nursery.

The attic space was divided into two rooms by an ornate wooden archway and swinging doors. The front room was a sitting area that looked over the walk and roadway. The middle was a bedroom with separate bath and dressing rooms.

However, what really intrigued the girls was the back balcony. It had once been closed in, but now it was open to the air, with long, ornate stone posts reaching for the sky-lit cavern ceiling.

The Skyling, as it was called, held a thick layer of water, HDP, and manipulated electrolyte minerals. Somehow, these Skyling minerals were able to imitate almost perfectly the sky above the Upland open air.

"This is the perfect place to practice defense." Tanya surveyed the rooftop.

"Let's do everything we can to get ahead in defense. I also want to work on the Mind Powers for Beginning Optimists text. I will not go into school with a limited village understanding."

Holly sat on one of the stone benches and ran her hands over the carvings.

"No way will I let some Cluster boy or girl get the better of me just because they live where they see this stuff all the time."

There was a telescope on a raised circular gazebo, so Tanya studied the view.

"Oh my... waves and muscles. AHHHH!"

"What?"

"It's Mitchell! He's doing some self-defense art that the Bacht do.

Wow, he's really good, too."

"Let me see."

"Um? No."

"Fine. Do you need a hanky to wipe the drool?"

"Probably. Uh oh, Holly, baby, your fiancé just entered the scene."

Tanya stepped back and nodded Holly toward the telescope. Holly tried to ignore the comment but decided to look anyway.

"That's a pretty grand house they have." Holly shrugged the guilt away.

"The house is grand? How about the owner? Although you could have been the lady of that house, so I understand your interest."

Holly backed off and sat on the balcony railing.

"I have to apologize. I can't leave it as it is."

"Well, now we know where he is, we can visit while Mema and Deda are otherwise occupied."

"Yes, but what of my slave labor with the healing potions?" Holly was glum.

"We'll figure it out together." Tanya, already scheming, winked at her sister.

The next morning, Salla burst in with her "tight morning" schedule.

"At second call, you need to go and register your shopping cards. We'll meet Deda at the third call, that's eleven in the morning, okay? We'll shop for your clothes then. I see you found your library books and have been working through them already. Maybe I should try to stop you from studying?"

"Wouldn't work if you tried." Holly kissed her mema's cheek.

"Besides, you know we only study what's fun."

"What isn't fun for you?" Salla lightly smacked her daughter's rear in jest. "Go on, dress, breakfast, and off to registration in two hours."

"Mema, can we take a walk around the circle before we go?"

"Okay. Just be back by seven-thirty. It'll take twenty minutes to get there." She bustled off.

"Voila! Apology to Marin arranged." Tanya bowed.

"Practical," Holly pointed to herself, "and resourceful," she pointed and bowed back to Tanya. "Together, we are unbeatable."

"Look out, Atlantis." Tanya grabbed her sister around the waist.

"Here We COME."

> Marina
>
> Fare Thee Well
>
> Registration
>
> Relative Freedom

Chapter 9

Marina

"I have never seen so much food laid out at breakfast before, and for only two people." Mitchell lifted the lids of all the exquisite silver serving dishes on the buffet.

"It's not for two, it's for three. My little sister is joining us."

Marin entered with a cute girl only a bit older than Mitchell. She had straight brown hair chopped to her chin and a grungy blue outfit that could only be a Defense uniform gone AWOL.

"I'm not so little. I could defeat you any day." The lithe figure didn't look that strong, but Mitchell thought it did look nice.

"You defeat me every day with that baby face."

Marin patted the top of his sister's head repeatedly until she held out her hand, wrist up and allowed a wavy blue light flow from her palm. It melted Marin's belt into what looked like water, but then froze solid.

"Hey, keep the Ice Queen acts for your suitors, okay?" He tapped the frozen belt and it steamed off in vapor.

"Oh, I am just going to have way too much fun here." Mitchell snacked on a sausage and nodded his joy to the girl.

"Not to interrupt, or anything, but, I'm Tambeaux Mitchell, L1 citizen as of two days ago," he saluted her showing his tattoo.

"A Bacht brother? Cool! But I am surprised you made it through our front hall without any of the family portraits jumping off the wall in protest. A Bacht in a Tambeaux house and not in chains is almost heretical."

She was looking nicer by the minute. "Marina's my name," she saluted him then winced, "and yes, it's Marin and Marina." She screwed up her nose and said, "Cute, isn't it."

"Yes, you're very cute."

Marin lightly tossed a knife into the wall next to Mitchell's head.

"Don't go there, or I'll have to kill you."

"Excuse me, Champion, sir?" An ancient grey Kobold in a blue tuxedo interrupted them. "There are two young ladies in the hall wishing to speak with you."

"Ten, whatever it is you call money, says it's Tanya and Holly."

Mitchell raised his glass in a toast to his new "brother."

"Fifty says I want it to be." Marin followed the grisly Kobold into the Hall.

"That wouldn't be Holly Dijex would it?" Marina smiled slyly.

"None other."

"Marin's been dreaming of meeting her for five years, ever since we heard of the dragon tea party."

"The what?"

"Ask Marin when he gets back, if he gets back. He'll probably propose to her."

"Already did. She turned him down and her dad nearly threw him overboard."

"Ouch, poor thing." Marina resumed eating, but fell quiet in sympathy.

Fare Thee Well

Holly, with Tanya as backup, stood in the marble hallway to await an audience with the heir to the exhaustive fortune of the Tambeaux family.

Tanya poked her sister's ribs. "Deda said this house is only one of many. How does one family gain so much wealth?"

"Ten generations of savings."

Jangling her purse, Holly's sister said, "Boy, am I behind."

Holly continued,

"They began during the Shifter Defense, 400 years ago. Their search for renegade Shifters took them all over the nation and they found it easy to make money as they hunted down and stole the property of anyone they wanted to accuse."

Tanya eyed the pictorial history in portraits of proud Defense Strategists that lined the Hall.

"Now there's a family history to be proud of."

Tanya, walking through the room, came upon a clear cabinet that encased a rather ancient relic. It was a pair of dusty hooves, cloven, and chained together by rusty old links connected to rings that pierced each toe of the hoof. Beneath this was what looked like an antique royal decree:

"Never forsake the bondage of the Shifters:

A Shifter is any such creature who chooses to change its form from that which it was born into. These 'prophets,' as they call themselves, appear only to spread dissention against legitimate Trevel royalty.

Though their numbers are rare, if they wear not the chains, the chains of Chaos will be thrown upon our entire Trevel society. Any who discover and destroy a Shifter prove their loyalty to all Trevel and will be richly rewarded in kind.

Any action that would aid and abet a Shifter is considered Treason, and will also be rewarded in kind.

By decree, King Erasmus II, devotee and High Priest of Poseidon."

In Tanya's mind, the portraits looking down on her became more threatening.

"But the Shifters have been gone a long time. What does the illustrious Tambeaux family do now?"

"Now there is little to defend, but there are always rebels. So, they continue their military travels and build on ten generations' worth of investments." Holly finished her history recital.

"How do you know all this?"

Holly stood in the center of the Hall and smiled at her sister.

"What do you think I did while I was mixing my aloe cocktail? The linknet is easy to browse by flowboard late at night, and I needed to practice my technical skills."

"No wonder you didn't make it to bed, then, if you were linked on all night."

Tanya came up beside Holly and wound her arm around her waist. Together they viewed the faces staring down at them from the walls. They were mostly Strategists, Trevel military. The ranks ranged from lowly primers up to champions, mentors, and masters.

"I feel very small." Tanya seemed to shrink beside Holly, who saw the glory of it all in the light of her proposal.

"It's austere, but there is warmth here." She let go of Tanya's arm and followed her curiosity around the hall, touching the walls and doors here and there.

The front door drew her attention the most. Glass and lead trickled around the window door, allowing waves of light to drench the floor with colorful visions of flowers and rivers.

Tanya sat on one of the dainty French fainting couches and watched her sister stare in complete, open vulnerability at the doorway. Holly's love for such beauty froze her into a pillar of adoration.

He was right behind her again.

"It tells a story." Holly held her breath and listened to him. "The story of the day my great-grandfather met his lady. He was forty-six and she was twenty-nine and they were married four hours after they met in that field of flowers. It is the only Upland wedding in my entire family history."

Holly turned and, out of awkwardness, curtsied.

"Would you like to sit in the conservatory with me?" Marin bowed and opened a doorway onto a dazzling green forest.

"I don't like plants that much. I'll stay here." Tanya stayed sitting on her hall couch, and Holly entered a world of such exhilaration that her feet barely touched the ground.

"My mother worked Floral Energies like you. All our homes have rooms like this one."

"I came to apologize, not to be enticed." She sat beneath a dormant cherry tree and it bloomed.

"Is that your final word?" Marin smiled and picked a blossom.

"I still want school."

"I still want a wife."

"Then I'm not who you want."

Marin stopped and looked directly into her eyes.

"Oh, yes, yes you are."

"Then you'll have to wait."

"If you leave here today, without me, you'll forget me for another."

"You're a little hard to forget." Holly relaxed some.

"I promise I'll be better for you, than he."

Holly became annoyed by the game Marin was playing.

"Who can possibly be more dazzling than you, Champion Marin Tambeaux? Who? Tell me of whom you speak?"

"No. Just remember that because of who I am, I know a lot of things. And this I know: if you leave me today, you sign your fate to another."

"Do you really love me, or are you just trying to save me from someone whom you think is not good enough for me?"

"I do only the things that my passion leads me to do. Will you have me?"

"I won't get on this circle again." Holly stood in the doorway, "I'm sorry my father was so poorly prepared to hear your request. I'm also sorry I allowed myself to get swirled up in the confusion and fantasy of that night and got drunk. I am going to school and I will not forget you. Perhaps we'll meet in Lemuria."

"Again, Holly, I swear to you." He raised his hand in a toast, holding the cherry blossom aloft. "May my family always love and protect your family, for as long as our blood holds true." He kissed the blossom and handed it to her.

She accepted the flower and, collecting her sister, exited beneath the glass window without a second look.

Mitchell joined Marin as a brother would, and Marin said,

"She'll take one look at him and forget this entire conversation, but he'll never be good enough for her. I don't care who he is. He'll never treat her as well as I would."

"He, who?"

"You'll find out soon enough."

He shook it all off and put his arm around Mitchell's shoulders.

"Well, what say we go and get you a livelihood?"

Registration

The Dijex family rode rickshaws pulled by oversized emus into Janeiro's downtown. The emus were remarkably well trained and quickly ran their regular route, slowing down at numerous points along the way, ready to stop if necessary.

When Hal and Holly, Salla and Tanya recognized the ANA Compound, they clicked their lips at the running birds notifying the fowl to stop at the next point. Each emu waited while its passengers clambered out, then continued on its route looking for someone else to carry.

"I am always amazed by the mismatching of styles in Trevel Clusters."

Raised in Upland Kent, England, with a Trevel father studying Bacht pharmacology, Hal was used to consistent symmetry and style in his surroundings. Even Latoona had one style, that of a typical Bacht jungle village.

However, here in Underland Janeiro, everything was different.

The Atlantis National Academy Compound was an Italian Renaissance castle complete with numerous stone buildings, grassy lawns and gardens, and a great wall surrounding the property. On top of the wall were Defense Strategists stationed at each of the four gates—north, south, east, and west.

The rest of the buildings along the street were from various eras. The Potions Store was English Tudor, the Water Power Company chose an early Celtic village motif, and an outdoor street mall looked like a Mexican market in the early nineteenth century. Further down the hill (the ANA compound was naturally on high ground) was a fairy-tale town complete with unicorns and singing maidens.

"I'm glad our house is in the English Quarter." Tanya gazed up and across the vast forty-foot-high, sixteen-foot-wide wall. It was not unlike the Upland Great Wall of China in design. "At least it's homey and not so imposing."

"Get used to imposing, my lady," a pretty primer guard saluted them. She was older, but nowhere near old.

"Welcome to Atlantis National Academy, the most imposing school in all Trevellia. The only place that is grander than the school is the Palace and Memorial Grounds of Royal Lemuria."

She directed the family to a smaller stone guard house in the wall of the gate.

"Here is your first registration stop. You will be measured here and then sent on to have your ability level tested. From there we will match up your scholarship, if you have one, with your ability level and send you on to the appropriate Collegian placing ground."

Continuing, the guard winked at them,

"If you have any questions, DON'T ASK, as all will be answered throughout the day. Write down your queries, and if there are any left when we are done with you, then you may fill out question forms and we will respond to them by flow mail."

The nameless guard ushered them into the small circular room, about twelve feet in diameter, to have their measurements assessed.

"But how will we access the answers?" Tanya was first to step into liquid HDP pool.

"DO NOT ASK." The guard smiled, then raised the silvery waters with a wave of her hand.

Tanya giggled as she was engulfed in a gooey mold and waved cheekily through the malleable plastic form to her family.

"Thank you, Lady Tanya, your uniform will be available at the Collegian placing grounds. Lady Holly, you're next."

The rest of the morning was a farce. Everyone testing the girls tried to act as if they were superior to these first years, but none could comprehend what stood before them.

In every area, the two ladies not only excelled, but also added something flashy of their own to the task. At one testing station, they each stood in front of what looked like a window box for flowers.

They were told to pull whatever they could out of the box, standing a full body length away. This was to discover not only their particular areas of Energy, but also determine to what level they were able to practice their talent.

Tanya stood on the left of Holly and they lifted their hands to feel out for what was in the box. Really, it was a bit of everything.

Taking a deep relaxation breath, they settled into their comfort zone and leaned out with their mind energies to take hold of their precious force and send it life, lifting it from out of the box into its own unique form.

Holly lifted twelve small stems of maidenhair fern, delicate new shoots that shivered and fluttered out tender circular leaves in tiny patterns of green whispers.

The testers "mm… mmed" their approval, so Holly smirked and, with a twitching of her fingers, caused each stalk to take on a color of the extended rainbow.

Awe swept over the judging table. Such excessive growth for a first year was amazing. Usually, one would raise one or two stalks. In fact, that was all that was there to raise. But Holly had not only induced artificial color, but she had also reproduced the plants, multiplying them in one moment.

Tanya took her turn. She winked at Holly and tickled the golden shoot that rose slowly out of the box. It danced, then splintered into thirteen stalks that stretched out like fingers and bubbled up circular leaves that imitated Holly's maidenhair fern. The leaves, however, were not of gold. Each leaf grew out as crystal does from rock, and the colors of the crystal also matched the rainbow of Holly's fern, with one black one added for pizzazz.

The judges expected a column or a simple flower, and that of one substance, but to join together gold and crystal, and create synthetic crystal from one seed, exceeded any textbook experiment. It was, indeed, a freakish, even frightening, power that existed in these two... monsters.

The Dijex sisters were immediately dismissed as the judges discussed possible expulsion before entrance was admitted.

Holy and Tanya sensed their reception and decided to finish the job properly.

"Thank you for your time, sirs, madam." Holly spoke with appropriate humility.

"We look forward to pursuing greater course for our skills." Tanya actually curtsied. Holly followed suit.

"Goodbye."

They waved and smiled, but as they waved, their ferns suddenly exploded all over the box and filled it overflowing with perfect models of the original creation.

The testers gasped, one of the men screamed, and the girls laughed as they walked out the door.

Finally, at the Collegian Placing ground, the girls received their dress uniforms to wear immediately, while the common school uniform and Laray sports uniform were to be sent on to their suite on the TSNS Atlantis travel ship.

The dress uniforms were midnight blue linen coats, fitted to their exact figures, with long sleeves, a closed lapel buttoned up to the neckline, and a hemline above the knee. Underneath, the girls wore a simple cotton tailored dress of the same dark blue with short sleeves and a straight skirt that ran down to their ankles.

Their shoes were black with a low one-inch heel. These shoes were fitted with an elastic material that covered the entire foot but left the ankle bones bare. Various stocking styles were offered from knee, thigh, and waist to full body length.

Tanya loved the body length, as it embraced her figure and heightened the effect of her curves. Holly loved the thigh length, as she was a romantic at heart.

The Color Guardian informed them,

"Just as many high schools divide the student body into teams for in-house games and competition, so does Atlantis National Academy. However, in an average school you would be divided according to alphabetical order, whereas, because your acceptance into ANA is based on your energy skills, so is your collegian assignment."

She gestured to the decorated wall.

"These are the colors of the four collegians, in one of which you will be placed."

Haryss was in goldenrod yellow, cerulean blue, and pearl (a white stone) with a mascot of a griffin for the Energies of Illumination, Electricity, and Air.

Faroush was in navy blue, chocolate brown, and amethyst (a purple crystal) with a mascot of a two-headed hydra for the Energies of Water and Fauna.

Bowra was in tan brown, forest green, and brass (an orange metal) with a mascot of a Pegasus for the Energies of Flora and Earth (mineral).

Chanton was in charcoal black, white and orichulum (a red metal) with a mascot of a dragon for the Energies of Fire and Metal.

This new Guardian woman was of the Faroush Collegian and looked typically so, with a long, flowing braid in her hair and long, flowing sleeves and skirt, so much like the fluid water and raw animal type Energies.

She advised,

"These Collegians are not the 'be all, end all.' They only benefit you in sports and common room events. There is no one better, but the one you are placed in is best for you."

She turned on what looked like an ultraviolet light in an archway.

"I will warn you that family members are rarely placed together. Tanya, I believe you are the older? Step though the arch."

Under the light, Tanya looked no different, but the light itself changed color. The whole arch shone orange in a brassy outline around the girl.

"That would be Bowra, the Collegian of the Earth."

A tiny seamstress threw a brown, green, and brassy emblem depicting a Pegasus onto Tanya's upper left chest, and brass button covers down the coat, that landed in perfect order. Then she spoke.

"Here are the rest of your colors. Simply lay out each uniform and throw the matching ribbons, button covers, and emblems as I have done."

The Faroush Guard need not have warned the girls of possible separation, for Holly was of Bowra, also.

"Here are your personalized flowboards and your scholarship access key."

The guard faltered a moment and studied the flat rectangular card.

"I have never seen an access key like this. It is made of platinum, so don't lose it. Present it to the man outside, and he will show you to your gate so you may shop for a trunk, casual clothes, and other necessities and novelties.

"Here ya go, loves." The man at the access gate shook their hands.

"Let's see that key of yours. Silver, is it? Then I guess it's the west wall, but I gotta test it, protocol an' all."

The plain-clothed man with brilliant bleach-blond hair took their keys and inserted them into his wall flowboard.

"That's not silver, is it?"

"No." Salla pushed forward as any mema would. "They said it was platinum."

"Platinum... not come across that before, let me check something."

He tapped on the keyboard a moment, then said,

"Well, then, that takes you to the north door. Off you go, the first stop is the trunk shop. The type of luggage assigned to you will tell you what is expected of you and what type of shopping has been made available to you. The Powers be with you."

With that, Salla, Tanya, Holly, and Hal jaunted across the open lawn to the North Gate. What lay in store for them was even more imposing than anything behind them.

Relative Freedom

The display window on street level celebrated the current Senate members and their relationship to King Darsaldain who, Mitchell learned, was the reigning monarch.

"There he is," said Marin, or Champion Tambeaux, as Mitchell must call him in public.

He pointed to a three-dimensional water cast of a powerfully charismatic figure in his mid-twenties, surrounded by adoring women.

"Who is he?"

"Our glorious, Powers keep him, Prince Hadigan, due to become Prince-in-One and heir to the throne, as soon as his father can convince the Senate that he is worthy and capable of the honor."

"Looks like a manipulator to me." Mitchell sneered as he watched the figurine work his charms on the surrounding crowd of water characters.

"I like you more every day, Mitchell." Marin looped his arm across Mitchell's shoulders and punched him with his right.

"Tambeaux!" A booming voice jarred the air behind them.

Marin groaned under his breath, but smiled in honor as he turned and exclaimed,

"Your Highness, was not aware you were in Janeiro?"

"Business takes me all over Trevellia, my friend. What about you? Are you not returning to Lemuria for this year's Championing?"

"Yes, sire. We are on our way."

Hadigan looked with disdain at the Bacht by Tambeaux's side.

The Champion nodded, responding,

"I was just explaining who you were to my young L1 here. Prince Hadigan, this is Tambeaux Mitchell. He entered Trevellia just this week."

A pained smiled oozed over an obvious sneer.

"An L1? I wasn't aware that we still sponsored them. You must be remarkable if Tambeaux admitted you. What do you do?"

Mitchell almost answered, but Marin nudged him and answered instead,

"He is brilliant with the Bacht computer system. He is capable of manipulating and creating any system to his own commands."

"Have you had a chance at our flowboards?"

Again, Marin nudged and answered,

"Of course not, your Highness. We would never presume such a responsibility. We are in fact here to find an L1 livelihood for him."

The prince surveyed Mitchell.

"You have a strong figure, but you should try cleanup. If you are as intelligent as Tambeaux says you are, you would completely waste away in a factory. Try a janitorial job that isn't quite as mind numbing as an assembly line." With that, the royal figure straightened, and Marin saluted him.

"Thank you for the advice, Your Highness, we will look to it."

Mitchell saluted also, displaying his new tattoo. His Highness paused, looking at it for a moment, then moved on his way.

"I look to see you at the opening season banquet in Lemuria, Tambeaux. I believe there will be some special ladies there this year."

They held the salute in a semi-bow till he passed.

"That's the he you were talking to Holly about, isn't it?"

"Keep your mouth shut, Mitch. Intelligence like that can only get you in trouble."

Tambeaux led the way through the automatic glass doors into a bizarre version of a government work assistance office that could only exist in Trevellia.

As dull and bland as the decor of a Bacht government office is, the Trevel work assistance office was brilliant and stimulating.

Everywhere, every kind of Trevel ability force was displayed. Plants, animals, statues of metal and precious gem, water pools, wind fans, rock gardens, and flaming torches all settled themselves in no apparent pattern. Even flowboards lay about, available for anyone to test their techno skills.

"Wait here. This L1 concept is new to everyone." Marin breathed deep and nearly looked nervous. "I'll take care of this. You just sit tight, and don't touch anything."

Mitchell stood watching everything in the room. He ignored Marin knocking on the door of someone obviously very important.

It was absolutely impossible for Mitchell to follow Marin's last instructions. A flowboard was blipping and flashing right at his knee. Mitchell was not fully aware of his legal limitations so he pretended he knew nothing; after all, it is better to ask for forgiveness than to first ask for permission.

He sat watching the flowboard screen. He followed the cursor and its images and began to rock slightly in rhythm with the movements of the information output.

When he reached out his hand, the keyboard flickered and proved to be a more complex version of the Bacht computer only in that there were fewer keys. He tried using the keyboard alone but did not get very far.

As he was beginning to understand HDP technology, he considered trying a touchscreen approach, then smiled, for it was indeed the way to communicate. He began exploring the techno language, as he called it.

Champion Tambeaux was gone for half an hour, but it only took Mitchell three minutes to translate the Trevel techno into something he was used to; after all, a binary code, is basically the same in any language. He delved into the programming and began to take control.

There was no concept of time when fingers met a computer, or now, a flowboard. Mitchell felt at home for the first time in this foreign world. If he had not been working so hard to figure things out, he might have even been homesick.

Briefly, he thought of his ex-girlfriend and wondered how his disappearance would be explained. Five years was a long time. Would she know him when he got out? Did he want her to know him? Did he want to get out?

These questions were knocked out of him when he hit the ceiling.

Champion Tambeaux, full of fury, had pinned him to the ceiling with all his power forces.

"Obviously, I have been lax in advising you of your limitations, boy."

"I'm not sure this will work, Champion," a short redhead Work Assistance guardian with long legs and almost no torso spat at Mitchell.

"I will take care of him, I assure you, and what better place to put him, really?" Champion Tambeaux dropped his hand and Mitchell thudded on the floor. "I can think of no better place with tighter security."

The short man sputtered, "I have a waiting line for this position. At least fifty pureblood Trevels want such a privilege as this, and you want me to hand it over to some ignoramus with no power whatsoever?"

"Yes."

That was all that Champion Tambeaux, of the ancestry of the Tambeaux Defense Strategists, needed to say to get his own way.

"Abide by the rules, L1." The legs were longer when the redheaded guardian stood over the breathless Mitchell. "If you don't, I'll petition King Darsaldain myself." He kicked Mitchell, then stamped into his office, slamming door.

Champion Tambeaux snatched his L1 off the floor and dragged him into the street. Outside, Mitchell was tossed against the building wall.

"You are never to touch or attempt to gain any Trevel knowledge while you are an L1. Is that clear?"

Tambeaux's hand gripped Mitchell's throat and their faces were inches apart. Glaring into Mitch's eyes, Tambeaux faltered momentarily and dropped his gaze ever so slightly, then flickered back up, intent on the depths of the large young eyes in his grasp.

Mitchell's eyes widened in astonished recognition, but the instant Tambeaux saw Mitchell read his secret, Tambeaux stepped back stone cold and brushed himself off.

"I don't want to have to teach you another lesson in public." He paused and whispered, almost pleading, "It's not good for the family name, okay?"

Mitch was immobile, shocked.

Marin continued on his way, nodding for the Bacht to follow him. Three blocks down, past the twentieth-century department store buildings and into the American Victorian home sector, Marin slowed down and Mitchell asked,

"What, exactly, will the Work Assistance man petition the king for?"

"To have you deleted from Trevel society."

"Death?"

"Or permanent memory destruction and placement in a Bacht sanatorium." Marin kept his eyes on the street ahead. "You get to pick which one."

"Oh, well, that's much better." Mitchell shook his sun-streaked hair with his hand and then flattened it by running his fingers through the thick curls.

"By the way, you'll start work as a stable boy at Atlantis National Academy on the first day of the school year."

By the tone of Marin's voice, Mitchell presumed that this was the privileged position in which he was meant to abide by the rules.

Great Expectations

After exiting the ANA compound and entering the Chinatown quarter, the first store the Dijex family was directed to was the Luggage store and the first trunk set that was shown to them was the base set.

The store manager, also the storeowner's son, assessed the girls by the simple, flowing lines of their crinkle cotton attire. He prided himself in his ability to guess which trunk set was assigned to each student, and today he presumed the base set of trunks would be theirs.

"This is the 'Enid Collection.'" Mr. Mancomb, as was the manager's name, lead them to their immediate left, into a large circular room full of doors, opened one of them and revealed a typical trunk luggage set. It was 'some kind of wood' covered with brown leather and nickel-plated studs. There was a sea trunk, a large medicine bag and a smaller one, a hatbox, and matching shoulder bag and money purse. It was elegant, well made and boring.

"I'm not sure this is…" Salla began.

But the well-oiled sales pitch of Mr. Mancomb interrupted her.

"Perhaps the Blyton Set?"

Hal burst out laughing.

"Do you have a love for Bacht children's literature?"

Mr. Mancomb sneered, "My father enjoys light reading. Enid Blyton is one of his favorite authors. I have not this taste for such Upland kitsch.

Tanya whispered, "What's kitsch?"

Mr. Mancomb replied,

"Kitsch, my dear, is a lower art form — if you can call it art — that is merely a filler for the real thing. It is a counterfeit to true art, a shadow, and an ugly thing. May I have your cards, please?"

The girls pulled out the cards and handed them to Mr. Mancomb.

Hal leaned in close to the girls and said,

"Kitsch is also fun and pretty. It is often inexpensive, and a way that the common man can enjoy beauty when the so-called 'great' arts are denied them by exorbitant prices. It has its place, especially in kitchens, thus, kitsch."

"Like the banana mobile hanging over the kitchen window?" Holly feigned innocence to the snobby manager who sneered with a raised eyebrow and upper lip.

"I love that mobile." Holly continued, "It reminds me of our dead mother." She emphasized the last two words.

Mr. Mancomb cleared his throat and moved on a few cupboards down.

"I have not seen such a card before. Let us try it in the Lewis."

The manager slid the card into a slot by another trunk set that had a hiking pack and a waterproof boating bag as further options. It was covered in burgundy leather and lined in black velvet with silver studs.

The empty screen glared at them and the card slid back out again. Mr. Mancomb assessed the whole family and looked confused.

"So, you perhaps have a sponsor applying for your scholarship?"

Hal stared blankly. "Why do you ask that?"

"No… I just… I didn't think… let's try George McDonald."

They were led almost completely around the circular room, passed other sets hidden in cupboards titled with such names as, "Donne," "Shakespeare," and "Tolkien."

Mr. Mancomb heaved a sliding pocket door aside. Inside the small room, draped with glistening green curtains and sitting on a smooth slate floor, were the most beautiful luggage pieces in the world.

There were two sea trunks, five feet by three feet, of golden oak inlaid with darker stained oak chips.

"You can have your initials inlaid in the top there." His comment fell on deaf ears as the family wandered around the display.

The inside of the oak trunks were padded with blue silk and silver studs. It held a top shelf for smaller garments and had silken ties to hold everything in place.

Another oak inlaid box stood three feet tall and one and a half feet wide. It had long doors and two silver handles that locked by a delicate silver-plated key with a sapphire insignia on the end. Inside everything was blue velvet and silver.

One side had various sized draws all the way down and the other had a long space for hanging something, with extra draws beneath. The inside panel of one door held a beautifully etched mirror and the other was padded velvet with silken ribbons crisscrossed over it.

"What's this for?"

"That is the jewelry cabinet. The padded door is for keepsakes and pictures to be held in place by the ribbons."

"What would I fill it with?" Holly smiled dazedly at the multiple draws.

"I bet I could find a rock or two to put in there." Tanya giggled and nudged her sister over to the leather luggage.

Again, what would they use it all for?

They noted the added hiking backpack and boating bag, but there was also a three-foot-long sports gear bag and a flow-board brief case, all in leather, though lighter and more flexible, and all in blue with silver accents.

There were also the basic large, medium, and two small suitcases that were solid at the corners and soft on top. They continued the blue and silver theme in leather color and stud-ware, with the option of monogramming.

Lastly, in a different style, was a five-foot-long hanging garment bag, also of the blue and silver theme, but instead of leather, it was a thick tapestry with a waterscape design. A shoulder bag, carry-all, hand purse, and money holder were also a watery tapestry. There were even hand-sized makeup and jewelry travelling purses.

Mr. Mancomb looked a pale shade of green and grabbed the card that slid back out of the 'George MacDonald' slot. He furrowed his brows and scuffled around the room, shoving the card in and snatching it back out of all the slots around the room. He returned to them and gazed sullenly at the jungle village girls.

"We have nothing for you here."

"I beg your pardon?" Salla's defense mechanism kicked in. "My daughters are on the Prince's Scholarship. You most certainly do have something for us, now go and find it."

"That is not possible. The Prince's Scholarship is being awarded for the first time in years, in fact it has not been awarded since Prince Hadigan attended ANA."

Mr. Mancomb pulled himself up to his highest point of snootiness. "I am sure that it is to be awarded to the Duchess Iphigenia Darsaldain, Prince Hadigan's only cousin." He sniggered here and continued while delicately flicking small pieces of nothing from his impeccable coat sleeves. "Return to your jungle village, dears, and live out your fairy tales there."

Salla, Tanya, and even Holly were about to explode, but Hal stepped forward and calmly asked, "Are you aware of which jungle village is home to us?"

"Some outcast place in Belize?"

"No, actually, it's a tiny village in the Amazon jungle called Latoona."

Mr. Mancomb shook his head in a 'who cares' gesture, but instantly, a thick back curtain flew aside and the elderly owner of the trunk store gushed forward.

"Lady Tanya? Lady Holly? My dears, you are most welcome here. Manny, get the coffee." Mr. Mancomb snorted in disbelief, but obeyed.

"Manny Mancomb?" The girls could not suppress a giggle.

"I was not expecting you today." Mr. Mancomb, Sr. glared at Manny, who re-entered wheeling in a coffee tray full of French pastries.

"Forgive my son, I did not tell him of the higher things. There are only a few of us that are informed truthfully about the Prince's Scholarship. Please, step this way."

He led them through the glistening green curtain from the 'George MacDonald' room, and then to a private viewing room.

"I thought this was for the Duchess." Manny wheeled the cart behind them.

"You thought wrong. Here she is, Ladies, the 'Charles Dickens' — the highest and grandest set of luggage this side of Royalty."

"Why the Charles Dickens?" Hal hoped to engage the elderly man in a conversation on the Bacht literature.

"The Charles Dickens design is made only for a Prince's Scholarship, for from those to whom it is awarded, is required a level of 'Great Expectation.'"

> Captain's Assistant
>
> Aboard
>
> Scholarship Perks
>
> Janeiroan Brat Pack
>
> A Horrifying Discovery

Chapter 10

Captain's Assistant

"Welcome aboard the Atlantis, Champion." The greeting officer looked like a cruise boat captain should.

"Thank you, Captain Cochran. It is indeed my privilege."

"Please, join me in my cabin for a drink."

Captain Cochran led Marin, Marina, and Mitchell to his extensive, luxurious cabin above the high class dining rooms.

Captain Cochran was of average tall height with thick, white hair firmly combed in place under his captain's sea cap. As today was only a preparation day, he wore jeans and a cream turtleneck ribbed sweater.

Mitchell hadn't seen any Trevel looking as much like a Bacht as the captain did.

"Your boy can stand outside." He nodded in Mitchell's direction.

"Actually, sir, he is my L1 brother and the reason for my visit."

"My grandfather had an L1. She was my mother's adopted sister."

The captain held the door open and ushered all three of them inside.

"Anyone for a drink?"

Marin explained,

"No alcohol for us, thank you."

Their host was startled.

"My sister and I are on duty, and Mitchell doesn't get that privilege."

"Of course." The captain hesitated, then poured even himself a soft beverage.

"Aunt Lily was her name."

The drinks were passed around and Marina asked, "Your grandfather's L1?"

"Yes. Used to go by the name Atette, I believe. Lovely woman."

"What happened to her?" Mitchell let his tongue go loose.

The Captain straightened in his seat and cleared his throat in a gruff, offended way.

"I'll forgive you, boy, for speak'en to me this once, 'cos I understand ya want'en to know 'n all, but you watch ya mouth or it'll get ya in trouble."

"Mitchell, you cannot talk unless you are spoken to, you cannot make use of Trevel technology, and you cannot do just about anything else unless you are ordered to."

Marin reviewed the rules of L1 servitude.

"You want to get my brother in trouble?" Marina glared at the L1.

"You mess up and his head is on the block." Marina then whispered to Marin, "It's so risky — do you still want to go through with this?"

"I know he will be great here." Marin looked accusingly at Mitchell.

"As long as you get rid of your rebellious attitude. Just wait it out, kid. It's not forever, and I know you can do this."

"And if I can't?"

"It isn't can or can't, it's will or won't. And if you don't, I lose everything, and so then, do you."

"Ah, that makes me feel much —"

"Better? Yeah I know. Just behave or you'll spend the next month sweating it out in the engine room." Marin slid his gaze over to the captain on these last words.

"So that's what this is all about?" Capt. Cochran leaned back waiting for the proposal. "What would you have me do with him, then, if not the engine room?"

"Mitchell, tell the good captain how old you were when you travelled from Sydney to Rio, and exactly how you did it." Marin sat back and Marina nodded in encouragement.

"Well, sir." Mitchell stood. "I was sixteen when I ran away on a series of cargo ships. I sailed around the south, west, and north coasts of Australia into South Asia, across the

Pacific Ocean to the west coast of Florida, USA, via the Panama Canal, then down the east coast of South America from Miami, USA, to Rio, Brazil."

Mitchell began to understand why Marin had him tell his story.

"All in all, it took three cargo ships, one rental car, and very little money, considering the experience, but the greatest opportunity I had on the entire trip was the privilege of being cabin boy on the last two ships."

The Captain took the bait knowingly.

"Privilege of being cabin boy, eh? I'm listening. Did you come into any trouble on these ships?"

"Yes, sir, we were attacked by pirates not far off the Panama Canal."

"Did they take anything?"

"Only injuries."

"And were any of your crew injured?"

"'Only one, sir, as he caught the cargo being dragged overboard by a fleeing pirate, he ripped a nail off his finger."

"Have you ever sailed beneath the ocean, young Mitchell?"

"Only on my way from Bacht Rio to Underland Janeiro, sir."

"What's your price, Tambeaux?" The captain rubbed his palms together.

Marin smiled and offered, "A three-week vacation for you and your family, up to twenty people, at my private Lemurian Estate. You name the time."

Their host raised his eyebrows. "And from me you want?"

"Mitchell's safe passage to Torres Entrance in one piece — and no excessive bruises. I would like you to be his guardian while I'm gone."

"Will you meet me there?"

"We'll both be there when you pull in, sir."

The Captain considered the proposal for barely a minute.

"I'll take the last two weeks of December and the first week of January this year."

"Agreed." Marin shook the captain's hand, and Tambeaux Mitchell's passage to Torres Entrance was settled.

Aboard

Candice and Katiel, the older girls from Latoona, dressed in their own suite. The rooms were lovely; they even had a small balcony on the fifteenth deck, counting down from the top, on the lovely cruise ship Atlantis.

Each suite was rectangular in shape, with a twin bedroom on each side of an open living area. The long bathroom, at the back, connected the opposite bedrooms and was divided into a shower stall and a separate toilet room facing a lengthy counter with two basins and an extensive, well-lit mirror.

Typical of the Trevel design, each suite had a different theme. These girls found themselves in a homey tropical jungle, loving every animal and bird that peeked its nose out from the wallpaper. The couches and pillows were overdone in animal skins and leafy tapestries, and even the shaggy carpet was supposed to resemble lush green grass.

The bathroom décor shone in brilliant green and blue tiles arranged in watery ripples around the floor and lower walls. There were even hanging ferns above the counter. The wall was painted with fish from the jungle pools, and the ceiling sported the occasional three dimensional waterfowl bottoms and reptilian heads as they fished beneath the faux surface.

Behind the cabin door, a tiny kitchenette and laundry room snuggled, barely visible, in the wooden cabinetry. It gave enough freedom in hospitality to allow the girls the option of missing breakfast and even lunch in the dining rooms without suffering.

Katiel's berth rested in the corner of the front wall. The top bunk berth was stowed away, and she had pulled the futon-style couch bed to its full double-sized capacity. Candice had done the same, and her bed lay perpendicular to Katiel's but was close enough so that each bed shared one foot of the other's side at right angles.

"Do you know where we pick up our suitemates?" Katiel stacked her books neatly on the shelf between bed and wall.

Candice sprawled out on her bed, not caring if she crushed her casual dinner dress, and sighed.

"Under Falk; we only pick up some boys in Under Buenos. You'll never guess who?"

"I know it's not the Stilwell triplets. They're safely terrorizing Under Eng."

"Did you know, as a matter of fact, that the Stilwells have an ancient claim to an old estate in Buenos?"

Katiel slumped on the floor with her knees pulled up and her hands over her head.

"I don't even want to know."

The two shivered and glumly headed out the door, smoothing their hair. Down the corridor, they ran into Tomey Stonewall.

"Hey gals, I came looking for you. Do you know where Holly and Tanya are?"

"We lost them on the dock, but I figure we'll see them at dinner."

"Well, as my father expects me too, I shall escort you ladies to dinner, but don't expect me to do it again."

Scholarship Perks

No one noticed Tanya and Holly board the Atlantis.

They had enjoyed a simple dinner of fish and chips, wrapped in paper, on the Quay Park. (The fact that the marina key, where the boats docked, was spelled quay and pronounced key was remarkable to Salla, but Hal reminded her that the English language often added vowels and odd letters here and there to enhance itself.)

The green and windy (under-ocean) Quay Park was on the Undershore, one mile in from the HDP barrier, and was set up high enough so that, looking through the public telescopes, the outer barrier was clear and you could occasionally see vast schools of fish or other great creatures of the ocean deep swim by.

"It's a little frightening to know all that ocean pressure is only a mile or so away." Salla licked her fingers clean of delicious salt.

Tanya set down her soda and whispered,

"It's even more frightening to know all that pressure of the P.S. expectation is only an hour or so away."

"The Prince's Scholarship expectation is nothing you cannot handle."

Hal smiled with fatherly pride.

"I am confident that either of you could succeed on your own, but together, you cannot be denied the brilliance that is yours to take."

"You sound like… I don't know? How will we ever know what could be ours if we spend our whole life masking and restricting what we are capable of?" Holly's frustration dug at her father in tones of disrespect.

"Watch that tone, young lady." Hal was serious and intimidating.

"You will at all times keep honor and dignity as your companions. If you do not, you will be feared." Hal waited for Salla to back him up.

"You've already experienced a little bit of that already, honey." Salla squeezed Holly's shoulders. "And that was by your neighbors who loved you."

Holly recomposed herself.

"I guess I would like to know when, if ever, we can let go?"

"I'd love to work in large amounts of stones and minerals." Tanya licked at the last of the crunchy chips at the bottom of the paper wrapping.

Hal remained serious, but smiled and said,

"Now is the time."

"Explain." Both girls drilled their father eagerly.

"You've been waiting to go to school, so go, be, and learn… but," Hal cleared his throat and looked uncomfortable. Salla rubbed his back for encouragement. He continued,

"There is a concern that we and Master Su have felt for some time and I believe now is the time for you to be perfectly aware of some of the danger you may be facing."

Tanya and Holly looked skeptically dubious.

"No," pressed their deda, "I mean it, and we have already seen this kind of trouble on the *Hera*."

Holly blushed.

"Master Su noted right after you girls awoke from the tears coma that there was a deeper maturity to you both. He believes that, not only were your energy skills enhanced by the tears, but your whole physiology has been advanced and, with that, possibly your age as well."

Tanya interrupted,

"I knew it!"

Salla looked at her daughters exchanging understanding nods.

"What did you two know?" she questioned.

Holly clarified,

"We have not felt the age of our chronology since the day we awoke."

Hal glanced at his watch and hurried them.

"I am sorry to have brought this up with so little time to discuss it. You are due on the Atlantis imminently. We will look into it further from our end and perhaps send you help once you reach the Royal Capital."

The family hurried off to the dock for parting tears and hugs and a final word of caution from their deda,

"Be wary around the men, girls… I mean, ladies. You still are unsure of how much power you possess there."

With that paternal warning, the overly confident girls boarded the Atlantis dreaming of freedoms unknown.

They left Hal and Salla on the dock and walked up the gangplank. Families were not allowed on board. This cut down on interfering parents advocating for better rooms as students were placed according to talent, not financial or social status.

The card-key they had received was all they needed to shop with, receive cash from bank stations, and acquire credit. Now, it was also their room key.

Their old jungle basket-weave backpacks were all they had as they pushed open the door of their room. Everything else was unpacked and ready for use in their suite, a suite that was set up like a luxury apartment big enough for their family and a few neighbors as well.

The floor was a spilled coffee-colored marble with ivory hand-woven rugs scattered around furniture pieces and doorways.

The furniture was all dark maple with creamy lacy doilies and cloth runners dripping from most surfaces. The wood designs were crisp and square with ribbed accents. For example, the low table between the lavishly puffy couches sat knee high from the floor with straight thick legs joined by a row of square "jail bars" half the height of the table itself.

This design was imitated in small segments around the longer edge of the table, which themselves were inlaid with glassy designs of jungle green and orange, as if autumn was being held captive inside a wooden jail. Brilliantly colored pottery, pillows, and pictures dotted the room like flowers.

"I could get used to this." Holly grinned and fingered the lacy table cover.

Tanya was halfway flopping on the couch when it suddenly occurred to her that she didn't see any bedrooms.

"Where are we sleeping?"

"Maybe the couches are fold-away beds?"

"My Ladies?" A cuddly woman stood in the doorway smiling like a grandma. "Excuse me, my dears, I am Mrs. Priscilla, your housekeeper. I can show you the rooms."

She walked toward the right wall. A large painting of a fairy captured in a tree glittered in beautiful agony. Mrs. Priscilla clicked the side bar of the frame and pulled the wall aside.

Foamy blue carpet bubbled under their feet all the way to a massive bed of cloudy comforters, pillows, and shaggy bed shawls. Tanya instantly disappeared into the white dream.

"I feel as if I'm in heaven," she mumbled lazily.

"That's right, dear. You are in Heaven's Parlor here. That is the design." Priscilla opened the curtains onto the long balcony running the full length of the room and overlooking the entire ship below, but for the private officers' quarters and entry levels above them.

"This is level three, the Top-Set Penthouse. Directly beneath us are the High-Set suites, level four and five, then levels six through ten are the common community decks, and on to the remaining Main-Set suites, levels eleven through sixteen. Level seventeen houses the animal stables, and below that, below sea level, are the staff living and working quarters. It's a bit rough down there, and the dances can be exciting, but I did not tell you that. You are on top of the world here, Ladies; nothing more to do here than make your own way higher than anyone has ever known."

Tanya and Holly looked with innocent delight at their grandma-housekeeper. They all made their way out onto the balcony that extended past the bedroom wall twice the length over.

"I have spoken to your parents," continued Mrs. Priscilla. "I, too, am from Latoona. I took a job here on the Atlantis after the bombing of the hotel and marketplace. I was to work at the new resort, but… anyway, I know what to expect from you."

"And what is that?" laughed Tanya.

"More than any have seen before."

"Priscilla," Holy was a bit distracted, "where do those doors lead?"

Holly pointed to identical sliding doors on the other end of the balcony.

"Those are your bedroom doors, dear, if Tanya has decided to take Heaven's Parlor."

"There's another room?" She rushed over and opened the doors and entered Sunrise Threshold.

The colors imitated those found in the paintings of the Bacht artist Maxfield Parrish. Fiery apricots and blazing oranges were offset by cool blues and blushing pinks. The woodwork and wallpapers celebrated the ancient Greek Trevel gods, a theme that recurred in various urns and plates that ornamented the flat surfaces.

Holly smiled. "Yes, I could get used to this."

"There is enough time to get used to everything, but now you must get ready for the first meal. You will be sitting at the captain's table, my lovelies, so dress carefully."

Mrs. P, or Grandma P as the girls eventually came to call her, opened the closets and drawers for the girls to rummage through looking for their favorite new outfits. She fussed around them at their bathroom mirrors, attending to their hair, and finally had them scurrying down the corridors to the common dining room for the first lavish celebration of the Atlantis Voyage.

Janeiroan Brat Pack

"Well, arrest me a Naiad, and look out for jungle fever, if it isn't Tomey and his harem." Daniella, of Janeiro's Defense Force brat pack, flicked her finger, shooting a gust of wind that did no more than ruffle the girls' dresses.

"Jealous that you're not by my side, are you, Daniella?" Tomey tried to walk the girls around the small crowd of elitist Janeiroans. Unfortunately, the hallway was too small and the dining room entrance just out of reach.

"What floors are your rooms on, twenty-seven?"

Candice snorted,

"I wouldn't tell you where I was if I were dying."

"My dear, with that dress, you would be better off dead." The mash of laughing noises quieted when the soft ting of the penthouse elevator announced the arrival of Holly and Tanya.

"Penthouse Ladies? Welcome, I was not expecting such an honor." Daniella curtsied and her friends followed suit.

Tomey, Candice, and Katiel were surprised, but not amazed. Really, it was to be expected. Tomey snorted, and scooting passed the crowd, disappeared into the dining room.

Candice smiled and mischievously nudged Katiel, who giggled back.

"Hi." Holly shifted her gaze to Candice and nodded to the bowing crowd with a look of "What the...? Get over yourself."

Tanya laughed openly.

"Are you the duchess?" Daniella was proud of her knowledge of secret details.

"No." Tanya moved passed the huddle. "Hey, where are you guys sitting?"

Candice swung her arm around Tanya and Katiel gestured and took Holly's hand. The four walked into the dining room together, enjoying the exhibition they had created.

A Horrifying Discovery

Tanya and Holly left their very jealous Latoona cousins at their corner table. Tomey still would not acknowledge the girls. Tonight, however, was too amazing for either to even care.

The Captain's table! How elite could they get? There were five of them: the captain and his wife, the captain's assistant, who just happened to be Mitchell, and then the Ladies Tanya and Holly.

The other officers were seated at another table, as tonight the captain wanted the ladies to himself, just to see what all the fuss was about.

Both the captain and his wife agreed. Yes, Lady Holly and Lady Tanya were amazing creatures of power and presence, but they were also just two twelve-year-old girls on an exciting adventure. They should be easy to care for.

After a wonderful dinner, the second officer asked Holly to dance. Tanya was surprised that her sister was asked first but hoped Mitchell would ask her before any of the other officers.

"Mitchell, do Bacht dance?"

"Is that an innocent question, or are you prompting me to ask you for the privilege?"

The captain and the first lady were already dancing, so there was no one to object.

"Do I look anything other than innocent?" Tanya unconvincingly batted her eyelids.

Mitchell had liked both girls ever since he met them, although he considered Holly to be not only way too young but off limits due to Marin's interest.

Tanya, the older sister, however, was enticing. Mitchell didn't have a girlfriend any more, and here was a young woman almost begging him to dance with her.

Mitchell smiled and inwardly growled at the opportunity set before him. He would take this lovely, obviously his age, maybe a bit younger, and taste her lips before the night was done.

His confidence drew her into his arms before she balked and motioned to the door.

"This maybe looked down on. Let's sneak out to the walkway."

Mitchell could not stop himself from nodding and almost dancing as he walked behind her out of the room and to the moonlit walkway.

What a perfect setting, he thought, and on the first night, too.

Tanya watched the starlight ripple on the water and said,

"The captain said we sink tomorrow at noon, right?"

Mitchell leaned back confidently on the open balcony railing.

"Noon tomorrow, and all the world will rise above and we will dwell beneath in the beauty of motion and peace."

"So the Bacht are poets, too?"

"Only when inspired by such beauty as yours." He turned and looked out over the water.

Tanya blushed and dropped her gaze under her free-flowing hair.

"I, ahh, I was wondering if you could tell me more of your life, outside Trevellia."

"What life?" Mitchell stared at Tanya.

"You know, where you were born, grew up."

"I don't remember. In fact, I don't remember anything before this moment here with you."

He stood up and leaned on the railing just an inch closer to Tanya.

Tanya held her breath and gulped quietly to herself; even if he was tacky in his approach, who cared? Her nerves were jittering and, although her deda's warning echoed in her mind, she was too thrilled to heed the warning so she, too, leaned on the railing an inch closer to Mitchell.

"Marin told me about his proposal to Holly," he whispered. "I think he asked the wrong sister."

Tanya was lost in her memory of watching Mitchell practicing his martial arts on Tambeaux's rooftop.

"If I were him, I would have asked the older sister." He stood straight and gently lifted Tanya's hair off her face and tucked it behind her ear.

Tanya was caught up in the moment she had scarcely hoped for since dinner began. A Trevel tangled up with an L1 was completely unthinkable. She would be expelled from school even before she got there. He was too old for her. At eighteen, he would be considered a thief snatching an innocent — not to mention a lady of such stature with a lowly stable boy.

There were so many reasons that this moment should not exist, but Tanya was just a girl caught up in a dream and Mitchell was ignorant of the pertinent details. Tanya straightened up and leaned back on the railing post.

"You talk pretty, for a Bacht. Are you sure you don't have some Trevel blood?"

"I'll be anything you want me to be tonight."

Tanya giggled and cleared her throat.

Mitchell broke the tension.

"So, exactly what type of learning goes on at this amazing Academy?"

"School stuff; higher-level learning, to be specific." He stepped forward and gently tapped her shoe with his foot.

"Exactly how high a level?"

She wanted so badly to kiss him, but calmly continued the conversation.

"Well, explain to me your school system and I will try to compare ours to yours."

She smartly tapped his shoe back and they fought a little, each one trying to stand on the other's foot. Mitchell pinned Tanya's foot by stepping close enough to nudge her arm with his elbow.

"There's infant school for five through seven-year-olds; primary school for eight through eleven-year-olds; high school for twelve through seventeen-year-olds; and college or university for eighteen-year olds and on."

He reached out and gently held her hand. She glanced up at him. He was so close she could hear him breathing.

Again he lightly tugged at the hair around her face and ran his fingers down her jawbone. Slowly leaning down he whispered,

"So where do you fit in?"

She almost didn't answer, but out of instinct, quietly responded,

"High school."

He grinned and snickered,

"What?"

"High school."

He blinked and straightened up a little.

"You're in high school?"

"Yeah."

Mitchell breathed out quickly. Twitching his head, he stepped back and surveyed the seeming woman in front of him.

"You're a first-year in high school?"

She smiled and shyly lifted her hand to tug on his shirt button.

"Ah-huh."

He dropped his head, covered his mouth with his hand and breathed in short breaths.

"Shi… oh… gee… Ah… Ohhh my, Goohahhd. Holy, fffree… ahh."

Mitchell totally stepped back and Tanya smiled guiltily with her head cocked to the side.

"I nearly kissed you." Mitchell walked backward to the ship's wall and banged into it.

"Uh-huh." Tanya slumped and looked up through puppy eyes.

"You're not going to anymore?"

"But you're so... Oh, you're just a little girl. I... ah...." Mitchell shook his head no and backed away to the dining room.

Tanya followed him inside and watched, deflated, as he walked directly to the captain on the dance floor, whispered something to him, and immediately left the room.

"I need to leave."

Tanya jumped as Holly bumped into her and nodded over to the officers' table as she whispered,

"It's your turn to dance with all of them."

"No thanks. I think I'll go to bed, too."

Holly was so desperate to leave the dance floor that she didn't notice her sister turn down the chance to flirt.

Falk's Landing

A Rush

The Stilwells

The Luau

Two Tutors

Chapter 11

Falk's Landing

The girls soon discovered the novelty of being a novelty wearing off. Every time they left their High Set decks and joined the rest of the students and passengers on the Atlantis in the common decks for shopping, eating, dancing, or swimming, they found many eyes following their every move.

The social director on board even took up a small gossip column in the ship's daily newspaper to follow the footsteps of the two young jungle girls trying to make their way as celebrities. It only took a couple of jealous, snide entries for Tanya and Holly to decide to restrict themselves to their own decks for entertainment and relaxation. This in itself caused gossiping jabs, as they were then accused of being snobs.

With Candice and Katiel avoiding the Janeiroan Brat Pack and Holly and Tanya avoiding all gossiping society, the four girls found themselves taking great advantage of the Heaven's Parlor and Sunrise Threshold balcony.

Snacking on delicate meat, cheese, and fruit platters and watching the ocean glide by an arm's length away behind the HDP barrier that surrounded the ship sailing beneath the ocean, each girl lingered in her own secret world of teen angst.

"What a sorry lot of lovelies you are." Grandma P bustled onto the balcony with an armful of backpacks.

She dumped one bag on each of the girls' laps and began clearing away the refreshments.

"I'm not done with that." Candice grabbed a last handful of provolone cubes.

"I was nearly asleep, and not really planning on going anywhere."

Katiel was polite and apologetic as she dropped the backpack on the floor under her deck lounge.

Grandma P, trays stacked up her arms, headed back through the glass doors and casually mentioned,

"We dock at Falk's Landing shortly, and the lines are already long. The beaches are faring clear and sunny with a slight breeze."

The glass door clicked behind her, and for a beat the four girls stared at each other. In one move, they became a scatter of moving limbs clambering for their hats, sarongs, and packs.

With her mouth still full of cheese, Candice challenged, "First one off the boat gets a full day's spa package courtesy of the other three..."

She was off the balcony in a flash with Tanya close on her heels. Holly dashed out after the two, with Katiel following closely behind.

They ran directly to the High Set gangplank and were running down a clear pathway to the dock within minutes, begging the porters to let them disembark before anyone else.

As they were trying all manner of flirting and bribing methods to get past the guards, Candice slid down the anchor chain supported by a rush of wind. She'd been practicing her wind energy traits that supported minimal levitation.

She jumped onto the dock in a flurry of dirt and flying hats. Turning to wave and blow a kiss to Holly and Katiel, she suddenly found herself in the solid arms of a burly young customs officer.

Hands cuffed as she was led off to the office, Candice called back,

"I was still first off!!"

She then turned her attentions to her arresting officer and smiled shyly at him. He couldn't help smirking in admiration.

Holly and Katiel were finally released and wandered onto the dock ahead of the Common exit crowd, keeping an eye out for Tanya, who was nowhere to be seen.

Tanya, thinking she had the upper hand, remembered the stable animals were released for exercise each time the ship docked and headed down to the zoology level.

Convinced she would make it off first, she raced through the pens, dodging the muck being cleared out and left in piles to be carried off the ship at the crew's soonest convenience.

As she rounded the cattle pens, she slipped and balked as a pair of huge Clydesdales reared their massive hooves and kicked them ferociously at her.

The sound volume in the stables was a high din of barks, shrieks, and all manner of animal protestations, but they could not drown out the scream that escaped the young girl's lips.

Not often startled, Tanya was surprised to find herself hiding her face behind an automatic reflex of a stone-skin shield extending from her forearm.

The barrier before her eyes was large enough to cover her whole presence as she crouched on the floor beneath the pawing might of the great horses.

She heard a soothing voice,

"There, there… you're okay. I won't let anything hurt you."

Tanya relaxed, and the rocky shield dissipated into a shower of the dirt and muck from whence it had risen off the floor.

"Thank you. I think I should be fine in a minute."

"Not if I have anything to say about it."

That previously soothing voice was sharp and curtly directed toward her. Mitchell stood holding the reins of both horses in one hand and calmed them with rubs on each of their noses.

He looked sternly at her.

"You could have really caused damage to both of them."

"Them? If it weren't for my defense reflexes, I'd have been eating hoof." Tanya raised herself off the floor and dusted off her curves, very aware of Mitchell's eyes.

Mitchell turned his back to her and spoke to his charges.

"You'd have put a nice hole in that silly little girl head, wouldn't you?"

He offered a handful of carrot chunks, and the two noses nuzzled his hands appreciatively.

"Silly-little-girl-head? Need I remind you, you nearly kissed this silly little girl head?" The scorned girl's indignation rose.

Mitchell paused, deliberating between continuing the game and admitting reality. Weighing his current disposable position in this new alien world, he thought games would only prove to worsen his situation.

Keeping his back to her, he spoke quietly,

"I think it best that a Trevel lady such as you should steer clear of this Bacht stable boy. It's not worth the complication to both of us."

He turned to lead the horses out the now open gangplank.

"And a small piece of advice… you may only be twelve years old, but you put off a lot more womanly essence than is natural. Be careful, not all men have the restraints on them that I am currently required to live under."

He reached out and tucked her hair behind her ear just as he had done before he knew her age and tapped her on the nose with his finger.

Out of the ship, his mighty equestrian charges followed him like lambs trailing a beloved shepherd.

Tanya whispered to herself,

"Thirteen," then pouted, following along behind the Clydesdales.

A Rush

Holly and Katiel lay out on the famous glittering black sands of Under Falk. Katiel kept looking up and down the beach.

"Where do you think Tanya ended up?"

Holly, eyes closed behind her sunglasses, mumbled, "Look for the nearest clutch of boys ogling some girl, and it's probably Tan."

"Does it bother you that she's always the center of male attention, and you're... not as much as she?"

Holly pulled down her sunnies and looked at Katiel.

"It used to at first, until Mema pointed out the type of boy she attracted."

Katiel considered the past and questioned, "You don't think she's... you, know... easy?"

Holly laughed outright.

"Good heavens, no." Sitting up, Holly began to run handfuls of rich, coarse, black sand over her legs. "Tanya can't help the attention she draws. She's a magnet—quite literally, actually, being an Earth Energy girl. Boys are drawn to her, but that doesn't mean she actually lets them get away with anything, or that she encourages them unnecessarily."

"How does that work?" Katiel, always the shy one, had little boy knowledge.

"I used to watch her with them. She's kind and generous to everyone, but if any boy crosses the line and presumes she's an easy conquest, she just laughs at him and walks away. Both Deda and Master Su have given her much advice on how to handle the attention with grace and safety. She has boundaries and an awesome backup."

At the word backup, Holly grinned and pointed to herself.

"But don't you wish the boys would pay more attention to you?" Katiel's secret pain was surfacing.

Holly brushed a little extra sand off Katiel's arm and said,

"Kat, you are a beautiful woman of substance. Boys that hang off Tanya are only out for instant gratification. They leave as quickly as they pile up. We both know that and give them little credence. The game of finding a guy who will hang around longer than the last breeze, that's where the best energies are spent."

"Not sure I'll ever find one like that."

"Be kind to yourself, Kat. Give yourself more credit." Holly hugged her shy friend. "You are worth effort, and if someone doesn't want to make that effort, then they aren't worth your energy."

Katiel sighed,

"You were right." She pointed down the beach.

A four-wheeled buggy heavily laden and leaking limbs trundled up the beach. It halted in front of the two and out tumbled two tanned surfer boys who clumsily fought over who got to hold Tanya's backpack as she stepped elegantly out of the pile of bodies within.

"Thank you." She smiled at both boys. "Perhaps we will all come to the luau."

A chorus of agreement and pleading exploded from the buggy, and Tanya dismissed them with a smile and a wave.

Plopping onto the sand next to Holly, Tanya grumbled,

"Ugh! Man-boys, cars, and sun equals smelly. Who made it off first?"

"Candice is improving her antigravity abilities and slid down the anchor chain — straight into the arms of her arresting customs officer."

Holly giggled.

"Haven't seen her since."

Katiel sighed in gloomy jealousy.

"She'll blow him over. Everyone loves a flighty Air Energist."

Tanya scorned Katiel's gloominess,

"Um... you can light up anybody's life, hon. I've seen you shine, Miss Light Energist."

Katiel dug up a fistful of black sand, and her hand glowed through it, causing the shine to dazzle off their sunglasses.

"I like glowing in the dark."

The sudden blast of an air horn startled a squeal out of her, and she clasped her heart as Tanya and Holly jumped to their feet, watching a speeding Coast Guard dinghy race up the shore before them.

A uniformed officer jumped into the shallow surf and pulled the boat onto the sand.

Saluting his civilian passenger, the officer balanced Candice as she stepped gingerly into the ankle-deep surf. She waved up the beach at her friends.

The young customs officer from the dock secured the dinghy's anchor in the sand, then followed Candice.

Candice dropped her backpack next to Katiel and asked with cocky pride,

"So, ladies, when is my spa appointment?"

"Being arrested should disqualify you." Katiel tried to be grumpy but couldn't help smiling at the young man adjusting his officer's cap to keep the sun from his eyes in order to better survey the four young girls before him.

"I wouldn't exactly call it an arrest, Miss. It was more of a cautious detainment interview." He winked at her.

Katiel blushed and pulled her sunhat down over her eyes.

"Merk, here, has invited us to the luau festivities tonight. He can get us VIP passes!" Candice slipped her arm through the young man's, showing him off like a new bracelet.

"Merk? Is that short for Mercenary?" Tanya couldn't help her flirting reflex.

He smiled.

"That depends entirely on my audience. If you were a tough smuggler coming in on the docks, it would be. But, the truth is, my mum has a thing for the gods."

Holly sat up quickly again.

"Not... Mercury?"

"At your service. Any messages you want delivered, I'm your man."

Bowing, he detangled himself from Candice's clutch and backed down the sand.

"I must be off back to the dock. Let me know if you want to sit with the Strategist contingent tonight. The luau is always on the itinerary for Atlantis passengers."

"Oh, I know I want to." Candice spoke a bit too blatantly and watched him collect the anchor, push the dinghy out past the waves, and speed back down the beach.

"What's up, Tan?" Holly eyed her sister.

Tanya was sitting with her feet and hands buried in the black sand with eyes closed and a look of consternation across her brow.

"I feel something."

"So do I." Candice was still watching the departing boat.

Tanya grinned with eyes still closed.

"No, I mean, I feel an oddity, something in the magnetics and mineral compilation of the sand."

Katiel read out from the tourist brochure she had been reading.

"The famous black sands of the Under Falk beaches are shipped in from the tiny mining town Hanain located under the Great Barrier Reef. The sand is the result of Hanain's deep mining process and contains the leftover sluff from precious mineral extractions."

"Hanain, isn't that the mining town that was so infamous with the mass rioting some years ago?"

Katiel continued her spiel.

"Hanain is famous not only for the tragic riots of 13 years ago, but for the Hanain Diamond, over whose discovery the riots were fought."

"Well, the diamond sluff accounts for the taste of sparkle, but there's something else I can't quite place." Tanya swam her hands through the sand.

Candice laughed.

"And what exactly is the 'taste of sparkle'?"

"You know, that metallic taste in the back of your mouth you get when transfusing HDP saline?"

"Yeah?"

"It's a bit like that, only more… sparkly."

Still skeptical, Candice queried, "You're telling me you can actually taste sparkle?"

"Yes, air-head; you levitate on the wind, I taste sp—" Tanya stopped midsentence and, forcefully quivering, tilted her head slowly to one side.

"Ah, Tan, you okay?" Candice was concerned.

Slowly raising her clenched fist out of the depths of the sand, she put it to her nose and smelled the aroma, undetected by anyone not Earth/Mineral Energy inclined. Even behind her closed eyelids, the girls could tell they were rolling back into her head.

Katiel reached out to grab her shoulder. Holly gently but quickly beat her back, shook her head, and came to kneel in front of her sister.

Rather quickly, Tanya came out of it, smiled and said,

"Wow, that was a rush," then giggled profusely.

The other three watched her expectantly.

Tanya, ever the drama queen, looked each one in the eye then directed her gaze to her fist as she slowly unclenched it. Lying flat in her palm, a black oval stone about the size of a thumbnail glinted of its own accord.

"Holy Parthenon, do you know what that is?" Katiel's eyes were enlarged greater than any the girls had ever seen. "That's a Hanain diamond."

"It's not possible that a Hanain diamond was just sitting hidden in the sand." Candice reached for it.

Tanya pulled her hand away and confessed, "Well it wasn't exactly in that form when I found it."

"Did you just reform a Hanain diamond from sluff?" Holly drove her eyes into her sister's victorious gleam.

"Sort of?"

Candice looked up and down the beach to ensure they were alone.

"Are we about to be ridiculously rich?"

"I doubt that. I didn't just make it from the sluff. I found some pieces of larger, raw sediment and blended them, 'tis all."

"Do it again." Candice was digging furiously in the sand looking for pebbles.

"I don't think I can."

"Why not, Tan, you okay?"

"Yeah, I'm fine, fabulous, actually. It was just such a rush I'm just a bit overly sensitive now. I can barely handle feeling the sand touch my skin."

Ever the tease and tester, Candice sprinkled a drizzle of sand down Tanya's back. She screamed like a banshee and shivered convulsively, then giggled uncontrollably again.

"That sensitive, huh?"

"I just hope you chill out by the luau tonight." Holly lay back down on her towel. "I'd hate you to miss out on the flirting because you were having so much fun on your own."

The Stilwells

The other three lay back down, imagining all sorts of visions of roast pigs, grass-skirted dancers, and flaming batons. It wasn't until Candice swore vehemently that anyone sat up again.

Katiel moaned in agony.

Tanya and Holly joined the upright crew and followed the distressed gazes.

From up out of the surf, like Neptune's own guard, three hard, bare chested black men cut through the waves, spears, masks, and fi ns in hand.

Tanya absentmindedly ran her hand across her racing heart and whispered,

"Oh my."

"Don't let the sweet wrapping fool you. What lies beneath is darker than their skin tone." Candice began throwing her things into her backpack, Katiel following suit. "Let's get out of here."

Holly was indignant.

"What? I'm not giving up my spot of delicious sun for anyone."

"You'll wish you had." Katiel swore this time as one of the three waved and blew her a kiss.

There was no escaping it now that the path directly to the girls was set in each young man's eye. The four bronzed young women sat entranced by the inevitable meeting.

"Happily met, my bevy of beauties, what delicious morsels do you bring me from out of your jungle home, this time Candy-Land?" The far left one absentmindedly ran his hand across his clear-cut abs.

"Good afternoon, Ham."

The far right one dropped his gear and joined Katiel on her towel, dripping all over her and causing her much grief.

"Sweet Katty, I missed you this summer. Did you miss me?"

"No, Shem, I did not."

Holly groaned in recognition, shielded her eyes from the sun, and addressed the central male.

"Please don't tell me your name is Japheth?"

"I see you are well versed in history." He, too, placed his fins and mask on the sand but kept his spear in his large fist. "Yes, indeed my name is Japheth. And as Candice is so slow to make the polite introductions, we are the Stilwells. Who might you be, lovely?"

"They are none of your business." Candice stood and snatched her backpack from behind Ham. "We were just leaving."

"Why so hot and bothered?" Ham stood too close to her. "You need cooling off." He picked her up and ran to the surf with her over his shoulder, beating his back and yelling at him the whole way.

His brothers laughed. Japheth glanced at Katiel.

"You been swimming yet? The water is not too cold."

"No, ah, yes, thank you. I don't wish to swim anymore." She was almost trembling.

Shem ran his fingers down her arm.

"No need to be frightened, my little lighting bug."

"I'm not," she gulped, "frightened. I'm mad at you."

Shem insistently ran his hand up to her neck and held her firmly.

"You know how I love making you angry. You glow deep in your passion."

"Shem," Japheth cautioned his brother and nodded to Ham in the surf with Candice, soundly dunking her under every second wave.

Shem scoffed, laughing, and stood up to make a show of rescuing the girl from his brother.

After he'd gone, Japheth consoled the others.

"They mean no harm really. Being biochemically engineered has caused the testosterone to fluctuate erratically, and the sight of you four only heightens the experience."

"You're biochemically engineered?" Tanya resurveyed the specimen before her.

"What? Kat and Candy-Land haven't told you about us?" He pouted.

"I'm hurt, Katty. Can you really forget me that easily?"

"I usually banish you from my mind as soon as you leave."

He stood rather violently and snatched Katiel into his arms. Holding her hand, he ran it down his rock-like chest and stomach, blacker than the sands he stood on.

"How can you forget this, baby?"

Completely focused on what was happening right in front of them, Tanya and Holly missed the approach of two massive Clydesdales and their rider.

"I'm quite sure the lady does not want such attentions." A deep, solid voice threatened from the vantage point of the equestrian height.

Mitch sat with Candice dripping and shivering on the horse next to him.

Ham and Shem came jogging up toward them, furious at losing their prey. Japheth turned calmly and stared at the intruder, the glaring sun apparently making no impact on his unshielded eyes.

"I'm quite sure a Bacht like you has no place wandering Trevellia unescorted."

Mitch's ride stepped closer and snorted hot air down Japheth's shoulders. He then addressed the girls.

"Do you ladies need a ride back to the ship?"

Katiel was already climbing up behind Candice with the assistance of Holly, who scrambled up behind her.

Tanya grabbed Mitch's forearm, and he hoisted her so heartily up behind him, she nearly went over the other side. He whispered to her,

"Hold on tight." Mitch then twitched the reins, and the giant horse reared and kicked out its hooves at the three "super" Trevels, barely missing their heads.

The treasure-laden Clydesdales then galloped down the black sand, leaving the fury fast behind them.

The Luau

"It's such a shame he's Bacht." Candice was spread-eagled on Tanya's fluffy white bed. "He came out of nowhere and ran right into them."

She rubbed her wrist, which was lightly wrapped in an HDP bandage. Grandma P held the bandaged wrist between her palms and closed her eyes.

"Ohh!" Candice twitched and grimaced.

Grandma P consoled her.

"It should be fi ne in about an hour, my dear, that paste underneath will soothe the strain." She patted her on the head. "It all sounds rather exciting, but I recommend you stay as far from those Stilwells as best you can."

She then looked at Tanya.

"I also suggest you warn the stable boy to steer clear of them, too."

"Oh." Tanya blushed at being addressed directly as the one to talk to Mitch. "Yeah, I will."

"I mean, it was like one those horrid romantic novels." Candice continued reliving her rescue, "Only it wasn't horrid in real life."

"I don't get why he ran into you. You could have been more hurt than just a sprained wrist." Katiel brushed her hair into ponytails for the evening's festivities.

"No, that's just it." Candice sat up, only too enthralled by her own story to retell it. "He ran right into Ham. Ham loosened his grip on me, and I was able to punch him in the stomach." She grimaced while she replayed the action. "I sprained my wrist punching the jerk."

Holly sneered in disgust.

"Biochemically engineered."

"But then," the rescued damsel spun around the floor, "the Bacht reached down and lifted me up onto the horse next to him." One final twirl and a long sigh ended in a flop on the bed again.

"He has a name, you know." Tanya dragged her brush violently through her tangled hair.

"Never said it didn't." Candice jabbed at Tanya's obvious annoyance.

Tanya visibly clenched her jaw but said nothing. The rest of the hour was spent dressing for the luau in relative silence.

In fact, the tension between the girls didn't subside until they reached the fire-lit beach and Candice's Coast Guard date led them past the rest of the Atlantis passengers, Stilwells included, and directly to the front by the stage's premiere seating. The four were seated with a group of Strategist champions and mentors and one elder dowager.

Merk introduced them.

"Ladies, it is my honor to introduce you to Champion Murphy, Mentor Faveri, Mentor McArthur, and of course the ever illuminate Dame Tambeaux."

Holly swallowed hard and dropped her gaze. Merk continued, oblivious,

"And these lovely ladies are Candice Blacc and Katiel Tcumah of Latoona, with the Ladies Holly and Tanya Dijex, also of Latoona."

Dame Tambeaux raised a pair of spectacles on an elegant gold stem. She gazed determinedly at the last two introduced and commanded,

"Which is Holly Dijex?"

Trembling, Holly curtsied rather clumsily.

"You... sit by me."

Holly obeyed and seated herself on the grand old dame's right. She glanced at Tanya, who immediately seated herself directly opposite the ancient grace in challenging defiance, refusing to be put off by her grandeur.

The festive atmosphere around the various bonfires was contagious, and there was laughter all around. Holly tried to relax but could feel the piercing eyes of the grand dame watching her every move in silence.

Tanya, having sized up her opponent, addressed her brazenly.

"Are you vacationing in the Falklands, ma'am?"

Dame Tambeaux granted her play. "I was, but I heard some rather distressing family news and am now on my way to investigate."

Holly coughed slightly on the drink she was sipping.

Tanya pursued,

"I hope all of your family is well." She paused only briefly and then decided to throw caution to the wind.

"Champion Marin Tambeaux, your nephew I believe, was well when we left him in Janeiro."

"Indeed he is well… since you left him. My concern is that you continue in this state of having left him."

Holly's anger was piqued by her interference and it gave her confidence to speak.

"Surely the champion is a man of his own and can choose to go where and with whom he pleases."

"That is where you are mistaken, my dear." Dowager Tambeaux adjusted her seat to settle in for the declaration. "My nephew, the champion, was the playmate and confidant of the future Prince-in-One, Hadigan himself. He was raised by a family of exclusive Strategist Defense Leaders and is set to become the right hand of a future king, should the present one ever decline his gracious presence from us."

The grandeur of Holly's denied beau heightened in her mind like the blush rising in her cheeks.

Dowager Tambeaux sipped her champagne.

"I'm not sure what happened. He's been away on tour for too long. When he returns this season to receive his promotion to mentor, he will be set right. And you will be nowhere in sight."

Holly closed her eyes, and placed her napkin delicately on the table. She smoothed her skirt with her hands and rose to her feet. Curtseying, she calmly smiled and said,

"I will be precisely where I need to be. Good evening, ma'am."

Tanya rose to follow her sister but couldn't resist the temptation. Turning back to the hawk eyes watching them retreat, she sneered,

"I must congratulate you on a new brother in your family. A rather remarkable L1 Bacht. He and Marin," she emphasized the familiarity of calling a mighty Trevel Defense Champion by his first name, "are quite close. They are famously influential upon each other."

Thus the two girls retreated as the Dowager, so proud and austere, suddenly looked weakened by a fatal blow.

"You shouldn't have told her that," Holly smirked. "You'll get them both in such trouble."

Tanya looked her sister in the eye.

"You know as well as I that both of those men are more than capable of handling themselves." She winked and put her arm through her sister's, and they strolled down the beach away from the crowd. "That's why we like them so much."

"I'll pretend you didn't say that." Holly's brow showed concern.

Tanya shrugged. "Just being real."

Two Tutors

The Atlantis set sail again through the HDP barriers of Under Falk not long after all her passengers had returned from the Luau. Tanya and Holly spent the night staying up into the small hours of the morning watching girly flickers and eating cookie dough ice cream in massive quantities.

The girls had not used their flickers option yet. They had always preferred to make their own story rather than watch someone else's on the big or small screen.

Falk was famous for its Trevel flickers, and most companies used these small Under Island Clusters for their home bases. In fact, many of the Flicker fans on board the Atlantis were able to visit a couple of flicker sets during shooting times.

Tonight, the girls wanted to escape. Holly tried to block out visions of the grand second-in-command-to-the-entire-Trevel-Nations asking her to marry him. Tanya allowed her mind to linger on socially suicidal activities such as dating a Bacht. The ice cream was therapeutic.

Thus it was in a sugar coma, curled up on the couches, that Grandma P found the girls and made desperate attempts to rouse them for a highly important meeting.

"Your ANA tutor is here. He's a famous life-coach and will not be kept waiting." Grandma P tugged the covers out from around the pair, and they both plonked on the floor, moaning.

"Seriously, I couldn't move if I wanted to." Tanya curled up under the mat on the floor.

"You will move, and you will do so with grace and style. Heaven knows I'll make you move." A male, somewhat effeminate, voice charged them and mumbled the last sentence under his breath as if no one could hear his perfectly audible statement.

"I'm done here for now. Tyal, they are yours." Grandma P walked out of the suite.

Holly peaked open her bleary eyes to see a remarkable specimen of a classically dressed gentleman dabbing his brow with a polka-dot lime green handkerchief.

He tapped her feet with his polished and spatted shoes. "Rise and shine, flora girl, holidays are over."

He stepped over her and kicked off the mat that was draped over Tanya.

"You too, dirt girl, it's time for me to work my magic."

Tanya, scowled down her nose at him. "And you are?"

"Nice tone, darling, but raise only one eyebrow, not both. It is more disarming." Tyal seated himself rather daintily on the puffy couch, careful to not crinkle his suit.

"Excuse me?" Holly crawled up off the floor and sat cross-legged on the couch opposite the intruder.

"Oh goodness," he tapped his own knees, "never cross-legged, my dear. That's far too open and vulnerable a position."

The two stared at him.

"If you don't know to whom you are speaking, never leave yourself open for anything." He stood and walked over to her, lifting one leg toward the other.

"Keep yourself closed off. Knees together... body language is eighty percent of what you communicate." Holly obeyed and adjusted herself into a side-saddle seated position.

"Much better. Now, raise one hand in the air as if you were holding a glass of some exotic drink. It poses the question, 'Who the hell are you?'"

Holly complied.

"There, now you scream snobbery and condescension, no matter how disheveled or hung over you look."

"Why would I want to look like a snob?" Holly checked out her reflection in the wall mirror.

Tyal gasped and clasped his heart. He glanced back and forth between Tanya and Holly to see if they were jesting.

"I need a raise; this is going to be more effort than I thought." Again, he muttered to himself, perfectly audible.

He checked his reflection in the mirror, smoothed his bald head and his coat and clapped his hands together.

"First things first, off to the showers, both of you. I don't care how long you take once you're in, but if you aren't dousing yourselves with water in three minutes, I'll strip you and throw you in there myself."

Tanya snorted and looked disgusted at him.

Tyal straightened to his full perfect posture and stared frankly at the girl.

"Don't think I won't. You don't get to be as fabulous as this," he gestured to his perfect image, "by having any interest in private improprieties."

The girls stood carefully eying him.

He watched them and shooed at them with his hands.

"Scoot."

Tanya turned around at her bedroom door and asked,

"Who are you?"

"I am your salvation. I am the only thing that will keep you out of the jaws of the wolves in the Royal Cluster of Lemuria. I am Tyal, your social tutor."

The girls slunk off, quite disgusted at the idea.

Tyal called out to them,

"And don't think you can get rid of me. I'm in the service of Atlantis National Academy. You will be presentable by the time we arrive in society."

The girls spent the morning going through their toilette with Tyal. He threw out everything they were used to and gave them a list of cosmetics, skin care items, and perfumes he required as replacements.

As they made their way down to the shops to purchase their homework products, they wandered past the gymnasium and became quite distracted by the sight behind the glass doors. Mitch was taking a moment of his free time to rededicate his routine to his daily katas.

As the girls had only seen Bacht martial arts once before, they stared in bewilderment. It appeared that much of the Bacht system for defense was based on physicality in strength, flexibility, and endurance.

There was an aura of determination and focus on the young man's face, but as it is a fact widely known that a Bacht accesses only a limited amount of its mental capacities, neither girl could imagine what effect his concentration would have.

Tanya raised her hand to push open the door. Holly pulled her back.

"You've become too attached to him of late. I think we should keep walking."

Unfazed by the hindrance, Tanya merely mumbled as she entered,

"Grandma P said I should warn him to steer clear of the Stilwells."

The heavy door made a loud click as they entered. Mitch appeared to not notice. The two sat on the bench by the door and studied him, fascinated by the precision and dedication he gave to each gesture.

In cyclical fashion, he worked his way around to all corners of the compass, reciting each stroke of his hands, arms, and legs with confidence and beauty. After a few cycles he stopped, stood tall, and bowed.

Stooping to pick a towel off the floor he said,

"You act as if you've never seen anyone work out before."

"Is that what you call it? Well, I haven't, not like that, anyway." Tanya nervously ran her hand down her crossed leg.

"What do the mighty Trevel do to keep fi t?" Mitch approached them.

Tanya giggled.

"I'm not sure about the mighty ones, but a Trevel Strategist's Defense is, well, physicality is involved, but it comes from more your core and exudes the power of the Energies."

"Show me." He held out his hand.

Holly raised her eyebrow, just as Tyal had taught her, but Tanya approached the Bacht.

"Try to hit me," she challenged.

Mitch shook his head somewhat condescendingly and said,

"I don't try to hit, anyone, especially not women." He wiped some dripping sweat off his chin. "I either do or do not hit, by choice."

"So hit me, stud," again she challenged.

Mitch smiled, chuckling. Tanya turned to wink at Holly and felt her ponytail being tugged. She whipped her head back around and saw Mitch standing still again winking at her.

"Oh, you gonna play like that, are you?" Tanya's competitive nature teased.

He shrugged.

She flicked her fingers at him and a pebble flew forth and hit his hanging wrist, causing him to drop the towel he held. He swore.

"Yeah, boy, it's a whole new ball game in this universe," Tanya teased.

"Expect anything."

Mitch shook out his disarmed hand and slowly bent down to pick up his towel. Suddenly he flicked it, snapping it on her arm, but she was too quick and blocked it with a mild stone skin.

She was expecting to see his surprise again; instead he was already placing his hands gently and firmly on her opposite wrist.

Tanya, proudly expecting to show off her earthen manipulations, found herself suddenly in his arms with one arm behind her back leaned against his chest, his other arm embracing across her front holding her waist.

"Perhaps you should expect a bit more from this lowly Bacht?"

Mitch whispered in her ear.

He held her for just a split second, then pushed her away and began to walk off.

"How did you do that?" Tanya was at a loss. Never had anyone been able to gain such an upper hand on her before. It frightened and enticed her.

Even Holly walked directly toward the retreating figure.

"Show me how you did that."

Mitch turned to gaze at them.

"I doubt I could teach you anything. You're of the 'Atlantis National Academy.'" He added quotation marks to the school's name with his fingers. "Don't they have defense lessons?"

A deep voice boomed across the gym from the quietly closing door.

"They have the best Strategist Training in the Trevel Nation. Would you like to see?"

Without further provocation, Shem Stilwell tossed his arm out, and a dagger sped out at Mitch's shoulder and stopped within inches of its fleshy target. Mitch, however, had already rolled away and stood two arms' lengths from where the dagger hung in midair.

"Not bad, Bacht, I'm mildly impressed."

"I'm not." Ham Stilwell ran at the trio. Tanya and Holly darted apart.

Mitch stood his ground, solid and nimble.

In one great leap, Ham rose up from the floor, letting a long sword slide out from out under his sleeve. He aimed it at the Bacht's heart and set to slam into the young man.

Mitch waited for his descent, dropped to the floor, and rolled backward, landing crouched like a cat, head-on with Ham.

A breath and they were in vise grips with each other. Ham used basic Greco wrestling techniques; Mitch resorted to some mixed martial arts tactics. Ham barely kept his footing.

Enraged that such a base creature as a Bacht could even stand in his or his brother's presence, Shem joined in from behind, fighting dirty: long sword and dagger verses bare hands.

Holly glared at Japheth, who shrugged his shoulders and tossed a pocket knife, at Mitchell who snatched it in flight.

Despite the blades flashing, no blood had yet been spilled until Shem and Ham, in practiced movement, attacked as one from opposite angles.

Mitchell had no choice but to take it from one of the blades and chose the dagger.

Impaled through his thigh, his determination to defeat both attackers only increased.

Tanya and Holly wanted to throw in their assistance, but the frenzy was so heightened the three were one mass. It is uncertain how long it would have continued had they not all been instantaneously frozen solid.

Captain Cochran stood calm and overbearing. He held Japheth in a twist of swirling water, immobile.

"The Bacht is in my charge. If you wish to make a complaint against him, you speak to me."

Japheth squirmed under the swirling rope.

"We're just playing, sir."

"Cool it," was the Captain's response. He shattered Mitchell's ice cocoon and let the water melt from around the heads of Shem and Ham.

"You get yourself to the ship's doctor." He nodded Mitch out the door. "Girls, your tutor awaits you up on deck." Tanya and Holly ran after Mitchell.

"You three, stay put a while." He froze up Japheth's bindings and left the three to chill.

Tanya caught up to the proudly marching but profusely bleeding Mitchell.

"You have to teach us how to do that."

Holly placed her hand on the open wound and a green slime covered the surface and stopped the bleeding.

Mitch shook his head, still refusing his training.

"You don't understand," Tanya insisted. "We will be in school every day with those three." She looked at him pleading. Mitch dropped his head then conceded, "Meet me in the stables tomorrow morning before breakfast."

Off he stalked.

A Letter

Sydney Port of Call

Science Expedition

Return to Snowy Mountain

Chapter 12

A Letter

The afternoon before they arrived in Under Zealand, Tanya was changing in her room after a vigorous workout with her new sensei.

She couldn't help smiling as she recalled the physical work. Sensei Mitchell would grab at the girls in ways the Stilwell boys might. Tanya managed to throw Mitchell a couple of times, and she glowed recalling his congratulations.

She hugged herself and felt something crinkle in her pocket. It was a note:

Meet me in the stables.

Her heart skipped a beat. Only Mitchell could or would give her such a note. What a situation to be in. Should she shower first or just run to him? She knew his schedule, though she'd never tell her sister, and knew that he only had an hour after their martial arts lessons to brush down the horses before he needed to help the captain prep for his dinner speech.

Tanya ran to the stairs rather than rely on the leisurely lifts. Straight to the onboard Laray fields, she then took the animals' express elevator directly to the science and zoology deck in the belly of the ship.

The hole was a zoo, literally and in the chaotic term also. The animals and pets all squeaked and screamed, hooted and made a mess as scientists and aides rushed about preparing for departure and the reloading of newcomers.

Tanya stole around to the equestrian quarter looking for Mitchell, but found herself pounced on and dragged easily into the tack room.

She sprang to life. Twisting in three places, Tanya nearly slithered out of her captor's grip and was about to mud pack his nose when she saw his curly sun-streaked hair. The door clicked quietly behind them and she was free to move.

"Nice moves. You must have a good teacher." Mitchell winked at her and held his fingertips to his, lips signaling for her quiet.

"You ought to know," she whispered. "What's with the secrecy?"

"Professor Mawkes is suddenly under the impression that I am his personal slave. I don't wish to move any more boxes around for him."

"Well, Sensei, how can I help?"

"I'm not here as Sensei, just as a friend in need."

"You don't speak to me for days except to bark disciplined direction at me in lessons. Now, suddenly you need my help, and we're friends?"

"I know, I'm sorry, it's difficult. I have to be tough to be professional."

"You could at least smile once in a while."

"No, I can't smile, because, it would drop my guard, and I can't do that, especially not when Tyal is around."

"What guard? You're not so tough, big guy." She pushed him playfully.

"No, I'm not… look… I, ah. Tanya, I dream about you almost every night. If I… if anyone… Tyal can never know. The captain would keel-haul me, really, he'd drag me under the entire length of the ship several times, not to mention among my people it's illegal for an eighteen-year-old to like a twelve-year-old."

"I'm thirteen. Holly's twelve, technically, anyway."

"Still, I understand Marin's torment. There is something about you two that makes you more than what you really are."

"Did you call me down her to tell me you love me or something?

Because you're really stinking at it right now."

"Actually, I asked you down here to ask if you could help me mail a letter. I didn't intend to say anything else."

Tanya reached for the door.

"Please, I haven't seen my family in three years and I just want to say goodbye."

"A letter?"

"I figured you would be the only one who might help me."

"Seduce me first, use me later. You really stink at telling a girl you love her. Give me the letter."

Mitchell handed her the envelope addressed to the Jaacks in the Snowy Mountains.

"First, do you have two more envelopes?"

Mitchell opened a shoe box with envelopes, paper, and writing pens. It also had what looked like a personal journal that caught Tanya's eye.

"The return letter is the trick. It needs to be addressed in two envelopes, the outer one to the nearest Bacht/Trevel post office, where the Bacht deliver it as they would normally. There, because of the P.O. Box number, it is earmarked to be opened. The Trevels open the outer envelope and mail the inner envelope, which has your Trevel address on it, which in this case is TSNS Atlantis." Tanya wrote out the addresses and put the envelopes in order inside the letter to be delivered.

"Now you just have to figure out a way to explain to your family why they have to mail it back to you this way. According to them, what secret branch of the government do you work for?"

"What?"

"That's usually the story the Bacht use. It's the most believable."

"I work for myself, as a private computer securities contractor. I hire myself out to various companies to improve their technological security."

Tanya just stared at him.

"Really, that's what I did before I came in."

"Really? Techno? Not allowed on a flowboard yet, are you?"

"Don't remind me. Thanks for this. It means a lot to me." Mitchell filled out a note to explain the return envelopes and closed the package.

Tanya tapped the top of the box and said,

"Now you just have to get it to the post office before it closes."

Mitch slumped and looked at the time piece on the wall and grunted,

"Yeah, time." He blushed in embarrassment and confessed, "I don't know how to tell time here."

Tanya giggled and said,

"I wondered if anyone had jumped that hurdle with you."

Mitch shrugged and shook his head.

Tanya continued,

"It's okay. Even some Trevel have difficulty differentiating between Upland and Underland time. I, however, being born in one of the very few completely Trevel Upland villages, am well equipped with a clear understanding of both. If you ask nicely, I might tell you." She pouted in her typical flirtatious manner.

Mitch continued, forcing humility on himself, and asked,

"Tanya, would you please help me tell the time?"

Smiling rather triumphantly, the young girl explained,

"Trevel time is set on a twenty-four-hour clock with minutes and seconds, the same as Bacht time. However, our hours are numbered differently. To begin with, the day is divided into four calls, as is the night. The first call (I) is at sunrise, which, as it is regulated by an artificial Skyling, is at precisely 5:15 a.m. Bacht time. The second call (II) is then three hours after that (08:15), the third (III) is three hours after that (11:15), and the fourth (IV) is three hours after that (14:15). Then begin the evening calls. The first (V) is at 17:15 Bacht time, and the rest are at three-hour intervals through the night as through the day (VI20:15, VII23:15, VIII02:15)."

She paused to see if he was calculating the differences in his head then asked,

"Make sense?"

Mitch stared at the clock on the wall, it read IV1:47. Mitch tilted his head slightly sideways, then said, "...-ish."

Tanya looked at the clock also and continued, "IV1:47 means it is one hour and forty-seven minutes after the fourth call of the day. That is, 14:15 plus 1:47 which equals...?" She questioned Mitch with her eyes.

Mitch quickly calculated and said, "Its 16:02, or just after four o'clock in the afternoon."

"Precisely," applauded Tanya. "You've got it now."

They stood around the tack desk in silence for a minute.

"Here, I'll mail that for you." She accidentally, as so often happens in these situations, placed her hand on Mitchell's and left it there.

Mitch slowly gave her the letter and closed the shoe box. Tanya leaned in, held his cheeks with both hands, and kissed him heartily on the lips.

"You owed me that one." Then she walked out, leaving the tack door swinging closed behind her.

Mitchell went to look for Professor Mawkes to haul more boxes.

Sydney Port of Call

There was a far-off, muddled thudding coming from somewhere. Holly mumbled from under her pink and blue covers, then squished her pillow tighter around her ears.

The thudding continued.

Groaning, Holly slithered to the floor and spasmodically detangled herself from her sheets. Her hair was half in but mostly bird-nested out of a ponytail and sticking out in all directions. She pulled herself up on her bed and stuffed on her slippers, stumbling out the door. Thinking the better of it, she returned for her dressing gown and pulled out the ponytail, semi-straightening her hair.

"Maybe Tyal is rubbing off… a bit," she mumbled. "Coming," she called to the eager thumper.

Still with eyes mostly closed, Holly opened the door of her suite.

"Can I help you?"

Marina Tambeaux stood, in perfect uniform, smiling cheerfully as if to burn the dead with her brightness.

"Good morning, Lady Holly. It is two hours past the first call on this fabulous morning here in the Upland world. I am Pre-Champ Marina, here as you and your sister's personal chaperone. We are going to tour Bacht Sydney today. Great place to see and be, mostly because Australian Bacht don't ask questions and don't care if you're a little eccentric. The stranger you are, the better you fit in Down Under. We love it here. So why don't you get dressed; I'll wake your sister. We need to be in the Darsaldain Banquet hall by I/2:30."

The Strategist was immediately thumping on the door across the hall.

"I have a personal chaperone, half an hour to get ready, and it's only I/2:00? Argh!" Holly flopped back on her bed and would have stayed there if the thumping had not started again, this time on her own bedroom door.

"Yes?" Holly slumped up against the door, not even opening her eyes.

"Your sister isn't answering and I have orders to see that both of you are up."

Holly opened her door, and the pre-champ walked through her room.

PC Marina was beautiful and looked slightly familiar, though Holly was too tired to pay much attention. She strode to the sliding balcony door and crossed over to Tanya's room at the other end.

In moments, the pre-champion returned with a concerned look on her face.

"Are you aware you sister is not in her room?"

Holly trundled across the balcony to her sister's room.

Tan's bed was made and PJs put away and the room empty.

Holly went over to the sand-and-rock planter sitting next to the bed and touched it. Unwittingly, a seedling grew. She picked it and put it in her pocket.

"The sand is cold, so she's been gone a while. I have no idea where she is. She's never been an early riser before… unless… she's seeing someone."

PC Marina dropped a contact over her eye from under her eyelid and reported,

"Lady Tanya is MIA, sir."

There was a pause as she listened to instructions. Her face clouded and smiled at the same time.

"She's with Mitchell," the officer told Holly. "You don't have much time, and I have a feeling you might want to look your best. There's a big surprise at breakfast for you. I can't tell you who, oops, I mean, what it is, but you should always find out the last name of someone you let into your apartment." She winked at Holly as she walked to leave, but stood at the door expectantly.

Holly blandly played along.

"What's your last name, PC Marina?"

"Tambeaux." She closed the door.

Holly froze, shook her head then dressed quicker than she ever had done before.

Despite Dowager Tambeaux's presence, Sydney was lovely. Holly, feeling awfully self-conscious, had requested that Candice and Katiel and even Tomey join them. Tomey declined the offer, as he was joining the zoological team's trip to the Tauranga Park Zoo. Tomey's art projects this year involved detailed drawings of birds, reptiles, and mammals. Candice and Katiel, however, were delighted to join them.

This turned out to be the best idea, as the grand old Dowager was a Light Energist like Katiel, and Katiel had a pleasant manner with the elderly, so when the shared interest was discovered, the two spent the whole day together chatting and practicing. Katiel graciously listened and asked for much advice and insisted she learned more from Her Grace in one day than she did in a year in class at ANA.

The other four girls—PC Marina, Candice, Tanya, and Holly— stood on the blowy prow of the Manly ferry as it sailed out of the quay.

The massive Atlantis in the international dock dwarfed the tiny ferry as it chugged passed the Sydney Opera House on the other side of the harbor. From the outside, the Atlantis looked like any other cruise ship, and Tanya smiled as she thought of all the Trevel secrets hidden inside, in plain sight of the Bacht world. She felt Holly nudge her.

"What were you doing up so early with Mitchell this morning?"

"Oh, that was nothing. He asked me to mail a letter, that's all."

"Then why are you blushing, and why is he staring at you in the window's reflection?"

Tanya spun around. "Is he really?"

Mitchell suddenly stared at his shoes. He had been intently watching the windows. Marin Tambeaux also appeared engrossed in the flying cloud patterns reflected in the windows in front of them.

Marin and Mitchell had been inseparable since Marin had surprised everyone with his early arrival in Sydney. He had not been supposed to meet them until Torres Entrance when they left the ship, but suddenly here he was.

The young men sat with their backs to the wind and the ladies, staring at the windows. Candice thought they were watching the Bacht girls inside, who were obviously watching them. Marina and Holly guessed better. Marina knew Marin had no interest in any powerless

Bacht women, and Holly saw Mitchell watching Tanya's reflection. She just missed seeing Marin watching her.

Marina reached for Tanya and Holly to hug them under her outstretched arms in a sisterly fashion.

"We'd better keep an eye on windy here." She nodded behind her to Candice, who was standing with her arms outstretched, "flying" in the wind. The problem was that with her Wind Energist powers, her feet actually were four inches off the floor.

Rather than bother her exalted mood, the girls huddled around her so it wasn't noticeable. They even stood on tiptoes to keep their height the same. When Candice landed, so excited to have finally achieved flight, the girls ran inside the cabin together, cheering, to buy juices in celebration.

When the ferry reached the Manly wharf, the sun was much warmer than on the open water and jackets came off. Tanya, Mitchell, Candice, Katiel, and Dowager Tambeaux all began walking across the street, headed straight for the beach at the opposite end of the Corso, but Holly hung back.

"What's up, kid?" Marina noticed her pause.

"I was hoping to go to the Ocean Museum. I wanted to check out the underwater vegetation there."

"I'll go with you. I am a Water type, so I love that idea."

"Really? Thanks, PC Marina."

"Just call me Marina when we're out here, okay? This isn't really Strategist business, anyway, it's more of a private favor."

Holly blushed and smiled, both because of the silent reference to Marin and because, for the first time that day, he was actually approaching her.

"Where are you two off to?"

"We're going to the Ocean Museum for a while. We'll meet you on the beach."

"No, I think I'll come with you."

"You don't need to do that, sir." Marina was suddenly straight and professional. "I can handle the assignment you gave me."

"I'm not questioning your abilities, PC. I am stating a fact. I am coming with you. It is necessary in this environment."

"I don't understand, sir." Marina's voice strained with annoyance.

Holly butted in,

"If it's too much trouble, we can just go to the beach."

"Nay, my dear." Champion Tambeaux smiled softly at her, and she blushed deeper than before. "You are never a trouble. PC Marina, however, may be mistaking basic safety for brotherly overprotection."

"We are perfectly fine without you, Marin. I'm supposed to be here to protect Holly's pure reputation from your overbearing presence. You don't need to be here."

"My what?" Holly looked at Marin amused. The brother and sister ignored her.

"I have already counted at least two, no, three groups of boys who would like to accost two beautiful young women. Not to mention all the single Bacht men who are blatantly staring at you. How do you intend to get in and out of there without a single date? Holly's too young for that, and you are on duty. You can't afford to get that kind of attention. My presence cuts down on that problem by 98 percent, and you know it."

"I wasn't too young for you." Holly looked Marin in the eyes, quite perturbed by being spoken about and not to.

Marin dropped his head and took a deep breath. He spoke so quietly, Holly barely heard him.

"Marina, please, can I just come. Don't make such a big deal."

Science Expedition

"Absolutely not." Marin dropped his newspaper and looked Mitchell square in the face. "You know the deal and swore to five years away."

"Yes, I did. And I'm willing to live up to that. I just thought we're so close…"

"No."

"…and I haven't seen them in three years…"

"No."

"…and they live in secluded mountains with lots of rocks and even a gold mine or two…"

"What? No."

"….and all the unique native plants."

"No."

"Plants that are singularly unique to that area only and one would not have the chance to see them anywhere else."

"You're evil."

"I know."

"The answer is still no."

"Uh-huh." He tuned to leave then stopped to ask casually, "How long 'til the girls meet Prince Hadigan at Hanain, again?"

"Get out," was the only reply.

Mitchell left with a smile on his face, confident his plan had worked. He winked at Tanya, who waited for him in the hallway, and together they left the Tambeaux apartments on the Atlantis.

They met Holly and Marina in the mid-ship lobby. Tonight was their last night in Sydney and they were going to Luna Park, an amusement park under the Harbor Bridge.

***　　　***　　　***

The phone echoed in the quiet mountain ranch hallway.

"This is Tom Jaack... Yes, we had a Wattle-Gum Gecko Mitchell as a foster child."

Jaack excitedly waved his wife over to him and she listened in on the telephone call.

"You'd like to come and see his early work? Yes, we still have all his work here. Why? You'll bring him with you? Yes! We'd love that...

What? Everyone but the two of us has to be gone, why? His brother's and sister's... top secret... yeah, sounds like Mitch. Okay. Tomorrow?

That's short notice, but I guess we can do that . . . How many? You'll bring gear. We're far up, but trailers work, we have roads . . . Righto, we'll see you then. Bye."

The Jaacks sat looking bewildered at each other, then hugged with tears in their eyes. Mitch was coming home.

*** *** ***

"Holly, concentrate! I want purple veined climbing roses on that arbor. These look like they have the plague. Tiny veins, none of this coloring with fading and blotching. Now focus, or do I need to send you to the focus room again?" Tyal certainly had his socks in a knot this morning.

"Forgive us, Champion, we are usually much better on command than this. I just don't know what has gotten into the girl."

"Perhaps we should all take a moment to remember that she is just that, a young girl." The distinguished Champion Marin Tambeaux soothed Tyal. "No need to be so hard, the roses are exquisite."

To prove him wrong, Holly waved her hand past the arbor and all the roses turned brown and dropped off.

"I'm no girl, Champion, I am Lady Holly of Atlantis National Academy." She stood beneath the arbor and bowed her head, closed her eyes and took a deep breath.

Flattening her hands in front of her facing them down, she slowly raised her hands sideways, palms facing outward, running them along the outline of the arches. Tilting her head slightly, she continued lifting her palms outward till they lay flat up at her head, by which time the entire arch was covered with white roses labyrinthed in tiny purple veins.

"That is lovely, Lady Holly." Tyal tapped his fingers together in quiet applause.

Holly picked a rose and handed it to Marin. He whispered,

"Holly, you never have to prove to me how much of a woman you are."

He bowed and kissed her hand. Then, turning her hand over, he blew gently into her palm and recreated a perfect replica of her rose in ice. Holly fished the necklace she was wearing out from under her sweater and took it off. Laying the chain across the back of the rose, she said,

"Here, blow on this."

Marin blew again and froze the chain to the rose. Holly then walked over to the HDP tank (for first aid use) and dipped the rose into it. Out came the ice rose, sparkling clean, clear, and shimmering in its water plastic covering.

"Now when it dries hard in about thirty minutes, it won't melt, and I can wear my necklace to dinner tonight." She smiled triumphantly.

Marin grinned and Tyal raised an eyebrow. He would have enquired further into such intimate behavior, but Tanya, who had been working privately with Sensei Mitchell — Tyal and Mitch swapped opportunities to work with the girls — came running in.

"Some scientists are headed this way. They have a message for you, Tyal."

"What have I to do with scientists?"

The door opened and the chief of the science lab, Professor Mawkes, stalked in.

"Is the Coach Tyal here?"

"Mentor Tyal am I."

"I didn't know you were military."

"It's an honorary title, anyway…"

"I have a request to work with your young ladies. May we talk in private?"

Mitchell winked at Tanya, who looked at Marin, who was trying not to look too pleased with himself as he stared at Holly. Holly blew on her necklace and showed it to Tanya.

"Bachtland!" Tyal belched from the corner conference.

The hushed whispering continued.

Tyal returned looking ill.

"Ladies, sad fortune has come upon us. It looks as if we are about to be forced to take part in reckless abandonment."

The champion interrupted,

"This is completely voluntary, Tyal. If you do not care to join us, you do not have to. The ladies will have their female chaperone."

"Truly?" Tyal was completely relieved.

"Then in that case, you may actually enjoy yourselves, knowing your habit of liking Upland air. That means I have the rest of this ship's journey off. I'm going to the spa, if anyone needs me."

With that, Tyal disappeared for the remainder of the Atlantis journey to Torres Entrance.

Champion Tambeaux nodded to the scientists as they left in a bustle of anticipation.

"We are off on a science expedition. South of Sydney, some way south actually, is a remarkable mountain scape with unique landscape and vegetation. The reason we are going on such a controversial expedition is due to a unique member of our party. We have an ex-local who is willing to be our travel guide. Not only is he highly familiar with the area and can communicate freely with the natives, but he will not try to escape or give us away, or we will kill his family and anyone who joins the expedition. So let's not go there, shall we, Wattle-Gum Gecko Mitchell?"

"Wattle-Gum Gecko?" Tanya and Holly in unison snorted, giggling, and turned to Mitchell.

Mitchell looked at Marin and said sarcastically,

"Oh, yeah them knowing that is much better."

Return to Snowy Mountain

Mitchell insisted he and Marin ride the horses up the mountain. The two saddled up while the girls helped load the last of the trucks and batten down the trailers.

By the time the convoy was ready to leave the lower town and head up the mountain, the two "brothers" were already disappearing into the mountain scrub, hollering at each other all the way.

Tanya sat in the front of the camper while Holly lay down above in the bed and watched out the windows. The trees were all ghostly white and the leaves were deep green, yet grey bark hung from the trees like murky and tattered tinsel.

The bush was anything but dark; the sun was blinding. It shone everywhere. The leaves even seemed to scream at each other as they scratched the air together, rallying against the arid temperature.

There was a constant hum, not a quiet hum of bees or a gentle chitter of birds, but a discordant protest against the heat. January in Australia, even in the South, was still just plain hot.

They arrived at the great wooden homestead only minutes before the two men came crashing through the underbrush on their steeds.

Holly was concerned the horses may have been too hot, but both man and beast were drenched and bare-chested after an obvious swim.

Mitchell jumped from his horse before it stopped and landed like a cat on all fours. He ran up the porch and straight into the arms of a huge man, who picked Mitch up and swung him round like a rag doll.

Next, Mitch tenderly kissed and hugged a tall woman crying her eyes out. She held him for a long time, and Mitch let her.

Marin slowly wound the horse's's' reins to the post and sauntered up the steps to shake hands with the burly man. He was greeted with a great slap on the back.

When released, Mitchell took his foster mother by the hand and led her directly to the camper that held the two spying girls. He knocked politely and waited for them to exit.

"You go first; he wants to introduce you to his mother." Holly nudged Tanya, who had joined her up in the bunk bed as soon as they had stopped.

"No, you go first and explain how old we are." Tanya couldn't take her eyes off the great man on the porch.

Marina spoke up from the driver's seat.

"How about I go first and tell them the Lady Wonders are too terrified to meet anyone?"

"No!" They both jumped down from the bunk.

Marina grabbed them before they reached the door.

"Whatever you do, do not tell them your age."

"Mum." Mitchell helped Tanya down the steps, then Holly. "I'd like you to meet Tanya, and her sister Holly. We work together, sort of... not in the same department, just with the same company."

"My, you're all so young," Mrs. Jaack said. "You barely look a day over seventeen. What is it you do?"

Tanya spoke first, as always.

"We work with the science crew. I'm a geologist and Holly is a botanist. We love nature and you certainly seem to have a lot of it up here. It's beautiful. How long have you lived here?"

And with that, age was forgotten and everyone was ushered inside for afternoon tea. They had sponge cake, black tea, coffee, and lime cordial. Tanya tried the coffee but ended up with lime cordial instead.

Holly quite enjoyed the tea. It was fresh, homemade herbal tea, and it made her feel really good — almost too good. Marin kept a close eye on her drinking habits.

That evening while the girls helped to clean up after dinner, Mitchell showed Marin his room. The rest of the team was out in the camp preparing for the next day's work.

"The Belle family would love to see this craftsmanship." Marin ran his hands over the woodwork.

"Who're they?"

"A famous family of architects. They did our Lemurian home."

"I did this room."

"No you didn't."

"No, I didn't." They laughed. "I can build a pretty mean cabinet, but not as beautifully as Dad. He's the one who built the house."

"Well, if they ever need somewhere to stay, they have a place and a job with me. What did you want to show me?"

"Behind those doors."

Marin opened what he thought was the closet and stepped back to admire Mitch's old computer room.

"How does it work?"

Mitch smiled and said, as if he'd been waiting his whole life to say it,

"You show me yours and I'll show you mine."

Marin chuckled.

"Nice try, kid." He sat down at the computer for a few seconds, then reached behind and turned it on.

"Smart one, aren't you." Mitch nudged Marin to scoot over.

"I studied Bacht technology in Strategic officer's training."

"Move over and let me show you what a professional can do."

The rest of the night, Marin and Mitchell showed off to each other as they built programs, played games, and even played guitar. The girls came in for a while, but the boys were so engrossed that soon they left for the open air instead.

"Boys will be boys." Mrs. Jaack smiled and brought them some peach tea. "I thought you'd like some fruit blend tea."

"Mrs. Jaack, do you have a garden?"

"I sure do, Holly, but it's best to see it in the day time. So how old are you Tanya, dear?"

"I'd be giving away all my secrets if I told you that, now wouldn't I, Mrs. Jaack," Tanya laughed, hiding her distress perfectly. "I will say I am younger than the boys, but that is why we have a chaperone. Marina is here to keep us safe from the evil ways of men," she joked and hoped to lighten the mood.

"Well, that's sensible. And I wouldn't laugh too much. I love Mitch, but I'm not sure what he's like around girls. He was always so secluded up here. He has quite a wild streak, too, so just be safe and don't be silly. You don't want too much happening at too young an age, love."

The mother sighed.

"I've seen too many mothers in their twenties trying to recover teen years lost to pregnancy. It is a sad thing." She stood up and took up the tea tray. "But look at me preaching to you, and I hardly even know you. I'm sure you're old enough to be sensible. Good night, dears."

"How long do you think she's been waiting to tell you that?" Holly giggled.

"Since she found out her baby Gecko brought home a girl." Tanya wasn't quite as amused. They walked back to the camper, past the window flashing with the blips of Mitch and Marin's computer game.

The Tube Takes Time

The Port of Hanain

New Management

Lord Deagan

Chapter 13

The Tube Takes Time

Secretly, Tanya hoped for some romantic moments in the mountains, but it was not to be. Mrs. Jaack stayed with them like a hawk. Mitchell appeared to relish the attention of a mother and constantly smiled with his arms draped around her or patting her. He even picked wildflowers for her. But as they were only to stay three days, the constant affection was endearing, not excessive. Besides, Professor Mawkes kept Tanya and Holly busy.

Mr. Jaack took a keen interest in Tanya's talents with geology. It was hard to think up reasons for him not to join them in their mountain walks. However, as Tanya and Holly were freely moving entire trees and cliff faces around for easier study access, it was a little difficult to take a Bacht along with them.

Holly smoothed some HDP fluid into her scratched and aching hands as she sat in her seat on the Tube station in Underland Syd, waiting for their ride to the Hanain Mines to arrive.

"You really worked hard up in the mountains. Let me cool your hands for you." Marina took Holly's hands in hers and blew on them a cool, wet breeze. A thin, firm layer of ice slithered over both hands and was just enough to bring relief to the burning sting.

"I wasn't expecting those spitfire caterpillar things to be so painful, or so plentiful. Thank you, the ice really helps."

"So, do you know what's going on between Mitchell and Tanya?" Marina tried to sound casual.

Holly grinned.

"Nothing, much to Tanya's disappointment. Mitchell is too disciplined to let anything happen. He still considers himself our sensei and knows that sort of thing is pretty much illegal for him right now."

Sounding much more unpleasant, Marina scowled.

"Smart boy. He'd be better off staying away from her altogether. He'll never be considered worthy of her. You would do well to advise Tanya to stay away from him. He's not good for her image."

Holly laughed, a little unsure.

"He's okay. There's no harm done."

"Not now, but I'd be careful if I were you. A decent career may be hard to come by for someone who has a Bacht in the family. And if you do want to marry, a decent man will be hard to find if he has to put up with that type of association."

Holly looked at Marina, about to point out her hypocrisy. Marina explained,

"An L1 brother is one thing; it shows condescension and generosity. A Bacht brother-in-law, however, shows a lack of discretion and respect for the Power of the Trevel way of life. Just a word of warning."

Marina left her in the windy tunnel. Holly and Marin were the only ones who remained outside as the rest of the party took shelter in the warmer waiting room.

After a moment's brief silence, Marin casually strolled over to where she sat and began adjusting the pile of bags and boxes next to her.

"What has my sister said to you that has you so depressed?"

But Holly had no time to answer as the tunnel filled with light and wind blasting around them.

A rounded, bullet-shaped blue engine appeared pulling six matching blue carriages behind it. They were all encased in HDP and glistened in the tunnel's lamplight. At the ends of each carriage, the doors opened up like wings hanging in the air above the doorway, and blue-coated porters came rushing out to check and load the baggage.

Under Syd was a central station, and dozens of people poured out of the waiting rooms and crammed themselves onto the platform, all wanting to go in opposite directions.

Marin took Holly's hand.

"This way," he said to her gently. Then in a loud, commanding voice, he said, "Make way, please. Champion Tambeaux of the Royal Lemurian Tambeauxs wishes to enter the Tube."

Immediately a path was made clear for him, and everyone bowed to both of them, saluting them as they passed.

Marin led them straight to the last car, which was marked High Set.

Tanya didn't have quite so easy a time getting to the carriage and arrived, rather tousled, to see her sister and Marin sharing quiet drinks in the corner.

She was about to interrupt when Marina slammed a suitcase down on the seat in front of her, blocking her path.

"After spending every spare moment you can with a lowly Bacht, ignoring your sister for the past month, you're not going to deny her one little moment of happiness with her man, now are you?" Marina sneered a little at Tanya.

"I haven't been ignoring her."

"No?"

"No, I haven't." Tanya sized up the lithe young militant woman.

"What is it that you don't like about me, anyway?" She had just pushed her way through a throng of station dwellers and was not going to sit down yet.

"I have no problem with you, Tanya dear. It's your choice in men that I have a problem with."

"But he's your brother!"

"My L1 brother."

"So?"

"So, when we get to the civilized world, you will understand just how important a difference that is."

"What difference does it make to you?"

"None whatsoever, but it affects everything that touches your sister, so don't be quite so completely self-centered just yet."

Marina picked up the bag effortlessly with her ice rope and tossed it into the overhead compartment. She then sat down with her feet across the aisle, barring the way to Holly. Tanya turned to go and sit with Mitchell, then changed her mind and sat by the window alone.

The train began to move away from the station. Mitchell beckoned to Tanya, but she pretended not to see and put her music threads in her ears, laid her head back, and closed her eyes.

Mitchell pulled out his journal to write, while Marina sharpened her knife. Marin and Holly continued their pleasant conversation, oblivious to the tension buildup in the rest of the carriage.

"Marin, may I bring up a sore subject?"

"I am willing to talk about anything if you wish to speak of it."

"You said I would forget you for another man... is that Prince Hadigan?"

Marin didn't smile. As if it were the most difficult thing to say, he gritted,

"It is he."

"Do you know him?"

"I know him well enough to not want to talk about him."

"You said you were willing to talk of anything I wished. I wish to know why you think I will fall so completely and blindly for the prince."

"Everyone else does."

"I'm not everyone else."

"You don't understand, and I can't explain it. It's as if that is his energy gift: having people love him."

"You don't seem to love him."

"I grew up with him."

"How is that possible?"

"I grew up in Lemuria. My father, my father's father, my father's father's father — all of them have been great Strategist ambassadors and counselors to the kings. As such, the family spent lots of time in the castle. 'Haddy' was a loner by choice, but he liked hanging out with the younger kids, because we would do as he said. Some said he was a born leader. I say he was a born bossy boots."

Holly giggled.

"See, that's what you need to tell me, so I won't fall for him."

"Don't you ever tell him I said that. If you don't fall for him, he'll know it's my fault and I'll pay for it."

"How? He can't do anything to you, can he?"

"You'd be surprised how much power he has. He could make it so I don't get this Mentor promotion, or he could demote me, or send me to somewhere like Kentari."

"Kentari, isn't that the Independent province under the British Isles and the Netherlands? It's thousands of miles away, he can't send you there."

"He'll be Prince-in-One soon, successor to the throne. He can do what he wants."

"So if I don't fall for him, he'll blame you?"

"Definitely."

"But if I do fall for him, I'll lose you?"

"Not if I know you don't want to lose me."

"I can't ask you to wait; that'll take too long."

"I have nothing better to do."

"I don't want to lose you."

"Then you never will."

Marina coughed up a hairball and dropped her head back toward them.

"That's enough saccharine. Think with your brain, big brother. You need to go do the commanding champion thing anyway."

"That would be why I hired her to chaperone." Marin smiled and kissed Holly's forehead. He stepped out of the seat, saluted her, and marched down the aisle through the door to the adjoining carriage.

Marina came to sit next to Holly.

"There are about thirty strategists in the next carriage awaiting his orders. But you and your sister now have to prepare to meet the prince. We'll be there in the morning, so I recommend you take Sulky over there," she pointed to Tanya, still listening to her music, "and go to your sleeper apartments at the back end of this carriage and get a good night's sleep. The prince is rather energetic and is known to tire people."

The Port of Hanain

The Underland Tube system flies through water tunnels and is covered in HDP. It is, therefore, extremely fast. The trip from Underland Syd to the Port of Hanain, underneath the Great Barrier Reef, took only six hours.

Thus, the girls' "good night's sleep" was only a four-hour nap. They weren't sure it did any good or if it made matters worse.

The science team groggily stepped off the blue tube and into the dark Port Station. It was, after all, only an hour after the fourth call of the night, IV/1:00, or 3:15 a.m. Bacht time.

The Station was at the end of the line, so they waited for the train to back up into the tunnel and disappear again.

All was quiet.

The soft "plash-plash" of the rhythmic waves at the end of the dock was the only welcome the huddle of cold expeditioners received.

"We were supposed to be here three days ago with the Atlantis to meet Hadigan," mumbled Marina.

Marin growled slightly, hoisted his bag and a couple of Holly's onto his shoulders, and then began walking across the tracks toward the lights of the Port Town.

He tapped the energized time horn on his upper right chest-pocket for light, but there was something in the mine's air that hindered the technology. Marina, also, couldn't get her equipment to work, and the only Light Energist among them was rather weak in his attempts to shed any light on their path.

It was a mile trek that would have been made in pitch darkness if they hadn't combined their Energies and used the HDP seal from the first aid kit. Off the station platform, they could barely see their faces.

Fortunately, Professor Mawkes and his aide were Fire and Light Energists. Tanya gathered some sand together and, with much quiet concentration, for this was a difficult task, she was able to form some small pieces of glass.

As she heated the sand in her hands, the Professor noted that not even he could burn a fire that hot. Tanya shrugged it off, saying only Earth Energists could match the wavelength of each grain of sand to liquefy it.

With that done, Marina and Marin froze the edges of the glass together in small lantern shapes. Everyone helped, sealing the seams with HDP. The flicker documenter (for there had to be a visual record of the expedition) was a Wind Energist, so he blew the lanterns dry.

They didn't have to wait for long. Holly formed some ropes to swing the lanterns from. Thus, they had small luminaries to guide their path from the Station to Port

Hanain's big gates. It was an effort well spent, as there were many pot holes and obstacles along the way.

New Management

"Is there some kind of construction going on?" Professor Mawkes tripped on another lead pipe.

"I am not aware of any, but it certainly looks like it." Marin stepped lightly over a pothole and leaned back to help his sister and the girls.

Naturally, Marina flatly refused his help. She scoffed,

"This would be the first time you weren't aware of something happening."

"I know." Marin's brow was creased and he looked at the looming gates. "That worries me."

Before they reached the massive entrance structure, a shot of flame was fired over their heads. Professor Mawkes and his aide screeched, and the flicker guy jumped on his camera.

The others, however, all dove behind luggage and took defensive stances. Marin stood his ground and commanded,

"How dare you fire on a Champion of the Royal Lemurian Defense Force? Prince Hadigan will have your necks for this. I command you open the gate and let us through."

A weasely voice mimicked,

"I command you let us through." It continued the mocking: "Oooh! Whatcha gonna do, royal poo on us?"

Cackling laughter burst over the wall from the gate's tower.

Marin was staunch.

"Who's your commanding officer?"

The mimicking again, "Who's your commanding officer? We don' 'ave none, but the Lord 'imse'f, an 'e don' wanna be disturb'd righ' now."

"I demand you wake Prince Hadigan and tell him his Champion Tambeaux is here."

"'Is champion is ya? Or are ya 'is chamber maid?" Guffaws of laughter and the sound of someone falling over came from the battlements.

A blast of ice had hit one of the helmets that was moving around and one of the laughing voices silenced. But then the others retorted.

"Pretty littl' Ice Queen down there 'as good aim."

Suddenly, a ball of color sounded and disabled itself from a spear on the castle walls and squarely hit the rock Marina was hiding behind.

It ballooned into a dome over the covering rock, Marina, and a couple of bags around her. Holly barely managed to scoot away from it. Marina tried to claw her way out of the oil rainbow, but it held fast, then BOOM, it imploded on her.

Cackles of laughter rang from the battlements.

"That'll teach her. Let's take Lazza inside. He needs ta warm up a bi'."

"I can warm him up."

"No way, man, you'll give 'im serious sunburn."

"Let him thaw out the slow way, I got tired of hearing him boast about that girl in the tavern last week."

"Let's steal his money."

The voices quieted down as everyone ran to see if Marina was all right.

She lay unconscious on the ground, splattered with the oozing rainbow oil substance. Tanya reached out to touch it, but Marin smacked her hand back.

"I have no idea what that is. This is different weaponry than any I've ever seen. Professor, do you have any gloves?"

The professor guided everyone in how to correctly collect and clean up the samples. The guys built a make-shift tent and the girls washed down Marina and redressed her in new clothes. She still lay unconscious, and Marin was visibly upset.

"If I knew more about that weapon, I could maybe know better how to help her." He ran his hands through his hair.

"She's sleeping peacefully," Holly reassured him. "We better just wait until she wakes up."

"That's a nice sentiment, but how do you know she's not dying?"

Tanya put her hand on his shoulder.

"Our parents are great healers. We know when someone is dying and when they are sleeping. When we drank the dragon tears, we were in a similar coma. You just have to sleep some powers off."

Marin wasn't satisfied. "I'm going to try and get in."

"What good is one ice man against a dozen guards?" Tanya tried reason.

"I'm damn good, that's what."

"We're here as guests, Marin. You can't go blasting into the house from which you seek hospitality." Holly took his arm and smoothed the hair with her hand. "Come sit with me. We will watch over Marina together. I will teach you a dragon song that always helps."

She led Marin like a lamb to his beloved sister's side and began singing,

"A dragon tear for you..." Behind her back, however, she signaled Tanya to go see what she could do.

The rocky landscape, outside the Gates of Hanain, was a welcome sight to Tanya. Playing hide and seek with Holly in the jungle was near impossible, and Tanya hated it. But here, on the bare hillside, Tanya took a deep breath and giggled in delight. She was about to make PC Marina proud… and Tyal not so proud.

She shivered herself into what she liked to call "stealth action." Her jeans and jacket color rolled off her and she blended perfectly with the dirt on which she stood. She scampered toward the cliff side at right angles to the Great Gates that towered menacingly over the tiny campsite.

The flicker guy, who was watching her the whole time, moved toward the gate, and called a distraction,

"Hey! You up there on the battlements. I'm making a documentary flicker on this expedition. Can I get some shots of you up there?"

"You're not coming up 'ere, we're not tha' stupid."

"No, can't pass that one by you. But can I just get a shot of you looking down at me? I'm over here, by the sand."

Thus, all the guards on the gate had their backs to the cliff walls and the camouflaged Tanya, had free range to scramble up the cliff, moving the flat wall face in fragments so as to grasp hand and footholds, then along to the battlements.

She managed to "borrow" one of the spears and slid it down the back of her shirt, tying a jacket around her waist to secure it. The guards were getting bored with the camera, though, and she only just made it back to the cliff without being noticed.

She climbed directly down the cliff wall to the lower window of the gate, as she'd heard a conversation that sounded interesting.

"But if Prince Hadigan finds out we treated him like this, he will kill us."

"Our lov'ly P-in-One is gone. Lord Deagan rules here now. We'll let 'im know in the mornin'. Unless you wanna go wake 'im?"

"No, thank you. I'll wait till morning. Did you see the prince leave?"

"Nah, saw 'is ship go though. 'parently 'e was ticked off as 'is littl' champion out there weren't 'ere on time. S'posed ta bring 'im somfi ng."

"What would you know?"

The three voices began arguing, so Tanya climbed back along the cliff to the camp. She had all the information she needed, not to mention the weapon.

Before she got to the camp, based on a hunch, she found a cave and took out the Hanain diamond.

She held it over the weapon and focused her energies through the diamond over the weapon. The spear lit up and hovered above the ground, alive. Using it like a vacuum, Tanya drew the energy from the weapon into the diamond.

A perfect rainbow of sticky oil arched from the end of the spear to the diamond, and the gem glowed white. It grew round and plump, almost juicy, no longer the size of a thumbnail but now the size of a golf ball. The weapon lay as lifeless as a rod of iron. Tanya then tried to reverse the operation. It worked.

The weapon hovered, terrifying, tantalizing. Tanya powered down the spear and retied it to her back, then climbed the rest of the way down to the camp.

Marina was sitting up, complaining about the choice of pastels the girls had dressed her in.

"Glad to know you feel better." Marin rubbed his sister's head.

She winced.

"Something still doesn't feel quite right."

She tested her ice skills. Nothing happened. Panic ran across her face. She tested again, and again, but still nothing, not even a squirt. She was completely dry.

"That weapon doesn't hurt you physically other than knock you off your feet. It will drain all your Energy abilities, though. That's its design," Tanya interrupted.

They all looked at her. She stood in the door of the tent holding the spear. Marin carefully approached her.

"Where did you get that?"

"I climbed the cliff and took it from the battlements. Rock beats ice on this terrain."

"You're only twelve and you could have been killed. What were you thinking?"

"I am thirteen, Holly's twelve. I can't be seen on rocks, and Holly had the same idea. She agreed that I should go."

"The two of you are…" Marin was exasperated.

"…Unstoppable, yes, we know." Holly motioned for Tanya to sit by her and Marina, who was sitting looking wide-eyed at the spear.

"What else did you learn, Tan?"

Tanya told them of Prince Hadigan's departure and of the new Lord Deagan. Then, to an astonished and much displeased champion, she showed them how she had experimented on the spear without them because she'd had a hunch.

Marin was furious.

"You had a hunch? Have you ever studied weaponry before, or warfare? Do you know anything of traps? Is there anything inside your head that might have warned you that what you did was the dumbest, most dangerous, stupidest thing you could have done?"

"Looking back, I can maybe see your point, but this is different. I have a diamond myself. I just knew."

Marin took a deep breath as Mitchell came up and put his hand on the champion's shoulder.

"Just promise that next time you have a hunch," Mitchell compromised, "you'll share it with someone first, okay?"

"How do I know you won't take it away from me?" Tanya excused.

"Fair enough," Marin suggested. "I promise to recognize that you and your sister are more powerful than most, if you promise to share your dangerous secrets with me. Deal?"

"Deal."

The girls saluted Marin in unison, and he saluted back.

"Now, can anyone transfer this power to and from the weapon, or do you have to be an Earthen?" Marin took over the investigation.

As it turned out, they could all draw energy from the diamond, but only Tanya could get the energy back into the diamond.

"Look," Marin checked his watch, "it's nearly first call. A weapon like this doesn't just go missing. They'll know we were to ones who took it. We'll have to find a way to get it back… No, Tanya, the way you got it is not the way it's going back. We'll have to be smarter and sneakier than that."

They packed up camp and waited for the gates to open. Another tube, some fishing boats, and a ferry had come in, so a small crowd was gathering outside the gates.

"Tanya, can you get a look inside the gates?"

Tanya shivered into stealth and out of obvious view. Everyone else made a lot of noise to detract attention from her as she stalked nearer the gates and spied through the cracks.

One of the fishermen must have seen Tanya and followed her up to the gates, because he was sloshed with day-old sea water and seaweed from above.

Laughter spilled over the battlements.

"Tha'll teach ya for gettin' too close before openin'."

The fisherman spluttered something about,

"What about her?" but no one heard him.

Tanya returned, dry, with her report.

"Just inside the gates is stunning. It's like a picture of the palace grounds I saw; all marble and green hanging gardens, flowers are everywhere, and if it isn't living, it's glittering with gold and gems. But that is only the first entryway. Past that, it looks like everything is under construction. I think I even saw what looked like a sphinx being carved."

"Sounds like this Lord Deagan is building his own kingdom down here," said Holly.

"With secret weapons," grunted Marin.

They followed the crowd up to the gate as it opened with great fanfare and a sudden rush.

"Holly, it kills me to put you in danger, but you're the only one who can do this." He handed her the spear covered in a towel.

"Try the first copse of trees just before the registration tent. Be careful, though, they're watching us." He looked up and around. Sure enough, almost every guard, if you could call them that, was watching them.

The guards could only be distinguished by the loose tunics tossed over their heads and the occasional spear, rifle, or pistols in their belt.

Everyone else was weaponless. The tunics were a deep brown, with tanned leather braided around the hem.

The emblem on the front of the tunic was a horned Viking helmet with a visor that looked like a fence of downward-pointing pikes. The rest of the face covering was shaped like the jaw of a bull, with only a narrow vertical slit in the center left open for speaking.

One wondered how the wearer would eat or drink through such a masked helm as this. Obviously, he wouldn't.

"So that is the design of our Lord Deagan?" Mitchell, quiet as he often was, except in Tanya's company, spoke without fear.

Holly giggled. "I wonder if he listens to the music of Wagner."

Passing the copse of trees, Marin stepped behind Holly to block her from sight as she shivered into her own version of stealthy camouflage and disappeared into the trees. By the time the slow line reached the opposite end of the tree garden, Holly had gently laid the spear against the table unnoticed.

"I always loved hide and seek." Her tummy did flippies as Marin wrapped his arm around her and squeezed her from behind to give the outward impression of an established relationship.

He whispered in her ear,

"We need to get a foot hold in this town so I can figure out what's going on here. Can you and Tanya pose as socialites, and I'll purchase some land here for you?"

Holly nodded, leaning against his chest, playing along with his pretense while secretly enjoying his closeness, and whispered back,

"I'll let Tan know, and we can buy the land ourselves, thanks to our anonymous sponsor." Holly then hugged her sister and whispered the plan to her.

They reached the registration tent, and Marin stepped up and tried a different tactic.

"Who are you?" asked the bored clerk.

"I'm here to register the sisters. They wish to buy a mine."

"So does everyone. Name?"

"Tanya and Holly Dijex," Marin responded.

"Occupation?"

"Miners, of course." Marin smiled.

The clerk smiled through a sneer.

"I mean outside of Hanain, what do they do?"

"They look beautiful, don't they?"

The clerk looked them over, then spoke as he wrote down, "Ladies of means. Do the ladies wish to put down any other address besides the one I'm about to give them?"

Tanya butted in,

"I'd like to choose my mine."

"My dear," the clerk crooned, "I know exactly what young ladies like. I assure you I shall put you near the latest shopping locations and theatres."

"That's not what I want at all."

"Nor I, thank you very much." Holly stepped forward. Together they were intoxicatingly beautiful and completely imposing. The clerk would have given them anything. Marin stepped out of the way and let them work their magic.

"W-w-w-where would y-you like to be?" the clerk stuttered.

Tanya drew herself to her tallest height, tossed her hair back onto one shoulder, and sat half on, half off the table. Holly slid gracefully around the table and stood right next to the clerk, leaning right over him in his chair. They both looked at the map for about a minute while the man's temperature rose.

Holly finally said,

"We prefer to be alone. Society is rather tiresome.

That is why we came here; to get away from it all." She whispered into his ear,

"You understand... a secret getaway."

Tanya pointed her finger vaguely above a hilly sector that hadn't been divided up yet.

"Is there anything out here?"

"No, nothing at all."

"That would be perfect." They both clapped their hands.

"No. N-n-no, you don't understand. There's nothing out there. Lord Deagan hasn't established that as a mining sector yet."

"Is it for sale?" Tanya pouted.

Marin whispered to Mitchell,

"Can she find stuff on a map as well as she can in real life?"

"I hope so." He responded.

The clerk looked through his flowboard to check and see if the property in mention was for sale. After much looking, he found that there had been a hold on the property and surrounding tracts, but he could find no reason why. The hold had been on too long anyway, and the ladies needed a place to stay immediately.

As he did, in fact, have the authority, he took the hold off, and sold Tanya one property and Holly another.

Marin stepped in again to buy the third adjoining property and was trying to convince Marina to buy the last one when Mitchell said,

"How good is Bacht money to you?"

"That's right, kid," Marin sized Mitchell up, "you're considered wealthy among your people."

"Can you transfer your cash into gold?" Marina questioned.

"Absolutely."

So Marin bought the last quarter of property in Mitchell's name.

"We'll see to you repaying me as soon as we get to Torres Entrance."

Mitchell was excited. He owned land!

Lord Deagan

Trumpets bellowed outside, and the clerk's face drained of all color except green. He sat at his desk begging someone, or something, to

"Please don't stop here, please don't stop here. Please don't stop here."

Mawkes, the aide, and Flicker, as the documentary camera guy liked to be called, were waiting for them outside the tent, so the four hurried out to join them and see what the noise was about.

Flicker had his camera on and was shooting everything around him, but he was smart: he was doing it all from the top of the largest tree. As a Wind Energist, holding on was not a problem; he just flowed with the breeze. The important thing was, he couldn't be seen.

A troop of sharply dressed Strategists came down the walk from the direction of the sphinx. Standing in a chariot pulled by four male lions was one of the largest Trevels any of them had ever seen.

He was a bull of a man, massive thighs and arms encased in shimmering orichulum chain mail. His chest, as broad as Holly and Tanya standing next to each other, was covered in thick leather plate, molded to outline the muscular vision that he was.

The grandness of the figure was further enhanced by the billowing tan fur cloak he wore, and all down his back lay long, thick blond braids blowing out from under his helmet.

Mitchell purposefully cleared his throat and Marin coughed loudly.

The girls closed their mouths quickly but couldn't help staring. Even with the masking Viking helmet, such a figure was a powerful attraction. Holly felt immediately guilty and hoped Prince Hadigan didn't look that good.

A massive gloved hand gripped the reins and pulled the lions to a halt. They roared in protest. The crowd squashed itself as far away from them as possible. They were not tame lions.

Thud-thud: out of the chariot Lord Deagan pounced. In his left hand he held a mighty staff with a massive Hanain diamond encased in the top. Tanya noticed that his diamond was raw and had not been processed for cleaning.

Lord Deagan stopped before a line of quivering guards.

"I understand you have news to report." The voice echoed deep and hollow from inside the mask.

"Yes, m'lord," squeaked a familiar voice. "We was attack'd last nigh' by a band o' rebels, claimin' to be Royal Champi'ns."

"Attacked? Did you sustain any damage?"

"Yeah, m'lord," a rather tall fellow pushed forward. "I was frozen solid, sir, for the whole night. They stole all my money, my favorite flask, and my spear."

Lord Deagan, to this point, had been patronizing, but at the mention of the spear, he went ballistic.

"What?" He lifted the tall guard off his feet with one ray of electricity and pinned him to the wall.

"B-b-b-but it's okay, we found it."

"Yes sir!" the first weasel voice squeaked in earnest. "All weapons are 'counted for."

Lord Deagan kept the tall guard pinned to the wall, but his eyes pierced through the one talking.

"How so?"

"I-I check'd i' mese'f. It went missin' off the bat'lements last nigh', but we jus' foun' it, now, by the trees, over there."

The first guard, pinned to the wall, hovering above his lord, was joined by the weasely guard, who squealed loudly.

"How do you suppose it got there? Did it go for a walk last night and then walked back through the gates by itself this morning?"

"We fink the ones we fired on stowl i'."

There was a silence as the weasel was drawn so close to Lord Deagan's mask that the sparks from the electric rope bounced off the metal. A low growl could be heard coming from behind the mask.

"You fired one of my weapons?"

There was no answer, for the weasel had fainted in terror.

Lord Deagan slapped him awake.

"I asked you a question. Did you or did you not fire one of my weapons?"

All the lackey could do was nod in affirmation.

Lord Deagan held the guard out in the air with the electric rope, then shot a blast of ice at him, freezing the Trevel completely on contact. He then grabbed the belt around the frozen waist and slammed the ice statue into the marble sidewalk, shattering him forever.

The girls screamed and grabbed each other, for they had never seen death come so finally to someone before. Marin and Mitchell automatically reached to comfort them. Marina laid her hand on her weapon hilt as the science aide stepped closer behind her.

"You will not fire my weapons unless by my direct order, is that clear?" Lord Deagan bellowed.

The guards and Strategists all bellowed back,

"Yes, Lord, yes."

"Now then," the lord said, turning back to the tall guard, who was crying. "On whom did you fire?"

The guard said absolutely nothing. He only pointed directly at Marina.

Following the finger, Deagan gazed at the young pre-champion poised to defend herself.

"Oh, you are a fool." He didn't take his mask from the direct gaze of Marina. "I'm not going to punish you. I'm going to send you to Prince Hadigan to tell him you fired on his best friend's little sister, and hit her."

"No, m'lord, please no..." The cries fell on deaf ears, and the guard was carried away.

Marina, brave and sometimes foolish, stepped forward and pulled out a hilt from her thigh brace.

After the night's rest, her energies had returned, and a blade of ice extended from the handle into a long and powerful cleaver. Marina walked toward the hulking Lord Deagan, dangling the cleaver by her side.

"They fired on me. What I'm wondering is if you are going to do the same. I'm not so unprepared this time."

Lord Deagan grabbed his heart.

"It appears, dear Miss Tambeaux that shots have already been fired, and you have hit my heart."

Marina gagged and looked much disgusted.

"Not one for poetry?" Deagan began sizing her up. "How about this, then?"

He compacted his wooden staff, and from out of the Hanain diamond came a long ice blade. It was Marina's cleaver versus Lord Deagan's great sword.

Marina smiled.

"My kind of poetry in motion."

They sparred playfully, and Marina looked like she was having more fun than she'd had in months.

Deagan allowed her to have the upper hand but then enjoyed his own surprise when in those few blows she actually did gain an advantage.

He struck back, testing her, teasing her, taking her closer to full attack.

They were not too uneven a match. What Marina lacked in bulk and strength she returned with agility and speed. Not that Lord Deagan was at all slow or inflexible; his battle skills were remarkably balanced, and he seemed to have no weakness.

"Has she forgotten how he just shattered the life out of one of his guards?" Holly was confused.

"Marina falls into a world of her own when she's fighting and has a tendency to forget everything." Marin stepped forward into plain sight.

Lord Deagan paused and bowed to his match.

"I think you brother would have us stop." He glanced at the two girls. "And, of course, your young lady friends are upset with me."

He returned his sword to its walking staff state and saluted them in the Trevel fashion.

"Forgive me, I am a hardened warrior. My ways are not the ways of civilians. If I had known you were here, I would not, for all the world, have tainted your eyes with such a sight."

He approached them as a gentleman.

"Lady Tanya, Lady Holly, forgive the harshness you have had to suffer at my ignorance of your presence. All will be amended. Come and ride my chariot."

The girls, much to their dismay, were ushered over to the lions, which looked as if they would devour any who drew near. But Deagan swayed them with a wave of his hand, and they calmed and followed him like playful kittens. The parade took them up the hill to a grand house on the hilltop.

Mitchell and Marin walked like victorious returning warriors either side of Lord Deagan. Understanding the softer side of the scientists, seats carried on the back of donkeys were arranged for Mawkes, his aide, and Flicker, who had surreptitiously reappeared.

They were treated as being as close to royalty as could be managed in the small, partially constructed mining outpost. Lord Deagan kept apologizing for the meager amenities and told them of plans for great motels and shopping malls.

Before they met him for dinner that night, they all agreed to refrain from divulging any information on their earlier purchase, as he spoke of the surrounding lands as if they were his. Marina was the only one wanting to give him the benefit of the doubt.

"He just thinks differently because he's a warrior."

"With what army?" Marin contended with his sister. "I've been around defense forces all my life, all over the world, and I've never heard of him before today. I think I'd have heard of a man like that if he'd been in any legitimate armies, and probably more so if he were in any illegitimate ones."

Marin looked out the window, watching the guards on the rooftops.

"What are you saying?" Marina argued.

"I'm just saying I don't know where he's come from, and Trevellia is a small world. Maybe he's been hiding in some of the Independent territories, or far North Kentari even, but I still say a man of that size and ability doesn't live long in the world without developing a reputation."

"Not to mention the blatant display of Chameleon Energy." Holly spoke what they were all secretly avoiding.

"Chameleon Energy?" Mitch questioned in his Bacht lack of Trevel understanding.

Tanya offered,

"A Chameleon Trevel is a myth, so I thought. Trevels only have access to one major Energy, possibly two in rare cases, but Lord Deagan has openly displayed a command of at least five of the nine already."

"Earth, Electricity, Vegetation, Ice, Animal... How many more are at his disposal?" Holly counted through their encounter.

"You either are Chameleon or not." Marin walked to the door. "I think it is safe to presume he can access all nine." He opened the door, and the party exited toward the dining hall in great trepidation.

Marina, bringing up the rear, muttered,

"You're just upset because you're out of the loop for once. Hadigan gave Hanain to him, so obviously he knows him. Your little royal friend didn't tell you something, and that annoys you."

"He rarely ever tells me anything." Marin shrugged. "Let's just get a picnic reprieve tomorrow and visit our land. We need to be as discreet as possible."

After two days, the team boarded Tambeaux's private cruiser, the Hera, in the Port of Hanain. By that time, Marin had set up a combined mining company on behalf of the four with the front name Jaack Mining.

By the time the girls would have made the last half of their journey to Lemuria and then on to Atlantis and high school at the National Academy, they would be well established in a plan to discover the intention behind Lord Deagan's secret weapons.

It seemed that Life, as it often does, had interrupted the simple plans they had made. All that was left was to respond as best as they could.

Holly wondered how much else could happen. Tanya already made scheming plans.

Her goal was to register all the larger diamonds, as was Hanain law, and to have them processed for cleaning. This essentially stripped them of their secret powers and rendered them useful only for the jewel market.

The undersized diamonds, which were usually discarded and sent to be processed as sluff for the Underland Falk beaches, would be filtered out and sent to her at school. They would be disguised as craft supplies. Tanya and Holly would develop a glitter fetish.

These undersized and unprocessed diamonds would then be grown by the Earthen Energy girl and sent on to Tambeaux sprinkled through Laray sports supplies via Mitchell in the stables.

This was the only way Marin could think to smuggle a supply of raw diamonds out of Hanain and into his own research facilities. He didn't like the idea of someone having a stock pile of de-energizing weapons without being prepared himself.

The plan had to work and remain hidden from all. No one knew who Lord Deagan was, but with secret weapons that sapped Trevels of all their Energy Powers, he was a threat to global security.

As Marin still did not yet know whom to trust, it remained only the eight of them.

Professor Mawkes headed up the mine. Even as a Fire Energist, he loved geology, and his aide stayed with him to oversee the separation and smuggling of the undersized diamonds. Most others would ignore them, and they planned to occasionally raid the sluff piles of other mines as well.

Their potential haul could inundate Tanya, so they hoped to find another talented Earthen that they could trust.

Flicker chose to stay as well as documentary specialist and chief smuggler, as his film canisters were the perfect place to stash the "glitter." If he was ever pulled up or questioned, he would blame it all on a prank to dump and run.

That is how, even before the girls began school at the nationally prestigious Trevel high school, Atlantis National Academy, they became involved in a dirty diamond smuggling ring, stockpiling secret weaponry just in case a war broke out against the Lemurian Royal Forces. They would have ammunition on hand against Lord Deagan's sapping weapons, but they hoped they would never need it.

Torres Entrance

Dating Games

Parting

Lemuria

The Garden and the Gardener

Chapter 14

Torres Entrance

Hera, the Tambeaux private cruiser, bobbed up onto the surface of the Underland Torres Straight Entrance Harbor.

The Bacht map places this in caverns under the continental shelf, directly beneath the opening of Torres Straight at the very tip of Queensland, Australia.

Immediately, amid the drips and drizzling of the draining boat, Holly and Tanya scurried outside and began waving to all the other Trevels passing in their own leisure crafts.

The girls wore their swimming suits under crocheted tank tops and breezy sarongs. Their straw hats had to be tied under their hair so they would not fly off in the wind. Yet the sun in the Skyling was gloriously warm, and cool drinks were soon ordered all around.

Marin entered the scene wearing long white shorts and a brightly striped shirt. It was the first time he'd been out of uniform since they'd met him.

"You look so different," squealed Tanya as she threw an ice cube at him.

He pretended to tip her chair back but caught it at the last minute.

She screamed and they all laughed.

"I'm on holidays. From now until school begins, I am officially off duty. PC Marina is the only working Strategist here, so if you need anything, ask her. I plan on being asleep."

With that, he lay back in the deck chair and closed his eyes for a snooze.

Marina quietly carried the ice bucket around to dump on him, but the sudden lull in conversation stirred him and he caught her first. Dangling her over the edge of the boat, he asked,

"Do you have any last requests, sister dear, or shall we just send you off to Lord Deagan?"

"Marin Mohave Ptolemy Tambeaux, put me down this instant, or I'll show Holly all your old school pictures."

Marin promptly put her down.

"I've hidden the worst pictures, so that was an idle threat anyway."

Holly repeated,

"Marin Mohave Ptolemy Tambeaux, that's quite a mouthful."

"What's your full name then?"

"Holly-Anne Dijex. Nothing fancy, just Holly-Anne."

"I like that, Holly-Anne." He pulled a strand of hair off her hat brim. "We beat the Atlantis," he said. "It comes in at first call tomorrow. So I was wondering if you would join me for dinner tonight, in town."

Marin was so casual, it was as if the question was the most natural thing in the world.

Tanya gleamed.

"The town looks exciting. I can't wait to go shopping."

"Actually, Tanya, dear friend," Marin didn't take his eyes off Holly, "I was asking if Holly would like to accompany me alone, on a date. Here in the civil Clusters, we, as a couple, would not be considered so strange."

"What would Deda say?" Tanya couldn't help herself.

Holly was defiant.

"Deda said to grow and be who we are. This is who I am now."

She held her hand out to Marin and accepted his as he pulled her up.

"Marin Tambeaux, I would love to go on a date with you tonight."

Off they walked to the other end of the ship, arm in arm. Marina watched them go and quietly said to no one in particular,

"I'm more concerned about what Hadigan is going to say."

"Well, Tanya," Mitchell spoke up, "my foster mum always told me I had a good eye for fashion. May I accompany you on a private shopping spree tonight, then maybe a movie—I mean, a flicker?"

Tanya stood before Mitchell with eyes wide in awe,

"You want to come shopping with me?"

"Yes, and I want to pick out some outfits for you to try on. I might even buy you some if I can get Marin to transfer my money before we go."

"I can do that for you," Marina offered. "I have to mail a letter in town anyway, so let me know when you're ready, I'll come in with you, do the money thing, then leave you on your own."

"What are you going to do tonight?" Tanya didn't really want to leave Marina alone.

"Don't worry about me." Marina cracked her knuckles and flexed her wrists, shooting ice and water pellets into the air. "There's an officer's club in town that has dueling competitions, and the trophy already has my name written on it."

*** *** ***

"Where is Marin taking you?" Tanya and Marina, who was slumping on the bed in the corner, were conspiring in Holly's little cabin on the *Hera* as she readied herself for her date.

"He won't tell me, but said he would send a clue for how to dress."

"Yeah, I have that clue." Marina sucked on a hard-candy stick as if she had not just said the most important thing in the world at that moment.

"Well?!" stressed the sisters.

Marina grinned, teasing them, then pulled a large, flat velvet box from out of the back of her jeans.

Holly squealed so high only the dogs on the mainland could hear it.

"It's a jewelry box!" Holly squeezed Tanya's hand.

"I know!" mimicked Tanya sarcastically as she squeezed Holly's hand back.

Marina opened the lid.

Inside lay an intricate wreath of sparkling rose gold flowers woven into a leafy emerald vine. It was about an inch wide, and the flowers were the size of a Bacht American dime. There were earrings to match, of course, and one delicate flower ring.

"You can borrow them for tonight only," Marina stressed. "They were my mother's. I haven't even worn them."

Holly looked horrified.

"It's okay," Marina assured them. "Gold just isn't my metal," she shrugged.

"Do you have anything to wear with them?"

Holly's eyes lit up. "Yes, yes, I do."

Dating Games

Mitchell sat and drank a dark soft drink, watching Marin working on the flowboard in the reflection of the ceiling. He had the keypad memorized by now and was quite sure he could figure out what almost all the keys did.

The basic function of the flowboard was, naturally, the same as a computer, but the actual programming layout was not quite upside down, or back to front, but different like that. He hadn't been able to figure it out at all until he saw the Trevel analog clocks.

Then he took the principle of the face of the clock being turned upside down and slightly to the left and tried that process with all his programming layouts. They seemed to work but needed more fine-tuning. He was, after all, working only in theory, without flowboard access.

There was a rustle of material and Marin looked up. In walked Marina, in dress uniform, wearing a skirt.

"You've had legs under those pants?" Mitchell commented.

"Shut up, L1, or I'll stick these legs up your rear end."

"No, really, Marina," Mitchell's voice softened, "you always look good; now you also look feminine and beautiful."

"I said, shut up." She smiled despite herself and smacked his head.

The next to enter was Tanya.

She was slicked up and ready to rock in a fitted, black denim pantsuit that showed off her ankles. A brilliant red T-shirt with "Rock Buddy" printed on it peaked out from under her open jacket, and a shiny bronze bag (the color of her skin) to match the strappy heels was slung over her shoulder.

To top it off, she had curled her hair and it hung down her back, thick and as full as Lord Deagan's lions' manes.

"You can be my rock buddy any day, Tanya." The L1 stood to receive his girl.

"As long as you just stay buddies, right, Mitchell?" Marin insisted.

Mitchell wasn't really listening when he said, "Uh-huh," but it didn't really matter, because Holly came in next.

Marin, who had been standing, sat back down again.

Before them stood a woman who radiated and looked as if she was in her mid-twenties. All her hair was piled on her head and looked as if it might cascade down her shoulders at any given moment, yet it stayed, obedient.

An embroidered silk dress fell gently to the floor, tilting slightly with the curves of Holly's young body. The brassy coloring of the silk and the black embroidery made her look like a Grecian urn: fragile, priceless, and exquisite. The green and rose gold of the Tambeaux family jewels could not have been highlighted better.

She was a piece of art, one that Marin barely dared to touch. He could not breathe. He simply took her hand and led her off the ship and onto the wharf.

They waved goodbye to the others as Marin silently handed Holly into the beautiful glass horse-drawn carriage he had hired. Holly smiled and hugged herself. Tonight would be a night she would never forget.

***   ***   ***

Marina was true to her word. She helped Mitchell transfer his Bacht funds into the Trevel world as cold, soft gold. She signed as witness for him to open an account at the bank and showed him how to use the key pen on the flowboard to access his money.

"This is the one flowboard you are allowed to use."

"Why do I need the key pen?"

"Because this flowboard is activated by energy flow, which you do not have, so the key pen provides that for you."

"So as soon as I pick up that pen, I show everyone I'm Bacht."

"No, as soon as we look into your eyes, we can tell. They are the windows to your soul, little brother."

"That is the first time you've called me 'brother'."

"So?"

"You're getting soft. Go beat up some officers."

They parted laughing.

Mitchell was more thrilled than ever to be independent and wealthy again. Now he could treat Tanya properly even if Marin looked down on it. What was Marin doing telling him what not to do anyway? He was on a date with a minor half his age.

           ***   ***   ***

After two minutes of silence, Holly could stand it no more.

"Is everything fine?"

Marin cleared his throat. "Sorry, having trouble breathing."

"Well, undo your top button, silly." Holly laid her hand on Marin's chest to point out the obvious solution.

Marin shied away, took her hand and put it in her lap.

Silence again.

"Did I do something wrong?"

"No, not intentionally."

"So I did do something wrong? Did I choose the wrong dress?"

"No, it's nothing like that… I can't breathe in here, it's so hot."

He began pulling at his collar and touching the windows, which were all closed, as the air was controlled. He banged on the roof.

"Can we have it cooler in here? It's like a steam room."

"Marin, are you feeling sick? You're heating up." She leaned in close to feel his forehead. "Mema always said the best way to test a fever is with your lips."

Holly stood up and leaned over to kiss Marin's forehead.

Marin, who was still wiping sweat from his face and palms and playing with his collar, opened his eyes at just the wrong moment. There was Holly leaning in, and there were her breasts right in his face.

He grabbed both walls of the carriage and slammed himself as far away from her as he could get.

"This was a really bad idea. I shouldn't have asked you out like this."

"Marin, what's gotten into you? It's just me, Holly." She moved over next to him. "You look delirious." She ran her hand down his cheek.

He closed his eyes and just smelled the perfume of her hand close to his face. She smelled like jasmine tonight. It was always some kind of flower, and yet there was that underlying familiar aroma, too. He drank it in and leaned forward for more—nearly so close he could taste the sweetness.

The carriage hit a bump, and something inside awoke him from his dream. He opened his eyes to see her, so sweet, so pure, hanging on his very breath, leaning against him with her face turned up and eyes barely open, expectant.

He swallowed. What was he doing? He had to get out of there. He backed up as quickly as he could, aching in every muscle.

Somehow the door opened behind him and he fell out. Throwing some money at the driver, he yelled,

"Take her back to the dock."

Then he ran all the way to the officers' dueling club. Blood would run tonight.

*** *** ***

"I'm glad we bought the last red sweater for Holly." Mitchell sucked up the last of his drink and tossed the container away.

"You are the sweetest guy. Are all Bachts like you?"

"Believe me, no. I am an oddity."

"I can't believe you bought me clothes, and my sister."

"Yeah, I'm quite a guy."

They'd made it all the way back from town and were walking up the moonlit beach to the wharf, at the end of which the *Hera* was resting.

"What's that under the dock?"

Mitchell picked up the pace and jogged under the wooden boardwalk. He bent down and picked something up, then waved Tanya over to him.

"Come see what I found."

"What is it?"

"Come and see."

Tanya walked under the little boardwalk, out of sight of the Tambeaux cruiser, and leaned in to look into Mitchell's hands expecting to see a shell. Instead, she saw nothing.

"I don't see anything."

"You don't? It's right there on the tip of my finger."

He held up his pointing finger and Tanya stared hard.

"What is it?" She was just playing along now.

"Just this…" He leaned in and kissed her.

He took her in his arms and really kissed her. He made up for all the times he'd wanted to on the Atlantis and hadn't. He made up for the time he'd planned to in the mountains and missed the chance. He kissed her because Marin said he shouldn't, and he kissed her because he'd wanted to do nothing else since she'd given him the flying horse pin on the very first day.

Mitchell kissed Tanya because he was five years older than she, and he would have to wait another five years before he kissed her again.

It was some kiss.

When he finally pulled away he whispered,

"That has to last until you graduate, if you still care to kiss me again by then."

"It's not going to last that long," Tanya teased.

"It'll have to."

Bells rang the second call of the night.

"Big day ahead. I love being around you, Tanya. I'll miss you. Visit me in the stables once in a while, will you?"

"I promise." Tanya kissed him again, then ran up the beach and along the deck to the boat. Mitchell followed.

Marina halted him before he boarded the cruiser.

"What were you doing under the dock, little L1?"

But he wasn't in the mood, so he pushed passed and mumbled,

"Saying goodbye."

Parting

Tanya floated into Holly's room to share her good news but landed with an awful thud when she saw the state of things.

The jewelry was dumped on the velvet box and the Grecian dress was tossed on the floor beneath shoes that looked as though they'd been ripped off.

Under a pile of quivering bedclothes came noises of heaving, sobbing, and much sniffling. Tanya cautiously approached and called her sister's name.

"Holly? What's wrong?"

Deftly, Holly threw back the covers.

"He ran away from me. That is what's wrong."

"What?"

"We were in the beautiful glass carriage, riding through town, when he got all hot and bothered for no reason. I thought he might be sick, so I tried to check his fever the way Mema taught us, but he jumped to the other side of the carriage."

Tanya nearly interrupted, but Holly continued, her voice getting louder.

"Then, get this, he nearly kissed me. I know he was going to, he leaned in, and then he opened the door and fell backward onto his rear end on the road, yelled at the driver to bring me back here, and ran, literally RAN away."

Tanya's eyes were wide.

"He can't kiss you, Holly. He's way too old for you."

"When was the last time you actually felt like you were really thirteen?"

Tanya, sensing the seriousness of Holly's question, gave some thought to her past.

She had been seven when she drank the dragon tears and now, chronologically, she was thirteen, but she knew she wasn't really that young. The dragon tears had accelerated not only their energy abilities but also their physical growth, their mental and emotional growth, and basically everything about them.

If Tanya was honest, the last time she had felt physiologically thirteen was when she had woken up a week after she had drunk the dragon tears.

Holly saw the recognition in Tanya's eyes and said,

"If I'd known how cursed we'd become after drinking dragon tears, I'd never have done it, not for all the vengeance or all the power in the world."

Tanya pulled her sister to her chest and they sat curled up in the covers together.

"For all I know, we're not even teenagers anymore, even after only living for twelve years."

"Thirteen." Tanya gave her automatic older sister response. "So, you really think that, in reality, we really are much older than our years?"

"Yes. Only, everyone else gets hung up on the chronological thing."

"Maybe if we graduate sooner, skip a couple of years at ANA?"

Tanya tried a couple of theories.

"I don't want to skip any years, or any chance to learn and practice more, even if it means re-enforcing the idea that we are who they think we are."

"I wish we could find a dragon to explain it all to us." Tanya stroked her sister's hair.

"I don't think they do that. You know, they're so mystical. They'd rather we figure it out for ourselves."

The girls heard the ship's outer door bang shut and Marina's horrified voice asking,

"What happened to you?"

Marin's mumbled response was barely audible.

"The duels weren't exactly between two." They heard him thump off in the opposite direction to his cabin.

"What are you going to do about Marin?" Tanya rolled over, determined not to tell Holly about Mitchell's kiss.

"Ask him why he ran away."

"That's kind of obvious, don't you think?"

"No."

"Honey, I know guys, and when they think a girl is attractive, they want to do one of two things: either nothing at all, because they're too shy, or they take her in their arms and let her know."

"So what's wrong with Marin? He's not the shy type."

"The problem with your man is that there is no problem with him. He's just trying to be a gentleman. He thinks so much of you that he won't let himself touch you."

"I hate being a freak like this. I am done. I'm going to go to the Atlantis tomorrow, pick up my stuff, and fulfill my scholarship duties."

She stood and hung up her silk dress. Tanya watched her clean up.

"If I see Marin," Holly determined, "I'll say goodbye. If I don't, I'll just forget him."

"But, Holly, he loves you."

"What good is he to me if he runs away and doesn't talk to me?

Champion, my foot, I want a man who will stand his ground, even if he is just a… a… a chemist!"

Before they left the *Hera*, Marina gave the official Tambeaux family farewell with excuses for Marin's absence. He'd apparently taken quite a beating and refused a healer. He was still in bed, and Marina thought he'd be there for a couple of days.

"If he ever wishes to stop running away, he may call on me at school, but I doubt I will be at leisure to see him." Holly stiffly said her farewell and left before she would allow herself to reveal any true emotion.

Tanya hugged Marina, and revealed,

"I know you've been corresponding with the Lord Deagan," she whispered into Marina's ear.

"Just be careful, he has more power in those mines than anyone realizes, but he knows it. He is a Chameleon, accessing all the Energies, not just one. He can sense, just as I can, the power in those diamonds, but he can also sense what Holly senses and what you sense, too, and who knows what else. Just be careful. That's my warning to you."

Marina nodded.

"I'm not stupid. At least, I'm trying not to be. I'll keep my eyes open and my heart closed… semi-closed."

Thus, the Dijex sisters left the Hera with Mitchell in tow, as he, too, was to begin his life alone at the Atlantis National Academy.

At the ship, *Atlantis*, Mitchell said his farewells briefly.

"I'll see you two there, after you're settled in. That is, if you come and visit me in the stables. My commission gives me a small bachelor's cottage behind the stables and a motorized cart, but I'm not allowed near the student residences, and I'm only allowed on campus proper if I have a specific job to complete."

"We'll visit, don't worry," was all Tanya could say without throwing her arms around him, which, of course, she could not do.

A grand parade it was. The caravan of royal peers, Senate families, and special guests from ANA drove slowly through the crowded dockside streets of Torres Entrance. Because it was a royal cavalcade on the way to the palace, which was a two-day journey inland, they had a hover-pass and made their way to the hover-pad.

One by one, the caravan of vehicles drove off the five-story building, straight out into the air. They flew on through the buildings of the busy Torres downtown and passed over the suburbs and country areas.

They had stopovers at quaint country estates, and the whole time, while the grand royal reunion celebration was going on around them, the two girls remained dejected and depressed. Tyal, who had of course joined them when they regrouped at the Atlantis, was at his wits' end.

"Obviously it's boy troubles. Nothing depresses a girl more. But I assure you, you are far too young to worry about some pimple-faced schoolboy that has caught your eye. There are far too many men in the world. You'll discover that when you grow up."

These comments only made the girls more depressed. They behaved their best, though.

When it came time to shake hands, smile and wave, take flickergraphs, and make speeches, as they had to do all the way to the palace, they did as they should and were shining examples of what an Atlantis National Academy Ambassador should be.

But back in their rooms, they returned to their misunderstood depressed state. Tanya wrote letters constantly, and as she always had a letter to Mema and Deda in front of her when Holly looked, Holly thought nothing of it. But Holly thought of nothing much other than her own woes, so Tanya could have been writing to Zeus on Mount Olympus and she would not have noticed.

Lemuria

The laborious two days of travel lingered until finally the caravan landed on the private hover-pad at the Royal Lemurian Palace.

The Royal City of Lemuria was a white-walled circle city. Each circle from the center at the base of the palace mound descended downhill and further out around the city. The more central circles were the High Set, and as the road wound further out and around, the quality and class of the buildings lessened.

Thus it was that the entry gates to the city were not the most hygienic of places to be. Most visitors to the city chose to enter via the various hovercraft platforms dotted along the city rooftops.

The palace was built on the east side of the Great Mount and wound itself upward in terraces and outcrop buildings, itself the size of a small village.

The throne room and central court were at the top of the Mount. It sat, shining red like the rising sun, on the lower, eastern edge of the plateau, dwarfed only by the massive Parthenon that challenged all the other buildings on the flat top.

The Great Mount sat at the southern end of Lemuria, set apart from the cavern wall. It was the furthest one could travel before stopping at the Skyling horizon that plummeted to the floor in a slippery eighty seven degree angle. In contrast, the terraced layers of the royal palace were grand memorials of the ancient Hanging Gardens in Babylon.

The walls of the palace were shining white marble, accented with gold, silver, and of course, Lemuria's favorite red metal: orichulum. Thus, the red of the royal court at the mountaintop came from the massive marble columns intricately covered in tendrils of orichulum-wrought metal designs.

The palace's glory was outshone only by the awe-inspiring Parthenon, which could only be suitable for a god. The rectangular building, lined with columns on all sides, some straight cylinders, some carved Trevel figures, imposed an austere silence on anyone who dared enter.

Inside the Parthenon at the south end was a massive statue of Zeus in his chariot with lightning bolts in hand chasing the sun. He was the mighty Thunder God and akin to another thunder god native to the outlying Kentari Nation, although recognition of the barbaric cultures outside the established Trevel nation, even if they were Trevel, was looked down upon by city cluster governments.

At the north end was an even larger statue of Poseidon, the terrifying Mer-King, brandishing his Trident aloft in his right hand. He was the God of the Waters.

"The Trevels had given over their Thunder God," said the uniformed man standing in front of the tour group at the door of the Parthenon, "in favor of Poseidon when we went under the oceans thousands of years ago."

The final event of arrival day was a guided tour of the Parthenon where Tanya and Holly dawdled behind their museum guide in awe of the grandness.

The guide recited,

"Under Zeus's rule, there was much squabbling and bickering among the Trevel kingdoms and nations. The mythologies that the Bacht tell as fairytales and legends are loosely true tales of Trevel attempts to gain divine power over the Bacht people."

Tanya interrupted.

"Are any of the Bacht aware of the truth behind their imagination?"

The guide responded,

"It is suggested that the truth is always known in their hearts, but the reality of Bacht experience limits what they choose to believe. Some of them are called dreamers in the Upland cultures and they whisper truths disguised in fantasy and when such delusional Bacht come in contact with the Trevel, it has been proven that they have the remains of ancient Trevel bloodlines in them."

The guide continued his recital.

"Most tales of the mighty men and women with powers or abilities beyond mere human capability are also found, in some form, in the Trevel history annals that are cared for by the Keeper of the Chronicles, Oliver Pascoe."

The group stopped before Pascoe's marble statue and the guide explained,

"Some of his favorite stories are ones he readily leaks to the Bacht; such as Nimrod, the mighty hunter; or Hercules, the son of Zeus, he is naturally Trevel, though his mother was Bacht; Arthur, son of Pendragon and the whole great 'King of the Round Table' characters."

The guide pointed to a massive portrait behind the central statue.

"Pendragon was a decorated Defense Strategist."

The group entered an ante-chamber with many other stunning portraits lining the walls.

"Then there was Merlin, Mab, Lancelot, and Guinevere, as well as Lady Ashtalot, a lesser-known character in this story. They were all Trevels attempting to aid the miserable Bachts in their pitiful existence at the time. The reason there is no record of descendants of these lines is that after their interference, which did little to aid and much to hinder, they were all called back to the Underlands."

Another collection of story pictures that decorated the walls in frescos and murals were pointed out as the guide interpreted them.

"Other Trevels, of which you may know, were 'fairy godmothers.' This fairy godmother program was also an aid mission that did not succeed, as the material assistance granted either blinded or hindered the growth of the Bacht in question. The program was cancelled after a few hundred years, although in extreme cases the occasional 'nanny' approach has been more successful."

The girls then followed their guide into another room that had dimensional models of multiple fantastic histories. The guide's face had a genuine smile and it was obvious that this was his favorite part of the presentation.

"Jack also was a Trevel, as was his brother Jack and his cousin Jack. In fact, some of the Jack family continues to live in Upland, perhaps even unaware of their Trevel ancestry. They were actually a family of rogue pranksters who liked to play their games on the wealthy, ignoble Bacht. The Jack Tales, although never endorsed by any Trevel government, are highly popular around the campfire."

Tanya tapped on the communication bracelet she wore and absorbed a few images into it for later discussion with Mitch, as she remembered the name of the family to whom he'd mailed letters.

The guide returned to his practiced droning as the tour continued through the halls of the Parthenon.

"Despite further interference and influence by the Trevel, the Bacht continued choosing to not believe in the Trevels as divine gods to be worshiped. For generation upon generation, the Bachts' free will would not be ruled unless they gave in completely to their faith. No Trevel has been able to hold that faith for too long. Thus, the Bachts lose interest eventually and usually just stop believing."

They descended into the lower levels of a dark room full of terrifying holographic portrayals of Upland tragedies.

The guide continued,

"The Trevel, tired of the faithless Bacht, have staged massive, corporate disappearances of their people in order that they may give the Bacht what they wished for: to forget their gods. The first time, at Atlantis, the disappearing island, the Trevel culture was almost completely withdrawn. The second time, at Pompeii, in anger and disgust, the Bacht culture that had mixed with the Trevel life was simply buried."

The guide became silent and allowed the group to absorb the horrible visions presented all around them.

A deep voice-over continued the telling.

"It was an unthinkable undertaking, disappearing an entire culture. It took all the godlike abilities and Titan strength we had. Our ancestors tore down everything piece by piece, then transported it to the Underland caverns beneath the unknown Great Southern Continental Shelves and rebuilt everything, stone by stone. Here, in the new capitals of Lemuria and Atlantis, we thrived undisturbed, then colonized and became so technologically advanced that we now continue to live as the gods and Titans that we are."

More pictures of present day Upland Trevel appeared,

"A rare few still live Upland, and even fewer intermingle with the Bacht races. Despite some Trevel disgust at such a thought, such intermingling is necessary, as both cultures do share this same Earth."

As images of Latoona, Rio, Venice, Sydney, and other pockets of Upland Trevel presence flashed across the presentation, another member of the tour party sneered,

"Why would anyone want to live out there?"

Tanya and Holly, for once, just kept their mouths shut.

It was in this grand history of a god-people and to this glorious setting of luxury and lush wealth that Tanya and Holly now found themselves encased.

The Garden and the Gardener

"These will be our suites, dears." Tyal glowed with pride. "I'm at the beginning of the hall. That way I'll hear if anyone comes up or if you try to leave. You shall be safe. I shall be your guard."

"Great," sighed Tanya under her breath.

"I'm sure we'll never be able to sneak past you." Holly checked the lock on the door.

"No, you won't." Tyal was serious. "There is to be no wandering around the palace without me. I insist on that. There are too many little places for big things to happen to little girls. This is not a chaperoned building like the school. And you never know where a courtier will turn up, not to mention Hadigan."

"Between the two of us, we'll be okay, Tyal."

"Ladies, listen to me." He sat them down on the swanky love seat in front of the open balcony and sat himself on the coffee table in front of them.

"I know I have been somewhat condescending about your Latoona jungle home, but believe me, I'm not just being rude this time. You are not at home anymore, and you don't know what it is like here in the palace."

Tyal warned,

"Almost anything goes here. If you don't have a chaperone with you, the men (and women for that matter) will think you are there to be taken advantage of, and they will not take no for an answer. This is a dangerous place. Do not leave this room without me. Do I have your word that you will obey me in this?"

Holly saluted him and said, "I swear I will not go out that door without you."

Tanya was not so quick to offer her promise.

"Surely you exaggerate, Tyal?"

"Surely I will call your father this instant and tell him what I just told you if you don't promise." Tyal knew the girls well enough by now to know exactly what threat would work.

"Fine," sighed Tanya, "I won't..."

Holly nudged her foot under the couch and Tanya thought on what Holly had said, then tried hard to suppress a smile.

"Tyal," repeated Tanya solemnly, "I swear to not go out that door without you."

Quite satisfied, Tyal nodded and left.

Immediately, the girls walked out onto the balcony.

"We must be in a tower higher than Rapunzel," Tanya grumbled.

"There goes that idea."

"I don't know why you're so grumpy, we can still get down." Holly was almost completely surrounded by the climbing ivy that rose up from the balcony railing.

Tanya looked down over the edge again.

"It must be at least forty four stories. I think I'll sit this one out. I'll let you know if I hear Tyal. You should have a few minutes from the time he opens his door."

Tanya rubbed her bare feet on the slate floor.

"I love stone floors, I can hear everything. Did you know Prince Hadigan has been flirting with twenty-six-year-old twins named Sula and Arula, and also a fourteen-year-old named Dalian? This is apparently the first time he has actually singled any females out. The king is having new caterers hired, he's so excited."

"Where did you hear that?" Holly was sitting on the outside of the balcony railing with the ivy nestled around her like a swing, caressing her and holding her up.

"There are guards on the opposite side of Tyal's room, and they are female. One of them has a huge crush on Hadigan and is quite convinced the prince should choose a wife from within the military." Tanya laughed and waved goodbye to her sister, then went to lie down on her bed.

She took out the Hanain diamond that she always wore around her neck and began pulling the energy in and out of it like a ball game.

Holly descended the ivy wall. Whenever she came close to other people on a terrace or balcony, she would wave her hand and the ivy would simply cover her up like a blanket.

At the base of the tower was an enclosed garden. Holly thought this was the perfect spot to rest and play awhile. She was barefoot, and the grass lovingly coddled her toes as she walked around what looked like the birthplace of spring.

The wall around the garden muted the sounds of the busy palace, so all Holly could hear was the growing of the plants. Not even a bird chirped here, though there were the tiny whipping sounds of butterflies flitting around the flowers, and bees hummed in harmony with the tinkling of the water features that rustled through the grass.

Mostly, though, Holly just heard the Green breathing. It was the most musical sound she'd ever heard. She began to hum along with the tune.

As she walked along the edges of the garden, the plants reached for her. She was the goddess of springtime, and all around her praised her as she walked. There was color behind her that had never been there before, and in front, there was a yearning as each plant, trunk, and stem, beckoned to her. Even the bark of the trees peeled back to show off proudly what was new and precious beneath.

He had tears in his eyes.

The tears flowed freely down his cheeks as he watched her, for he had never seen a more beautiful thing in all his life. He wanted to sing with her but did not want to frighten or startle her away, so he stayed silent.

He knew she would see him soon. He was such a dirty thing against such purity as she. Knee-high in mud, wearing only a pair of rough overalls and rubber boots, he was shucking out the next patch of weeds to make way for another seasonal garden.

The gardener, the tender of the glory around him, was covered in the muck and refuse left behind in the creation of such a rare and precious place. No shirt covered his smooth skin and muscles; only splattered mud clung to the dark hair that curled lightly all over the tight, much-exercised body.

Holly stopped her singing and stared at him. He whispered without moving,

"Please don't stop, they love you."

Holly looked around at the trees that were shedding their old bark, the grass that was at least an inch longer, the flowers dotting the scene, and smiled.

"I hope I'm not trespassing."

"If you are, please, continue." The gardener smiled. He put down the hoe he was using, wiped his hands on a towel, and came forward to greet Holly. As he saluted her, a wild rose whipped a long strand out to smack Holly's face, but she ducked and blocked with a bark shield.

"Taliamaland! That is enough of your jealousy," the gardener scolded the climbing rosebush. "Forgive her. She seems to think that all women are out to take me away from her."

"Taliamaland?" Holly stared in awe at the vivid orange rose. "I've never seen one in real life before. She's gorgeous." Holly bowed to her as she would a queen. "With deepest respect, Taliamaland, if I may call you by your name, I would never steal your gardener from you. He is obviously too mighty a man for me."

The rose bush shivered and caressed the gardener's cheek.

"I think you're wonderful too, Tali." He gently brushed the plant aside. "It makes dating in your own garden awkward when your plants are jealous of you."

They laughed together. This time he did salute her and said,

"You can call me Andrew, and by watching you sing, I'd say you are more powerful than I."

"Lady Holly at your service," she curtsied. "Who cares whom is more powerful, I'm just a freak of nature."

"Power is a special thing, m'lady, don't take it for granted. I am honored to meet the palace's special guest. You're even more beautiful that the rumors say."

Holly blushed. Andrew continued,

"Did Tambeaux really run away from you? I wouldn't have. Then again, maybe that's a bad thing? But at least I would not have let you go without saying goodbye."

Holly was shocked. "How did you know about that?"

"You, Lady Holly, are top gossip news in all Trevellia, and gossip travels fast. Did you know he took on twenty officers that night, and won? All for you, but he still couldn't face you the next day. Tut-tut. Strange what some men can and can't do, isn't it?"

"And what can you do?"

Immediately he took a step closer to her and reached behind her ear. In the clichéd fashion of an amateur magician, he pulled from behind her ear an exquisite miniature purple iris.

Holly took in a sharp breath.

"They're my favorite."

"I know," said Andrew in a quiet voice.

"But how could you know? I don't tell people that sort of thing."

"I'm a gardener. That's what I do." He smiled down at her from underneath his dark curls. Holly had a compulsion to wipe the splattered mud from his cheeks but refrained.

"You also like..." Andrew held her face in his hands and searched her eyes for a moment, "sunflowers, preferably the orange Mexican breed because they have a wild look to them." He paused for dramatic effect. "And you like that."

"You're amazing..." she faltered. "I mean... that's amazing.... Where did you learn to do that?"

"What? Read flowers, or seduce young women in lonely gardens?"

Holly blushed furiously.

Andrew led her back to the ivy vine against the wall.

"The court is expecting you soon. I think you should probably get back to your room. Besides, if you stay here much longer, I'll end up kissing you."

"That's okay . . . I mean, yes, okay, of course. I need to go." Holly bumbled back onto her ivy swing elevator. "Will I see you again? I'd like to learn more about Taliamaland."

"Of course you would," winked Andrew as he waved up at her.

"Don't worry, you'll see me around." He stepped out of sight underneath the lush cover of the trees.

No Chance

Gash Arabol

Poolside

Laray

Hadigan in Motion

Chapter 15

The First Night's Ball

Tanya was nervous for the first time.

She held her hand, unconsciously, to where her Hanain diamond lay flat against her chest. It glowed through her gold dress, making a shining circle catch Holly's eye from across the room. Holly walked to her sister and gently rubbed her bare arms.

"You'd better turn your diamond off."

"Hmm?"

"Your diamond is showing through your dress." She lightly tapped Tanya's chest where it was glowing.

"Oh, thanks. I guess I'm pretty nervous, how about you?"

"No, not really."

"What? I thought you were all tied up about meeting the charismatic Prince Hadigan."

"Not anymore."

Tanya's eyes widened and she took in a long, loud breath. "You met someone in the garden at the bottom of the tower didn't you?"

Holly smiled mysteriously.

"You little minx, I thought I was supposed to be the flirty one."

"Just don't let Tyal know. I'm sure he wouldn't approve of me falling for the gardener."

"So you didn't just meet someone, you fell for him, too?"

"Oh, Tan, I couldn't help it. He was so lovely and so handsome and so talented. He could read my favorite flower right out of my eyes."

"Holly, stuff like that is written down in all the teen magazines in the kingdom."

"What's my favorite flower?"

"The iris."

"What color?"

"I don't know."

"Exactly," said Holly triumphantly. "I've never told anyone what color was my favorite, and he knew. He also guessed my other favorite flower, which I have also never told anyone, because the reason I like it is embarrassing, and he guessed the reason too. I was an open book to him."

"Sounds serious," teased Tanya. "What did he look like?"

"A maple: strong, supple…"

"I'm going to throw up if I let you go on, aren't I? Thankfully, Tyal is on his way with a band of Strategists. Are you ready to go?"

"I just need my shawl."

"No, you don't."

"I might get cold."

"Then ask a good-looking young man to borrow his coat. Keep your shoulders bare, we are in the palace and this is the First Night's Ball."

Against better judgment, Holly obeyed her sister and hoped she wouldn't regret it.

The trumpets were blasting and the crowds were oohing as the Dijex sisters paraded down the aisle with all the other special guests.

They had at least chosen the right colors to wear, as many others in the crowd were wearing the gold of Tanya's dress or the varied greens of Holly's.

They had been unsure of the style so decided to go with simple and classical. They both wore identical floor-length togas that pinned on opposite shoulders and tied around their bodies from ribs to thighs with golden cord. Tanya looked perfect in all gold. It heightened the bronze tones of her skin and hair. Holly always preferred the verdant colors, so her toga was layered with spring greens.

Just to cause sensation, they decided to wear their hair identically, too. That, after all, was what everyone was expecting tonight, something sensational, so the girls were going to give it to them. They wound their long, dark hair in gold cord in long, loose ponytails down their backs, with plenty of curled tendrils allowed to fly free. They both looked like Roman goddesses tonight, and the effect was exactly as desired. The crowd gossiped in loud volumes until the girls walked by; then slowly, from back to the front, the voices died down as everyone stared at the stately women.

"I thought they were only twelve."

"So did I."

"Someone at the magazine is going to be fired for that mistake."

The whispers of disbelief followed them down the aisle. The ladies walked taller the further they went.

They made it to the central archway. The doors were already standing wide open and the parade didn't even pause, but a second blast of trumpets and loud music made with instruments the ladies couldn't name began playing.

The crowd of parade participants in front of them was quickly disbanding as the master of ceremonies guided everyone to their appropriate positions. Tyal, Tanya, and Holly were the last in line.

"These are the Ladies Holly and Tanya," announced Tyal when they reached the archway.

"I know exactly who they are Tyal. That is my job. Thank you, the Lord Prince Hadigan says your assistance will not be needed tonight. The ladies will be quite safe in the inner sanctum. Tyal, your place is over to the far right by the statue of Venus. There is a waiter there who will take care of you for the rest of the evening. Enjoy yourself."

Tyal looked as if he were to protest when a Strategist Primer stepped up to him.

"Would you like me to show you where you are going?"

"No, thank you, that won't be necessary. I used to live here; I know exactly where Venus is." With that he huffed off.

"My dear ladies, please wait just a moment." The master of ceremonies turned and took a small cup-sized megaphone filled with HDP and spoke to the crowds both before and after the archway.

"Your Majesty, and His Royal Highness, senators, special guests here this evening, and ladies and gentlemen, it is my greatest honor to introduce to you on this our First Night's Ball the Ladies Tanya and Holly Dijex."

Then he whispered to the girls,

"You will notice that I, unlike Tyal, announced you in correct birth order." He winked at them.

"It is my job to know these things." Then he smiled, bowed, and gestured to the Grand Promenade.

Holly swallowed rather hard and took Tanya's hand. Tanya was sweaty and shaking, but together the two were more confident.

They stepped off the red carpet and onto the elaborately tiled aisle. It curved around the thick columns of the archway to the right for what seemed like forever. Finally, they reached the inner sanctum of the Great Throne Room; it was black and red and gold.

"Obviously lacking a female touch," Tanya giggled under her breath.

This made Holly feel much better. She too giggled, and they dropped hands and walked forward as Tyal had trained them. For the past month, he had trained them for this very night. They would not let him down. They knew he and all Trevellia were watching on private screens in the courtyard or in their homes.

Tanya smiled with ease at all the people, all the people! There was such a sea of people surrounding them. The Top and High Set had come out in swarms tonight, and here she was, half of the main attraction. What would be the main event tonight, she wondered?

Holly, curious and unable to help herself, strained without looking like she was to see if she could tell just what the prince looked like. He was not yet named Prince-in-One, heir to the throne, as King Darsaldain had not been able to convince the senate of his worthiness, but it was expected.

The king, as a gentleman, stood before his throne, dressed in a black Strategist suit lined and highlighted with red. He wore an old-fashioned metal sword at his side, for he was a Metal Energist, and a fearsome one at that. He looked fearsome, too.

No wonder he was still alive, although he was nigh on one hundred years. He still looked seventy, lithe and strong, with dark hair, dark eyebrows, and dark eyes underneath, but he was smiling in welcome.

Next to him, draped in shocking pink, the only one in the room, was a young woman who had the look of boredom edged neatly into her mouth. She yawned and played with her dress and nails.

On the other side of the king, a couple of feet away in the center of the dais, supposedly was the prince himself. It wasn't too hard to guess this, as at the foot of the dais were several young ladies ignoring everything that was going on and trying to attract his attention with their fluttering and cooing.

He was dressed completely in red from head to toe. His headband – pointless, for it did nothing to hold back his dark curling hair – was deep orichulum red leather, and his fitted Strategist knee length coat was also the same deep orichulum red leather, as were his fitted leather pants, boots, and gloves.

Even his leather belt and leather hilt for his Energy weapon were deep orichulum. He was a slash of blood standing on a black stage. He was not smiling. He stared at the floor, his hair over his eyes as if wishing he were not there at all.

The king saw this and his smile clouded. He walked over to his son and whispered something vehemently in his ear. The prince tossed his hair back and stood straight. He winked at the girls at his feet and they quietly squealed, arguing over at whom he had winked.

By this time, Tanya and Holly had made it within ten feet of the dais, and Holly was distracted by something on the left side of the raised stage area. She couldn't put her finger on it, but something didn't fit the scene.

"Something isn't right," she whispered to Tanya.

"You're just nervous." Tanya smiled and waved to a young male courtier, who bowed lustfully back at her.

"Yes, I'm nervous and my senses are heightened. Just be wary, okay?"

Tanya took her sister seriously, as she knew Holly wasn't the dramatic type.

They slowed their step and began shaking hands with some of the ladies and older gentlemen around them to give Holly more time to sense what was wrong. She surreptitiously inhaled deeply through her nose, trying to test the air.

"There's so much perfume, it's hard to tell, but I'm sure I can smell nightshade somewhere to the left of the dais, a lot of it."

Tanya smiled and put her arm around her sister for a flickergraph that one of the guests wanted to take.

"What is a poison like deadly nightshade doing in a gathering like this?"

"Nothing good. It's not on metal, but soaked into wood, whatever that means."

The two moved back into the center of the aisle within five feet of the dais. Tanya stopped and bowed. Holly followed suit. Tanya whispered while bowing,

"Pinpoint it now."

Holly closed her eyes briefly and focused on the odor and the waves of poison that wafted through the air.

As they stood up, Holly whispered,

"The Strategist standing on the third step has a wooden dagger under his cloak, and it's dripping with deadly nightshade."

As the king addressed them, the girls kept their heads down in a shy, respectful pose so they could keep their eyes on the Strategist with the poison dagger.

"Ladies Tanya and Holly, we welcome you to Lemuria." The crowd applauded.

King Darsaldain continued,

"It is our great pleasure to have you stay with us these next two weeks until you arrive safely at your new school to begin your journey of wonder in education at my great alma mater, Atlantis National Academy."

The crowd applauded again.

"We hope that you will give us a favor now and entertain us a piece by showing some of your great talents, of which we have all heard a great deal."

The king gestured off stage, and up walked the Strategist in question. He had bent over and picked up two small glittering chests to bring them toward the king.

"Just keep those hands full, my poison friend," hissed Holly, so totally on guard that Tanya thought her skin was turning green.

The poison Strategist deposited the boxes at the king's feet then went to stand by Prince Hadigan, who shook his hand and hugged him.

Two Primers came forward and picked up the chests. Holding them out to the girls, they beckoned them to climb the steps. Holly walked up the steps away from the king and the prince, and Tanya walked in the opposite direction. This took the Primers by surprise, they expected the girls to come to them, but the girls wanted to keep the royalty and the poison in their line of vision by standing on either side of them. Holly didn't take her eyes off the hidden dagger.

The Primers were about to correct the girls when the king said,

"Well, go to them. They are the entertainers."

Each girl received her chest and opened it without looking inside, but reached out with a hand. Again, neither took their eyes off the king, the prince, or the poison dagger that continued at the prince's side.

Everyone just thought this was all a part of the girls' concentration. It was quite thrilling.

"Who is that with the prince?" whispered Holly to the Primer.

"Mentor Farrington, the prince's best friend."

"Does he have any reason to hurt the prince?"

"Why do you say that, Lady?"

"Just wanting to verify some gossip." Holly played with the seedling she had found.

The seedling was floating in mid-air before she grew it into a tiny shrub. The crowd was oohing and applauding. Tanya was pouring the sand from one hand into another, where it turned into a miniature rock robot that began dancing like a puppet. Everyone laughed and cheered.

"You be careful with the accusations you make, even in gossip, m'lady, a Mentor is a powerful man, especially a friend of the prince. You could be put to death for mentioning such a thing."

"Sorry. That's why I wanted to verify what I had heard."

"You hear anything more like that and you tell the nearest Champion. We'll nip that in the bud. Ha, no pun intended, hey."

Holly had just sprouted five different colored carnations on the one flowering bush, and the rock robot was picking them to give them to the king's lady.

That's when Holly's nerves shot through the roof.

It was moving, slowly at first, then with a sudden movement…

Holly didn't have time to think.

Prince Hadigan's back had been to her the whole time and now the dagger, she could see in slow motion, was headed directly for it and through his heart.

She reached for it and grabbed it with her extended energy hand. She still stood three feet away, but with her energy force she held onto the dagger and fought to turn it with all her might.

Screaming like a banshee, Holly plunged the dagger backward into the only place she knew it would be safe from ever hurting the prince, into the heart of the one who had attempted the assassination.

Suddenly the rock robot expanded and grappled the slumping assassin. Tanya was there for her. Holly could count on her sister, even in a blind rage. Holly flung forth her other hand and bound the dying Strategist to the rock robot with a vine. Her energy kept the dagger within inches of his heart, keeping him alive just long enough to see his would-be victim safe and know his plan had failed.

Mentor Farrington, bound and frothing at the mouth and heart from the poison, looked confusedly at his prince, then at Holly. He dropped his hand from off the dagger's wooden hilt and said,

"What went wrong, Haddy?" Then he died.

The energy force that held the dagger in its fatal place returned to Holly, and she looked at the shadow of blood on her hands.

She had just killed a man, the prince's best friend, a Mentor of the Defense Force.

She ran from the room.

No Chance

She didn't stop running until she found her way back to the garden. There she fell on the grass and cried, groaning in agony at the horror she had just committed.

Nothing in the world could save her from what was to come now. Hadigan's justice was always swift. Sure, she may have saved his life, but she had no proof of that because when it came down to it, it was her energy holding the dagger: a wooden dagger with a plant based poison. Naturally, they would think she was the guilty one, not the best friend and Mentor.

She was curled up in a fetal position when she heard his voice.

"Holly?"

That was all she was waiting for. She'd hoped to find him there. Without opening her eyes, she threw herself into the gardener's arms and cried and sobbed, heaving till there was nothing left but quiet tears.

"Andrew."

He held her and rocked her gently. He smoothed her hair, and she knew that everything would be all right if only she could stay right there with him, for always.

"What am I to do? Hadigan will have me executed."

"No."

"Yes." She tried to open her eyes, but they were swollen shut and it was too bright, so she kept her head down on his chest.

"He will do no such thing," Andrew consoled her.

"How can you know that?"

"Holly, look at me." He gently tilted her head and combed her hair off her face with his fingers.

Holly squinted at him and whimpered,

"I must look hideous." His beautiful face was blurry through her swollen, teary eyes.

"You're a bit blotchy, but you're still beautiful." He smiled at her, and she blinked back some tears. His hair was slung over his eyes, and she tucked it back into the head band.

"Why do you wear a headband if it doesn't pull your hair back?"

"It comes with the uniform."

He stood up and circled to show her the whole orichulum red leather strategist outfit he was wearing, from the coat to the gloves to the boots.

Even his weapon had a red leather hilt.

Holly frowned and looked at him.

"Is that uniform for a certain section of the Defense Force?"

"Nope, it's one of a kind."

Holly stood up and backed away.

"Andrew?"

"Yes, Hadigan Andrew Hades Darsaldain, at your service." He bowed.

Holly didn't move, or make a sound.

"Boo." Hadigan leaned in close to tease her immobility.

"He said you'd do this, and I didn't believe him. But you did, so quickly, so easily, and so completely," Holly mumbled.

"Who said what?" Hadigan wiped a tear from Holly's cheek.

"Marin. He said if I left him, I'd have no chance but to fall for you. He was right, no chance at all."

"Is it so unfair of me to want to steal the greatest beauty in my entire kingdom?"

"I'm no great beauty. You just want me for my power."

"But if you know and accept that, my young one, then your beauty is even greater than I thought."

"How old are you, Your Highness?"

"Please, in private, you can call me Andrew, and I'm twenty-six."

"I know you know how old I am."

"Yes, I do, but unlike Tambeaux, I am not a dirty old man. I have no intention of beginning anything with you just now. Instead, I will send you off on your merry little way to school. I will tell you to study hard, have fun, and I'll see you when you graduate. Then maybe we can discuss your future."

"You would wait six years for me?"

"I've waited this long. Besides, I have too much to do right now, to be distracted by any woman."

"What about Sula, Arula, and the other fourteen-year-old?"

Andrew laughed out loud.

"I see you've caught up with the gossip. They are merely instruments with which I can play my dear father's heart. We have an interesting relationship, he and I. I am not allowed near him, and he is allowed to bicker about everything I do, or don't do, as he pleases. Unfortunately, as a result, I have begun to take great pleasure in 'playing' him. It is more entertaining than watching the silly ladies that come to sit at his side."

"You're not allowed near your father? Why?"

"The Senate does not trust the offspring of their sovereigns. For some reason, they think I might kill him. Preposterous, really, anyone can see I'm not ready yet."

He winked at Holly, and she presumed he was joking so she laughed.

Andrew took her arm and guided her back to the Grand Throne Room. Tanya caught up with them and consoled her sister. The mess was completely cleared away, and no one said anything.

Gash Arabol

The king had already retired and the feasting was beginning, so Holly sat to the right of Prince Hadigan, and Tanya sat on his other side.

Holly's appetite did not allow her to eat much. She still had awful visions of the assassination catastrophe.

To Holly's right sat a man a few years younger than Hadigan. He was nothing compared to his host. He had a slight build and straight black hair trimmed to his ears. He wore glasses that were quite attractive, but he didn't say a word all evening, and Holly thought him rather rude.

Just before they rose from the tables he cleared his throat and stuttered,

"L-L-Lady Holly, c-could I speak w-with you?"

"Yes, sir?"

"I was w-wondering," he paused and Holly had the impression that this was about to be a very important question. "W-what do d-dragon tears taste like?"

"Oh?" That was certainly a new question that had never been posed to her before.

"They're smoky," she said, and looked at the man a little closer. "Do I know you?"

"Perhaps, I have seen you in the village marketplace before."

"Do you mean Latoona?" Holly was suddenly animated.

The man brightened.

"Yes, I live ten miles from your village."

"Have you been there recently? Have you seen my parents?"

"I was there just a week ago, and they were quite healthy. In fact, I had scraped my knee tripping over a silly rock and your mother patched me up. A perfect job she did, too."

"She's a great healer. Oh, I miss home. How did you get here so quickly?"

They were walking out onto a small balcony, and the man lead her over to a secluded corner.

"I took the yellow bullet sub-line. I hope I don't alarm you, bringing you to such a secluded corner."

Holly was suddenly alarmed because she hadn't noticed till it was brought to her attention. She even shivered in the cooler evening air. The gentleman offered her his jacket without a second thought.

He continued,

"I don't like company much, but I wanted to ask you some questions about your experience with the dragon tears. You see, I am a biochemical and medicinal engineer. I have been studying dragons for just a couple of years, and I'd love to get your first-hand impressions."

Holly agreed, and soon they were deeply involved in an animated conversation about dragons, Latoona, the Amazon, plants, and poisons.

They were so engrossed in each other that they didn't notice Hadigan slowly approach, watching them.

***   ***   ***

"Gash Arabol, what are you doing with my Lady Holly?"

"My Lord Hadigan!" Gash, the man sitting with Holly, bounced up guiltily and dropped his pen. "I was j-just interviewing the Lady Holly on her f-first-hand experience with d-dragon tears, for my research, sir."

Hadigan lightened up a little.

"Ah, you're working. I was worried for a minute that your interest in Holly was due to something else."

"N-No, sir, of course not, I n-know your intentions v-very well, sir.

I would never think of such a th-thing."

"Good. Lady Holly, will you join me?"

The royal couple turned to leave, but Gash had one final question.

"Holly, do you know how old you are?"

Hadigan frowned at Gash and pulled Holly inside. Taking off Gash's jacket, which had been draped over the Lady's shoulders, Hadigan tossed it aside.

Holly, however, realized that she had finally found someone who understood her true age. She tried to maintain eye contact with Gash through the archways and windows and between the trees, but Hadigan whisked her away too quickly. Holly was determined to find him again and ask him what he knew.

"Gash." Hadigan had called Gash to come and see him before he retired to bed after the festivities were over. Gash had obviously been dragged out of bed to be seen.

"Yes, m'lord?"

"What did you mean by asking Holly how old she was?"

"The dragon tears, Lord Hadigan, accentuated more than just her abilities. They accelerated her growth. By my rough guess, physiologically, Tanya and Holly are in reality somewhere near their early twenties by now."

"How old will she be when she graduates?"

"Hard to tell without biochemical calculation, but I would guess at around late twenties to thirties."

"Perfect," cooed Hadigan. "I want you to detail exactly how to do these tests to find their real age and how quickly they are progressing.

Then leave me the instructions and return to your jungle home by noon, today."

"My Lord? May I ask, why so soon?"

"No, you may not ask anything. But I may ask why you, who don't speak to anyone, would suddenly decide to become," at this point Hadigan began losing his temper, "completely enamored with the one girl I told you, no, you pointed out, as an excellent match for me? Why would you do that?"

Gash paled.

"I promise I was only interviewing her about the dragon tears."

"And boasting about your latest findings with your poisons garden. She was oh so proud of you and impressed by that."

Gash balked. He hadn't realized Hadigan had been listening in to quite that much of the conversation.

"She has a curious mind and was asking a lot of questions. She misses her home, so I mentioned a few things that might make her feel more comfortable. It had been a difficult evening for her."

"At the same time, almost completely destroying everything I set up in the garden for her. Do you realize just how much work I have done to gain the favor of the girl? First Tambeaux, now you? Will all my closest friends come against me to pull her away from me? I will have Holly, she is mine."

"If I may, m'lord, why are you so intent on Holly, w-why not Tanya?"

"She is tainted. She's fallen in love with a Bacht."

"How do you know this?"

"I have my ears everywhere, I know everything."

"The tests are difficult to calculate accurately."

"Then it is good you are an excellent teacher and I am the perfect student." Hadigan dismissed Gash, saying, "Detailed instructions by noon, and you gone. Oh, and Gash, if I ever see your letterhead, or even smell your ink near ANA, I will kill you."

Poolside

Hadigan Andrew was the perfect host.

Holly was a marked woman.

Tanya was slightly jealous.

Holly complained,

"Have you noticed that the men here don't even look at me?"

Holly sprayed some more coconut water over her legs and watched a couple of virile, young Strategists, (off duty), walk passed the sunbathing sisters and dove into the pool in front of them. They smiled at Tanya and quickly looked at the ground so as to not catch Holly's eye.

"It's not that I have a problem with you and Prince Hadigan," Tanya wasn't listening to her sister, "I guess I'm happy for you."

"Look, those two smiled at you and ignored me." Holly emphasized her point.

"It's just that he chose you awfully quickly."

"Do I have an 'X' on my forehead or something?"

"I was expecting at least some kind of competition of sorts."

"Maybe a scarlet 'A' on my chest?"

"I mean why you so definitely, and not me?"

"What about Mitchell, have you forgotten him so quickly?" Holly was listening to her sister.

"NO, I haven't forgotten him. I am just curious as to why the prince chose you so suddenly without even blinking an eye at me. It's just not..."

"Not what, normal? Thanks a lot. Just because you usually get the boys doesn't mean I can't have my turn. Maybe," Holly began jokingly pretending to be a butterfly, "I have just come out of my chrysalis and am now more beautiful than ever, and you are still a worm." She poked her sister in the ribs.

Tanya shrieked at being tickled and squirted Holly with water. Holly squealed back. They laughed together and looked around, as they had drawn the attention of the surrounding pool crowd. They giggled and settled down. Holly pulled a hidden sheet of paper from Tanya's notebook. It was a letter to Mitchell.

"So you haven't forgotten him."

"Give that back!"

Holly scanned the page briefly while Tanya stood up, trying to snatch it back. Holly let her take it, then stared at her accusingly.

"What?" Tanya pouted.

"You kissed?"

Tanya looked guilty.

"When were you going to tell me?"

"Right away, but Marin had just run off and I didn't think you wanted to hear about me just then."

"That was a week ago. Apparently I have a new non-boyfriend now."

They smiled at the joke together, and then Holly continued, hurt.

"Were you ever going to tell me?"

"I don't know. There just didn't seem to be a right time."

"Do I need to talk to you about all the problems and reasons not to get involved with a Bacht?"

"NO."

"Just checking."

They were silent for a while, each soaking in the sun and swimming in her own thoughts.

Tanya spoke quietly.

"So you are black marked, and no male is ever going to look at you for fear of death-by-Hadigan. Are you planning on staying loyal to him for six years?"

"I know it sounds impossible, but yes. I fell in love with Andrew in that garden, and I'll do anything for him, no matter how long it takes."

"Hmmm," Tanya pondered.

They spent the rest of the afternoon soaking in the sun.

*** *** ***

Hadigan Andrew found them by the pool just as they were packing up to leave.

"Have you ladies enjoyed your day of luxury?"

"Yes, my prince," said Tanya, "your swimming facilities are more beautiful than even the river back in Latoona."

"I doubt that, Lady Tanya. I've been there, remember. Your mineral well makes up for all the beauty here. I'd sell this whole terrace if I could just bring back the well. But as I can't, I shall have to keep the terrace for you to enjoy."

"I can have Mema send you some mineral water, if you like," Tanya casually boasted. "She knows how to bottle the water to keep it fresh."

"Really? Perhaps, we will talk more on this, then. There may be profit in such a conversation."

Tanya looked scandalized.

"Forgive my big Cluster ways, Lady Tanya, but I am a businessman. I like profit. Think of all the benefits Latoona may have with a prosperous well. She may be able to have that resort she's been wanting for so long."

Holly cleared her throat.

"My prince, since the explosion was an attack on your life, we primitive and superstitious jungle folk" Holly sarcastically emphasized these words "believe that any attempt to rebuild a resort will be cursed by the royal family."

"Not if the royal family is backing the project."

Holly looked, amazed, at her prince.

"You would take such an interest in a tiny Upland village?"

"I have a distinct interest in that village now, don't I?" He saluted her. "Shall I escort you ladies back to your tower? I have dancing and shopping on the agenda for this evening."

"Are the women courtiers coming?" Holly sighed with her nose turned up.

"Yes, you don't like them?"

"They don't like me. Of the court, the men ignore me, the women gossip cattily about me behind my back, and the children run away from me, afraid I'll turn into a dragon and breathe fire on them. I don't like courtiers."

"We'll see what we can do about that, don't worry. Just don't count on any of them being real friends and you'll be safe. Take them as what they are: leeches and scavengers. Then you get along with them fine."

"Great, that sounds much better." Holly rolled her eyes, and Tanya giggled to herself at Mitchell's familiar phrase.

"So where have you been these past few days?" Holly tried Tanya's flirting tricks and looked up at Hadigan Andrew through her eyelashes.

"I've missed you, sitting out here with no one but my boring sister to keep me company." She pushed out her lower lip with a pouty turn. It must have worked, because she could see him melt.

"I've been busy, unavoidably busy, and I'd much rather have been with you than with a bunch of sweaty men running around an empty field all afternoon."

"What were you doing?"

"Laray practice. I'm on the Defense Companies national team."

"You play Laray?" Both girls were instantly starry eyed.

"What position?" Tanya asked.

"Trout, of course," the prince boasted.

Laray

Tanya began to yawn behind a forced-closed mouth and tried not to roll her eyes as Holly sat in rapt attention while her dear prince bragged on and on to the girls of his battle-hardy conquests on the Laray field.

"The Laray field is set up differently with each game and is laid out somewhat like a cross-country steeplechase. The obstacles are many and vary from waterfalls, mazes, horseshoe turns, and climbing walls to jumps, pipelines, road waves, rivers, and other such creative devices." Hadigan unnecessarily over-explained the game.

Holly closed her eyes recalling the flickervision games she'd seen of HDP-covered courses that were dangerous, thrilling, and mildly safe as the hydro-plano that lined everything created a cushion should someone fall, although gravity did always get the upper hand.

Hadigan continued,

"The teams consist of two front runners who lead the race, or chase. Five bront runners who circle and defend or attack, and one trout rogue who plays as a scout and sniper. The trout is the best position to play. I've always played trout."

"Swimming upstream to spawn?" Tanya inquired with feigned innocence.

Hadigan focused his attention upon the adoring Holly and ignored her sister and continued over-explaining. He enjoyed the sound of his own voice.

"Each team member rides (like a surfboard) standing on the back of a stingray that is specially fitted with an HDP harness that allows it to breathe and fly at low altitudes, just a couple of feet above any surface. The stingrays add an extra improbability to the game; they are still wild creatures that need respect and understanding, and only the best Laray riders are Trevel, or -at one- with their rays. But all the rays thrive on the speed and excitement of the game."

Holly interrupted.

"How long have you had your ray?"

"I raised him from a tyke and have had him for nine years now. His name is Mahntin and he's the meanest ray in the game," Hadigan answered with pride.

"Wow," drooled Holly. Tanya stood with apologies, needing to use the facilities.

Hadigan continued, ego pumping.

"The object of the game revolves around the tack, a diamond-shaped leather ball twelve inches in length and six inches in width. The team races in the same direction, attempting to gain possession of the tack by catching it when it is passed or snatching it when it is dropped. Most of the game is spent attempting to dislodge other players from their rides without touching them. Forced physical contact between players constitutes a foul, but accidental or "natural" contact is relative, and it is a fi ne line that is drawn between the two."

He winked at Holly in a you-know-what-I-mean acknowledgement before diving back into his explanation.

"The goal of Laray is to complete all laps of the race and have all team members cross the finish line with the tack in that team's possession. If at any time a player falls off the course, he must be replaced by a reserve player, who enters the field from the start and must complete the whole circuit himself."

"So how many laps in a race?" Holly asked with genuine interest.

"Depending on the level of difficulty, each race may consist of two laps, or ten. On the national level, some obstacles change mid-play and are extremely fast with hard falls; thus, the players rely heavily on the HDP walls and floor for cushion and bounce."

Hadigan paused and looked at the wide eyed girl before him and thought, By Hades I hope you're older than your chronology. He studied her face a moment longer, and then shook his resolve and continued with a more pedantic distance in his voice.

"Atlantis National Academy is well known for its outstanding Laray teams, and the National Laray League often pulls from its graduating students."

Holly had played Laray only on foot because there was no stingray access in her jungle home. But she had watched many NLL games on flickervision, so it was no wonder that she was much enamored with the idea of having a real National Laray League player explain the game to her.

Hadigan in Motion

Hadigan Andrew was more than willing to give details of his victories. It thrilled him, perhaps too much, to see Holly's eyes shining, hanging on every word he spoke. He found himself staring at nothing, thinking of her looking at him with that adoring smile. In her eyes, it appeared as if he was a god who could do no wrong.

He'd seen that look in other women's eyes before, but it didn't have the same effect on him as it had when Holly looked at him. He would walk to Hades and back with bare feet for her.

He shook his head. What was he thinking? Such thoughts were for lovers, and he had no time for that. He was a warrior, not a lover.

He picked up his whip and began practicing. The vine that came forth from the weapon hilt was Taliamaland. Her beautiful orange roses spewed forth, drenching the whip in gold.

"Not tonight, my sweet," spoke the gardener, "I wish to do damage."

He pressed a button on the wall with the hilt end, and a combat practice dummy appeared in the center of the room.

Taliamaland shed her roses as quickly as she donned them. In their place were cruel curled thorns that dripped with a sweet orange liquid.

Hadigan swung his whip around and stung the dummy once. Taliamaland clung to it jealously and barely allowed herself to be torn from her place. She took with her much of all she held and left behind a soaking of the orange liquid. It spread quickly to eat hungrily at the cloth and hay, easily dissolving it.

But what it did to the metal plate mail was what intrigued Hadigan. The drips clung to the metal and ever so slowly crawled down the plate. It its wake, the drips left trails of faint orange lines that began to deepen. At first, they looked like rust, then burned metal, and then the holes began to show through.

"Ah." The vine curled lovingly around the gardener's neck. "Tali, you can do more than I had ever hoped. Lord Deagan will be glad."

He picked one of the thorns and turned it into a stunning long stemmed orange rose.

"Primer!" he called to the guard outside in the hall, who entered immediately. "Have this taken to my father's latest lady. Don't say who it's from, only say it's a gift for looking so unique tonight."

The Primer nodded and left.

Hadigan stretched, smiled, and went to bed. He slept very well that night.

Shocking News

Marina's Orders

Lemuria

Hadigan's Silvertongue

Laboratory Discoveries

Physiochemical Recognition

Last Night before School

Chapter 16

Shocking News

When Tyal came to collect the girls the next morning, Holly met him in the living area.

"Tyal, could you deliver a message for me?"

"Sending love notes to your prince already could be deemed desperate, my dear."

"It's neither a love note nor addressed to the prince."

Tyal raised a quizzical eyebrow and took the folded page from the young girl.

"Gash Arabol? Jolly Jove, the girl has a death wish," he mumbled in his usual fashion, then handed the note back to her. "No, I will deliver no such letter."

"Excuse me?"

"Ohh, nice condescension." Tyal always took his duty as teacher of snobbery very seriously, no matter the situation. "Try tilting your head slightly off kilter when you say that.

It gives an air of scrutiny and can add to the discomfort of the receiver of such attention."

"Tyal!" Holly was frustrated by always being trained but rarely listened to.

Tyal sighed.

"Truly, are you that oblivious, or has your sister not yet told you the most recent rumor?"

Tanya entered.

"You mean about the death of the king's latest lady?"

"What?!" Tyal was shocked.

"Her body was just discovered quite dead in her bed."

"How do you know this?" Their tutor was remarkably flustered by the news.

"I... just heard it... around." Tanya subconsciously rubbed her foot on the stone floor.

"It can't be? She was barely in place long enough to make enemies," he mumbled to himself, pacing and running his hands down his suit lapel. "Are you sure she's dead?"

"Tyal, did you know the lady?" Holly was concerned.

"She was my cousin."

"I'm so sorry." Tanya came over to comfort him. "I wouldn't have said it so abruptly if I'd known."

"No, you mistake my concern. I'm not sorry for her loss so much. She always was a wretched bore. Dreadfully pretty face, though. No, I'm more concerned about whether her death was at the hand of the king in anger and if he is angry enough to wreck vengeance on her whole family."

"Tyal, you don't think your life is in danger because she's dead, do you?" Holly's gaze connected to Tanya's.

"Stranger things have happened in the palace."

"It wasn't by the king's hand." Tanya confessed sheepishly.

"What do you know?" Tyal was intense.

"They don't know how she died. They just found her dead in bed, no forced entry, no struggle, nothing. It's as if she just lay down to sleep and died."

"Perhaps it was a peaceful passing, then. Poseidon take her readily."

Tyal breathed a sigh of relief and went to leave. "We exeunt for the Champions' graduation in fifteen minutes."

"Tyal?" Holly pressed her request and held out the letter to be delivered.

Tyal walked back to her and took the letter.

"Gash Arabol has been banished back to his jungle hideout. He's been commanded to make no contact with you on pain of death by Prince Hadigan's orders."

He held the letter in his palm, and a searing light began glowing around its edges. Instantly, the paper combusted in a flash and was gone.

"Whatever reason you have to contact the chemist is not enough to threaten his life."

Holly was shocked.

"Seven minutes now. Look exquisite; this parade is visualized via flickervision out as far as Trevel power is accessed."

Marina's Orders

The girls were hoisted up onto a float decorated in hundreds of fresh flowers and fruits. The colors were brilliant and the fragrance was exhilarating.

They moved out in fine fashion in a long trail that wound its way through the inner city circles down around the winding road. The further downhill and away from the palace they travelled, the more conspicuous the security became.

By the time they reached the base of the city and were in sight of the massive gates, most of the float passengers had pulled the curtains to block out the sight and smell of the grim surroundings.

Tanya and Holly insisted the curtains remain open and watched appalled as grubby, half-naked urchins ran alongside begging for some compassion, yet waved with such delight and hope despite their circumstances.

Both girls were moved to tears.

In unison, they reached for the decorations pinned in place around them and began tossing the grapes, oranges, and mangoes to the upstretched arms jostling for a place next to the glorious vision floating through their daily nightmare.

Such a flurry of activity surged on their float that it wobbled dangerously on its HDP rudder, and the guards had to descend with force, pushing the crowd away. The girls were so distressed they nearly called for a cease in the parade. But it was not to be. The king's float was only three places behind theirs, and they steamed forward out onto the grassy, sloping plains before the massive white walls of the glorious

Lemuria.

The parade fanned out across the grass, and the girls were flabbergasted by the vision before them.

In a show of force seen only once every two years, almost the entire Trevel Defense Force stood in row after row, platoon after platoon of Strategist Warriors.

The entire gathering wore midnight black dress pants with the same in a dress jacket, but for the highlighting stripes and accents of specific Energist colors. They also all wore a colored beret and a cape that was ready to be tossed back over one shoulder, exposing the inner lining that was also the color of their specific ranking.

The Energy ranking colors were in blocks of: Metal in charcoal black; Earth in tan brown; Flora in forest green; Fauna in chocolate brown; Water in navy blue; Fire in scarlet orange, Air in cerulean blue; Electricity in golden rod yellow; and Illumination in ivory."

Holly stood to scan the crowd. Putting on her sun shades, she looked for the telltale singular red uniform but found her eyes adjust and rest only on a black-and-navy blue uniform close to the main dais.

Champion Marin Tambeaux stood at attention, gazing straight at her, or perhaps only in her general direction, as chance had her float located directly before him.

A sudden guttural "HOO" punctured the air as the mass of Forces greeted the entrance of that one red uniform Holly sought.

The future Prince-in-One, His Royal Highness Prince Hadigan, erupted from the city gates on a massive white stallion and raced down the ranks of troops. Again, as he passed each color guard, they "Hooed" in unison, raising their left hands in salute, straight fingers under left eyes. Capes draped over these left shoulders fluttered open, flashing their colors in a rippling sea of hues.

The king's float descended from the hill and halted at the dais. He stepped onto the royal platform and left his newest lady sitting in the shade, looking slightly nervous in her brand-new position.

The circle of HDP on a stand at neck height amplified the king's already massive voice, and he was heard clearly across the entire field and up into the royal city itself.

"My fellow citizens of Trevel, the Powers be with you."

The crowd cheered.

"My fellow Strategists, Guardians of Trevel, the Powers be in you."

The Strategist Militia "Hoo-ed" with gusto.

"Today we are gathered to celebrate the passing on of those who, for fortune's sake, have chosen to climb the ladder of Energist Development."

At this point, a small band of Strategists without cloaks separated from the mass and stepped up before the dais.

"In past Trevel Kingdoms, this opportunity has been open to only those privileged by birth and wealth. However, in my father's father's time, this opportunity was opened to all who found within the talent of being -at one- and determination to step up and defend our grand and glorious life that is the Power of Trevel.

"In memory of those simple men and women who fought alongside their king during the dark days of the evil Shifters, we honor their sacrifice by allowing anyone to take the Rite of Champion.

"Men and women of Trevel, I present to you your latest Pre-Champion contenders."

The crowd went wild.

The Pre-Champion contenders bowed and, in perfect unison, stepped through an amazing display of precision and force prowess that could only come from a lifetime of practice.

Tanya and Holly recognized Marina Tambeaux on the mid-right of the line. Her brother, an already recognized Champion, could not take his proud eyes off his sister.

Holly let a tender smile cross her lips as she watched Marin drink in the family pride of the moment.

Prince Hadigan, seated on his steed, watched this and took note. The horse stamped uneasily, sensing the tension of his rider.

Holly snapped her attention to Hadigan's eyes and lowered her vision only enough to keep his gaze over the top of her shades. He held her blatant stare hungrily.

Only the final shout of determination from the line of Pre-Champions broke the visual connection.

The afternoon pulled on in the heat, and the mass of Strategists shimmered in the distortion waves that rose from the hot grass.

Throughout the ceremony, young honorary Strategist youths wandered among the warriors and the crowd, casting their own talents in soft sprays of water and gentle breezes to keep them cool.

Each Pre-Champion was given the opportunity to show individually her or his command of Power. When Marina Tambeaux was announced, Tanya and Holly straightened up, cheering. She began with basic moves of water spouts and ice carvings forming from her hand.

Then she surprised everyone with her own unique moves that only Holly and Tanya recognized. It would seem Marina had also taken advantage of her association with her L1 Brother Mitchell. She proceeded to complete the Bacht martial arts katas that Mitchell had taught the girls for form and physical preparation. She also added her own flare of water/ice manipulation, ending in a show of physical strength and flexibility not familiar to the Energy-dependent Trevel crowd. Her popularity among the people was loudly obvious.

The distinguished Champion Marin Tambeaux could barely contain his demeanor as he smiled, bursting with familial pride. Prince Hadigan raised an eyebrow and watched, rather mesmerized as well.

As the roar of the crowd shook the city walls, Champion Marin Tambeaux, friend and boyhood companion of the prince and heir to generations of mighty Trevel Strategists, stepped up onto the dais and began reading out the first orders for each of the new Champions as the king pinned a shiny status medal on each breastplate.

The orders were all issues of leadership. Platoons and legions were placed under the new direction of each newly recognized Champion, but for one.

Even Marin faltered slightly as he opened Marina's orders. Marina was visibly shaken with rage as he read,

"Champion Marina Tambeaux, you are hereby ordered to your new post of... Royal Ambassador to Hanain."

The Dijex sisters sat with mouths open. The rest of the crowd, presuming this was some mighty posting, glorious and privileged, cheered with gusto. Marina stepped forward and snatched the roll of parchment from her brother's hand and stepped out of his reach briskly.

Then came the rolling call.

One by one, each Energy Guard unit raised its hilts in a final salute of triumph.

The ringing of metal flashed above black uniforms, followed by the thunder of rock cracking against rock as stone daggers were raised. Vine whips cracked, and in a massive display of impressive visual Energy, the Animal Strategist lifted empty hilts that spontaneously poured forth translucent blue forces in the shapes of all types of animals. Some Strategists stood with eagles flying above their heads, while others had large cats and reptiles circling their feet, and others stood dwarfed by massive bear and dragon forms standing behind them. Next, the flowing waterfalls thundered over the top of violent burning explosions. Tornados and spiraling air currents of the Air Strategists whirled around, Lightning strikes and frazzling electricity amidst laser beams and sunbursts that blinded the crowd by the Illumination Energists.

Yet despite this show of awe and grandeur, neither Tanya nor Holly missed the concealed argument of brother and sister as Marin tried to convince Marina he had nothing to do with her orders and had no idea where such a castoff deployment would have come from.

Hadigan's Silvertongue

Marina disappeared in the night. She didn't stay for the celebratory banquet, nor did she talk with anyone before she left. Her humiliation of being the only new Champion to not receive a leadership commission was felt more powerfully with her absence.

Holly queried her prince when he joined them for the post-banquet brunch the following midmorning.

"Good morning, my lovelies." Prince Hadigan winked over Tanya's head to the twins Arula and Sula just to keep the scandal and gossip mills running. "You two look remarkably fresh this morning."

Tanya, still put out by his blatant favor of her sister, muttered,

"We didn't stay late, which you would have known had you actually talked to us at all last night."

The prince paused, not used to being scolded by anyone, especially one so young. He considered warning her to hold her tongue but changed tactics in honor of Holly.

"It is satisfying to me to know you missed my presence, Tanya."

He reached for a jug of syrup.

"I thought there was some negativity between us."

Tanya glanced at him as he continued to casually pour the sweet, fruity juices over his pancakes.

"Perhaps we can put whatever bad footing we started on behind us and move forward into a new friendship?" He replaced the jug and directed his gaze with slight menace toward her.

"Ay?"

Tanya opened her mouth with a sneer and Holly kicked her under the table. She took a breath and responded,

"Of course, Your Highness, I would never want to be the bad apple of a batch."

"Excellent, and in good time; I have an exciting discovery planned for you two today."

"My prince?" Holly interrupted.

"Yes, my dear lady?" He took her hand and kissed it.

Holly blushed slightly. "May I ask the favor of your understanding?"

"Anything you wish to know... if I know it, I will reveal it." He soon learned the folly of such promises to one as intelligent and confident as Holly.

"Why was Champion Marina not given a leadership commission like all the others, but rather banished to Hanain?"

"Banished!" the prince exclaimed in surprise. "I had hoped after your own visit to the flourishing mining town, you might have seen for yourself the importance of such a placement."

"How important can one feel when all your peers are granted hundreds of troops beneath them and yet you are sent to a tiny, infamous outpost to play lackey to a gregarious puppet?" Tanya expressed a never before-present loyalty to Marina.

Prince Hadigan laughed out loud.

"Gregarious puppet? Well, tell me who you think could be pulling the strings as puppeteer? Lord Deagan even puts me off a little. I'm sure his blatant use of varied Energy access did not go unnoticed with you?"

"You seem to have granted him vast favor." Tanya didn't know when to stop.

"You recommend my consulting young high school subordinates when making state decisions?"

Holly quickly interjected to break the tension.

"Forgive our fervent loyalty to our former chaperone, my prince. We are women of like nature and seek to band together in unity. You, as a mighty warrior and leader of nations, can understand the passions of brother-, or, in this case, sisterhood?"

The future Prince-in-One eased into a smile.

"I would have it no other way and could only hope that I should earn such loyalty from you myself someday."

"You have mine, Andrew," Holly whispered so only he and not even Tanya could hear her.

He magically pulled the petal of a purple iris from behind her ear and breathed in its soft fragrance, then changed the subject.

"So how old do you two think you really are?"

Holly and Tanya stared silently at each other. Prince Hadigan rose from the table and extended his hand to them.

"Shall we find out?"

Tentative with hope, confusion, and a yearning to know, the girls followed the prince through the many corridors and covered walkways of the palace grounds to an odd, shiny building amid the rock and carvings of the ancient replicas.

The modern man of Trevel waved to the simple silver structure with an odd futuristic look to it.

"One of my own special projects: my mad scientist lab."

He laughed an appropriate maniacal laugh.

Even Tanya couldn't help but giggle.

"Is there a bathroom nearby?" Holly scanned the lobby as they entered.

As Tanya paused in the doorway that Hadigan held open for them, he leaned close to her ear while Holly's back was turned and whispered,

"I'd like a short chat in private."

Then he directed Holly to the bathroom.

"Down the hall on the left, my dear, to powder that pretty little nose." He tapped the tip of her nose lightly and winked at her.

"Tan, you coming?" Holly began walking off in the appointed direction.

"No, I'm good."

"We'll meet you under the central chandelier, you can't miss it." He nodded in the opposite direction, then guided Tanya off in that direction with a gentle hand on the base of her neck. Tanya felt the hairs there prickle.

They passed a couple of young workers in white lab coats, and as they bowed, the prince smiled generously at them and casually opened a side door to a small office. He steered Tanya inside.

The door closed with an uncomfortably loud double click.

Hadigan had his back to her in the darkened room.

"I may be wrong, but I'm getting the distinct feeling you are jealous of my favor toward your sister over you."

Tanya scoffed a little in self-defense.

"Do not think for a moment…" He turned and stepped uncomfortably close to her. Tanya backed up to the wall, "…that my choice is based upon a lack of interest in you."

He pressed his entire body gently against her lithe figure. Slowly he dropped his head and ran his cheek against her hair.

"Every plant needs some Earth to put his roots down in."

Tanya shivered slightly. She could barely breathe.

A long, soft vine slowly wound its way out from under his long sleeved cuff and caressed her neck, ever so slowly creeping down her shoulder along the V neck of her shirt. It paused at the edge of her cleavage, and he gently brushed it aside.

He backed up and said with clinical coldness,

"Unfortunately for me, your choice in male companions is a tad unscrupulous for a prince of Trevel."

Tanya remembered Mitch for the first time since she'd entered the room with the handsome royal. She dropped her eyes in shame, not sure of what exactly she was ashamed.

"If, however, you find yourself in need of planting, you only need let me know."

He took the door handle in his grip, and the vine extended itself around her hips and the top of her jeans.

"But don't come to me for your first time." The vine dropped ever so slightly beneath the button of her jeans, and Tanya gasped.

Hadigan opened the door and walked out. Tanya, partially double over, gently pulled her jeans down to expose her hip.

A small incision dripped a tiny drop of red blood mixed with orange pollen dust onto her finger. Taliamaland had left her mark.

***   ***   ***

Hadigan was conversing on his ear-horn phone beneath the largest black and red chandelier either of the girls had ever seen. Holly entered the central room and joined Tanya, who was casually wandering the edge of the room surveying the massive frescoes that collared the walls.

Holly took in the sight of the grand light and the even grander prince beneath it. She sighed like the high school girl that she was.

"He's just so handsome. But even more than that, he's such a gentleman."

Tanya kept her back to the subject of Holly's admiration. "Yeah, a gentleman."

"Look," Holly squared her shoulders to her sister, "I know you're usually the one who gets all the male attention, but can't you just be happy for me for once?"

"I'm just not sure he's the gentle gardener you fell in love with."

Tanya glanced at him, absentmindedly ran her hand across her hip, and turned her back to him again.

"He's a great prince. He is required to have some duality. I mean, he can't expose his real nature to just anyone. He has a reputation and a royal honor to uphold."

"And you think he's exposed his true nature to you?"

Holly froze in angered defense.

"At least he has a nature to expose. I'm not even sure Bachts are capable of having true depth of person."

"Excuse me?" Tanya was horrified by her sister's snobbery.

"I'm not interrupting, anything am I?" The noble prince laid his arms across the shoulders of both girls.

Holly grinned.

"You are never an interruption, rather a breath of fresh air."

She ignored her sister and didn't notice that at the touch of the prince, Tanya's hand flew to her hip and she almost lost her balance.

Her eyes rolled back into her head and her breathing became shallow. The prince held her up without even looking at her as he guided them off.

Laboratory Discoveries

"We're off to my experimental technology lab. I'm developing a Chitton Chamber. Do you know what a chitton is?"

Tanya was still stumbling slightly as if dosed on a magnetic medicine.

Holly boasted her knowledge proudly.

"Chittons are the physiochemical particles that make up the cells of a Trevel. They hold the equation of one's make up in personality, chemical disposition, physical structure, and energy connection."

"You're definitely well read." He squeezed her shoulders and continued to guide the two. "The studies I'm conducting in Chitton technology will have vast applications. I am working mostly in the medical healing fields."

"Isn't that dangerous?" Holly was intrigued, "Experimenting with energy on a smaller than cellular level seems to me to be rather terrifying."

"Fear is not a good enough reason to stop doing something. Besides, I would only use it for good. And, right now, we only use it to calculate the progression of time in the Trevel energy flux."

He led them into a sparse, softly lit room.

There was a young couple, the woman of which was with child, and a lab technician in the quiet room. They all rose to greet the prince with a bow and salute.

Holly was quite taken with the partially organic, partially flowboard structure in the center of the room. She stepped immediately forward to place her hands on the mossy exterior of the machine.

Hadigan didn't take his eyes off her but gently deposited the drunken Tanya on a stool and stepped over to Holly's side.

Tanya swayed slightly, shook her head, and suddenly felt very clear. She took in the scene and smiled shyly at the young couple still standing with heads bowed.

"How far along are you?" she inquired.

The young woman smiled broadly and said,

"We're about to find out exactly."

The technician looked at the flowboard screen and then at the open benchtop of the machine.

Slowly forming in the translucent blue of HDP was a tiny figure curled in a ball. It was the form of a partially developed fetus. The woman softly moaned in delight and approached it, entranced. The young man blew out hard and held his chest.

"Baby, it's our baby!" The woman tilted her head slightly, and even Tanya and Holly couldn't help approaching to study the solidifying formation.

The flowboard screen blipped and the technician excused himself.

"Pardon me." He grinned at them and reached out to the image. He tapped the skull and "pulled out" the brain and central nervous system of the floating fetus reflection and set them aside separately. The "empty" curled fetus hovered and rotated on the benchtop delicately.

Using swift and fluid movements the technician expanded the form of the brain and stretched out the central nerve as long as it would reach.

He flipped a switch on the bench, and a light began to scan from the top of the brain from all down the long spinal cord. The flowboard screen blipped once more.

It was a fascinating procedure as every nerve ending and capillary was highlighted in distinct formation. The pulse of the blood flow could still be seen pushing though the tissues even though they were separated from the form of the heart left inside the floating fetus next to it.

"Not long now."

Again the technician grinned at the awed couple.

The young woman couldn't resist holding out her hand to the clear blue form while laying her other hand on her round self. The form responded to the touch on her belly and squirmed slightly. The woman cooed.

"And, there we have it."

The young man jolted slightly into reality.

"Already?"

"Five months, four days, twenty-two hours, and two, three, four, five seconds." He passed a readout to the young father.

A tear dribbled down the deda's cheek as he grasped his wife and kissed her. The fetal form kicked out and he stepped back, holding his abdomen.

"I felt that!"

The couple kissed again.

The technician reset the machine and ushered the delirious couple out into the waiting room and left the royal trio alone.

"That was amazing." Holly ran her hand over the moss and walked around the walls of the Trevel technological marvel.

"Oh! There's a pool back here." She motioned to Tanya, who was completely clear of mind now and torn between the beauty of what she had just witnessed and her own confused stirrings within.

"That is how we contract the readings." The prince joined them by the open tub. "Who's first?" He nodded into the HDP liquid.

"Oh, that would so be me." Holly stripped of her shoes and grabbed Tanya's shoulder to get her balance as she lifted her leg toward the knee deep solution.

Hadigan laid his hand on her exposed knee.

"Why don't we let Tanya go first... age before beauty, y'know." He winked in light-hearted teasing.

Holly giggled and stepped back. Still, in awe of her grand and openly expressive royal suitor, Holly continued not to notice the obviously subdued nature of her usually bold sister.

"Go ahead, Tan. Oldest first..."

Tanya grinned reluctantly, but eager to discover just how much older, she slipped off her own shoes and stepped into the liquefied gel.

She had one hand on Holly's shoulder getting in, and just as she lifted her second leg into the pool, Hadigan casually and gently lifted his arm to steady her elbow. Down she went.

I was quite an unceremonious plop under the solid, wavering gel that swirled sluggishly around her. Holly squealed and laughed hysterically, grabbing at her sister and pulling her up out of the slush.

Tanya pulled herself up and began sputtering until she realized that all parts out of the liquid were rinsed dry.

"Holy Jove, what happened then?" Holly steadied her kneeling sister.

"Did you slip?"

"No." Tanya looked dazed. "My legs just completely gave way under me."

"Are you okay?" The prince kept his hands to himself and studied her with deep curiosity, mistaken for genuine concern.

"Yeah." Still confused, Tanya settled herself back into the HDP.

"Yeah, all good, let's do this."

She submerged her entire body after taking a deep breath and heard Hadigan mumble something, but the HDP had already enclosed her ears, and she was encased in a lush silence.

The liquid still waved up and back slowly, and she rested in the gentle rocking. Without thinking, she breathed out and expected to see bubbles but was surprised as the liquid simply absorbed the exhalation. Tanya sucked in a slight breath accidentally and found the HDP surrendered the necessary oxygen to her lungs without a gurgle. She could breathe easily.

Bliss was hers floating in the soft gel. She felt a tingle along the cut on her hip and recognized the healing sealing up the open wound.

As her mind was perfectly clear now, and she pondered what had happened as she stepped into the tub.

She had been perfectly balanced until she felt Hadigan's hand on her elbow. He hadn't unsteadied her; in fact, he barely touched her. But at his touch, her hip pulsed and she lost all feeling in her legs.

Then she remembered the sensation in her hip as Hadigan had his arm looped over her and Holly on the way to the lab. A pulsing began with a slow rising deep in her abdomen, a burning with no pain. Only pleasure ascended from the base of her spine all the way up to between her shoulder blades. She had barely been able to resist arching her back as they walked.

Completely inexperienced in such sensations, Tanya was totally lost as to what had been happening, but some tiny voice within wanted it again.

His deep voice interrupted her contemplation.

"We're done, Tanya, you can get out now."

She shivered slightly and rose up out of the sweet quiet.

***   ***   ***

As Tanya had lain down in the liquid, the prince had said, "Relax and breathe in there."

Holly looked at him quizzically. He answered,

"The HDP is a constant connection to its surroundings. All energy, gas, and even liquid forms flow freely through it. Thus, it will take in your breath and give back oxygen just as if it were natural air."

"That's amazing." Holly ran her fingers in it.

"You have a delightfully inquisitive mind." He was studying her.

She blushed and dropped her head. He was such a beautiful specimen of a Trevel. Holly briefly compared him to her first suitor, Champion Tambeaux, but there was no comparison. The prince was such a completion of all things perfect.

"What are you thinking?" He ran his fingers across her brow.

Holly blushed deeply and couldn't answer. He rose up from his stool and pulled her off hers.

"I promised you I wasn't some dirty old man and that I would not move on you until you were older."

Holly swallowed hard in innocent nervousness. He was so in control.

"I just want you to know how hard it is for me to do that."

He held her chin in his hand and ran his thumb tenderly across her lips.

"There is something about you, Holly-Anne Dijex that defies chronology. You have such innocence, but such essence of power, as to make any man of any age crumble in adoration before you."

She held his gaze openly. He dropped his face closer to hers.

"I am your servant. Tell me anything and I will obey you."

The flowboard blipped and Holly opened her mouth to speak, but nothing came out. He placed his fingers on her open mouth.

"Hold that thought." He walked back to the flow board and spoke into it. "We're done, Tanya, you can get out now."

Tanya sat up.

"You know you can breathe under there?" Tanya shared the discovery with her sister.

"He said that as you went under. Didn't you hear him?" Holly was switching places with her.

"No. It's fantastically quiet in there." She took both Holly's arms.

"Watch your step." They grinned together.

As Holly went under, Tanya, alone again in the prince's presence, felt an awkward tension rise. She avoided his gaze by watching the formation of her own figure in translucent HDP come to life on the machine's open countertop.

Hadigan busied himself pulling out the brain and central nervous system, stretching it out and setting the scanner to do its work.

"Chemicals are a fascinating study," he said blandly. "It constantly amazes me what the addition of one solution can do to a compound."

She barely saw it, the tiny green thread of a vine caressing the prince's hair around his collar. Had Tanya been delusional, she might have thought it waved at her.

"I've never seen any Energist so devoted to his channeling that he carries his source with him everywhere, all the time."

The vine descended from his collar more prominently now.

"Tali and I are very close."

"Tali?"

He reached up and pulled a stunning orange rose from the vine that now caressed his hand.

"Taliamaland, my own creation and life work." He placed the rose into his lapel. "I'm surprised Holly didn't tell you about her. They met in the garden."

"My sister doesn't tell me everything."

The prince steadied his gaze into her eyes and slowly reached out to tap her chin.

"I'm sure you hide some things from her, too."

Again, at his touch, her knees went weak, and she staggered and had to catch her breath.

Hadigan ran his fingers around the rose petals and whispered to himself,

"Fascinating."

Tanya stepped away from him, but he wasn't that easy on her. He followed her as she backed through the room.

"Just imagine your response to me if I gave you more."

Tanya gulped and glanced at the open pool, readily showing Holly lying as if sleeping peacefully in full view.

"You need to stop."

Hadigan smiled unconcerned and shrugged.

"Just food for thought."

Then he paused and reached out to touch her again. This time he ran his hand across her hip where Taliamaland had left her mark.

Tanya buckled and gasped out loud. She caught herself on the wall, panting, confused, and furious.

"Don't touch me," she hissed like a cat in heat.

Hadigan chuckled to himself,

"Totally fascinating."

He returned to the flowboard and spoke into it.

"We're all done, my dear. Please grace us with your lovely presence again."

Physiochemical Recognition

Holly sat up and stretched as if rising from a refreshing nap.

"That was lovely."

She saw Tanya leaning up against the wall panting heavily and sweating.

"What happened to you?"

Hadigan commented, "She just had to run to the restroom. Come see what you look like inside."

Tanya pushed herself away from the wall and regained her composure.

She knew her sister would never believe the truth of the situation. She'd just have to watch and wait… and stay out of the prince's reach… maybe?

Hadigan worked Holly's form as he'd done with Tanya's, and the scanning commenced. The flowboard blipped in unison, and a readout rolled out of the flashing opening.

Taking the paper in hand, Hadigan grinned at Tanya. He whistled,

"That explains a lot."

"What?"

Holly ran to snatch the paper from his hand, and he held it over her, teasing her with it. She jumped and giggled at him. Tanya nearly gagged at her goofiness.

Hadigan dropped the page just enough for her to reach it, and she snatched it and read the text greedily.

"Oh my freaking Jove! We were right, we're not twelve." Holly stared at her sister.

"Thirteen." Tanya's automatic response precipitated her expectant wait.

"No, Tan, you're nineteen."

"Get the flip out of here." Tanya strode over and grabbed the paper to read for herself. I missed six years?"

"No." Hadigan sat looking like a Cheshire cat, all too pleased with himself. "You have absorbed six years at a more rapid pace than the average Trevel, or Bacht for that matter."

"Holy Zeus, I'm nineteen years old." Tanya considered a moment.

"Yeah, yeah, that's actually about right." She smiled and laughed.

Holly hugged her.

"We always knew, didn't we, Tan. I guess that makes me eighteen. Maybe?"

And with all the coincidence of the best of Dickensian novels, the flowboard blipped again and surrendered another readout to be snatched up by Hadigan. Holly tried to chase him down, but he jumped up onto the open counter space and stood there with the floating HDP forms of the girls hovering around and through his legs.

He read briefly then stopped and read more intensely.

"What?" Holly watched him. "What's wrong?"

"Holly, tell me how the dragon tear ceremony went," Hadigan interrogated her.

"We said our little pact and drank together. Why?"

"Can you replay it for me?"

Tanya and Holly looked at each other. It wasn't as if they'd forgotten the episode of some five years ago. They had just never been asked much about it before. That, and they'd never actually told anyone what the pact was all about, either.

He stepped off the counter and folded the paper into his pocket.

"I need to see it to maybe explain something."

The girls sensed the importance of the moment and dropped all other things aside to step into memory.

In their mind they were there again. They pantomimed the event with eyes closed, seeing within, the crater, the tea set, the blanket, and the red cloud…

> The girls set up their blanket and tea set right in the center.
>
> Tanya pulled a small red crystal bottle from her pocket and set it next to the teapot.
>
> "I've never stolen anything before."
>
> "I know. I've felt sick all afternoon."
>
> "Let's just do this." Tanya poured the clear, thick liquid into the pot.
>
> "Let me stir the dragon tears, you sing." Holly swirled the teapot around and around. Tanya sang gently,
>
> *"A dragon tear for you,*
>
> *A dragon tear for me,*
>
> *Will you ever see-*
>
> *Dragons come to tea?*
>
> *The song will rise above*
>
> *The new song down below,*
>
> *See the dragon come,*
>
> *See the dragon go."*

The girls paused a moment to let the atmosphere build, then Holly poured into Tanya's bright little sunflower teacup and Tanya poured into Holly's.

Together they raised the cups high and chanted,

"As much as the parents who live are ours, so also the parents who died are ours, and together we vow to destroy the one that took their life from us."

They drank.

There was a beat of silence back in the lab, and a look of horror flashed across Hadigan's face just before the two beautiful Trevel Terrors before him opened their eyes.

They took in a deep moment of oxygen and momentum. Holly tilted her head as she questioned her prince.

"Does that help?"

"More than you know."

He blinked slightly then, reached into his pocket and took the readout in his hand again.

"You see, from what I understand, and I have definitive access to an expert in such matters, dragon tears are an extremely heavy liquid. If they are still even for a second, their potency settles."

The girls looked confused.

"The moment you stopped swirling the pot, they began to settle, and as Tanya's portion was poured first, it came from the top of the liquid and Holly's portion came from the bottom... where the potency was stronger."

"What are you saying, Andrew?" Holly was lost. "I'm not eighteen?"

"Nay, my dear, you are twenty-three."

Last Night before School

A publication was circulated and an official announcement was put forward, from the king himself, declaring the scientific discovery of the actual physiochemical age of the Dijex sisters.

On pain of death, the girls were now to be addressed by all as the young women they were at the ripe ages of nineteen and twenty-three.

Tanya took it rather harshly that she was no longer the oldest. Holly couldn't apologize enough and so gave up, devoting herself to her precious prince. Tanya wondered why everything official had to be on pain of death.

Tyal was dismissed, as the girls were now both more than of age, and he left with a final warning.

"I've already told you that to walk around the palace alone will only attract the attentions of those looking to take advantage." He smoothed his suit coat as if remembering a past darkness. "Don't think that has changed. In fact, it's more a problem now than before. Don't be deceived into believing that being a full consenting adult means anyone will actually ask for your consent."

Then he stalked out of their lives without a farewell, nose in the air, as proud as ever.

The night before they departed to travel the last miles to school in the neighboring trade city of Atlantis, Holly descended her tower vine to the garden beneath, leaving Tanya alone.

Since her encounter with Prince Hadigan and her all-too-invasive introduction to Taliamaland, Tanya had been puzzled and confused by the stirring within her. The tiny cut had healed completely in the HDP tub, but occasionally, Tanya still felt the heat inside her hip, usually when the prince was near.

She managed to avoid his touch, and he stopped pushing the matter. In fact, he was completely ignoring her.

There was a knock at the door.

A young Primer in black and green stood holding a single orange rose out to her.

"What is that?" Tanya backed up with a hand on her hip.

The Primer bowed and said,

"It is a farewell gift from Prince Hadigan for you, Lady Tanya."

She didn't move but stared, horrified by the sight of the flower.

"He sends a note with it."

"I don't want it."

The Primer balked.

"I am commanded to give it you."

"I don't want it." She tried to close the door.

The Primer was too quick. He had his foot in the door.

"You will at least take the note." He pushed his arm through the door and pressed it into her hand.

She slammed the door on his retreat and threw the card on the floor.

She paced back and forth with her breath getting shallower and more rapid. Hands on hips, she bent over slightly to catch her breath and paused, spying the card by the corner of the door.

She snatched it off the floor and read it by the light of the burning fireplace.

"Is your first time out of the way yet?"

She growled and screamed in anger, ripping the page furiously and vehemently throwing it into the fire. Tanya wrenched open the door and stepped over the rose lying on the threshold. She stalked off into the corridors and dark places of the palace with her Hanain diamond glowing brightly through her top.

The rose turned brown and dissolved into ash. The dust of it blew off in the breezy hallway.

***   ***   ***

Holly alighted in the garden. This is where she always came to refresh and be with him. He openly loved her in the garden, though he remained a gentleman. Here she knew him best, not as Prince Hadigan, not as the grand Strategist Director, but as Andrew.

He was sitting with his journal, writing notes on his lovely Taliamaland. The rose shivered as Holly drew near.

"She misses you almost as much as she misses me." He smiled proudly and kissed her full on the lips.

Just with the acknowledgement of her full age, Holly had blossomed and was indeed a young woman of twenty-three.

"I can only hope to be able to produce something as beautiful and full of life as Tali." The rose wound through her hair and gave it a playful tug.

"I think you will do much more than I ever could, but very differently."

"Really?"

Andrew set about weeding and digging.

"Men and women function differently."

"Oh?" Holly set herself up to receive some teasing comment about being a mere woman.

"I'm not saying better or worse, just different." He dug the shovel deep into the earth, and Holly enjoyed the rippling effect of his strong, muscular physique.

"You see, men, like me, hone their focus like a laser. I have one major life work that I perfect. If I'm not working on it, I focus entirely on something else and perfect that. Men like to have one solid laser beam, focused, channeled, and unstoppable, like one point; direct and penetrating." He winked at her.

"Women, however, now there's a magnificent mystery; they are more radar focused."

Holly looked quizzical. He studied her.

"Look at you, right now, you sit there watching me, but I bet you can tell me which flowers are blooming on your right and how many inches the grass has grown, and how much time you have left until you need to go, and... who knows what else?"

She laughed.

"The hyacinths, bluebells, and wattle; three point two inches; forty-five minutes and... I love you."

He tossed the shovel aside and wrapped his arms around her in a passionate kiss. Pulling back slightly, he brushed her hair off her forehead and whispered,

"The radar focus with all things, always present, missing nothing. You enthrall me."

She kissed him this time, with every ounce of passion in her growing deeper, more intense.

He pulled back and gently pushed her away.

She was upset.

"Andrew?"

He walked back to his digging and delved into it vigorously.

She sighed, exasperated.

The silence of the garden was no longer one of peace, but rather the hush before a storm full of tension.

"Hadigan Andrew Hades Darsaldain..."

He grinned up at her.

"Now, I'm in trouble," he teased.

She continued and closed the distance between them.

"I am yours."

Holly's skin was tinted a slight olive, as it always was when she was in the height of passion.

"Why won't you just take me?"

His hand found her waist and pulled her into him. He breathed in her scent and lost himself in her taste for but a moment. In her ear, he whispered,

"Some things are worth the wait."

Her eyes glistened with disappointed tears.

"Have patience, my love." He kissed each eyelid.

"You will be my queen."

*** *** ***

There were nine of them, as was typical.

They stood smoking by the stone entrance to the clifftop. Tanya had found she was making her way up to the Parthenon with an urge to sit in the presence of Poseidon and Zeus. They greeted her as any retinue of bored militia would.

"Hey there, pretty lady."

"What are you doing up here all by your little lonesome?"

She barely grinned at their presence.

"No need to be so rude, love."

"We're here to take care of you."

Two stepped in front of the entrance and, with practiced ease, two stepped behind her.

Tanya considered being afraid, but something stirred inside and she actually felt enticed. "I have some prayers I would like to make to the gods. May I pass?"

"'May I pass?' Now, those are some lovely manners."

One behind her stepped in and fingered her hair. "I always like it when they ask first."

She smiled.

"What would you have me ask next?"

He crackled in electric energy and zapped her neck with his tongue.

"Ask me to shock you."

Tanya turned to face him full on.

"Please shock me… if you can…" She raised her eyebrow exactly as Tyal had taught her.

The sweaty oaf grabbed her head with both hands and planted his flabby lips on hers in a sloppy kiss, but then pulled back, choking, unable to breathe, with sand pouring from his mouth. He crashed to the ground unconscious.

Tanya daintily wiped her lips of sandy drool and looked at his mate, beckoning him with her lusty grin.

He flashed a watery whip around her waist and lasciviously sneered as he dragged her forward. He began leaning forward as the weight of the water rope in his hands became too much for his grasp, and he dropped it as a muddy sludge slowly slid down Tanya's legs.

She stepped out of it and kicked it at him. He fell, choked also with his own rope, thick with mud, strangling him.

In a flash, a fireball exploded before her eyes. She raised her arms in defense, and a swirl of thick dust wound round and round the fireball, smothering it and blasting it back into the Strategist's face, knocking him down.

Tanya's hair began swirling around her, blocking her vision, and she felt vines wrap around her body while at the same time an intense light focused on her eyes.

She closed her eyes and listened. The wind was coming from the left. Wind is always noisy.

The vines around her were tugging from the right, and she laughed as she remembered every tie-up game her sister constantly played on her.

The light, however, that was harder to place, except for the fact that it traveled in a straight line and was right in her eyes.

There was a loud thwack and sudden stillness.

Tanya stepped out of the slack vine and straightened her hair, surveying the three men lying with bloody heads beneath the large stone bricks protruding from the previously flat walls behind them.

She felt a cold shiver of metal run across the back of her neck, and a deep growl rumbled at her feet.

Yet still, one of them leaned against the wall watching as his last two mates circled her. She ignored the two and addressed the one.

"What's your preference, limestone or granite?"

"Shale."

He stood up and walked toward her as his mate with the great sword held her in place against the snarling body of the very real hyena poised to spring at her feet.

"Many underestimate that one as too flimsy, but I find that, if carved correctly, it holds a mighty sharp point."

He ran his grey dagger down her arm to prove this. It left a thin, faint scratch. Tanya didn't flinch.

With a sudden crack, a tall rock column rose up from the stone floor and caged the hyena, at the same time crunching its handler under the chin and knocking him unconscious.

Another solid black wall also rose up behind her, capturing the great sword blade in its tight grasp.

She turned to address the Metal Energist.

"I presume your name's not Arthur."

He grinned and gripped the sword hilt.

"That's just coal, love, not gonna do any good against me." He tried to pull his sword out, but then jumped back.

The coal was crushing down on the sword and getting clearer. With actual physical effort, Tanya clamped her hands together, and the blade was suddenly and permanently held by a massive diamond.

Whether it was his shock or his greed that got the better of him she could not tell, but either way, he never saw the tumble of rocks that fell from the ceiling and left him prostrate on the ground.

"Not bad," said the opposing Earthen. He inspected the great shiny rock. "Pity it is synthetic."

Tanya shrugged. "Short notice."

"I know who you are." He leaned up against the mighty diamond and ran his blade across his shirt sleeve. "I've actually been studying you. You really are quite the freak."

Tanya hated that word, and he knew it.

"So you've enjoyed the privileges of being the oldest all your life, but now your little sister, who not only stole the prince who should have chosen you, is also your senior by four years."

He pushed all the right buttons.

"That's gotta grate."

"And your point is?"

"My dear, you may be declared an adult now, but there is no substitute for experience."

"So what's stopping you from giving me some experience, now that I've weeded out the weak?"

With a sudden rush, he pushed Tanya against the wall and an iron loop enclosed her neck.

She grasped it with both hands.

He smirked at her.

"Weren't expecting that, were you? You see, some of us guards in the palace are bastard cut-offs of lonely kings. While this is no help socially, it can have its benefits."

He held his shale dagger blade against Tanya's breast. She watched it as threads of shiny steel grew down it and formed a sharp point at the end that dug into her skin.

He began untying his belt.

"I'm going to really enjoy this. Just consider me a substitute prince. We do have the same father, after all."

He suddenly stopped moving and a stunned look overtook his face. Tanya watched, unsure, as a small spot on his forehead began to glow. It got brighter and larger, then bam, a solid beam of light burst through his skull, splattering blood on her face as it hit the wall next to her head.

The last of the Energists slumped to the floor, very dead where the others were only unconscious.

Tanya stared open mouthed at Tyal, who stood with finger poised directly where the head of her captor had been.

He took his silk handkerchief from his breast pocket and wiped her face clean.

"Will you ever heed anything I taught you?" he mumbled.

"Keep your mouth closed, dear, you look like a blow fish." With the flash of his laser, he cut through the metal, and Tanya gasped for a deeper breath as she fell away from the wall.

"You killed him?"

"Well, yes, I did."

"Why? I mean, won't you get in trouble?"

"Let's just say, I've had the not so pleasant opportunity to meet these gentlemen, specifically the dual bastard, myself." Tanya grimaced at the thought. "And there is no trouble when there are no witnesses."

He aimed his laser finger at the encased hyena and fired one fatal shot.

Tanya whimpered.

Tyal took her hand and led her back to the tower. "Remember that 'almost anything goes here' applies only to royalty. If there's no royalty around, then it's just 'anything goes.'"

Tyal looked at the shocked girl as he dragged her off to safety and asked rudely,

"Aren't you a metal head too? Couldn't you sense that in him?"

Tanya just nodded her head in agreement but was too bewildered by the experience to respond clearly.

The Stables

Bonjour!

Marina's Match

Bowra House

Settling In

Chapter 17

The Stables

The Atlantis National Academy in the City of Atlantis was located below the Temple levels on the far northern slopes. Here the city spiral roads did not embrace the full circumference of the circle. They twisted back on themselves as the ANA compound was the only place where the boarders ran all the way down to the beach.

Tanya and Holly arrived rather unceremoniously at the Atlantis National Academy. The long black limousine dropped them off at the front gates, and the driver gave them strict instructions to go straight to the office of Principal Zanne while he took their luggage to their dorm rooms.

Naturally the girls had a variation of that plan. Tanya suggested they split up and sneak in separately so they could get a good look around before the hype of their Prince's Scholarship caught up with them.

Holly remained oblivious of Tanya's true intentions and agreed, making her way to the gymnasium, hoping to check out the defense floors.

Hadigan Andrew had encouraged her, even charged her, to learn all she could of Energy manipulation for defense purposes. He'd said it always gave him something to clear his mind when times were difficult.

Holly's sister had something else in mind.

Tanya breathed the thick air deeply. Wet hay smelled so good in the morning. She closed her eyes, drinking in the horsey smells of hay, oats, leather, and…

"Freeze!"

Tanya stopped her breathing and held her pose, mid-step, eyes still closed. Strong arms enclosed her, picking her up.

She could smell his scent of sweat and leather. Smiling, she snuggled into his arms and whispered,

"I miss that smell."

"Of road apples, miss?" A red headed boy of eighteen deposited her gently on the floor away from the pile of horse manure she was about to step into. "Keep your eyes open in the stable, miss, I wouldn't want to mess up those pretty little toes." The boy nodded to her heeled sandals that showed off her glittered toenail polish.

Tanya's eyes, wide open, stared at the boy.

"I'm sorry; I thought you were someone else."

"No kidding." He bent down and picked up the shovel that was leaning against the wall. "And I thought you'd gone and fallen in love with the smell of my sweat." He shoveled up the manure and tossed it into a wheelbarrow.

"What's going on here?"

"None of your Joving business, Bacht, shove off and let me entertain the little lost lady."

"Sorry, Jake, I don't mean intrude." Mitchell turned around 180 degrees, then paused just long enough to let Jake think he'd won. Then he turned back around and said,

"Of course… we could let the lady decide who she wants to show her around, just a thought." Mitchell suggested this because he knew of Jake's jealous and competitive nature and liked to bait him.

Jake, thinking he had the upper hand in the situation because he had already met the lady and saved her from a foot full of poo, agreed readily.

"No worries, Mitch," he sneered. Then, bowing mockingly to Tanya, he addressed her chivalrously. "My lady, which of us would you like to show you around?"

"Hi, Mitchell." Tanya ignored Jake, and smiled directly at her target.

"Hey, Tanya." Mitchell nodded and stepped forward, taking her hand he helped her maneuver her way through the "road apples" of horse manure on the floor.

"How was your trip since you left us at Torres?" Tanya inquired.

"Pretty much a nightmare, I'm sure you don't want to hear about it."

He tossed his head and threw a passing thought back at Jake. "Could you finish shoveling the manure? More students will be coming down to visit, and we don't want to see any more pretty little toes dirtied."

"Stuff you," snarled Jake as he went back to shoveling.

Mitchell guided Tanya into the staff break room next to the tack room in the center of the stables and shut and locked the door. Tanya threw herself into his arms. He grabbed her and firmly tossed her into a chair, then stalked to the opposite side of the room, making herbal teas for them both.

"What are you doing here?" he growled.

Shocked, she croaked,

"I came to see you."

"You shouldn't have."

"But you stopped writing, and I... What's wrong? Don't you love me anymore?" Shining water trickled down her cheek, for when she was really upset, Tanya's tears glistened with heavy minerals.

"You seem to have forgotten I said goodbye under that pier in Torres Entrance." He handed her a steaming cup. "That means we can't see each other until you graduate."

Realizing Mitch's ignorance of recent developments, Tanya left her cup on the table and sauntered over to the door on the far wall. Opening it she asked, "Is this your new tack room?" She walked in and through to the far door and turned, leaning up against it, locking it behind her back.

Mitchell followed her and closed the door behind him, glancing around nervously.

"You can't be here."

Tanya inhaled the leather smell. "That scent will always hold good memories of our first kiss."

"Your kiss. I didn't kiss you then, remember, you kissed me."

Casually Tanya slipped her cardigan off, exposing the bare shoulders of her strapped shirt. Mitchell, now standing three feet away leaning up against the mending bench, dropped his gaze to the floor and folded his arms across his chest.

"It's stuffy in here. How thick are these walls?"

"Solid." He grinned and nodded to an oddly placed drum kit amid the bridles. "Jake likes to practice in here where it doesn't bother the horses, or anyone else, for that matter. He kinda stinks at it."

Tanya raised an eyebrow and pulled herself off the door.

"Sound proofing? That's cool."

Mitch furrowed his brows and suddenly felt more uncomfortable.

"What do you want, Tanya? I thought we had an agreement."

"I believe the agreement was," she circled across him and leaned against the bench next to him, tilting back onto her elbows, "to steer clear of each other until I was older."

He couldn't stop himself. His view was too clear across her low-cut top. He swallowed and didn't move for fear of doing something he'd regret. He mentioned hoarsely, "Which we agreed to only a month ago."

She turned to him and "accidentally" brushed against his arm.

"You haven't heard?"

He was transfixed.

"It's not like I get a direct link to the universe in here."

Tanya smiled, and an odd, familiar throb beat in her hip. She tried to ignore it, but it compelled her forward.

"We did some tests at the palace." She flipped her hair back. "It would seem Holly and I had quite the reaction to those dragon tears five years ago."

"How so?" He did his best to maintain a calm exterior, quite the opposite of what was going on within.

Tanya developed a slight itch on her neck that slowly travelled in a downward motion. She scratched it.

"Well, dragon tears enhance and transform the physiochemical systems of your most basic makeup." She looked up at him, leaning in to make sure he was paying attention. "Make sense?"

He just nodded, not taking his eyes off her.

"These tests we did proved that not only our mental development and Energy abilities were enhanced, but that indeed our age was progressed as well."

Mitch straightened slightly.

"So the official word from the Royal Palace of Lemuria is that I am no longer thirteen, nor am I to be considered as such by anyone."

She ran a finger under the edge of his short sleeve and pulled on the tightness of it against his oversized biceps.

"How old are you, then?" He was still immobile.

"Funnily enough, I'm nineteen, which makes me a year older than you."

That was all he needed to hear. His arms were instantly around her, lifting her onto the bench behind her. As he lifted her, his hand gripped her hip and she gasped. A look entered her eyes that he'd never seen before, and she pounced on him. He was very grateful for locked doors in a soundproof room. She was passionately wild.

Bonjour!

The gymnastics building was six stories tall with a glassed-in ceiling for the fifth and sixth floors, which in essence were one floor.

It was the indoor Laray training track; thus, it required the two floors to hold the quintessential cross-country track field for the Laray racers to train their rides — being live, trained sting-rays — and practice their skills on.

Going down, respectively, the fourth floor was for such games that even the Bacht enjoyed, like basketball, volleyball, racquetball, and indoor cricket.

There was also a section for cardio and weight training, which was rarely used except by the Bacht familied Trevels. The third floor was the defense floor, where all the martial energy training took place.

The second floor was a myriad of theory classrooms, and the first floor consisted of offices and a large gathering lobby for glittering receptions whenever there was defense recognition within the school — for example, at the end of the year when the first years received their first weaponry hilts and discovered what their weapon of choice would be. A great family ceremony was held that was both delightful and embarrassing all at once.

Next to the gymnasium was the Energies extension, a circular tower of nine floors with one floor for each of the energies, starting with the heaviest at the bottom and ending at the top with the lightest: Metal, Earth, Flora, Fauna, Water, Fire, Air, Electricity, and Illumination.

Despite the plant Energy floor's strong call, Holly decided on exploring the defense floor first, so off she went to the third floor of the gym.

She climbed the steps quietly amid the random students. Most seventh graders were going through registration processing and finding their rooms or being escorted around campus by eleventh graders who were showing them off proudly; precisely what the girls did not want.

However, as Holly really did appear to be twenty-three years old, no one bothered her, a benefit she thoroughly enjoyed.

There was a small group of girls gathered around a topless, tall, black-skinned boy whom Holly recognized immediately. Ham, the oldest of the Stilwell triplets, was showing off his prowess with his wooden practice hilt. Another young girl was trying to imitate him with a water sword and giggling hideously.

Holly stood by the school's rack of practice hilts and watched. The practice hilts were available to anyone who did not have his or her own personal weapon hilt, particularly the seventh graders. Each hilt held just enough of each of the nine Energies to be worthy of a practice weapon.

A Trevel would grasp the hilt and transfer Energy through it to create a weapon like a sword, whip, mace, or such. If they were metal Energists, then the metal was usually not sharp enough to cut, due to the lack of power within the hilt itself.

As Holly watched skeptically, Ham looped his arms around the water girl to show her how to hold and swing her weapon at the wooden combat dummy.

"Now you try," he encouraged her.

When she hit the dummy, the sword exploded like a water balloon and the group of girls squealed, splattered in water.

"You need to focus, Jordan. That's the only way it will stay solid."

Ham was trying not to allow his frustration to show through his voice.

Jordan just giggled.

They tried again, but this time as well as being sprayed in water, from the next combat dummy over, they were sprayed by a soft shower of daisy petals.

They all spun around and saw Holly staring at a splintered wooden sword hilt.

"Dark Persephone! Sorry, I still can't stop the swords from shattering." She shrugged vaguely apologetic shoulders.

"Argh!" Jordan yelled in anger and rubbed her hands over Ham's naked chest and arms.

"You could have really hurt us!" To the bare-chested boy, she asked,

"Are there any splinters?"

"Holly, right?" Ham brushed the girl off. He obviously recognized Holly just as she had recognized him.

"That sword shattered and you caught every splinter turning it into a petal?"

Shrugging, Holly smiled and replied,

"That's the easy part. Stopping the stupid sword from shattering — that's the hard part."

"What wood are you using?" Ham took her hand with the hilt in it and inspected the weapon.

The group of girls giggled and Ham rolled his eyes. Holly raised her eyebrows and extended an intricate maple sword carved in the fluid hieroglyphics of her Amazonian home.

"That's your problem right there." He took the handle of the rounded sword firmly, then snapped it over his knee. "You're using maple. It's too soft." He snorted quietly. "Typical of a girl, you're going for looks over practicality. You need to use something stronger like oak or, even better…" He pulled out his own hilt and extended a dark grey sword. "Deadwood. Here, feel this."

He held the hilt in his hand so the sword wouldn't disappear but let Holly feel the weight of it.

"But it's dead?" Holly was rather repulsed. "And I thought you were metal?"

"I'm a dualist, metal and flora. Japheth is metal and earth. Shem is metal and fire." He winked at her.

"But the deadwood is petrified, and is therefore much stronger than your flimsy maple." To prove it, he swung back and, with all his muscular advantage, slashed his sword through the wooden practice dummy which itself disintegrated under the pressure of such might.

Everyone ducked, and Holly put out both hands, immediately turning the splatter of foreboding splinters into a fragrant shower of daisies.

"I knew you were going to do that," he said, leaning on his deadwood sword with a devilish grin.

Jordan, the girl Ham had been trying to teach earlier, stalked over and kicked the sword out from under him. He stumbled and snickered, recognizing the jealousy.

Brushing his fingers through his dark, sweaty hair, he introduced her to Holly.

"Holly, this is my girlfriend Jordan Conception."

"Bonjour," smiled Jordan

"Bonjour," replied Holly smoothly.

"Oh? Parlez-vous français?" queried Jordan.

Holly looked puzzled and replied, "Je ne parle pas français."

Jordan continued in French,

"If you don't speak French, then how is it you are speaking perfectly in my language and understanding me so clearly?"

Holly replied in perfect French,

"I don't know what you're talking about."

Turning to Ham, Holly spoke in clear English,

"What's she talking about?"

Ham laughed and looked at Jordan, who was furious at being mocked in such a manner. For if it was truly known... Jordan Conception had been born and raised by a French mother in Under Frisco.

Although she had holidayed in France and Underland Par for three weeks before attending ANA her first year, she was actually as American as apple pie.

Ham explained to Holly, "You're speaking French beautifully—better than me, and I've had a tutor all my life."

"I do not like being mocked," hissed Jordan in her best French accent.

"I don't speak French. Jove! I am speaking French? When did I learn French? I need to tell Tanya."

Marina's Match

As the Tube pulled into Hanain Station, Marina pulled herself together despite her humiliation. She had determined that for whatever reason, she had been sent to Hanain strategically. She would not only make the best of her situation but make her own way here. After all, Hanain was most infamous for those who came to seek their fortune by whatever means possible. She would use every resource she could find.

The door of the High Set carriage swung upward and her ears were met with a musical blast, and fireworks with waterworks exploded in her vision. Nearly all of Hanain was crammed onto the station and surrounding platforms.

At first, Marina glanced around to see what all the fuss was about. Then a bulky soldier in the tunic of Lord Deagan's Militia stepped forward and saluted her.

"Champion Tambeaux, Hanain salutes you."

The fuss was all for her?

She cleared her throat and saluted back but remained silent, taking in all the splendor that had spared no expense.

The Hanain Militia lined the path and held back the jostling crowd, who were all waving Hanain flags with the symbol of Lord Deagan, a bull Viking helmet on a tan background. Some even had homemade banners proclaiming welcomes to the new royal ambassador. Marina was stunned but maintained a cool demeanor. She was, after all, an Ice Queen.

An exquisite white and gold fainting couch shone, terrifyingly feminine, in the morning sun. It sported golden rings on the legs with large, thick poles lying through them. Marina was horrified as the guard directed her toward it. It would seem she was supposed to sit upon it and be hoisted upon the shoulders of the massive Strategists waiting to carry her up to the palace.

It then occurred to her that the members of Lord Deagan's Militia had received an upgrade. No longer were there any scrawny misfits fumbling with weapons they knew nothing about.

Each Strategist was of massive form, with obvious confidence in manner.

Marina was so shocked by all she took in that she barely noticed herself sitting on the couch and being borne up to the great gates in style befitting only a royal concubine.

Through the gates, the gardens and lavish splendor of the new downtown Hanain shone in completion. Even the finished sphinx glared down at her, full bodied and ferocious.

How Lord Deagan had managed to complete his Empire in a few short weeks baffled Marina, and she began to see the importance of the position she was to fill. Someone had to keep an eye on Lord Deagan. He seemed to have unlimited resources and limitless gall to do whatever he wanted.

When they reached the palace gates, the crowd was left outside and the Strategists deposited her in a spacious, empty hallway.

"Lord Deagan will attend to you momentarily." The hulking guard saluted and the retinue exited in backward steps, bowing.

The hush of the quiet hallway was broken only by a trill of birdsong. At the far end of the hall was a lorikeet in a gilded cage. It whistled to her.

Lord Deagan entered from another door on the right of Marina. He was still wearing his bull Viking helm.

The down-pointed spikes over the eyes hid all but a glint of life behind them. The massive jawline was punctuated by a thin slit that formed an open mouthpiece in the center of the biil-faced helm. His blond dreadlocks cascaded down his back, all but covering the cloak of a Strategist Director of unknown Energy. Marina remembered his display of at least five energies and thought her brother wise to assume he could access all nine.

He bowed on bended knee.

"My Lady, Champion Tambeaux, Royal Ambassador to Hanain, it is my privilege to welcome you to my world."

He took her hand and touched the forehead of his metallic Viking helmet to it. He then rose and walked to one of the massive knee-to ceiling windows and gestured out of it.

"All I have is at your disposal. Should you need anything, please do not hesitate to ask."

She remained silent and followed his hand out the window to survey the grandeur of his kingdom. It was somewhat daunting.

"You are welcome here, and this room is our neutral ground."

She looked quizzically at him.

He gestured again to the door she'd been carried in through.

"Those doors lead to my throne room, the conference rooms, and places of Strategic leadership." He then gestured to the doors he'd entered through. "Those doors lead to my private chambers."

Then he guided her eyes to the door at the far end of the corridor by the lorikeet's cage.

"Those doors lead to your private and personal chambers, into which I, or anyone else, will never step foot without your direct invitation."

Marina began to wander toward her exit.

He called after her.

"Again, if you have need of anything, please do not hesitate to ask."

Marina stopped a moment and finally spoke.

"There is one thing,"

He was attentive. "Anything..."

"My entrance... the couch... the parade... I can't figure out if I was brought to you as a concubine for your bed, or a suckling pig for your table."

She could hear him smile behind the pointed spikes of his helmet.

"That, my dear, is entirely up to you." He saluted, bowed, and swept out of the hall into the public rooms whence she had entered.

Bowra House

"Did you know we speak French?" Holly bustled through a busy open air corridor of new students looking for rooms and showing families around. She talked excitedly to Tanya on her new HDP mobell phone.

"Not sure what you're getting at, Hols." Tanya answered on her phone and made her way toward Holly through the same crowd. Both were getting buffeted well and good.

The mobell phones the girls were using were standard issue of their not-so-standard Prince's Scholarship. They looked like key rings when not in use, resembling a fair-sized coin shape of HDP that the user could poke and pull out into the shape of a horn.

This horn part settled in the ear hole and curled around the ear to hold itself in place. The narrow end pulled further down the jawline for a mouthpiece.

When dialing, the tip of the narrow section was tapped and a circular list of numbers appeared to be tapped in succession to request the appropriate number.

"I just met a French girl and out of the blue, I promise, out of the blue, I start speaking French right along with her. I didn't even know I was doing it."

Holly was sitting in the sun on a wooden bench by the agriculture building explaining all this when Tanya whispered into the phone,

"Freak. Duck!"

Trusting her sister's instinct and being casual about it, Holly leaned over and wiped the grass off her shoes.

She asked,

"You see the principal?"

Tanya was across the courtyard, hidden by a group of Haryss house members battling each other with tiny tornados.

This may have seemed like a good hiding place for an expert like Tanya or Holly, but regular students who are learning to use their skills... not so good a spot.

"Yeah, the principal is walking across the center gazebo, looks like she's looking for someone." Tanya dropped her hand down to hold her skirt, which was beginning to flap wildly in the blowing of the tornado battle.

Holly glanced through the fringe of her hair and then over in the direction of the gazebo. She followed the line of Principal Zanne's gaze and hissed into the phone again.

"You'd better move, or it's too late for us."

Instantly, a fireball landed at Tanya's feet, bounced, there and then whipped across the yard to swing around Holly's waist.

Principal Zanne collected both girls onto the gazebo with her fireball and scolded them.

"You girls are expected at Bowra House. No more skipping out on your Prince's Scholarship duties."

"But..." the two young women rebutted with no effect.

"No 'buts.' You are expected, staff of the house has been called out to meet you. You're the only seventh graders allowed to live in the house, so take this privilege seriously."

"Where do all the other seventh graders live?" Holly questioned the principal while dodging through the crowd, trying to keep up with the column of fire that lead the way.

"All the seventh and eighth graders live in Heart Tower above the dining room. The ninth through twelfth graders live in their specific collegiate houses."

The Principal lead the two girls across the campus toward the Ziggurat Hill where the four collegiate houses sat. As she walked briskly, she gave a proud description of Heart Tower.

"Heart Tower is a residence hall style of living as opposed to a dormitory style, where each two rooms share a private bathroom forming a suite. Each suite has four students, and the bathroom has two sinks and one shower and a water closet."

The Principal continued bustling the girls through the crowd to the beat of her recitation.

"Heart Tower consists of two actual towers — one for male and one for female students — with a large common room on each floor and six suites: four students per suite, built on ten floors."

Holly and Tanya absorbed it all as they stared wide-eyed at the elaborate structure they marched passed.

Principal Zanne detailed,

"Thus, there is room for 480 seventh and eighth graders. To supervise these students, each floor has a single room with private bath for a staff member. There is also a laundry and vending room on each floor."

Principal Zanne turned and gestured to the grand tower, now behind them.

"The unique aspect of Heart Tower is its shape, as each of the towers makes up the shape of the Atlantis National

Academy symbol, the Heart's Eye. The towers are joined in the basement, where there is a common dining area open for all students."

"Where do we fit in?" Tanya squeezed up to Principal Zanne and reached out to touch the fire column leading their way through the crowded grounds.

A hand of fire formed in the column and slapped her hand smartly. Tanya withdrew her hand quickly, shaking it and sucking on it.

"There is a VIP room in each collegiate house. You and Holly get this room in Bowra House."

The girls looked at each other dubiously. What would the other members of Bowra House think of them camping in the VIP room?

Tanya whispered to Holly,

"So much for quietly sneaking into the social life here."

Principal Zanne stepped down the steps outside of the Collegiate Ziggurat Hill and simply stated,

"There will be no sneaking around for either of you." She stopped mid-step and turned to face the girls.

"Everyone is excited to see you, and the next couple of weeks will be rather grand for you. Just be aware that all fads die fast."

The principal raised their chins with her hands. She looked like a super Trevel with the fire behind her, imposing and terribly beautiful. But as the two looked into her eyes, they saw the compassion.

"I just hope your maturity will show through when the novelty runs out." She smiled at them, linked her arms around their waists, and smoothly walked them down the last few steps of Ziggurat Hill and the collegiate houses.

All four houses were grand homes built upon the top of a massive low-lying ziggurat. There was a great moat between the ziggurat and the level ground, which functioned as a sunken courtyard.

Steps leading down into the moat provided an entrance to the courtyard that was hidden under wooden arches covered in vines and plants of many kinds.

To walk through the sunken moat was to enjoy a ceiling of flowers with all the Energies of the world existing in harmony.

Waterfalls lit by flame torches chuckled under electric Jacob's ladders, (two metal rods with bright electric charges running up between them), zapped around metallic statues. The stone floor was carved, and tiny woodland creatures—squirrels, chipmunks, and rabbits—rustled around in the leaves. Light streamed down through the vines in diagonal beams as wind chimes tinkled in melodious charm.

Each of the houses sat atop Ziggurat hill like a Mayan temple overlooking the courtyard on one side and the zoology stables at the other side on the east end of the school, south of Heart Tower.

On Ziggurat Hill, the ninth through twelfth graders lived in great luxury. They shared two students per room with a private bathroom.

The house was rectangular, with an entry hall in front on the west side. The house staff rooms resided above the entry hall. Each wing was lined with the private rooms — men on the north side, women on the south. The east side consisted of a large common room and practice floors above it.

In the center of each house was an open-air central garden with both a pool and grass croquet lawn. There were ten rooms per wing, a large dinning/ballroom in the basement, five floors, and a small attic over the practice rooms for VIPs.

Each house had room for 400 students, times four houses. That is 1,200 ninth through twelfth graders, plus 480 seventh and eighth graders, equals a total standing of 1,680 ANA students, not including the small number of students who lived off campus. Thus, it was the largest and still most exclusive high school in all of Trevellia.

Every one of those students anticipated Holly and Tanya's arrival in her or his own way. So when Principal Zanne walked the two girls through the densely populated sunken courtyard, all eyes were on them.

Even the squirrels, chipmunks, and rabbits seemed to stop skittering around in the leaves, and there was a rather awkward pause in birdsong.

Principal Zanne slightly squeezed the girls' waists and whispered,

"Continue, continue, continue."

Settling In

The staff of Bowra House lined the grand steps leading up to the veranda. Tanya and Holly were required to shake hands with each one and were painfully aware of the occupants of both Bowra and the three other houses scrutinizing them from every vantage window above and along the top of Ziggurat Hill.

They smiled at the snooty house captains and prefects, who showed no sign of acceptance.

Principal Zanne escorted them up to the VIP rooms and helped them settle in. She sat, rather casually, on the end of Holly's bed, smiling in secret solidarity with them,

"I don't envy you. Change is a process."

The girls continued rummaging through their already packed drawers and closets looking for personal items.

"Most new students take a couple of weeks to adjust to the bustle of a school's schedule. But you two have to adjust to a new age, new school, and new pressures of popularity and expectations not asked for."

Tanya shrugged.

"We've always known we were older than our chronology. It's a relief to finally have everyone else acknowledge it."

Holly chimed in,

"Besides, we have good support in high places."

She smiled, remembering her royal suitor.

"It is a weighty thing to be favored by royalty and rarely turns out how you expect." The principal ran a tiny fireball through her fingers distractedly.

Tanya couldn't help but allow a grunt of sarcastic acknowledgement to escape her lungs. She scratched her hip without thinking about it.

Principal Zanne noted this in the corner of her eye.

Holly flopped on her bed happily.

"I know! I'd been warned that the prince might take an interest in me, but I never expected him to be so grand and kind."

"He is a charmer." Principal Verity Zanne smiled with a knowing grin.

Holly sat beside her.

"You weren't principal while he was here, were you?"

"No, I was deputy principal, which meant I was in charge of student discipline—or, as we prefer to call it, student redirection of Energy."

"Andrew needed a lot of 'redirection,' did he?" Holly coyly questioned while Tanya gave a "no kidding" eye roll behind her back.

"Prince Hadigan was a shining example of exemplary behavior. Unfortunately for most of his companions, however, a lot happened around him, and although nothing was ever proved in all his six years here, whenever something went wrong or mischief erupted, Hadigan's presence was always… felt."

"But nothing was proved?"

"If I were to give a summation of our prince's personality strengths, I would say he was an excellent delegator."

Tanya spoke from the bathroom out of their sight.

"You think he got others to do his dirty work for him?"

Principal Zanne laughed. "I know he did, but I could never prove it. His followers are decidedly loyal."

"Seriously?" Holly was skeptical.

From the bathroom again, Tanya asked,

"How do you think he gained their loyalty?"

Principal Zanne admitted,

"Other than being a charmer, I have no idea." She stood to leave. "It was almost as if he could exercise his influence over anyone he wanted."

Holly was ever defending.

"Well you seem to have escaped his 'poisonous' touch." The young girl used the two-finger quotation gesture and scoffed at the thought of her prince being negative in any way.

Verity Zanne dropped her head slightly.

"What makes you think that?" She changed the subject. "Don't be late for class, eat and rest for overall health, and exercise both mind and body. These are the keys to good success here." She stepped out the now open doorway. "And be not deceived, I have never known Hadigan Andrew to do anything that didn't give a greater advantage to himself."

Holly flopped back onto her bed and looked at the little HDP image she had of her prince sitting on her bed head.

"I don't care what she thinks. You can have all the influence you want over me." She smiled as the little translucent blue Hadigan blew her a kiss.

Tanya stood before the mirror and looked at herself. A quiet tear dribbled over her eyelid. She brushed it away, shook her head, and surveyed her outfit.

Running her hands down her full figure, they paused on her hip. She lifted her hand and undid a couple of buttons on her shirt, exposing a more buxom view of her figure than usual. She smiled a lascivious grin and, straightening up and putting her shoulders back, walked out of the bathroom.

Holly was reading on her bed and didn't look at her sister.

"You never said where you were before the Zanne found us."

"Oh, I popped down to see if Mitch was settled, like I said I would."

"Figures. How is he?"

Tanya took off her jeans and stepped into a form-fitting miniskirt.

"He seems to have found a place to fit in." Fluffing her hair out, she added, "I feel the need to expend some more energy. I think I'll head down to the gym extension."

"'K." Holly continued ignoring the new appearance her sister was expressing.

Tanya walked down to the central open ground of Bowra House. Stepping outside, she stopped an avid game of water polo among some of the young boys of the house and caused a near commotion, parting the crowd of young Strategists kicking a small HDP hacky sack around.

She smiled to herself and continued parading through the school grounds, counting every eye that turned to appreciate her passing.

Lord Deagan Revealed

Mail Call

Courtesan Court Case

Engineering vs. Mutation

A Shock

The Defense Secretary's Secret

Chapter 18

Lord Deagan Revealed

Marina was up before dawn, bribing the palace staff to let her know the regular and irregularly scheduled movements of Lord Deagan. She knew her assignment as royal ambassador was a position with no precedent, and she was determined to establish her power immediately.

Lord Deagan ate his breakfast alone on a terrace overlooking a private section of the Hanain coastline. Marina found a clifftop overlooking the same sight and seized the moment to attract his attention.

She stripped down to a moderately attractive bikini that left as much to the imagination as was exposed and dove off the cliff in a spectacular display of form and precision.

He was watching.

She swam through the surf and casually walked out onto the beach before him. The Skyling glowed in the early morning behind her, leaving him blinded by only a little more than its rays.

She didn't realize at first, as she was so focused on presenting him with a good show, that she nearly balked openly when she saw he was sans armor.

There was a reason he wore a bull Viking helm.

Pulling together all the interrogation and psychology training she'd ever had, Marina relaxed as if it were the most natural thing in all the world to come upon a Minotaur snacking on a fruit-and-pork breakfast platter and sipping sparkling water.

She strolled up the beach toward him under his direct and intense eye. He didn't move but watched her every chitton-based atom flicker through her body.

She stood at his side and raised his glass of water to her lips. She blew into it, forming ice cubes, and sipped the cool refreshment. She handed it back to him wordlessly.

He took it, and she actually scratched under his furry chin. As she retreated through the palace back to her quarters, Lord Deagan the Minotaur smiled to himself and continued snacking.

Her staff was waiting in the neutral hallway, and as she donned a heavy robe and dried off with a thick towel, Marina found herself accosted by the Militant Guard who had met her at the station the day before.

"Lord Deagan requests your presence at Court today at II/2:00, being 9:45 a.m. Bacht time."

"Anything of particular interest this morning?"

The military man smirked.

"One of the courtesans is on trial for theft."

"I see."

Marina walked back to her lorikeet-guarded doorway, but not before she heard the soldier mutter,

"You will indeed see, little miss, that you will."

Mail Call

Instead of heading down to the gym extension, Tanya headed over to the common rooms below Heart Tower.

Principal Zanne had been right. It was a process to adjust to her "new" age. Tanya had always known in her heart that she was older than thirteen but was in the habit of allowing others to treat her as such, and in the habit of associating with others that age. So it was only natural that she felt an inclination to seek out a younger crowd.

Tanya entered the seventh- and eighth-grade common area and found it full of all ages. In fact, it looked like the lobby of Heart Tower was the place to be seen.

Seen she was.

Many heads turned her way. The sneers of the High Set girls, obviously well tutored in the ways Tyal had tried to pass on to her, made Tanya feel distinctly ill. This feeling, however, was complemented by the pulsing of excitement that rushed through her as she saw how many of the boys stared openly at her.

An excited squeal caught her attention.

"Oh my triple-threat Trident! Is that the new Sassy-Rose miniskirt from the autumn line?"

A gorgeous and full-figured young man in ANA uniform came rushing at her from behind a half door in the wall. He looked as if his bloodline was a combination of Indian and Arabic and was, in Tanya's appreciation, as hot as his homeland was.

Tanya couldn't help but giggle a little in her backward jungle-girl surprise as she noticed that complementing his uniform were the colors of his eyeliner and sparkly earrings he wore all the way up both earlobes.

He circled her, clapping.

"It is!" he yelled back through the half door that looked like it led to a mail room, set in a wall of post boxes.

"Misty, you have got to see this!"

Two more heads popped over the half-doorway. One was a shock of pink and purple pigtails sticking up all over; the other was just as shocking in white blond and straight to the shoulders.

"Nu-ahhh!" The pigtailed girl looked scandalized. The blond just looked wide-eyed and... blond.

The door flung open and an Irish accent spoke out in discord with the rainbow hairdo.

"I know you aren't wearing a Sassy-Rose and a Calvin Klein in the same outfit, girl!"

"Excuse me?" Tanya looked baffled.

"I can't believe you're wearing a Calvin Klein at all, here in this place." The blond ran her fingers to the back of Tanya's shirt and checked the label.

Tanya still looked entirely too confused.

The boy sighed,

"Oh, look sweeties; she doesn't even know her crime." He patted her on the head like a lost puppy. "Wearing Bacht fashion is one thing; wearing Bacht fashion at ANA requires either total ignorance or complete gall. Either way, I love it."

"Not to mention matching it with the hottest Trevel designer this side of... anywhere." Pigtails put her arm around the boy. "You know what we're going to have to do, don't you?"

He looked from his girl back to Tanya a few times.

"There's nothing to be done. We simply must take her in." He saluted her in the typical Trevel style. "I am Joshun. These delicious gurlies are Misty and Breezer."

The two girls saluted in kind.

"It's a good thing you met us. We'll take care of you."

"If you want to be taken care of by the trash of the school."

Shem Stillwell stood a little way off, surrounded by an adoring crowd.

"You'd be better off allowing a stable boy to take you." Tanya smiled at the secret irony. "Well, I do prefer a horse to an ass."

The crowd gathered in a combination of admiring oohs and scandalized aahs.

Shem Stillwell rose to the challenge.

"Then it looks like my ass is one you'll be seeing a lot of." He walked passed her. "Feel free to kiss it as I go by."

He continued walking toward the door.

"No thanks, I'd rather watch the door slap it as you leave."

A sudden wind blew up and did just that as he walked out. He slammed the door open again and glared at the blond.

"Careful, Breezer, I wouldn't let too much air out of your head, it'll implode with the vacuum." He slammed the door himself to avoid the blob of molten lava aimed at his head. As the lava dribbled down the door, catching the paint on fire, Joshun doused it with water from his own fingers.

"Misty, you really need to learn how to get revenge without staining the paintwork."

"He just makes my blood boil." The brilliant pigtails shook violently.

"Ignore him," Joshun comforted her. "He is, after all, just a jackass, right Tanya?"

Tanya smiled then looked quizzical again.

"You know my name?"

"Lordy, gurl, where've you been all your life?" Joshun clapped his hand over his heart and Breezer suddenly disappeared behind the half door again.

Misty whipped her arm around her waist.

"We work in the mail room and have access to all the latest magazines... You've been on the cover of the last four Teen Trevel issues alone."

"Speaking of mail..." Breezer came back with a package in her hand. "This came for you yesterday."

Tanya took the package and saw Professor Mawkes's handwriting with the return address of Jaack Mining Company, Hanain.

"Thanks. I've been waiting for this."

The three looked at her expectantly.

"It was nice to meet you." Tanya smiled at them and casually popped the package under her arm and turned to leave. As she walked off, the three looked a little disappointed. Tanya paused and turned back to them. "Where can you eat a meal with friends not in your school house around here?"

Joshun pointed to the ground.

"Below, in Heart Tower dining hall. It's the only place everyone can meet in peace."

"What time to do you guys eat?" Tanya looked slightly sheepish as she invited herself.

Misty smiled big. "We'll meet you in the ziggurat courtyard at V/1:00."

"You guys don't live here?" Tanya had presumed her new friends were younger.

"Nah, we're in ninth grade." Misty pointed to herself and Joshun.

Breezer waved.

"Tenth grade."

"Grand. V/1:00 it is."

Thus, much satisfied with her new friends, Tanya took her package back to Bowra House.

Courtesan Court Case

When Marina was escorted into the courtroom, Lord Deagan was again a vision of masculine splendor in his mighty armor, massive helm, and dripping blond dreadlocks.

Marina wondered how uncomfortable his boots must be, but rethought that perhaps hooves had no feeling in them except for the deep center, so massive false boots were probably not painful at all.

She was seated at his right on a level just below his own throne. There was no jury, only a typical peanut gallery that consisted of drama addicts, journalists, and what appeared to be family and friends of the accused.

The walls were sprinkled with guards, and the massive cathedral-style colored windows smattered everyone's faces with odd stripes of yellow, blue, green, red, and black.

The accused was practically dragged into this circus by the familiar militant man, who seemed to believe he was the ringmaster.

She was a beautiful young redhead of Gypsy blood. Jangling gold was roped around her hips, ankles, wrists, neck, fingers, and toes. Her hair was barely pulled back under her silk scarf, and although it was obvious she'd spent the night in a filthy dungeon cell, her glamour and familiarity with luxury were evident in her style and carriage.

The militant tossed her onto the floor before Lord Deagan, who asked,

"Her charges?"

"This courtesan," the militant raised his voice to fill the whole circus space, "this woman," he used the word as if it were a disease, "has enjoyed the generosity and kindness of our good Lord Deagan for over half a year now, and how does she repay you, my Lord?"

He bent down and hissed at her,

"She takes what is not hers. She is a thief and must be punished to teach her, and all others like her, a lesson in humility."

Lord Deagan surveyed the woman who sat fearfully before him. He noted she had more poise than most would in her present circumstances.

"The evidence?" he questioned her accuser.

With sweeping grandeur, the militant revealed a necklace of heavy glittering beads and shining silver.

"This was found under the woman's bed two nights after it was reported stolen by one of the upstanding citizens of this great city."

Marina sputtered a small chuckle.

The militant spat at her,

"Do you find something amusing in thievery?"

Marina shifted in her seat.

"Not particularly, but if any of the citizens of this great city are upstanding, I'm a fire-breathing dragon."

"Treachery!" The militant pointed at her with a dramatic finger.

"How dare you despoil our Lord Deagan's great creation with such despicable slander?"

Marina turned to Lord Deagan and asked,

"Is he for real?"

Lord Deagan nodded.

"I sense you have your own interpretation of these accusations?"

"I do, my lord, if you would allow me?"

Lord Deagan waved the floor open to her.

"By all means."

Marina rose from her chair and stepped down between the courtesan and the militant.

"It is obvious by the look on this young girl's face that she distains her accuser."

The girl spat at him on cue.

"It is also obvious that Mr. Militant here wants nothing more than to have her for his own." The soldier looked disgusted but couldn't help ogling the young Gypsy.

"I believe that this young girl's only crime is to have turned down the attentions of her accuser."

"Do you accuse me, the Chief of Lord Deagan's Guard, of lying?" the militant snarled.

"I'm surprised that such a thought should surprise you when, after all, you are accusing me, the royal ambassador, of slander."

"And what of the evidence?" He shoved the shining silver necklace into Marina's face.

"Yes, well, that's rather obvious, too." Marina took the necklace and walked nearer the girl, who shrank slightly from its presence.

"Look at her, soldier. What do you see?"

"I see a slut who doesn't know what's good for her." He dropped his pretense slightly.

"Take a closer look — at what she's wearing, not what you're trying to see underneath…"

One of the other guards unconsciously verbalized his realization.

"You there," Marina pointed to the ahh-ing young guard. "What do you see?"

The guard covered his open mouth and looked, terrified, at his commanding officer.

"It's okay," Marina assured him. "We're in a court of law. The only thing you need fear is untruth." She glanced at the militant accuser. "Am I right?"

He grimaced.

"What do you notice about our young supposed thief?" Marina questioned the young guard.

"She's not wearing silver."

Marina smiled.

"Indeed she is not. In fact, nearly her entire body is covered in gold."

Marina reached into the depths of her tom-boy demeanor and spoke like any woman might when faced with a style faux pas.

"Everyone knows that silver clashes with gold. In fact, I wouldn't even be surprised if a Gypsy girl, with as mysterious an ancestry as Gypsies have, is not even, shall we say, 'allergic' to silver?"

With a relieved look of mutual understanding, the young Gypsy threw herself at Marina's feet.

"I beg you have mercy on me. You truly are a seer. I will give you the loyalty of my whole family, only please save me."

The militant began applauding slowly.

"Do you believe that such evidence will stand for even a moment in this court?"

Marina rested her hand on the girl's head.

"No, actually, I don't. But your dramatics are beginning to bore me."

Marina raised her hand and sent a shock of ice spray over the militant and froze him solid. Then she lifted the girl to her feet and whispered to her,

"Don't fear, you are not on trial here. I am."

Marina then, with all her power, kicked backward and smashed the soldier into a shattering of ice all over the floor that shot shards of cold, hard rock all the way up to Lord Deagan's boots.

She addressed her new lord.

"I'm disappointed, m'lord. I'd have thought a man," a word she overemphasized, "of your culture would provide a higher class of entertainment than this fiasco."

Lord Deagan parted his hands in farcical surrender and pronounced,

"Case closed." He exited the room, crunching ice beneath his massive feet.

Engineering vs. Mutation

Holly found she'd fallen asleep. The weeks of traveling had taken their toll. In fact, Tanya was able to quietly sneak into the room, hide the package from Hanain under her bed, and then leave without Holly noticing.

It was the click of the closing door that woke her. Holly stretched, wiped the drool off her cheek, and looked out her window. The cracking of whips caught her attention.

Below Ziggurat Hill were the zoology stables. A young man was training a horse on a long lead, cracking his whip behind the colt to keep it trotting in a circle. It took just a moment for Holly to recognize the L1 stable boy. She called and waved to him, but he seemed lost in a world of his own.

Holly grabbed a set of binoculars and brought into focus the goofiest grin smattered across the boy's face. She watched a moment as he juggled the whip and led into the one hand and dropped the other in his pocket.

Checking to be sure he was alone, he pulled something small out and admired it.

Holly lowered the binoculars, but not before she saw the wiry Pegasus broach that Tanya had made Mitch at their first meeting.

"Oh heavens, Tan, what have you done to the poor boy?"

Holly went exploring her new home, Bowra House, and found some young women in the practice rooms.

"Excuse me? Is there a way to get down to the stables from here?"

There was no response.

Holly questioned them again a little louder.

One of them spoke.

"I heard you. I'm just ignoring you."

Holly moved on down the stairs, noticing the determined avoidance of the other girls in the hallway.

In the back common room, Holly moved through the dusty rays of sun to glance out the big bay window, checking to see if Mitch was still training. He was.

"Your hero does seem to have a way with beasts."

Japheth Stillwell stood watching behind her.

Holly smiled at his familiar face.

"He's not my hero."

"Yes. Tanya is the rather Bacht-enamored one, isn't she?"

"It would seem everyone knows everything about us." Holly sat on the bay cushions in the sunshine.

"Not everything." Japheth gestured to the space next to her. "May I?"

Holly nodded.

"What isn't public knowledge?"

Japheth leaned against the white window pane, his black skin shinning dark in contrast.

"Well, I'm pretty well read on the subject of the Dijex Dragon Sisters, but there is one question no one has ever answered for me."

Holly laughed at her title.

"And what would that be? Or are you just interviewing me for some gossip column?"

"No interview, this is purely for personal interest."

Holly questioned him with her eyes and a sly grin.

He asked,

"Does the Lady Holly, predestined to be owned by our great Prince-in-One to be, Hadigan, actually want his attentions; or might she be distracted from such royal adoration?" His dark eyes looked admiringly at her through the warm rays that made her skin tingle.

Holly was cautious in her answer. She recalled the threat against Gash's life because of his kindness toward her, and as one not accustomed to flirting, she thought the better of even beginning something that might prove Hadigan

Andrew to be less than the gentleman she wanted to continue believing he was.

"I am determined to wait for my prince. I will be his."

"Determined? Will be? They don't sound like the words of a woman in love."

"Well, I am. And you would do well to not start something that could hinder the continuance of your life."

"The prince doesn't scare me. I was engineered in a laboratory of the highest Trevel technology. No one has the potential that my brothers and I have." Japheth boasted in his confidence.

"Power cannot be manufactured. I would be more wary of ones who gained their power through freak accidents rather than ones who'd had it calculated into them."

Holly had been running her fingers over the fern that was climbing the sill decoratively. But now Japheth found himself plastered to the wall by such a riddling of fern stems and leaves that he could not even speak.

Holly stood and leaned into Japheth's shocked face.

"You seem confident because you know what you can do. It has been analyzed and the data processed for you."

She pulled a small stem of green off, and the remaining fern blackened in decay and dissolved off the boy. Placing the vibrant stem in a button hole Holly stated,

"I am confident because I know that I have not even begun to understand the extent of what I can do."

Changing the subject drastically she asked,

"Can you get down to the stables from here?"

Japheth tried to grasp at composure but couldn't hide his mild horror.

"Not legally. You go down through the front of the moat and around."

"That won't do." Holly turned to leave after a quick glance back at the now-empty stable corral. "Steer clear of us, Japheth. I'd hate to shake the foundation of your belief in your greatness."

A Shock

As Holly climbed the staircase back up to her room, she felt someone following her.

The hallway to her room was lined with indoor topiaries, so Holly had the top balls of three plants bound off their perches and hurl themselves back toward the not-so-stealthy follower.

A loud crackling exploded, and the hallway was lit up with a sizzling shield of crooked lightening. The balls of leaves disintegrated.

Silence highlighted the young girl walking toward Holly with all the elegance of a princess. She was not threatening but held an aura about her that prompted respect.

Holly felt the hairs on her arms rise as the young Lightening Energist walked nearer.

"You're rather shocking, aren't you?"

The girl smiled.

"I saw you with Japheth. I like the way you handled him."

Holly felt oddly nervous in the other girl's confidence.

"He had it coming." She grinned and shrugged her shoulders.

"The three of them do; the other two brothers even more so." She crossed her arms. "Thing is, no one's ever given it to them before."

Holly laughed at herself.

"I'm not no one."

"I know exactly who you are." She rolled her eyes. "Jove, everyone knows who you are. But there's a difference between knowing and understanding."

Holly was about to object that no one understood her, but the young girl held her hand up to stop her.

"I'm not saying I do understand you." She turned her hand from the stop gesture to an open palm up. "But I would like to offer you the chance to let me try."

"You want to be friends with the dragon outcast?"

"No. I want to be friends with you." She took Holly's hand and shook it. "I'm Lexa, Lexa Belle."

Holly registered the famous name.

"Belle's Architecture?"

Lexa smiled. "We all have some family history we're trying to reconcile."

"Nice to meet you, Lexa, I'd like a friend." Holly then realized how out of place Lexa was. "How'd you get in here? Electricity is Haryss House, not Bowra."

"I came looking for you… and it pays to have access to the man who designed the blueprints for the school."

"You have the blueprints to the school?"

"No, that would be illegal." Lexa put her arm around Holly and steered her down the hallway. "But I do have many fond memories of sitting on Daddy's lap eating cookies and milk while he worked on the plans."

At the end of the corridor, she admired the wood carving of a mare and foal.

"It would also seem I inherited my daddy's perfect graphic memory, too." She reached up and twisted the foal's raised hoof. The panel behind the statue fell away and a darkened staircase fell in front of them. "You wanted the zoology stables, right?"

A smile of true respect and appreciation spread across Holly's face.

"Should we explore?"

Lexa's confidence shone in a wry grin.

"Why not?"

The two stepped into the staircase and the panel slid silently back behind them.

The Defense Secretary's Secret

Prince Hadigan met with the Defense Secretary for a private luncheon.

The future Prince-in-One had not forgotten about the L1 brought in by Champion Marin Tambeaux. He had some serious concerns, not because the boy was Bacht, but because Marin had agreed to sponsor him and kept him lose with family ties. Hadigan knew Marin. They knew each other well. They were once great friends until Marin became too smart and saw right through Hadigan.

"I know you did it." The sixteen-year-old Marin calmly strung another ice arrow to his bow.

His mentor and friend, Prince Hadigan, or Haddy, was a strong champion in the service of his royal father. He was practicing archery with the teen as they often did at the end of the day.

Haddy strung his own wooden arrow to his bow and casually asked,

"What's that?"

"The Latoona tragedy. We've been studying it in school, and I know you did it." Marin took aim.

Hadigan breathed calmly taking aim also, focused and controlled.

Marin continued his aim and said,

"I just haven't figured out why yet." He shot true and hit rim of the bull's-eye.

Haddy took his shot and landed the dead center. He stretched and asked,

"How has this conclusion come to you?"

Marin pulled back his bow string again as another long, jagged ice arrow formed from his fingers. He responded,

"You were there. It happened. Therefore, it was you."

Haddy laughed and said,

"I think you give me too much credit, my friend."

Marin took aim again.

"Do I?"

Haddy aimed a new willow arrow that looked too flimsy to hold any strength, and confirmed,

"I say you do."

"Then I must," conceded Marin, letting his ice fly. It landed dead center with such force as to penetrate through to half way up the shaft.

Haddy let his willow fly and it wiggled and wobbled through the air as if on the wind. It missed his mark completely and blew off course landing sideways against Marin's ice arrow, shattering the shaft in half.

"I'm sorry," Haddy apologized. "I'm still in the testing stage with these ones." Haddy smiled sincerely at his friend. "I'm still learning exactly what kind of damage they do."

Marin fell silent and nodded.

It was from this point on that Marin and Haddy continued together in the dance of wild bucks: the young strong buck testing, sniffing, and watching for his moment when he might truly challenge the king of the bucks. Each warrior let his antlers grow high, ever stretching forth to the sky, seeking how they may best maintain their reach.

They played to personal strengths and the other's weaknesses. They learned from each other and became such perfect friends that the nemesis inside was hidden room all but themselves. They were famously inseparable; enemies kept closest to heart.

Thus Prince Hadigan was determined to discover just what it was that Marin saw in the Bacht Mitchell, and he was intent upon joining in encouraging the boy. He would support the unlikely human and keep him exactly where he could keep his eye closest upon him.

"Your Highness," greeted the defense secretary. "You are looking most full of power today."

"I always am," was the prince's reply.

The defense secretary cleared his throat in uncomfortable agreement.

"Do you have the information I requested?" Hadigan cut straight to the point.

"Yes, sir." He passed over a thin, hand-held flowboard.

Hadigan took it and began scrolling through the data. He demanded,

"And this is the only record of such a history?"

"Yes, sir."

Hadigan paused and raised his eyebrows in reading. He looked intrigued at the defense secretary and asked,

"So, it's the grandmother?"

"Yes, sir." The messenger shifted uncomfortably.

"So close a tie is disconcerting." Hadigan shifted his research to a chart of a family tree. "I expected at least a few more generation separations."

He stopped and stared at the chart, his jaw visibly clenched in anger. Then he growled,

"But Father's first wife died before the child was born."

The defense secretary nervously offered,

"Some premature babies survive miraculously."

Hadigan screamed in rage, then spewed his vehemence.

"It may be miracles that rescue premature baby girls," he said as he lashed out with his vine whip, sans thorns, and struck the defense secretary across the face continuing his rampage, "but it is not miracles that deposit baby girls into the safety of the barbaric Bacht."

The defense secretary cowered before his prince.

"None of us knew, my Lord. That information has been covered up for decades. It is only with the registration of the Bacht's blood that the information surfaced in the chronicles."

Hadigan forced himself to calm his breathing.

The defense secretary asked the only question he knew to ask,

"Do you want your successor challenger to be destroyed like the others?"

Hadigan's whip slashed around the poor man's throat and pulled him within spitting distance of his face, then whispered,

"He is not a challenge to me. He is not worthy to be recognized as even half my blood."

Haddy let the whip fly and threw the man to the ground.

"No descendent from Father's first wife, grandson or no, will ever see light of recognition in this Trevel Kingdom."

Haddy calmed and smiled in self-control.

"He will continue to live. I will watch him. I will take from him what he loves dearest, and if he ever discovers his true heritage, then and only then will I laugh as I take his life. For then he will know just how much he has lost."

Mitch's Appointment

Lord Deagan at ANA

The NLL Arrives

Fur and Metal

Tanya Touched

Chapter 19

Mitch's Appointment

The tunnel into which Lexa and Holly ventured was lined in HDP; thus, Holly presumed, its hidden nature.

She ran her fingers along the shining, silky walls.

"This is too amazing. How many of these are there?"

Lexa smiled as she led on, a small crackling of lightening sizzling in her hand to light the way.

"They're all through this place. The school, the palace, the city… are all riddled with these passages."

"Hades burn! Seriously?" Holly was dumbfounded.

Lexa made the lightening brighter so Holly could see the delicately carved walls of the tunnel.

"Don't forget, this civilization was preplanned and rebuilt stone by stone from a previous ancient culture. The aim was to protect the Trevel way of life from the onslaught of Upland Bacht overbreeding. Every secret this entire Trevel world has ever had is held within the bowels of the City Clusters, and upon these mysteries our modern culture has become stabilized."

Holly breathed out slowly.

"And I was so proud of my tiny jungle village because of a mysteriously refreshing water well."

"Don't downplay the village outposts." Lexa came to an end in the way and moved her hands along the wall carvings. "Nothing in Trevellia is not purposed and preplanned, even the Upland outposts."

She ran her fingers under a flickering mane of a brumby rearing its stony head out of the wall.

"Here 'tis."

The wall shifted, and Lexa stepped through a shield of glistening HDP.

Holly stood alone in the dark tunnel, staring with wide eyes at the force field in front of her. She jumped as Lexa's disembodied arm shot through the wall at her, gesturing to follow. Holly took an uneasy step forward, and the arm floating in the glimmering HDP grabbed her and pulled her through.

Holly's eyes blinked in the brilliant Skyling sunset. Lexa smiled and pointed ahead.

"Zoology stables, voila!"

The two made their way down the hillside in the twilight. Lexa nudged Holly and nodded toward another lone figure walking toward the same destination.

Holly stopped in her tracks and stared at her sister's scanty attire.

"What in Hades?"

A young stable hand came out to greet Tanya and was obviously enjoying the sight that she was flaunting. Holly felt like she was watching a horrible teen flicker as the flirting on the boy's part became braver and Tanya, although not encouraging, was definitely not dissuading.

Holly quickened her pace and began stomping down on the scene. She pulled up short, though, and Lexa nearly ran into her, when Mitch came out looking terrifying.

If anyone could take on the form of a raging stallion, it was that young Bacht. He strode briskly up to the two and stood eye to eye with the opposing stable hand, who did not back down but stepped in, chest to chest.

There was a challenging, mocking shrug and a lascivious leer at Tanya, then Mitch hauled out and slammed his fist into the other's jaw.

He staggered back a bit, and Holly was terrified there would be an all-out brawl.

But instead, the challenger dropped his head ever so slightly and, looking at Mitch from out of the tops of his eyes, an evil, triumphant grin expanded across his face. He snorted. Holly had broken into a run when Mitch reacted and was now close enough to hear the threat.

"You're mine now, Bacht. I'll rip that dead heart out of your soul and eat it for afternoon tea, perhaps with a glass of mineral water on the side."

Here, he let his vision penetrate the lack of cloth on Tanya's form. Mitch tried to pounce, but his competitor was ready for him this time, and a swarm of Energy-created mosquitos flew from his hand and entangled Mitch in a buzzing mess of stings and confusion.

"You won't see me coming, but, oooh, you'll feel my sting. Get used to that." Then he wiped the blood dripping down his lip and sauntered back into the stables.

A loud zap flashed above Mitch, and Lexa rid him of his pest cloud. His knees buckled slightly and Tanya rushed in to help him catch himself.

Holly exploded,

"What the cruck, Tanya!"

"Excuse me?" Her sister snapped back.

"Have you been walking around campus dressed like that all afternoon?"

"Are you okay, babe?" Tanya's focus was on Mitch and the welts that were starting to form all over his arms and face.

Mitch was dazed looking at the damage.

"How can an immaterial Energy form cause such real injury?"

Tanya smoothed some hair back off his face and instructed him,

"Energy is what is reality here, no matter what shell it comes in. Material or immaterial, the outcome is always from the energy, not the casing."

Tanya bent down and spat on the dirt, forming a tiny spot of mud. She stirred it with her finger and it grew to the size of a handful that the girl then dug up and began dabbing on the welts.

Mitch looked with a curious wrinkling of his nose,

"As gross as that seems, it's actually soothing nicely."

Tanya grinned.

"Earth and mineral girl with a mother well trained in the art of healing."

Mitch grinned back.

"Well, now then, that's much better."

As the stings began to be soothed, Mitch's head cleared, and he could not help staring adoringly at his healer.

Suddenly he remembered something. "Oh, hey! You'll never guess…"

"What?" Holly was still disgruntled and puzzled by a strange difference in the atmosphere surrounding her sister.

Mitch didn't even notice the tension and babbled on with his great news.

"I've been asked to design the programing for the NLL Championship Field."

"What?" Tanya was ecstatic.

Lexa stepped up.

"Wait, what?"

Mitch continued, not quite aware of the stir he was about to cause.

"The National Laray League was given a tip that I had a knack for programming and has given me the chance to work, fully supervised of course, as the main programmer for setting up the field course and working the course changes and adjustments during play for the championships that'll be held here in two weeks."

"I'm sorry? NLL Championships are to be held here, at ANA?"

Lexa was still skeptically hopeful beyond all her wildest dreams.

"Yeah." Mitch stared at her, then realized, "Crap, that's a huge secret isn't it."

Holly, not much of a sports fan, didn't understand Lexa's intensity.

She mumbled,

"That'd be cool to see a real game."

Lexa sputtered and giggled and regained her composure.

"Holly, 'cool' is not quite the most appropriate of words that comes to my mind."

Mitch nodded. "The NLL Championships are kind of a big deal, so I've been told."

Lexa lowered her head and breathed very slowly in and out. Holly and Tanya watched her obvious struggle to maintain her calm socialite demeanor.

"The National Laray League is the closest thing that we, divine gods of Trevel, have to our own *religion*."

The two outpost jungle sisters looked puzzled.

Again, Lexa took a deep breath.

"Discovering the location of the NLL Championships is as much a betting game as the event itself. To be a Laray championship player is to be," here Lexa's proper attitude began to crumble as her tone gave way to her secret passion, "a hero, adored by every living Trevel in history.

To actually attend such an event is to experience the greatest climax of life this Energized earth can offer."

Tanya raised her eyebrows.

"So, you are a bit of a fan, then, are you?"

Lexa exploded.

"A bit??? My dad has designed the stadiums for the NLL Championships for as long as I can remember. I have gone to every building, every practice, and every game since my mother carried me within. Every love I have ever had has been with the iconic poster of the latest Laray hero. They're coming here!!!"

Then she lost all decorum.

"Olympus descend! Please, Bacht boy, please let me work with you… I won't get in the way… I promise. Maybe I could arrange that I be the Trevel to supervise you? I mean, the officials already know me through my dad, they'd trust me."

Mitch stared at her.

Lexa tried her last card.

"And I could keep that mosquito boy from bugging you…"

She nodded in the direction in which the other stable hand had disappeared and flashed a crack of lightening toward it.

"Done, for my part anyway. I'll ask if you can help me with your architectural background, but the final permission doesn't come from me. That comes from my boss." Mitch held out his hand to shake Lexa's.

She looked slightly puzzled by the gesture but took his hand and let him grip it and give it one solid shake.

She then agreed.

"Permission I can get through my dad. He'll be there for construction overseeing anyway."

"Well, now that everyone is all happy, I think it's time we all go back and dress for dinner." Holly still eyed her sister's exposed thighs and gaping cleavage.

"Actually," Tanya casually ran her fingers through her hair, "I think I may stay here just a few more minutes to make sure the stings are healing."

Holly raised an eyebrow. Tanya continued,

"I'll be back just before dinner to change, I promise. I was thinking we could wear those dresses we bought in Rio at the mall?"

"See you back in the room in an hour, then?" Holly wanted a time confirmation.

Tanya busied herself checking a couple of Mitch's sting spots.

"Will do."

As Holly and Lexa strolled back to Ziggurat Hill, Lexa's excitement softened and she spoke quietly.

"You know he's sleeping with her, right?"

Holly laughed out loud.

"Don't be ridiculous."

"Maybe so," said Lexa, "but I do know that no man looks at a woman the way he looks at her unless he's already familiar with the form underneath."

Holly spun around and just caught a glimpse of Tanya leading Mitch into the stables. Mitch raised his hand slightly and lifted his fingertips under the hem of her mini skirt and gave it a teasing tug. Tanya just giggled and batted her eyelids at him.

Lexa had to gently steer a numb Holly all the way back to Bowra House.

Lord Deagan at ANA

Tanya knew she was in trouble as she walked down the hall toward her room and saw that all the topiaries lining the walls were splattered in overgrown blasts up the woodwork. Her door was alive. The wood itself was breathing and pulsing with a dark energy from within.

Tentatively, she slipped off her shoes and walked calmly through the live wood opening that bade her enter.

Holly was sitting on the window sill, legs hanging bent, barely touching the floor. The ivy that climbed the outer walls of Bowra House had entered via the open window and was encasing the young Flora Energist in a fluid wave of leaves.

Her eyes were closed and her breathing slow, but Tanya knew better than to think her sister was anywhere near calm, for her skin was a verdant, luminous green.

Tanya didn't break the soft rhythm of growth. Rather, she simply moved to her closet and coaxed off the vines slithering their way across the cupboards with a handful of rich volcanic soil. They released their grip and dove into the luscious minerals.

The Earth Energist changed into the sundress she'd promised she would.

"Don't think I can be so easily appeased as my extensions." Holly spoke quietly.

"I would never presume to merely appease you, dear sister." Tanya turned to face her.

The living green curled itself off its goddess as a second skin might peel off a dragon. Holly, too, wore the matching Rio sundress. She walked into her sister's personal aura and looked into her eyes. Tanya gazed blankly back.

Holly adjusted her focus and straightened a random strand of her sister's hair.

"Is Mitch feeling any better?"

Tanya didn't blink.

"Much."

Holly paused a moment, then moved out of the room.

"We shouldn't be late for dinner."

Tanya watched her sister's skin drain of green and walked behind her, her own hand absentmindedly rubbing her hip.

Lexa met up with Holly on the veranda and condescendingly raised an eyebrow when Joshun, Misty, and Breezer bounced up to Tanya in the courtyard.

However, before any discussion could ensue between the social classes, a commanding voice penetrated the grounds.

"That has to be the moteliest gathering of ragtag associates I have ever seen."

Both sisters' faces lit up as they recognized their past chaperone's voice, and open greetings of embraces and cheek kisses were shared by the three.

Holly looked slightly sheepish, and Champion Marina soothed her.

"Not to worry, hon," she rubbed her hands on Holly's nervous shoulders,

"I'm not here with my brother, but with my ambassadorial associate."

Tanya started.

"Lord Deagan is here?"

"In the flesh and as large as ever," the young champion grinned.

"He's making a special announcement tonight to all who are lucky enough to happen to have dinner in the Heart Tower Common Dining Room. You look like you'll be some of the lucky ones."

Joshun sidled up, sensing the excitement.

"Who's Lord Deagan? He sounds powerful."

Marina raised her eyebrow and gently flicked Joshun's dangling earing.

"I think you'll probably like him." She winked at the boy.

"Well," Joshun grabbed Misty's arm, "I'm ravenous, anyone for dinner now?"

The excited anticipation dissipated any tension that previously stood between the odd collection of students, and they walked off together, turning more than a few heads.

Tanya stepped up next to Marina's side.

"How are things going with your… ambassadorial associate?"

Marina smiled and dropped her head slightly. She sensed a secret affinity with Tanya despite their past disagreements.

"He's still quite guarded, yet completely open, and at every moment encourages me to pursue learning to work well with him."

Tanya smirked.

"How well?"

Choosing her words carefully, Champion Marina admitted what Tanya really wanted to know behind a diplomatic mask.

"An offer has been alluded to as being expected, but not yet time to be realized. He is, if anything, full of purpose and preparation."

"And your acceptance of this offer?"

Marina breathed slowly.

"Resistance… is… unlikely."

Tanya slipped her arm around the elbow of the strong military woman, who for a brief moment looked incredibly vulnerable.

***   ***   ***

The buzz in the Heart Tower Dining Room was as electric as the shock Lexa used to clean the table before she sat to eat with a cloth placemat, real silverware, and a linen napkin that she carried in her handbag.

Lord Deagan's presence had purposely been leaked, and the flicker crews were outside hoping to capture glimpses of the newest wonder of the Trevel gossiping world.

Champion Marina left Holly, Tanya, and their crew at the dining room entrance. When she re-entered, it was as the adorning military escort for the massive beast that was Lord Deagan.

Principle Zanne lead the parade that caused a loud hush to descend upon the overcrowded room as each step taken by Deagan's massive boots brought him closer to the communal curiosity of the student body.

Joshun whispered to Tanya,

"Does he ever take his helm off? I so wanna see the face of such a form as that." He tapped his chest with open palm as his heart fluttered in thrills.

Tanya grinned but didn't take her eyes of the great plated shoulders as they passed.

"He didn't while we were in Hanain, not even to eat."

"He ate through that tiny slit? That's gross." Lexa turned up her nose.

Holly forced herself to look away but maintained an acute awareness as to his movements.

"No, he never ate with us."

Principle Zanne, accustomed to having to gain the attentions of the students, paused at the front but noted that everyone was already riveted to her and her guest, so she began,

"Evening, students, we have a distinguished guest tonight. He has a particular announcement to make, so without further ado, it is my honor to introduce Prince Hadigan's right-hand Independent Strategist Director and Regent of Hanain, Lord Deagan."

Lord Deagan didn't approach the stand or even need the HDP amplifier. His voice was as large as everything else about his person.

But he paused a moment in silence, and his gaze began wandering down the wall that displayed the school's Laray team portraits.

Everyone was watching him. He surveyed the various trophies, then on to the furthest portraits of the current teams for the inter-house Laray competitions on campus. He bent in close to study the faces, then turned and surveyed the crowd before him.

His eyes, trained and clear, peering through the Viking bull helm, picked out each of the students present. He caught their eyes and they, compelled by his unspoken power, slowly rose to their feet. He nodded to each one.

When sufficient tension had risen due to his silence, he spoke.

"Anyone want a game of Laray?"

The student body erupted in whoops, hollers, and cheers. It was time and everyone was looking for the announcement. The bookies had all their bets in, and it was imminent that someone would announce this year's location of the NLL Championship Game.

That announcement followed as,

"Two weeks, right here at ANA. Be ready."

To thunderous applause and eager offerings of hand slaps, Lord Deagan exited and Marina followed.

One overeager young boy reached out and slapped the beautiful young champion on her rear. It all happened so fast and was nearly disastrous beyond repair.

Marina's left hand gripped his wrist instantly in a cold hold of rock ice. But out of the corner of her eye she saw it coming, and had she not been so well trained... Her right hand instantly rose up and flattened out in a torrential gush of water that barely had the strength to knock the massive blade that descended from its course.

The water ceased and Marina's hand grasped the handle of the great sword, her fingers clenched around Lord Deagan's. She had saved him from a reaction that would have destroyed him. Her eyes penetrated the helm and stopped his heart.

The common room was gasping in silence.

Lord Deagan stood straighter and sheathed the now empty hilt. He spoke with a voice of depth that rattled the quaking bones of the nearly handless schoolboy.

"Little boys' hands should never venture where even the mightiest of men dare not reach."

He bowed to his ambassador, and she led him out.

The seventh grader rubbed his wrist as the developing bruise began to surface.

The NLL Arrives

That very evening, the entire student body simultaneously appeared at the Laray fields. The two competing teams in this year's National Championship were the Lemurian Legions and the Kentari Knights.

Both teams arrived for their first warm-up practice to the thunderous applause of teenage hands. No one outside the school was allowed near the field, and many flicker crews were tossed out as they consistently tried to sneak in to the closed practices. But due to the close relationship that Atlantis National Academy had with the National Laray League, the students were admitted at will. Lexa was beside herself in excitement.

She dragged an extremely apprehensive Holly to as many practices as she could and did not understand why anyone would not want to be present every time the teams were flying through the course. At the end of classes, Lexa dragged Holly to the field again.

"Come on, Holly." Lexa bustled past other students as they all crammed in to see the play.

"Seriously, Lexa, we've been here five times already today." Then it happened: the meeting Holly dreaded in secret. She ducked behind Lexa and held her head down.

"Hallo, Ladies. I recognize you. Miss Belle, isn't it?"

"Holy trident, yes, you know me?" Lexa's eyes were all stars as she gazed longingly into the gorgeous eyes of her current favorite Laray sportsman. She was a diehard Lemurian Legions devotee.

"Your father designed the family chapel on my home estate, and I've seen you here on every class break for the last two days." The grand champion winked at her.

"Who's your friend?"

"Oh!" Lexa blushed as a true socialite caught with her manners lax would. "This is my dear friend…" she stepped aside and pushed her companion forward.

Champion Marin Tambeaux finished Lexa's introduction with a throaty gulp.

"Holly."

Holly dropped her gaze, then tried to regain her composure.

"Marin, I mean Champion Tambeaux. It's a pleasure to see you recovered."

Lexa no longer existed, nor did the crowds.

"How have you been?" he asked.

Holly felt the disruption in her soul and lashed out against the rising awkwardness.

"I am singularly well, thank you."

"That's not what I hear."

There was a pause as both sought for something that might flow as easily as it once had. Marin broke in,

"Congratulations on your new age."

"Thank you, it's an adjustment.

Even Lexa was caught up in the dialogue, out of shock, recognizing an unknown connection, that not even she saw him coming. The massive bull ray slid right above the champion's head and nearly took his scalp.

There was a great laugh.

Circling back around, the flying ray hovered at eye level and gave Marin a friendly tap on the back of his head. The rider, Prince Hadigan, jested,

"Still trying to win my lady away, friend?"

Marin was immobile and kept his back to the prince.

"I was merely enquiring as to the lady's health." Then he turned and jumped on his waiting ray and soared off in the direction of the stables.

Hadigan kneeled on the ray's back and gestured to Holly.

"Care for a flight, my dear?"

How could she refuse?

They cruised across the field, avoiding the other players practicing in flight. But Hadigan Andrew couldn't resist flaunting and slowly flew by the Laray stables where Marin was unsaddling his ray. Hadigan saluted him triumphantly. Holly dropped her head and couldn't meet his flaming eyes.

When they'd passed, Marin lost it and threw his saddle against the wall. It fell at the feet of a young student in ANA uniform adorned with dangling blue earrings. Joshun smiled as the saddle slid across the floor.

"Do you need help saddling up?" The young boy suggested.

Marin paused, his breath crushing through his lungs in rage-filled passion. He surveyed the lusty figure in front of him, then went about his business of soaking down his ray.

"The stables are no place for a lonely boy like you."

Joshun bent forward and picked up the saddle.

"I've always found places full of sweaty men to be the perfect place for me."

He stood too close to Marin, resting the saddle on his raised knee.

"Did you want this?"

Fur and Metal

Tanya was sitting in the stands with Breezer and Misty.

"Where did you say Joshun was?" Tanya questioned her new mates as she watched the practice through her HDP magnifying glasses.

Misty scoffed,

"You're seriously sitting there perving at the manly men players wondering where Joshun is?"

"What, is he trying to get a closer look?"

"Let's just say he wasn't interested in either the Skyling or the animals when he said he wanted to go catch some rays."

Breezer pointed out onto the field.

"Isn't that Holly?"

Tanya adjusted her glasses' focus and saw her sister standing with arms stretched out on the back of a massive bull ray, Hadigan behind her with his hands steadying her waist. Tanya dropped her glasses with a sneer.

Breezer was watching.

"You don't like the prince, do you?"

"I don't like his tendency to behave as a multi faced politician."

Her mobile key ring rang. She flipped the coin-shaped circle of HDP into a long horn and slung it around her ear. "Y-ellow!" She listened.

"We're halfway up in section D, hon. Come join us." Her face scowled a little. "No, Holly is otherwise occupied. I'm here with my new friends from the mail room." She grinned. "Not to worry, I'll come meet you by the entry. See you in five."

Tanya stood and tucked her mobell disc onto her bracelet holder.

"One of the other girls from my home village is joining us. She's kinda quiet, so we may have to loosen her up a bit."

"Katiel or Candace or Tomey? 'Cos he's a bit of a girl, too, if you ask me." Misty took Tanya's glasses and began scanning the crowd.

"Do you know where everyone is from?" Tanya laughed as she began jumping down the bench seats.

"Just the ones who live near supposed dragon sightings." Misty focused on a young boy doing burnouts on a motorized scooter.

"What a sandal."

Tanya tossed a final comment over her shoulder.

"Nothing supposed about it, I can attest to that."

Breezer wrestled the glasses from Misty.

"What's going on?"

Misty reluctantly gave up her sight.

"It's that stupid seventh grader who nearly lost his hand to Lord Deagan. He's still looking for trouble."

Breezer watched, disgusted.

"Little boys like that really are nothing more than sandals: only worth tying up on my foot."

Tanya pushed through the crowd streaming through the entry steps and heard the loud buzzing of a tiny, over pressed motor. There was a girly screech and the motor muffled to a low rumble.

Katiel was sprawled on her face with her books scattered around her. Even from where Tanya had emerged, she could see blood droplets beginning to form on her scraped hands and knees.

She rushed to help but was, herself, nearly bowled over by a massive Energized form of an arctic wolf. The wolf slowed and prowled around Katiel's limp figure and bared his teeth at the reckless scooter driver.

Katiel sat up, gingerly nursing her wounds, but moved slowly more out of fear of the great fur force pacing in front of her.

In fact, Katiel was so focused on the great wolf that she allowed another startled squeal escape her trembling lips when a rough but gentle hand offered her a support.

Tanya, well-practiced in the art of attracting men, slowed her approach and watched as the blond athlete bent gracefully with great strength to lift Katiel to her feet and inquired,

"I see you're hurt. Can you stand?"

Whether it was due to her injuries or her sudden weakness at the sight of the school's favored sports star standing over her, Katiel's knees buckled under her, and he lifted her deftly in his arms and seated her on a nearby bench.

The reckless youngster called at her from behind the wolf.

"Sorry, luv, I didn't see you there."

The wolf barked viscously and Roland, Katiel's rescuer, growled at him.

"You can't see anything when you're only looking at yourself."

Nikkos, the motor head, snapped back,

"Yeah, well you and your dog here can munch on this…" and he made an extremely rude gesture.

The wolf aimed its snapping jaws at the boy as if he would indeed snack on the offered appendage.

A metal pipe instantly materialized in Nikkos's hands, and he struck out at the wolf's head.

Roland lashed his hand out, and the energized wolf moved in sync and pounced. Nikkos lay flat on his back with the translucent blue energy jaws clamped around his neck in a very real grip.

Nikkos squirmed, trying to grip the metal pipe in his hand that was also pinned by the energized wolf's paw to the ground. He shouted in a constricted voice,

"Too scared to fight me hand to hand? Gotta use your shield dog, huh?"

Roland looked at the scrawny kid and shook his head. He glanced back at Katiel, who was now accompanied by Tanya and was allowing the offered healing to soothe her scrapes.

"I don't think you want to go there, mate."

Nikkos continued his defiance.

"A pretty pansy like you could do with a good thrashing."

Roland laughed and called his wolf to heel. He released his prey and ran back to sit beside Katiel.

Nikkos jumped to his feet with his metal pipe gripped securely in his hand.

"Why don't I show you how we bite on the low streets?"

Roland smiled. "I'd like to see you try."

Nikkos swung, rolled onto his back, and swung again at Roland's knees. Roland calmly jumped and landed on the pipe, smashing Nikkos's hands into the gravel. Nikkos grunted and let go.

Roland stepped off the pipe and kicked it up into Nikkos's hands again, then beckoned to the kid for another try.

Tossing the pipe into the air with one hand, Nikkos propelled his other hand forward, and two darts no bigger than his fists lashed out at Roland.

Roland leaped aside in a backflip over Nikkos and snatched the pipe out of the air before the boy even realized there was no target to land the darts into.

The patient wolf bounded into the fray and caught both darts in his mouth. Wagging his tail happily, he fetched the darts back to his master's hand. Roland shucked the pipe under his arm and studied the metalworking of the points.

"Not bad, kid. Nice workmanship. Where'd you grow up?"

Nikkos was stunned.

"Third level street, outer Lemuria."

Roland nodded and queried,

"Abner's crew, right?"

The boy's mouth dropped open in disbelief.

Roland stepped to the kid and handed back his weaponry.

"I'm with Mason, second level street Atlantis." He held out a fist to the boy, who pounded it automatically.

"Dude," he spoke with reverence to Roland, "I'm sorry, man, I had no idea. You're such a...." He let his voice trail.

"A pretty boy? Yeah, I know. I can't help it, and it has been the bane of my entire existence growing up as a street urchin."

"No crap." Nikkos was in wonder. "You must have had that face plastered on the street more times that you can remember."

Roland shrugged.

"They have to catch you before they can beat you. But enough of the camaraderie, you owe the jungle lass an apology."

Nikkos immediately saluted Katiel.

"I am sorry, stupid of me really. I hope you're not too hurt?"

All Katiel could do was ask Roland,

"You know I'm from the jungle?"

Roland blushed a little and smirked.

"I'm aware."

Tanya Touched

Tanya, Holly, and Lexa stood with Mitch in the programmer's bunker of the Laray stadium. They had a perfect view of not only the whole field, but also, via, flickervision, they could easily watch the activity in the stables and field's undercarriage, where the mechanics of the course obstacles were managed.

Mitch worked the flowboard like a concert pianist, coaxing rhythm and flow from the technology.

Lexa wondered out loud,

"Can you surveil the locker rooms as well from here?"

Mitch grinned.

"I have the ability to do so, but I didn't want to burden you ladies with the sight of nasty smelly men in pregame preparations."

Lexa cleared her throat.

"Oh, well, of course not. I was just curious as to how all this works."

One of the screen corners began flashing with a slight alarm.

"Crap." Mitch leaned in for a closer look. "I'm going to have to go out there." He gathered up a handy tool belt and instructed, "I'll only be a few minutes. There may be a slight loss or delay in the power flow, but sit tight and I'll get it under control."

Lexa looked concerned.

"Not to worry, Lex." Mitch ruffled her perfect hair. "It'll all run perfectly on the day of the match."

Lexa was scandalized by his familiarity and her now messy hair.

"Ugh! Seriously?"

Tanya piped up,

"You need a hand?"

Mitch smiled and mumbled,

"I can always use your hands…"

Holly bit her lip as the two slunk out the door together.

Lexa was horrified.

"Will you not say something?"

Holly defended her silence.

"She doesn't listen to me, never has when it came to boys."

"Well, she better listen to someone soon, or she'll destroy not only her life but the lives of everyone around her!"

Holly gently laid her arm on her electrified friend.

"Look, I know Tan. This will blow over. It always does. Mitch will just be a bad choice in slumming it that she can have a laugh over in a couple of years."

"I hope so, for the sake of all her associations."

"You'll see," reassured Holly.

Mitch and Tanya held hands as they wandered down the lonely corridor under the Laray field. There were twists and turns, and they should have been more careful, as they couldn't see who was coming.

When Mitch pointed out a circuit breaker in a dark alcove, they snuck in and made a moment of the quiet darkness. They were not long distracted by each other when they felt a presence looming over them.

As massive as his form was, Lord Deagan had a remarkable ability to maintain silence. Tanya balked and awkwardly wiped her mouth.

"Lord Deagan?" She curtsied nervously just because she had no idea what else to do upon having been caught so red handed.

"Can I help you, sir?" Mitch was cool and unapologetic.

"These are dark tunnels. Do you know what you seek?"

"I do." Lord Deagan's voice rumbled deeply. "But I think the better question is, 'do you know what you will find?'"

"Sir?" Mitch would not back down but challenged with his question.

"Trouble, Bacht, more than you know what to do with."

"The only trouble I'm concerned with right now is what will happen if I don't get this current flow fixed in time."

"Look to it, Bacht." Deagan turned to leave.

Mitch called after him,

"I'll be turning the lights off for a few minutes, Lord Deagan. You look to being careful in the dark."

The massive bull helm turned slowly to face him. Neither could see any glimmer of eyes behind the mask.

"Good advice," he said, then turned and walked into the shadows.

"He's so creepy." Tanya smoothed her skirt across her hips.

"Look, I need to get this fixed or even Holly will break her silent complaint against me."

"I can deal with my sister."

"I know you can, sweetie. But right now, I need you to deal with the circuit breaker down the hall."

Tanya questioned him visually.

"In the opposite direction to Lord Deagan's exit is another alcove, like this. I need you to go there and flip this switch for me." He gestured to the breaker on the wall.

"'Kk."

"The power will shut down for a bit and it will be dark, but only for three minutes. Come back here when the lights come on again."

"'K, baby." She kissed him and wandered happily down the hall.

She found the other alcove easily, flipped the appropriate switch, and was immediately plunged into deep darkness. Tanya fingered the Hanain diamond she always carried around her neck, and it glowed just enough to illuminate the alcove and highlight the fact that she was no longer alone.

Her hand snatched at her hip and she startled.

"Prince Hadigan!"

"How funny to run into you so alone, dear Earthen."

He approached and she backed up against the breaker but felt the rising as her knees weakened. He was in her aura and she could not open her eyes.

She felt his breath whisper in her mouth and her lips unwittingly beckoned his. He granted. She swooned.

"That's not good," he whispered, and she felt a surge of life fill her. "I can't have you unconscious. That would be taking advantage."

The young woman breathed in a deep breath and opened her eyes. His magnificence was before her, in her grasp, and she lunged at him. He laughed as he pulled back a little from her desperate kisses.

"I see you've done your homework, like a good girl."

She whimpered and leaned into him. He glared hungrily at her.

***   ***   ***

Lexa spoke in the darkness.

"For how long were the lights supposed to be out?"

"Mitch said just a bit."

"Does time run slower Upland or something, 'cos this 'just a bit' has been almost fifteen minutes by my count."

Holly stumbled over to the console and groped while Lexa brought her fizzle of lightening closer so she could see better. They both spied the well labeled "emergency backup lights" slide at the same time and raised the bar.

It was all so unclear. In the green haze of the backup lights, neither was sure what exactly it was that they saw; first, the slumped body of a young Bacht in one alcove, then a flash of moving flesh in another just before the light extinguished to darkness on that screen.

Both girls darted frantically down the low-lit hallways.

*** *** ***

Hadigan was in charge and fully ripe. Tanya was in an ecstasy she'd never known before.

He growled in blind passion,

"Mhhmmmmm, Holly!"

Tanya's eye's flashed open in wicked mocking.

"Oh, *Marin Tambeaux*, give it!"

Hadigan stopped and pure evil flashed across his face. He grabbed her hair in one hand and slammed the back of his other hand across her cheek. She banged up against the wall, but he did not let her go.

The pain shattering her consciousness threatened to blacken everything.

"No!" Hadigan cried. "You will be awake."

Tanya was completely unaware if it was in pain or in pleasure that she screamed.

*** *** ***

Lexa pushed Holly on as she stopped at the alcove where Mitch lay unconscious. Holly wasn't sure her legs would make it down the rest of the hall to where she just knew she'd find her sister.

She felt broken glass crack beneath her feet and reached out to find the wall, but there was none, and she fell forward. As she fell, her arms waved for something to regain her balance in the darkness. Her hand landed hard on something soft and cold.

"Tan?" Holly felt around her sister's writhing form.

Tanya moaned and shuddered.

The lights came on and Holly found herself holding a thrashing Tanya, disheveled and obviously ravaged.

Holly screamed.

Colonah's Offering
Parental Protection
A Strong Fulcrum
Championship Lineup
A Key Assignment

Chapter 20

Colonah's Offering

The central bonfire spit flames into the air that whirled around as the circle of dragons beat their wings in time to the song.

The great red mother, Colonah, and her smaller blue sister, Tantra, led the song as they circled the fire. There were only a small number of dragons in the circle, and each one shone in the bright colors of the surrounding Amazon jungle.

The bulls were there, too, for ritual, barely keeping in line with the code of the pack. But Colonah maintained full control, no matter how unwillingly it was given.

Tears flowed freely down many of the scaly faces. Each bleary-eyed creature raised a crystal vial to her or his eyes to collect the precious water. Tantra gathered the vials and the song ended.

One of the bull dragons, obviously of highest seniority, approached Colonah.

"I have business with you, Great Mother."

The red dragon scoffed a laugh.

"I do not believe it is business you intend, Halion, and I have greater matters to attend to just now."

Halion grabbed her arm with gentle force.

"What greater matter can there be that keeps you from my visit?"

"Preventing chaos, my love." She placed her clawed hand gently on his cheek and held his gaze a moment. "The song calls." Colonah then departed gracefully into a dark cave.

Halion turned to leave but warned Tantra,

"I will not keep coming back for what is denied me, even if it is rightfully mine."

Tantra slunk low and shrugged nervously. The grey-green bull dragon plunged his wings to the ground, stirring up all that was round about, and shot into the night air.

Tantra shivered and followed Colonah's steps into the cave. There at the end of a short tunnel, the blue dragon came upon her red sister.

Colonah was tenderly pouring all the crystal vials into one single container.

Her sibling broke her concentration.

"He is impatient for you."

Colonah paused only briefly.

"Impatience is a burden we must all bare."

"He won't keep coming for you."

Colonah snapped,

"Did you not hear the song tonight? The pact has been set irreversible."

Tantra was horrified.

"I did not hear... I ... we must call forth Shifters."

"And plunge the entire Trevel world into tragedy and trauma again?"

Colonah finished her pouring.

"They have known peace for over 400 years. I would do everything to maintain that."

"But," Tantra insisted, "If he ... continues on his course, there will be such an unbalancing of power as to affect the Bacht as well."

"If..." Colonah smiled at her sister. "I wait for him to find his peace and claim his grace."

Tantra whispered,

"And if he does continue on his current setting?"

Colonah turned again to her pot of tears.

"Then Shifters will be called, but that is our last course of action." She lifted a toy, sunflower teapot, freshly full of tears, and placed it on a ledge, well protected.

"What if Holly and Tanya cannot complete their pact?" Tantra questioned.

Colonah answered,

"Then it will be up to the foretold boy and girl." She encouraged her sister, "There is always a hope and a future."

Parental Protection

Tanya was still unconscious. Holly paced the healer's room with her father. Salla sat on the bed and tried to calm the fevered twitching. Master Su stood with outstretched hands hovering lightly over the invalid.

He spoke with eyes closed, studying the unseen aura.

"The physical damage is healing quickly and well, but..."

Salla waited expectantly. Hal exploded, "But what?"

Master Su continued, his concentration unbroken.

"There is much more at work here."

Holly interjected,

"Can you at least find who did this? There must be some evidence left behind."

Master Su studied and frowned, perplexed.

"That is the difficulty, my dear. Other than the physical wounding, there is no evidence that there ever was anyone else."

Salla was mortified.

"You're not saying Tanya did this to herself, are you?"

Master Su stopped to address Salla.

"Do not put words into my mouth by jumping to vague conclusions." He rested a gentle hand on Salla's shoulder. "That path is taken by gossipmongers."

Hal gripped the end of the bed to steady his churning stomach.

"But if there is no evidence, then that is what will be reported."

"I'm afraid so." Master Su retreated to mixing some healing tonic.

Holly's exterior control began cracking.

"There is no way she would do this to herself."

"Again," Master Su emphasized, "I do not say such a thing."

Hal, too, was crumbling.

"Then what?"

Master Su took a slow breath.

"There is no evidence of another, but there is a suggestion of a 'lack' of evidence."

He was met with distraught confusion, so he continued,

"Where there should be evidence, there is now a void of evidence." He paused to allow the thought to clarify in their minds.

"Someone took the evidence?" Holly suggested.

"It is more troubling than even that." The master returned to Tanya and began force-feeding her twitching mouth with a thick liquid. "An exchange has taken place. I cannot prove it, but I see the results of it."

"An 'exchange'?" Hal growled in disgust, "Well, that's bloody obvious."

Master Su continued,

"Tanya appears to have 'absorbed' all evidence of external influence; with it, she has also absorbed high levels of toxicity that I believe are the by-product of a chemical exchange where someone else has pulled energy out of her."

Holly's eye's narrowed.

"You mean, like something drained the energy from her?"

Master Su noted recognition in Holly's eyes.

"If such a weapon existed, that might be possible."

Holly resumed her pacing.

"What if I could prove that such a weapon did exist?"

Silence descended like a thud. Then Hal spoke with a quaking voice.

"What have you two been up to?"

Holly suddenly burst into a short sputtered laugh.

"No! Tanya and I aren't into making weapons."

Hal and Salla breathed a deep sigh of relief.

Master Su studied his young student.

"But you have seen such a weapon?"

"Yes, we both have." Holly's eyes dropped to taking in the visual of her sister still twitching in fevered pain.

The potions master turned to watch nothing in particular and spoke to no one in particular.

"I am aware of one who might be able to do such a thing, but I thought his focus lay elsewhere."

A soft moan snapped them all to attention.

Salla wiped the sweat off Tanya's forehead and spoke softly to her.

"Tan, baby, Mema's here. You're safe now."

Suddenly Tanya sat straight up in bed as if a string pulled her up from her chest. She screamed with a deep, growling cry, mouth wide open and eyes bulging.

Then the moment was gone as if it had never come, and Tanya sat quivering slightly from a chill. She was fully conscious and aware.

Master Su didn't show any surprise and merely asked,

"Feel better?"

A Strong Fulcrum

"Yes, thank you, I feel much better." Tanya ran her hands nervously up her arms.

Holly exploded into tears.

"Jove surrender, Tan, I thought I'd lost you."

Salla and Hal joined in the familial hugging.

"We all did." Hal looked as if he'd never let his little girl go again.

From the depths of the body pile, Tanya's muffled voice spoke steadily.

"Air would be good right about now."

The family giggled as one does in nervous response to a tragedy. Salla held her daughter's face in her hands and looked deep into her eyes.

"Can I get you anything?"

"A massive meat banquet pizza would be great. I'm starved."

Smiling, Master Su recommended,

"Perhaps you should resist such temptations for now, and fill your body with regeneration, not empty waste." He held out another glass of thick liquid.

"Well, that looks appetizing." Her tone gave way her opposing opinion.

But Tanya took the glass offered and sniffed tentatively. It was pleasant enough, and so she tasted and found it quite delicious and fully energizing.

The four spectators watched her finish her beverage with impatient smiles, each one bursting to question and defeat the unspoken problem.

Tanya was never one to ignore silent issues, no matter how elephantine, so she spoke after her last gulp.

"I know you are all dying to ask me, but I don't really know what happened."

Hal questioned gently,

"Do you remember anything?"

There was a soft tap on the door and Mitch poked his head in.

"There are a number of well-wishers hoping to see her if she's up…"

He smiled at her.

A rather large crowd juggled around the Bacht, hoping to send their smiles through the door, too.

Master Su reassured Tanya,

"You can take as many visits as you feel comfortable with."

Tanya smiled at the familiar faces and beckoned the crew in. Misty, Joshun, Breezer, and Mitch pushed over to her immediately.

Mitch took his confidence to a strong level as he sat on her bed beside her and held her hand. Lexa entered graciously but couldn't help sneering ever so slightly at the allowance of such Bacht familiarity.

Katiel followed with apologies for Candice and Tomey, as they were neck deep in final-year studies, but the ANA athletics star, Roland, was with her and had another youngster in tow behind him.

Roland saluted in greeting.

"While I am here representing the Academy, I am also here as a friend." He bowed. "This," he gestured to the young boy, "is Nikkos. I'm his peer-mentor, but I think you have already met."

Nikkos lifted Tanya's hand to his lips and kissed it.

"My lovely Lady, I am sorry for your trouble."

Tanya smirked cynically.

Breezer cleared her throat and spoke up.

"We've been talking outside, Tanya, and we've come up with a plan."

Surprisingly, every one deferred to the usually ditzy girl and listened intently. She looked nervous.

"Like, we were saying, that if you, like, needed a bodyguard… we wanna join together with you and, like, kick butt on whoever did this to you."

There was a brief pause as the family took everyone in.

Breezer continued,

"We're all represented."

Breezer then pointed to each of the schoolmates standing around the bed, and they smiled in turn and offered up their specializations.

Misty began,

"Fire."

Joshun,

"Water."

Lexa,

"Electricity."

Katiel,

"Light."

Roland,

"Fauna."

Nikkos,

"Metal."

Breezer concluded,

"I'm Air, and with you two, Earth and Flora, we make the complete package."

Mitch then spoke up.

"And I know most of you don't count me for much, but I add Bacht physical and technological expertise to the mix, which can only help."

Tanya was rather stunned, but Master Su spoke resonantly,

"I hear a song in this." He packed up his belongings and headed to the door. "I will consult with Colonah."

He surveyed the room and noted Hal and Salla's shocked faces.

"Do not fret the workings of the world in your daughters. I sense a shifting, and this unity may just be the fulcrum upon which all turning finds its balance." He left.

Tanya was deeply grateful.

"I don't know what to say."

Holly squeezed her hand and was about to speak, but the door to the healing room opened with a burst and two young Primers entered demanding,

"Stand tall!"

Hal stood suddenly, but only to rebuke,

"What is this? There are no Strategists here. Get out!"

He had barely finished his sentence before he instantly backed down and everyone else rose to their feet respectfully and nervously.

Prince Hadigan entered with a calm but austere presence. His personal Secretary spoke for him.

"His Royal Highness, Prince Hadigan, future Prince-in-One and Regent of the City of Atlantis, wishes to grant his condolences to his dear friend and sister of his Bride-to-be. Lady Tanya Dijex, please accept our deepest sympathies as we profess that the Powers be with you in a speedy recovery and full regeneration."

Tanya slowly rose to her slightly unsteady feet. Those near her rushed to aid, but she shunned them all forcefully. She stood straight and stepped slowly up to the prince and with all her strength, curtsied in full grace, and spoke in a steady voice.

"I thank you, dear sir, and I am pleased to inform you that I am quite well and ready to continue wherever I am needed."

The power of her presence overwhelmingly silenced the atmosphere.

Prince Hadigan nodded slowly and addressed her father, Hal.

"I wonder if I might have a brief moment alone with the Lady Tanya."

Everyone immediately began filing out of the cramped room.

Holly smiled as she passed her prince, glowing at the public reference to her future union with him. He took her hand and kissed her fingers tenderly as a truly devoted and honorable lover.

Tanya did not move from her power stance until they were alone; then she sat on the end of the bed and waited.

"I must say," Prince Hadigan began, "you surprise me, but I am delighted to see you so strong."

"One only grows stronger in tribulation." Tanya kept her eyes down and absentmindedly brushed her fingers over the familiar throbbing in her hip.

"I should like to research the growth of our little planting."

He moved in close and Tanya shivered and whispered,

"I am yours as you will."

He touched her chin to lift her eyes to meet his. Her body jolted as if shocked and she trembled but met his gaze.

The prince studied her eyes.

"Indeed, I see that you are."

Championship Lineup

The public had been admitted to the ANA Laray stadium to watch the iconic pregame selection process for the championship Laray final.

The nine friends sat close together in the crowded bleachers. Mitch, of course, was below in the tech bunker. Tanya would have preferred to watch with him, but everyone agreed it best that she display a front of strength to combat all the horrendous rumors that were flying around the entire Trevel world.

The journalists reported that she had suffered a freak energy surge and was recovering well with the aid of the royal physicians. The gossipmongers reported she'd staged an attack on herself to get back at her sister's newfound fame as Favored One to Prince Hadigan. Others created even more disgusting versions of said event and, unfortunately, the more horrible they were, the more they were believed.

The nine didn't talk together much but focused on the game at hand. Katiel surveyed the field and groaned in recognition as she saw the Stillwell triplets enter the Laray Legions base in the uniforms of Prince Hadigan's private defense agents.

When the Kentari Knights and their rays flew onto the field in a rush of thunder, the entire stadium jumped to its feet in frenzied excitement.

They circled the flat field and skidded to a dramatic halt center field. There was a pulse of black light and the frenzy increased as the ANA musicians announced the entry of the home team: the Lemurian Legions.

Prince Hadigan led the pack as was his royal right. Champion Tambeaux was fast behind him, focused and fierce. The other eight team members were just as ferocious and ready to slam the competition out of their way.

As there were ten members on a team, but only eight places in the game, the selection process, although usually sorted beforehand, was played out in a spectator-focused pregame challenge. The players bantered back and forth with their teammates in a supposedly friendly competition for each place in the game line-up.

The Kentari Knights were already running through their tricks and formations, and their display of effortless synchronicity delighted the crowd with a promise of an equal match against the Lemurian Legions.

The Legions played out their part in a seamless selection and the five bront runners and two front runners fell into place with a surprising twist.

The spectators and Holly were surprised as the Legion front runners flew into place on their smaller eagle rays, and the favorite, Champion Marin Tambeaux, was nowhere near them. She leaned in to Roland, who was more knowledgeable than most about the game and asked,

"Where's Champion Tambeaux going to be in all this?"

Roland scanned the field and shouted back over the crowd.

"I don't know. He always plays front runner."

The crowd hushed slightly as the announcer spoke.

"Trevels of Power, tonight we have an extra special treat for you as the position of trout for the Lemurian Legions is under challenge."

The crowd wailed in delight as two massive bull rays entered the field. Both teams retreated to their bases and the flat field began to rise with obstacles.

The announcer continued,

"His Royal Highness, the future Prince-in-One, Hadigan Darsaldain is being challenged for his treasured trout position by his own best friend and team favorite, Champion Marin Tambeaux."

It would not be unrealistic to say a number of Trevels nearly passed out in excitement, and it wasn't just the females of the population that were so affected. Such a challenge was unheard of, but no challenger was better favored for the feat.

Hadigan stood tall on his massive, black, flowing ray, both arms raised in the air in his usual crowd-pleasing conducting, charismatic, gregarious, and ever a show stopper.

In contrast, Marin stood straight, focused and determined. He gave a short nod to the crowd and waited, hands resting in preparedness behind his back.

In the age-old fashion of chivalry, each competitor was granted one salute to a particular favored one in the crowd.

Hadigan flew smoothly to where Holly sat and bent to one knee. He saluted her and threw her a kiss. Holly couldn't help feeling awkward as everyone stared at her image on the massive flicker screens.

Tanya put an encouraging arm around her sister's shoulders after Holly saluted back at her prince with a gentle, blushing smile. The crowd cheered and turned to see whom the champion would choose.

Marin's ray, a great grey flyer, hovered while Hadigan return to his place beside him. Stoic and unmoving up to this point, Marin finally broke rank and with a sideways glance at his prince, he also, flew directly to Holly and stood above her.

The crowd was nearly silent as he slowly raised his hand in Trevel salute to her. With definite distinction, Marin dropped his hand to point at her, his hand turned slowly palm upward in a move showing submission, not power. Such a thing is never seen in the ranks of the Strategists. He then flew off to the starting post and ignored the rage emanating from the prince.

It was game on!

The two bull rays "swam" three feet above the starting line and hovered in place, waiting in static tension for the starting flash.

There was the customary flash of black, then crack, lightning struck and the field was immersed in darkness, with only the running lights on the rays and the soft glow of the HDP-lined obstacles offering sight to the riders.

Hadigan was a master rider, as he and his ray were one in thought and action; neither liked to play fair. In the split second of darkness before the start, Hadigan's black ray had looped its tail around the tail of Marin's grey ray, and as Hadigan took off in sudden flight, the opposing grey felt the tug from behind and was sent into a flat spin at the starting post.

Marin nearly lost his footing but dropped to his knee and steadied his ride. They also were connected well and soon set off with a renewed determination that fast closed the gap across the obstacles chasing down the prince.

At the horseshoe bend, Marin raced at speeds that almost saw him fly right out the top of the loop. Hadigan, proving his expertise as trout and sniper, waited at the sharpest point in the bend and flew directly in front of Marin as he rounded. He flew upward across Marin's path, exposing the underbelly of his ray and flashing with full force the running lights directly into Marin's eyes.

Marin balked and his ray shied away from the sudden brightness. This time, Marin did lose his footing and flew off his ride, but the ray expertly doubled back and caught his master before he hit the floor.

Hadigan taunted him and shot a vine-whip at Marin's head. Marin ducked and caught it around his arm. He wound it tightly up his forearm, drawing the two closer together.

Then as the tension of the crowd frenzied, expecting hand-to-hand combat, Marin sprayed frozen water with such a force that the vine shattered, setting him free. He stared the prince down, tapped his foot, and he and his ray were off instantly in the lead.

Hadigan was only enraged more and pursued close behind all the way to the tower. Here each rider lay flat as his ray swam up the vertical limits, defying gravity only so far as they stayed within three feet of the HDP lining of the obstacle.

At the pinnacle of the tower, Hadigan, from behind, reached out to the tail of Marin's bull ray and grasped it, snatching it away with great force from the wall. The grey ray suddenly tipped backward, and Marin felt the fall begin.

He scrambled desperately to bring his ray back under him again, but the black ray jerked and blocked the move and

Hadigan kept a tight grip on the grey tail. Marin hung by only one hand, and the black ray swung its tail up in a quick sweep that severed the harness from Marin's grey. Hadigan, the great humanitarian that he was, held tight to the grey ray tail so as to stop it from falling, but Marin plummeted to the surface.

The stadium inhaled a gasp of horror as one, and Holly (and Joshun) cried out loud. The thud echoed off the HDP and rippled as Marin lay motionless.

Hadigan smoothly crossed the finish line, carrying the grey ray to safety. His victory was cheered, but rather less vigorously than he desired as Marin was carried off the field, motionless.

A Key Assignment

In the hallways deep beneath the stadium, Hadigan was shouting orders to his new agents, the Stilwells, and healers ran every which way. Marin was groggily coming to and moaned in pain.

Holly and Tanya pushed through the crowd, and when the Stilwells sought to keep them out, Holly threatened,

"If my Prince Hadigan finds out you've manhandled me, and I assure you he will find out, your head might as well sever itself from your neck." And without further hesitation, she pushed past.

The new agents considered blocking Tanya's entry, but she laughed,

"Oh, I don't think so," and forcibly made her way, also, to the limp form of Champion Tambeaux.

Mitch wasn't too far behind but was forced to join the remaining seven companions on the outside of the barriers.

Lexa looked ill, so Mitch comforted her.

"The course surface is supported by a layer of HDP cushioning that absorbs impact. He'll be sore, but nothing should be broken or permanently damaged."

Lexa snapped,

"I've been around Laray fields longer than you. Don't you think I know that?"

Mitch backed off a bit perturbed.

"Sorry, I just thought…"

Lexa continued,

"Well that's your problem, then, isn't it Bacht? You thought."

Mitch shook his head and walked away, but Lexa pursued him.

"Your precious naïve Tanya isn't here to defend you now, so let me just enlighten you as to your real predicament."

She grabbed Mitch's arm and pulled him up next to an empty wall covered in a mural depicting the Shifter Wars.

"You are the scum of the Earth, Bacht. Every Trevel resents being banished to the Underlands by a people of no power and no knowledge of us. No one here is ever going to accept you into any society or safety once Marin lifts his protection off you."

She paused to see if he understood.

"You are bound to serve the Trevel for the next five years, and if Marin was to die, you would be left to the gracious mercy of the Trevel Nation, of which there is no mercy, gracious or not, for any Bacht living among us."

Mitchell glanced back at where he saw the healers bustling around Marin in the background and began to feel decidedly uncomfortable.

"If you were to ever consider the impossibility of joining yourself with a Trevel in any way other than through servitude, not only would you be in danger of losing your life, but you would destroy the life of the one you were connected to, and the lives of her family and ALL her associations."

Mitch's mind clicked.

"You're not really concerned about Marin or Tanya or Holly are you? This is all about your precious social standing."

"No." Lexa squared her shoulders against the wall. "This is about you."

Mitch saw the looming figure of a Medusa painted behind Lexa and thought the likeness amusing. Lexa snarled at his grin.

"This is by no means comical, Bacht. I am the only daughter and sole heir of five generations of brilliant Trevel architects. I have the entire reputation of Belle's Architecture resting on my shoulders. My family name rests on buildings like the Atlantis National Academy, the palace of Lemuria, and the Parthenon itself. I will not have you undermine all that I am."

"If you and your family name is so great, then one little lowly Bacht shouldn't have any influence on it." He stepped away from her, hesitated and turned back, looking at the wall.

Lexa thought he had a final reply and waited to pounce on a rebuttal, but instead, Mitch walked back toward the wall counting his steps.

At the wall, he stopped and looked up and down the length of it, then back over his shoulder at the far wall, and looked puzzled.

"Something's not adding up."

Lexa was disgusted.

"What on earth are you talking about?"

Mitch kept sizing up the length of the passageway about him.

"The math here isn't right. There should be another room here."

Lexa rolled her eyes.

"I assure you there isn't."

"I know, but there should be."

Lexa sighed.

"You are daft. I have seen the blueprints of this entire place. I sat on my deda's knee as he drew them. This is all there is."

"No. You're wrong."

Suddenly, Principal Zanne was by them with her hand on Mitch's shoulder.

"Marin's asking for you."

Mitch was off in a flash. The principal scooted Lexa off after him and glanced up at the Medusa snarling down at her. Ms. Suzie Bore, the stables' guardian, came alongside her and whispered,

"It's too smart."

"Hush," said the principal. Then she turned and looked over to Mitchell seated beside his now recovering brother. "I have word from Colonah."

     ***   ***   ***

In the Tambeaux private suite, Principal Zanne sat opposite the champion on a bright balcony requesting an audience with the L1.

Marin nodded to the family Kobold, who scurried off to fetch the boy.

"Might I know the reason for your interest in my brother?"

Tambeaux was concerned there was an issue with his placement already.

Principal Zanne sipped her tea and commented,

"As guardian and protector of Atlantis National Academy, it is my business to make everyone my business, especially when there is an anomaly about."

"Anomaly?" Tambeaux was intrigued, but Mitch entered and saluted.

Principal Zanne gestured to a chair and studied the Bacht.

"I have been familiar with the family Tambeaux for many years now and I am fully aware that the champion, here, does not offer his favor to any who do not deserve it."

Marin shrugged in affirmation.

"And now, I have witnessed firsthand a rather dangerous intelligence about you."

The brothers questioned each other.

"Based on the trustworthiness of the Tambeaux name and on the recommendation from Prince Hadigan himself that you should be used for janitorial work, I am entrusting these keys to you, Bacht Mitchell, as I require you to perform the privilege of cleaning the mural in the lower catacombs beneath the stadium."

Here the Principal stood, brushed of her skirt and turned to leave.

"It has long since been left dormant and it has been brought to my attention that now is the time for such matters to be attended to. Thank you."

With that, she handed Mitchell an intricate key ring and exited the suite.

Marin looked from the keys in Mitch's hands and back to the now empty doorway.

"I sense you best guard those keys well, and tell no one of this interview."

Mitch nodded, curious and cautious.

Cupid's Contract

A Clean Discovery

The Big Game

Halftime

Who's the Rogue Now?

Chapter 21

Cupid's Contract

Marina entered Lord Deagan's private suite at ANA with the mail. She deposited the letters and various packages on the center table and hesitated as she heard the water beyond the bedroom turning off. She called to him,

"I have your correspondence, my Lord, it is on the table."

He called back,

"Thank you, Ambassador." As he rounded the door, he spoke directly to her. "You are consistently trustworthy."

Marina froze and tried desperately to shift her gaze off him.

He stood in all his furry magnificence with only a towel draped around his waist. His physique comprised the defined and cut body of a man, covered in the short fur of a red bull, the width of a tank. When his bull head shook, water droplets smattered off his long blond dreadlocks and his ears flickered sensitively against the curved horns.

Marina had never seen anything so appealing. It shocked her. She stuttered,

"I... it is-s-s only m-mine to s-serve." He stepped closer to her and she swallowed, continuing nervously, "And my honor to serve where I am needed."

He casually pulled the towel from his waist and dried his hair with it as he walked past her to the table, exposing fully the back of his figure.

Marina could not take her eyes off the muscular form and blushed at her inability to do so.

He kept turned away from her, looking through his mail, and commented,

"This form does not seem to raise fear in you as it does so many others." He turned slightly, but still modestly.

"Indeed, I could be mistaken, but it seems to please you."

Marina finally dropped her stare.

"It is a curious form, my Lord, one I am unused to. I find it interesting."

"Interesting?" He turned fully to face her. "But not pleasing?"

Her exterior iced over in professionalism.

"Pleasing is not the word I would choose," but her insides melted and she could barely stand.

Lord Deagan moved his back to her again and walked to survey his view from the glass doors over the balcony. He changed the subject.

"I have purposely secluded myself from the Trevel world and continue to hide my true figure from prying eyes, but the gossipmongers are restless to find a new fascination.

Does it bother you to remain in Hanain, away from all society other than musty miners and moneygrubbing mercenaries… and myself?"

"It is my duty and privilege to serve where I am placed." Marina spoke her champion code.

Lord Deagan turned and approached her slowly.

"You prove your worth as Ambassador well." He ran the back of his red fingers across her jawbone. "Ever my ice queen."

He walked past again back to his bedroom, and as he closed his door, Marina whispered barely audibly for his pricked ears,

"I would prove there is enough fire for you beneath all the ice."

Lord Deagan stopped and asked,

"What is more frightening to you, this form or the knowledge that I have another form, more compatible to yours?"

Marina walked to him. Standing close behind him, she whispered,

"My passions erase any fear and would embrace any and all that you are."

Lord Deagan stepped away from her closeness and pulled a blindfold from his dresser drawer.

"What if you may never see my other form?"

Marina responded,

"To see only with my heart is enough."

The Minotaur smiled and held out the blindfold. Marina took it and securely bound her eyes. Then, feeling his hot breath on her neck, she allowed the touch of his furless hands to take her.

A Clean Discovery

In the quiet hours of the afternoon before the championship game, Mitch distracted his nerves with the task Principal Zanne had bestowed upon him. Using the key ring he kept hidden around his neck on a long chain, he opened the doors to the catacomb chambers that lay deeper under the stadium grounds where the healers had attended to Marin the day before.

These walls were covered in the same HDP as the tunnels Lexa had showed Holly and were thus hidden from the knowledge of the general public, who presumed they were there but had no documented proof of their existence.

Indeed, the only Trevels who had factual knowledge of such places were those on the ANA higher council and select members of the Belle family who had access to the original blueprints. Presumably there were members of royalty and the National Senate who had access to such information also, but it was of no use to them, so they bothered little with it.

There was only one section of the walls that was not covered in HDP, and it was here that Mitch's curiosity had first been raised. There was a certain symmetry to the catacombs. They all looked alike, and it was impossible to tell the tunnels apart but for the labeling signs that hung about, except for that mural depicting the Shifter Wars.

It was the only oddity, and to one whose mind ran in mathematical forms and equations, it stuck out as stark as the number nine would in a list of primes.

Mitch had learned that the best method for cleaning such ancient artistry was with the now very familiar HDP fluid. He had a weak solution in spray form to apply to the wall, and while it was still wet, he would dust it down with an absorbent powder, allow to it dry, and then brush it off carefully with delicate bristles.

He set about this task, beginning on the nearest end and methodically moving up and down along the long wall in manageable columns.

He studied the pictures on the wall in detail. It was typically "religious" in nature, with light beams shining on the Trevels battling the terrors of the raging Shifters.

Images of the Shifters were many, varied, and realistic enough to satisfy any nightmare. There were fauns, toads, hydras, dragons, snakes, centaurs, werewolves, Medusas, and any number of other creatures who, in a different light, may have looked beautiful. But unicorns with blood-drenched flanks and horns and fairy folk clawing at faces were enough to turn anyone off the idea of happy nursery rhymes.

It was altogether gruesome.

About two-thirds of the way down the wall, Mitch tossed the absorbing powder as usual and found a small puff returning into his face on a tiny shot of wind. After coughing and clearing his eyes, he looked to find what the culprit was.

He slowly sprinkled another handful of dust along the fanged and fire breathing-face of a crying dragon. Its ear blew the dust back out again.

Mitch raised his flash lantern up to the face to study the black paint spot and saw it was not void of color after all, but rather void of wall. He ran his finger over it, testing the opening.

Fishing for his keys, he studied the small metal musical note that he'd originally thought to be just a decoration. It had an inscription that read,

Dragon Tears must hear the Song.

He inserted the musical symbol into the dragon ear, and it slid in easily. He tried twisting it, but there was no turning. He jiggled it some and felt it slip down as a lever. There was a jolt in the dragon wing as it jumped from the wall. Mitch wrapped his fingers under it and pulled.

A door, big enough to allow entry to any of the mighty Shifters on the wall, opened, and the suck of air rushing into a long-forgotten chamber pulled at Mitch. With the key ring back around his neck and flash lantern in hand, Mitch entered a place abandoned some 400 years previous.

It was another underground stadium. Although there was little seating for an audience, there was enough room for any amount of movement on the ground or in the air. There were basic training obstacles and other combat-related props lying around in much disarray.

It looked to Mitch like a training gym, with some sections roped off for small hand-to-hand bouts, weights and hanging bags for one-on-one training, and even a running track around the edge. There was a trough running along the wall with a liquid mixture siting dormant within.

He sniffed it and recognized the primitive scent. Thankful for the odd combination of modern Trevel technology and primitive Energy, Mitch opened the flash lantern he carried and exposed the live flame to the trough. It ignited, racing open flames all along the outer wall, down some side branches, and under and up into various posted lights. The open arena, awash in the dull orange flame, glowed in welcome.

A carving over the entry behind Mitch read:

> SHIFT NOW IN PEACE AND PREPARATION,
>
> FOR TOMORROW
>
> THE WORLD WILL SHIFT AGAINST YOU.

The Big Game

Tanya felt the extra jostling in the crowd as she, Holly, and their other seven schoolmates pushed through the crush up the stadium bleachers before the NLL Championship Game. Tanya turned and was surprised to see Mitch at her elbow.

Lexa squealed,

"Mitch, what are you doing here? Who's running the Course?"

Mitch laughed and assured her,

"Nothing to do for a while yet, it's all on auto until the game begins." But he pulled Tanya aside and whispered into her ear. Then he nodded at Holly and disappeared before anyone realized there was a Bacht on the loose.

Holly quizzed Tanya with her eyes. Tanya responded with a look only a sibling would understand. The two jiggled around their seats and found a way to get next to each other. When everyone else was occupied, Holly snuggled into her sister and listened as Tanya spoke in hushed tones.

"Mitch says he's found a secure solution for our storage issue." She fingered her chest where Holly knew her Hanain diamond always lay out of sight.

The girls had been receiving one package a week from Jaack Mining and were in need of hiding places away from house monitors who came through the rooms to check on in-house cleanliness.

Tanya continued,

"He says we're to meet him in the tech bunker at halftime."

Roland was watching the girls' quiet conversation. He leaned over Holly and said,

"You know we can keep you safer if you keep us all in the know."

The sisters exchanged nods in recognition of true support. Holly spoke behind her telescope glasses.

"We'll need to get there separately, but tell the others to meet us in the tech bunker at halftime."

Throughout the course of pregame banter, the message was passed along and the nine were in agreement.

***   ***   ***

The National Laray League Championships and its flickervision images cast all around the Trevel world began with a bang.

A crash of thunder jolted everyone out of their seats and lightning flashed as the royal cavalcade entered the arena.

Holly and Tanya had originally been scheduled to be included in this pomp and ceremony, but due to Tanya's recent illness, they were excused. The young women sighed deep relief as they watched the spectacle from their anonymous perch in the crowd.

King Darsaldain gave his typical droning speech of inspiration, to which few listened. Then the announcer called forth the players and every set of eyes became riveted on the field.

The Kentari Knights entered to the usual dull, roaring cheer, as the crowd expected them to receive a good walloping. They paraded the course field under the banner of green and gold, heads held high, defenses sharp, and their responses swift. The tails of their rays practically shivered in excited anticipation of a good run.

The Lemurian Legions entered amid deafening tumult under their banner of red and purple, ferocious, proud, and expecting victory. Their rays' tails slowly twitched back and forth, seeking whom they might slice.

Champion Marin Tambeaux stood tall on his smaller, brown eagle ray in the position of right front runner. Prince Hadigan brought up the rear on his mighty black bull ray. He waved to the crowd but kept rank and did not break focus.

The teams lined up at the start line: the two front runners of each team on either end, the five bront runners mixing together behind them in agitated defense, and finally, a space behind, the two teams' bull rays floated in trout position.

The lights dimmed and all hushed. A single spotlight burned from halfway down the length of the field to highlight where the tack was perched precariously, waiting to be captured by either team and carried across the finish line.

There were to be ten laps of the field, with the course obstacles changing at least three times mid-play, five laps per game half. Mitch had to be on his toes to move the entire field in a fluid transition that caused the least amount of danger to all players in the field—although the players were held responsible for their own injuries, never the tech support.

The sudden black light flash startled screams from many in the crowd, and lightning cracked the start of the race. The lights fell, and only the soft blue glow of the HDP-lined course and the running lights under each of the flying stingrays lit the way for any to see.

Holly gripped Tanya's arm, not sure where to cast her eye as the front runners neared the tack first. The running lights on both trout bull rays had been extinguished as soon as the race started, and no one knew where these rogue players were.

Marin came to the tack first, but instead of reaching for it, he flew right over it directly into the oncoming front runners of the opposing team. The other Legion front runner dove at the Knights bront runners and flashed his running lights at them as Hadigan had done to Marin in their pregame match. The five Legion bront runners circled the tack together, and it was impossible to see who snatched it, but instantly they accelerated to the first obstacle.

The Legion front runners circled their bront with the tack, and as the Knight bront runners wove in and out of them to dislodge the riders, the tack was expertly passed among them all. The Knights could not get possession.

After the first lap, suddenly the tack went flying as its possessor was tossed mercilessly from his stand by an unseen force. The Knights' rogue trout runner flashed on his headlights, snatched up the tack, and immediately tossed it to the Knights' left front runner, then disappeared into darkness again.

The Legions pursued with fierce power, and the Knights had difficulty maintaining possession.

Roland suddenly swore loudly and grabbed at the telescope glasses. Joshun even cried in dismay and said in too loud a voice,

"He's losing it."

Holly and Tanya tried to see what the commotion was as it became obvious that others in the crowd were concerned in a similar manner.

One of the red-and-purple-decorated eagle rays was off on its own, flying as a trout might, away from the rest of the pack. It flashed its light on a large black spot ahead, and the crowd realized Marin was chasing not the tack but his own trout runner!

He had flown on past the teams fighting for possession and was climbing a waterfall obstacle fast behind what was now obviously the Legion's rogue trout runner. There was a sudden jolt in the pattern of the eagle ray's flight path and a flash as it stopped instantaneously in midflight.

The HDP lining on the wall beside the waterfall flared up as if it had been hit, and the crowd followed the ragged descent of a ray tumbling over and over itself all the way to the bottom of the obstacle.

A howling whistle blew and the lights came up. Prince Hadigan's ray was perched at the top of the waterfall, and Champion Marin Tambeaux lay in a bloody heap with a broken-winged eagle ray flopping on top of him.

The other team members pulled up and separated, the Knights still in possession of the tack. A foul was called against the right front runner for the Lemurian Legions due to anti-teammate-ship, as he had revealed the location of his own trout runner.

Marin was carried off the field, a replacement front runner flew up to the starting line, and the game continued as the lights dimmed again.

Holly, without a look back, ran off to the tech bunker, and Tanya followed with a quick backward glance. The others nodded her on, and she knew they'd meet up again at halftime.

Halftime

Holly flew past the tech bunker into the catacombs where she remembered the healers working on Marin before. Mitch had the bunker door open and nodded to Tanya, who had stopped in the doorway.

He was working in purposed fervor as the first obstacle change of the evening was underway. The first course series melted into the HDP and the second field course rose up to meet the riders, who barely missed a beat. One of the Knights was nearly sideswiped by a rising wave, but his ray was careful and switched course in time.

Tanya slipped inside and quietly closed the door, watching her Bacht conduct his technical concerto with focused ease. Once complete, the riders still had two laps remaining until halftime.

Mitch ran his hands through his blond curls and said with a grin,

"There, that's much better."

Tanya grinned weakly and took Mitch's offered hand. He left the course in the care of his attendants, and the two ran into the catacombs to find Holly and Marin.

Marin was thrashing about under the pressure of his healers and making a dreadful fuss.

"Marin, please," begged Holly, "be still so we can help you."

"I'm fine." Marin pushed himself up from the mattress they were trying to strap him to. "It looks worse than it is."

Mitch rested a hand on his brother's shoulder.

"Then that must be pretty bad, mate, 'cos you look awful."

Marin grasped Mitch's hand, and whispered,

"Get rid of the healers, brother."

"They're just trying to help—" Mitch was cut off.

"Get rid of the healers, just for a moment. I have to speak to Holly."

"I'm right here, Marin." Holly moved into his line of vision. One of the healers tried to push her away.

Marin exploded and gripped the wrist of the offending healer with such force as to nearly break it.

"You, don't touch her!"

Mitch stepped in and begged a moment of quite conversation, with the healers finally granting Marin the tiny space he needed to speak.

"I need to talk to you Holly. I need to see you somewhere he can't."

Holly's eyes were large and full of tears. She looked at Tanya and Mitch in desperation.

Mitch said,

"I have somewhere. I'll take the girls there now."

Marin began to protest, but Mitch scolded him,

"You play nice with the healers and get them all out of here, and by the end of the game be back here alone." Marin's senses began to register reason again. Mitch continued, straightening up, "But for now, play nice." And that was all the warning they got before Prince Hadigan swept in, overly concerned for his teammate.

The halftime entertainment celebrations had begun.

Marin recomposed himself into silence and allowed the healers to carry him out to a more substantial place for healing, and Mitch saw the seven others slowly filtering into the shadows, waiting for them. He backed away from Hadigan, not wanting to start anything, but he hadn't gotten too far when Hadigan spoke to him.

"Are you supposed to be out of the bunker without your attendants?"

"I was concerned for my brother, Your Highness."

Crack. Hadigan backhanded Mitchell so fast he nearly lost his footing. The prince stepped in close to Mitch's now bleeding nose.

"You will never address me directly again, Bacht."

Mitch backed down in a bow that was overly humble and wiped his bloody lip with his middle finger in a gesture of rudeness only the Bacht would understand.

Hadigan nodded in conceited satisfaction and turned to address Holly.

"I hope you are not too distressed by the rough accidents of this game, my lady." He kissed her hand.

"Nah, my prince." Her voice was slightly strained. "I am only glad you are safe."

In a gesture of uncommon familiarity, Prince Hadigan Andrew swept Holly into his arms and kissed her till she swooned, and he promised her,

"If you love me, I am invincible."

Holly sighed girlishly as he put her back on her feet, and Lexa came out of the sidelines to steady her, equally starry eyed in the orbit of the prince.

Hadigan surveyed the ten companions lingering in the hallways and spoke after a brief silence.

"You're quite the rag-tag collection of fellows, aren't you?"

Everyone bowed politely. The prince paused a moment and restudied each of them.

"Yet I think, perhaps, not so unbalanced as would first appear; interesting."

He straightened himself in a disconcerted air and said,

"Be off with you all, then."

And they all filtered out of the corridor back in the direction of the bunker. The prince turned to the opposite direction while Tanya tried to attend to Mitch's nose. But he brushed her off, saying,

"Let me check something in the bunker. You all meet me by the mural." He ran off quickly.

He had dashed into the tech bunker and flicked a few switches to secure things until he could get back when he double glanced at the screen showing the mural and his friends.

He looked closer and saw Tanya was not in the group. He flipped through a few screens until he came back to where he'd left the prince.

Tanya was there, looking like a prize trophy as Prince Hadigan circled her, licking his lips. She was trembling and shivered violently as he traced a familiar finger up her inner thigh.

Mitch's heart lurched.

Hadigan leaned in to kiss but lingered centimeters from her lips, and she leaned into him, but he pulled away and snapped his head back as one of the Stillwell triplets called his attention, and he walked off without a second glance at her.

Mitch stared in disbelief.

Tanya was immobile, still searching for a forgotten touch. Then a tear slipped down her cheek and she grasped her hip and doubled over.

Mitch didn't know whether to run to her or catch her through the screen.

Tanya slowly stood again and glared after the exiting royal with eyes full of hate. She shook off the struggle within and limped off toward the mural.

Mitch's fist shattered the glass on the console and his blood-encrusted lip quivered in rage.

He reached the mural at the same time as a perfectly composed Tanya, and she smiled at him but kept her hand lightly resting in her jeans hip pocket.

Wordlessly Mitch unlocked the dragon song door and ushered everyone inside quickly.

They were aghast, but Mitch didn't allow them time.

"We have four minutes until I need to be back."

Holly pulled her backpack off her shoulders, opened it, and passed everyone a small cloth bag, explaining,

"There was a room inspection at Bowra House so we've been carrying these around all week."

Tanya interrupted,

"They're Hanain diamonds that have not been processed. They are essentially the only weapons a Trevel cannot defend against, as they suck you dry of all energy you might possess."

The seven were dumbfounded. Lexa began to interrupt, but Holly stopped her.

"Lord Deagan is stockpiling these. We've seen his weapons with our own eyes, and this is all the Trevel Nation has to counter him should he attack."

The party members studied their sacks gingerly.

"We need to hide these now." Mitch addressed them and began stuffing a bag into a hanging punching bag. "Find a place here, and don't forget where you put yours." The group stared around in a daze.

"Do it now. We have to be out of here before the game begins again."

Everyone rushed about and did as bidden.

Who's the Rogue Now?

Several members of the crowd booed and jeered as the nine friends found their seats late. The game was beginning again. The Legions had possession of the tack and a two-minute head start off the line in accordance with where they'd completed the last lap at the end of half one.

The black light flashed and they were off. Hadigan instantly disappeared.

The nine tried to look focused on the game but kept buzzing back and forth with each other as Tanya and Holly sporadically relayed all they'd come to understand in Hanain.

The first course change was underway almost immediately into the first lap, and one of the Knights lost balance and was sent hurtling against the side HDP wall. He slithered off the field quickly and was immediately replaced by the reserve flyer at the starting line.

The replacement runner paid no heed to the battle over the tack, as he was required to complete all ten laps by the time his team finished, so he set about a speed race like no other.

The Legions' royal trout came out of hiding in a desperate attempt to hinder him, but surprisingly, speed was this runner's forte and Hadigan had a hard time keeping on him.

The tack was passed along and dropped a couple of times when the new player caught up, but the Legions had possession and there was just over one lap to go.

The crowd's tension was tangible as everyone guessed what was about to happen. Mitch certainly knew how to build a good game. He'd waited for the final course change until the field runners all entered the last lap, hoping for a smooth run home.

But the obstacles began moving, and their flight paths were constantly changing in directions they could not guess. Prince Hadigan was up ahead and called to his front runner, who had possession. He saw the chance and threw a mighty cast across to Hadigan, who dove into the air in order to catch it. There was a tense pause as his ray swooped around underneath him and caught him deftly and triumphantly only meters from the finish.

Hadigan, unable to contain himself, waved at the crowd just as a great wall crashed up through the floor and tossed him ten feet into the air and the tack careened directly into the arms of the waiting Kentari left front runner.

Hadigan thudded to the cushioned floor, the wind knocked out of him and his pride cracked. He scrambled to his feet with his ray nudging his legs behind him and watched in horror as the entire team of Kentari Knights sailed over the finish line, tack held high.

Mitch pulled his hand off the controls, breathing slowly and steadily.

His attendants looked at him horrified. One of them squeaked in a strained voice,

"If he finds out you did that, you'll take a terrible long time to die."

Mitch growled,

"If he finds out you didn't stop me, so will you."

Out of Sight

Face-Off

Unlikely Rescue

Marina Breaks Trust

Chapter 22

Out of Sight

Mitch was closing up the tech bunker alone (his attendants had fled in determined silence) when the nine students clambered down to meet him. He slowly flickered off each screen showing the now flat field a tumbling mess of partying revelers.

The Kentari Knights were instant heroes, and Prince Hadigan was giving a pleasant congratulatory speech that only a true politician could pull off. Lexa was breathless and babbling incessantly about the game.

Mitch pushed them out and instructed,

"Go wait by the dragon. I'll be there in a bit." He couldn't even look at Tanya. She lingered behind.

"Tell me you didn't do that on purpose," she joked with him.

"I didn't do that on purpose," he recited and fell silent.

Tanya became concerned and approached him.

"I know he's rude but, please, tell me you didn't just sabotage the biggest game in all Trevellia over a bloody nose."

"I didn't just sabotage the biggest game in all Trevellia over a bloody nose."

Tanya pulled his arm and jerked him around to face her.

"Mitch."

She looked at him in horror.

"I expect more of you."

Mitch grabbed her around her hip and dug his thumb in too deep. She couldn't help cry out in shock as her body pulsed and convulsed.

He looked her in the eyes and said,

"Just as I expect more of you."

She faltered and glanced over his shoulder to the screens, all blank but one smashed screen that showed through the broken glass where she'd had her last encounter with the prince. Her face flushed and tears welled in her eyes. She stuttered,

"I-I c-c-can explain…" She paused.

"No, I can't explain. I don't even know what it is."

Mitch took her face in his hands.

"I saw it all." She tried to look away, but he held her and continued, "I saw it all, which means, I saw the way he looked at you. I saw the way he manipulated you. I saw you tremble and I saw the hate in your eyes when he left."

Tanya allowed the tears to flow in the peace of being understood.

Mitch kissed her and whispered,

"And for that I sabotaged the biggest game in all Trevellia." Tanya's eyes widened. "He's lucky for the HDP. I wanted to kill him."

Tanya stared at him.

"You can't kill the Royal Prince-in-One, heir to the throne of all Trevels."

Mitch gathered his things and closed the door behind them.

"Not yet I can't."

"Wattle-Gum Gecko Mitchell Tambeaux, Bacht! What are you saying?"

"What?" shrugged Mitch, "He's not my god."

They ceased their conversation as they met the others. Mitchell ushered them all in and stood outside to watch for Marin, who limped in only minutes later.

Mitch smiled at him.

"You still look like crap, and you're late."

Marin slapped him affectionately on the neck.

"Not late. I'm on Champion time."

Mitch walked him through the door, and as Tambeaux wandered into the Shifter training grounds, eyes wide and amazed, Mitch asked,

"What the hell is Champion time?"

"I'm Champion, it's my time." Marin recited his all too familiar response, then he gazed in awe at all he saw.

He then exclaimed, "Holy Zeus on Mt. Olympus, if my family had known about this generations ago, the Shifter Wars never would have gone on so long."

"Then it's a good thing your family didn't find out, isn't it?"

Prince Hadigan stood smug in front of the nine companions, all bound, gagged, and unconscious in the pollen mist put off by the beautiful flowered vine: Taliamaland.

Face-Off

"I always thought a good, long war was a great cleansing for a nation,"

Prince Hadigan taunted the champion.

Marin snatched at his weapon hilt—too late, as Hadigan whipped it out of his hand.

Mitch was on alert, darting his eyes all over, quickly analyzing and adjusting to the terrain and sizing up the true threat of his opponent.

Though Marin's hand was forced, he didn't back down.

"What in Hades do you think you're doing, Haddy?"

"'Haddy' again, is it?" Hadigan sauntered to his friend. "You try to steal my woman, steal my game, and steal my pride in a matter of moments and suddenly we're backyard playfellows again?" He glanced at Mitch. "Although I believe you are the one who stole my pride tonight, aren't you, boy?"

"It's just a pity the HDP stopped me from stealing your life," Mitch hissed.

Prince Hadigan cracked his thorn whip at Mitch, and he jumped aside, but not before she'd scratched his shirt open and left an orange and bloody trail across his shoulder.

Mitch flinched under the sting but kept his footing. Haddy giggled at him.

"I told you not to speak directly to me, and now it looks like you may never speak again." The mad prince tilted his head and watched as the orange juice soaked into the boy's skin.

Mitch grimaced slightly and lifted his hand to his shoulder, but Hadigan warned him. "Oh I wouldn't touch it if I were you, it will only spread."

Marin rushed to his brother's side as Mitch's knees buckled under the intense heat and pain emanating from his shoulder. The orange juice was slowly corroding his skin and threatening the muscle tissue.

Marin demanded of the royal,

"What have you done?"

Haddy replied,

"It's still in its testing phase, but I believe I've found the perfect corrosive that eats through anything and doesn't stop… unless of course you apply the antidote." Here he pulled out a delicate vial and rolled it along his fingers.

Marin walked to Hadigan slowly,

"If that bleeds through…" His voice broke, "Please, Haddy… Your Highness, please let me heal him."

"You know I've always known that about you, Marin." Marin's face paled. The prince continued, "The question is, have you told anyone else?"

He snapped his fingers and Taliamaland tossed Holly out of the pack slowly rousing to consciousness once she landed outside the puff of pollen filled air at Hadigan's feet

Marin froze, and Mitch called out in a strangled voice,

"Don't do it, Marin."

"Awe, isn't that sweet." Hadigan stepped around Holly as she steadied herself up off the floor, then he bent over, grabbed Mitch's face, and looked deep into his eyes. "No, you love Marin only as a brother…"

He stood and faced Marin. "That's gotta hurt. I bet bringing him into Trevellia and your personal household was the hardest thing you've ever felt, isn't it, lover boy, or is it lover of boys?"

Holly looked at Tambeaux in slow recognition.

"Marin?"

"Oh, don't be dismayed my soon-to-be princess… he loves you. He's just not the type of man who is, shall we say, biased in his affections."

Marin pleaded again, "Hadigan, please." He held out his hand. "Give me the antidote."

Hadigan continued his monologue,

"Y'know I've always been curious about your lack of preference. I mean, is there a preference?" He looked at

Holly, then at Mitch who was failing miserably in his attempts not to writhe in pain. "Shall we see?"

Before Marin could do or say anything, Taliamaland whipped out and slashed Holly across her back. She screamed and fell to the floor.

"Now then, Champion," Mad Haddy surveyed his victims, "which one are you more likely to tear open to save the other one?" He pulled Holly's face close to his and kissed her, then said, "Open wide," and held the vial as if to force its contents down her throat.

Marin pounced on the prince with all his might, and the two rolled on the floor in violent thrashings while the vial of antidote rolled further away from all of them.

Hadigan had Marin pinned and was pounding him mercilessly with his fist. Marin kneed Hadigan's back with just enough force to off balance him and wrestled him to the ground again.

Marin's hands were around Hadigan's throat, and he gargled in suffocation when Holly whimpered and pulled on the vine energy of Taliamaland, as she was wavering close to Marin's throat.

Taliamaland was furious at being pulled on. She whipped out to grasp Marin's neck and jerked him up off the floor, dangling him in the silence of hanging.

Hadigan stood and brushed himself off, Marin hanging and struggling for breath above him. He clicked his tongue in disappointment at Holly.

"Never piss off a plant, my dear, you ought to know better."

The next thing that occurred cannot be explained, only stated:

Hadigan in one moment stood in his madness scolding them all like a mother hen; then suddenly he was a trunk of deadwood.

Unlikely Rescue

Holly screamed, not believing her senses, but then crumpled, whimpering under the pain of her corroding back. Mitchell was nearly blacked out in pain. Marin was nearly dead. Lord Deagan caught Marin as he fell, for Taliamaland shriveled and fell to dust.

The unconscious companions slowly began coming to.

The great warrior gently laid Marin down as he gasped for breath. Then he swiftly reached for the antidote vial and poured a few drops onto Holly's back, stepped over to Mitchell, and did the same to him.

Groggy and shocked, the companions stood motionless, except for Tanya, who instantly clambered to her sister's side.

Lord Deagan rested a soft hand on Tanya's shoulder. She looked at him with teary eyes and he assured her,

"It looks like a fast heal. I can handle this one, but your boy over there needs more tender care than I can offer him."

Tanya hesitated only a moment before rushing to Mitchell, who was still moaning and twitching in agony. She applied one or two drops more of the antidote, then began singing a healing song her mother had taught her. He soon calmed and lay more peacefully in her lap.

Nikkos knocked on the deadwood statue of the prince. Lord Deagan suggested,

"After what we've heard of him tonight, I'd recommend destroying that."

Nikkos obliged by hurling an axe at his head, and Misty blasted a fireball. Lexa was horrified at the idea of destroying royalty.

"You can't kill a prince!"

Lord Deagan, confident that Holly was healing well, told Lexa,

"Can and did."

They each looked at the statue that seemed to shun their attempts to destroy it.

"That, my sweet lady, is not a prince anymore. It's now deadwood, and there's only one way to destroy wood if it's petrified."

Lord Deagan bent before the giant trunk and hoisted it onto his massive shoulders.

Roland whistled and whispered to Katiel,

"That thing must weigh more than five regular trees that size."

The mighty bull-helmed warrior staggered to the edge of the level they stood on, grunted loudly, and shifted the trunk into the air on straight arms; then, with all his might, he threw the tree upon the rocks below, where it shattered like brittle glass.

Marina Breaks Trust

It was a miserable trip. The sudden murder of the Prince-in-One ricocheted around the entire Trevel world, both Underland and Upland.

The injustice of losing such a vibrant life and beloved hero was sharply felt by everyone — except the companions now smuggled under the tarpaulin of a Gypsy caravan.

It was raining, cold, cramped, and stuffy. Nikkos commented that it was just good that Lord Deagan had decided not to smuggle himself out and was sitting up by Champion Marina (who was driving), not hiding with them in such close quarters.

Lexa complained,

"He's the one everyone knows murdered the prince, so why are we the ones being smuggled out?"

Roland snuggled closer to Katiel and laughed.

"Because I doubt even King Darsaldain himself would dare challenge Lord Deagan."

Holly glanced out from under the covers to the Gypsies following behind on foot. Lord Deagan wasn't the only one not hiding his escape.

Champion Marin Tambeaux also walked out in the open, though no one would recognize him.

Holly watched the downcast figure trudging in the crowd. He no longer wore any recognition of his military status, not even in his gait.

Instead, his shoulders were slumped, his head downcast, and his eyes never left his feet.

Holly winced as they hit a bump and Mitchell Tambeaux moaned groggily. Marin glanced up at the covered wagon and caught Holly's eyes watching him out of the darkness. He dropped his gaze back to his feet.

The reason they were all fleeing was because of the wounds Holly and Mitch had sustained. Taliamaland was a terrifying poison.

The only one who might be capable of manufacturing more vials of antidote was Hadigan's private scientist, Gash Arabol, from out of the Amazon jungle. They had arranged to meet him halfway in Hanain.

Holly tried to sleep to escape the pain. She almost envied Mitch's state of semi-consciousness. Another jolt and she rolled off her side to her stomach to find some comfort, but the caravan stopped completely and the Gypsies bustled about, preparing to set up camp.

Lord Deagan spoke from behind his bull mask.

"You'll be safe here. You can get out now."

Roaring fires, freely shared alcohol, and savory meats lightened the spirits of the ten companions. Breezer tried to invite Marin to join them, but he sullenly hung off to the side, then stalked off after his sister when he saw she was without her Lord Deagan.

"Marina."

Marina paused and sighed.

"I'm just going to the loo. Can I please have a moment of privacy?"

"You don't seem to care for privacy when Lord Deagan is around."

"Fine, let's have this out now." Marina turned to her bother.

"What exactly do you know about your precious Lord Deagan?"

Marin whispered conspiratorially.

"Marin, you have misjudged him from the start." Marin began to protest, but Marina would have her way. "No, listen. Just because the new kid on the block is someone you know nothing about and you are out of control and out of the loop for the first time in your life, you're threatened by him."

Marin clenched his jaw as Marina continued.

"And now that he not only saved your life but also killed the bane of your existence for you, where you could not, you absolutely refuse to trust him."

"You're right, I don't trust him, because a man like that doesn't just pop out of the ground, or come from nowhere."

Marina adjusted her gaze.

"Is this because he likes me instead of you?"

"What? No! It has nothing to do with that."

"You selfish bastard, you're just cranky because he only likes women, this woman, and you want a piece of that fine specimen and you can't have him."

Marin could not speak through his anger, so he turned and stalked off. He stopped mid-step and came back to her, spitting the words,

"I know he doesn't let you see him when he's with you. Don't you wonder why? Where's all your Defense Strategist training while you're blindly whoring yourself out to him?"

Marina slapped him in the face. She looked at her bother in disgust.

"You never did allow yourself to truly understand love."

He walked away from her and sat facing the fire opposite Breezer, Joshun, and Misty who were playing a loud game of chance. He didn't even flinch when Lord Deagan walked out of the camp holding Marina's hand, entering a dark cave with her.

Nikkos, however, watched after the giant man and lithe young woman and spoke the silent thought.

"How does that work, exactly?"

Lexa turned up her nose.

"I don't even want to know."

The trio playing chance squealed in drunken delight. Roland threw a pillow at Nikkos.

"Time you went off to your own fantasy land, don't you think?"

"Absolutely... Do any of you ladies care to join me?"

Breezer spat out the drink in her mouth in laughter and Misty said,

"Yeah, right!"

Joshun responded,

"Not tonight, love, I'm not into little boys."

Nikkos snorted,

"I said ladies!" He turned to Lexa. "How about you, babe? Ya want some metal to ground your lightning?"

"Great Jove," Lexa covered her mouth, "I think I'm going to be sick."

Breezer did throw up and then promptly passed out in drunkenness. Misty giggled and snuggled together with her under a blanket. She patted the spot behind her and said to Joshun,

"Keep me warm, babe?"

Joshun glanced across the fire at the eyes that had been staring at him all evening.

"Sorry, hon, I need to go visit the forest fairies first." He stood up and wandered into a darkened area of the surrounding woodlands.

Nikkos sighed and stared at Breezer passed out, Misty nearly snoring, and Lexa daintily laying her solo blankets out smoothly by the fire. Tanya was sleeping between her drugged sister and the Bacht, and Roland already lay comfortably, cradling Katiel's sleeping head on his chest.

"A man just wants a little lovin'," Nikkos pouted. He heard a hiss behind him, and a young gypsy girl poked her head out from under a nearby wagon. She winked at him. Nikkos smiled. "Now that's what I'm talkin' about." He quickly slid under the wagon.

Marin stood and tossed some more wood on the fire, turned, and wandered off into the dark woods in the same direction as Joshun's search for forest fairies.

In the cave, Marina was filled and satisfied with her love. Her blindfold was secure and her heart was free. She nestled in his arms and stroked the smooth skin on his chest. He breathed deeply and soundly.

The voice of her brother nagged in her mind.

"I know he doesn't let you see him when he's with you. Don't you wonder why, where's all your Defense Strategist training…"

She shook her head to silence him and her blindfold fell slightly limp.

She rushed her hand up to keep her eyes covered, then froze and lay still. Slowly she rolled her head toward her love, and with her eyes closed, she felt the material slip down. A quick glance wouldn't hurt. It had fallen off naturally, after all. She couldn't help what happened in her sleep.

She fluttered her eyes open and shut.

Her brain would not register what it saw. She did it again, but this time her brain did register and she sat up suddenly gasping.

He woke.

Seeing her look him full in the face, he shivered back into his full Minotaur form, and in all the power and rage of a man just betrayed, he roared at her in fury.

She cowered and cried, shaking her head, not allowing herself to believe what she'd just seen.

Hanain Refuge

Funeral for the Ages

Psyche

The Unraveling

Chapter 23

Hanain Refuge

The Gypsy camp was startled awake just before dawn by what seemed to be a violent wind storm. The dirt was stirred up around about them and blinded the hung-over travelers. The covered wagons began tipping and Tanya screamed trying to hold both Holly and Mitch as they rolled unconscious onto the pre-dawn dew.

Then an earthquake hit, but almost immediately all was quiet. In the silence, the piercing scream of Nikkos's young bed-fellow terrified them more than the sight of the great grey-green bull dragon newly landed in their midst.

No body stirred and the scaly face surveyed the crowd before him. He sniffed the air, testing it then twisted his head toward the cliff caves.

A sudden movement saw his massive clawed paw punch through the rock wall and retract holding a stunned, and rather worse for wear Marina Tambeaux.

Lord Deagan came raging out of the cave in full view of the entire camp revealing the true nature of his Minotaur form for the first time to all in attendance.

He rushed at the dragon, who calmly reared up on his back legs, cracked the air with his wings, and took off with Marina as his prize.

Lord Deagan tossed his staff, now a mighty scythe, at the scales, but it plinked off and fell impotent to the ground. The dragon and Marina were gone.

The Minotaur roared in despair after his mistress. Marin fell to his knees, blinded by tears, staring into the Skyling above.

"Get the wagons standing, we leave in fifteen minutes." Lord Deagan threw himself against a wagon and raised it to its wheels alone. Tanya rocked on her knees, gripping the hands of her drugged loved ones. She moaned.

Lord Deagan roared at them all again,

"Get up, I tell you! We need to be in Hanain in two days, or they die."

Tanya's quivering lip only mouthed her name.

"Marina."

"She will not be his for long." The Minotaur slumped slightly, and said, "All in good time." Then he set his warrior focus to the duty at hand.

The strain on Lexa was too much for her to remain calm.

"What are we to do? Where will we go?"

"You will go to Hanain." Marin handed her the bedroll at her feet. "You will see to Holly and Mitch. And you will wait until we know what more will come of all this." Marin then shouldered his pack and began walking into the forest.

Joshun called,

"Where are you going?"

Marin responded without turning back,

"My sister needs me."

Roland stopped him.

"You do not stand alone in this, Champion."

Marin shook him off.

"I'm no one's champion now."

And he left.

Funeral for the Ages

The white circle-city Clusters of Lemuria and Atlantis were, by Royal Decree, painted red as they mourned the royal blood that was lost. A nation of mighty gods fell to its knees as its king bent to the agony of having to bury his only son.

The declaration of guilt attributed to the crazed Shifter, Lord Deagan, stirred up the Defense Forces in a restless readiness. Rumors of frightening new weapons ran rampant and curfews kept the Cluster streets quiet after the Skyling went dark.

The day of the funeral saw the weather manipulated accordingly to a steady rain that soaked the cold hearts of the once reveling crowd of sports fans.

The procession from the palace was slow, and Tanya and Holly kept the curtains closed on their carriage as they descended through the rotations of the main road.

Gash Arabol sat opposite the girls and watched Holly in deep concern. She was healing well in body, but her spirit was considerably dull. Tanya, also distracted, held in her heart deep agony, as she'd been required to surrender Mitchell to the slave hospital. He was now alone without a sponsor.

King Darsaldain had called the nine ANA students out of Hanain, offering them places as heroes. It was broadly known how the nine had suffered at the wretched hands of the mad Shifter before and after he murdered the Prince-in-One in cold blood, then kidnapped them as the only ones brave enough to try and stand in his way.

Lord Deagan pushed them to accept the offer and try to regain their lives.

The carriage halted and the girls winced, listening to the pomp and wailing of a nation attending the funeral grander than the wedding that they had all hoped for. Gash leaned forward in the quiet carriage.

He laid his hand on Holly's knee and stuttered, "I-I am no p-prince, or Champion, but, I c-c-can offer you s-s-some peace…"

Holly stared at him with vacant eyes.

He continued,

"Y-you can s-s-stay w-with me in the B-B-Blue C-Castle n-near Latoona."

Holly turned to stare out the covered window and flatly refused him.

"I promised them I'd finish school."

Gash retreated, but Tanya asked him,

"What will become of Mitch?"

Gash said,

"Unless someone pays to sponsor him, he'll be sent to the weapons factory. War is brewing, weapons are needed."

There was a knock on the carriage door and Gash opened it up to Lexa. She climbed in and sat close to Holly.

Holly asked her,

"What did she say?"

Lexa recited,

"Principal Zanne says all will 'continue, continue, continue' as best as possible like before. The Atlantis National Academy did not crumble during the first Shifter wars, and it will not crumble now. Classes resume in a week; all in attendance are expected to return."

Katiel then burst in through the door.

"Isn't it great news?" She squeezed Tanya's hand and smiled, expecting returned happiness.

Tanya looked at her puzzled.

Katiel prompted,

"About Mitch…"

Tanya looked accusingly at Lexa and asked,

"What about Mitch?"

Lexa apologized.

"I didn't have the chance to tell them, yet."

Katiel burst out,

"Principal Zanne had ANA buy Mitch's sponsorship. He's to return to the stables as soon as he's fully healed."

Tanya glared at Lexa, but turned and opened the curtain. Looking out at the rain, she smiled and squeezed Katiel's hand back.

Psyche

The rain drenched her broken body and Marina gasped awake as shock set in and her frame rattled uncontrollably.

She lifted herself as well as her broken ribs would allow and saw around about her nothing but water and rocks. She'd been tossed from the sky onto the outcropping on the rocky island, and apart from a small pool of rainwater by her side, there was barely room to stretch out.

In her blurred vision, she saw something red on the horizon, and her blood began to run colder still as her vision opened up to reveal another dragon coming upon her. It began to descend, and Marina, weak and still numb from the visions of her last night in civilization, did nothing to defend herself.

The red dragon landed softly with its four legs creating a cage around the limp girl. Marina began to feel the heat emanating from the depths of the dragon.

Her senses returned to her in the warmth and she thought she heard a song. But from under the cliff where she lay, a great fire boiled through the water, and the waves crashed over her as that grey-green bull dragon rose up out of the water. The young woman heard a muffled growling and barely made out words from the depths of each of the scaly beasts.

"Colonah, you cannot attend to my prey if you do not attend to me."

"Halion, my love... what have you done?"

The bull roared,

"Do not mock me. I am no more your love than you are my lover."

"It was you, all along. I have searched the hearts of many and found the answer lay but a beat away from my own heart."

"I am not one to be trifled with, waiting for that which is rightfully mine. You will have my attentions."

"At what cost?"

"Whatever it may be."

"But do you not see that by your manipulations and by your calling forth that which was not yet needed, you have destroyed any hope of gaining that which you seek."

Halion struck at Colonah and grasped her neck in his mighty claws, yanking her up off the semi-conscious woman.

"You are mine."

"Nay, my love, I never will be now."

She scorched his face with the lava-hot breath that billowed up from within her, gingerly picked up the broken Marina, and flew off, leaving Halion dropping into the waves to cool his flaming eyes.

Colonah circled the island rock and Halion tried blindly to follow her, but her wings beat quickly and the air spun around them at such speeds as to suck the very waves up into a water spout.

The clouds, too, descended in a funnel, and as they met, a portal opened. Through it, Colonah soared into the dimensions beyond. Marina breathed her last breath and was still.

Colonah carefully laid the lifeless woman on the open Elysian Fields. She allowed a single tear to drip from her eyes and be absorbed into the forehead of the dead girl.

"What are you doing, Mother?" A beautiful dark-haired woman of timelessness approached in concern.

"This one shares your blood, my sweet Psyche, and now she also shares your fate." Colonah bowed to her.

Psyche knelt before Marina's still, lifeless form and kissed her forehead. She gathered her into her arms and whispered,

"With what love I lost and was once abandoned as you are now, I give you my spirit. Return to your love. Let not history repeat her pain, only her joys."

Marina's blue-tinted skin began to glow warm with fleshly life. She moaned and her eyes fluttered open. Slowly she stood and looked around.

The Fields were beautiful, and her eyes followed the soft road leading onward and upward toward Mount Olympus.

"Am I to stay?" Marina asked.

Psyche smiled and said, "I am offering you the chance I had not: to return to your love, if that is what you wish."

Marina looked at the woman and the dragon and asked, "You know who he is?"

They both nodded.

"He does not frighten me." Marina placed her hand on Colonah's neck and stepped up into a riding position. The Red Mother Dragon rose up from the Fields of the afterlife and returned to the Trevel domain.

The Unraveling

There was no closure.

No one had the chance to tie things up neatly and carry on with life.

Even King Darsaldain found he had not even the energy left to die. The world of the Trevels quieted itself in what their descendants would later call the calm before the storm.

School at Atlantis National Academy reopened with fervor, and all in attendance found the load grueling and gratefully distracting.

Holly and Tanya faced their futures with much less enthusiasm and lost their drive to explore all the vast reaches of their yet-to-be-discovered powers. They realized duty and responsibility were heavy burdens that required sacrifice and survival.

Lexa withdrew as it became clearer that Tanya's affinity with the Bacht was not some passing fad as Holly had professed. In fact, with the pressure of her family's associated reputation laid upon the shoulders of the heiress, Lexa decided to finish out her first year at ANA, then returned home to Under Frisco, where she attended a slightly less exclusive school but began taking on the duties of the family Architectural Empire.

Roland graduated a year early due to summer school attendance through all five years and was taken up quickly by the Lemurian Legions Laray team as the youngest and most promising player since Prince Hadigan himself. He was immediately played as front runner in place of the missing Tambeaux, but all knew he was intended for trout within the next year.

Despite his national Trevel fame, he maintained a home in Atlantis and engaged himself to his high school sweetheart, the shy Katiel of Latoona.

At her ANA graduation, Breezer shocked all her friends by being accepted to the Defense Strategist Officers' Academy and went into training as a Pre-Champion. She graduated top of her class and honored her family with orders of a Champion's Legion Command within the Lemurian Royal Guard.

Joshun and Misty stuck it out together as always. Some say they discarded their privileged schooling by becoming simple tradesfolk. The reality, however, was that they pursed their dreams and opened up what quickly became a chain of the most exclusive designer clothing boutiques in Atlantis, much to the dismay of Sassy Rose, the current Trevel style guru.

Nikkos never felt comfortable in academia and had a rough four years that probably would have been cut much shorter were it not for the frequent intervention and encouragement of Roland on his behalf.

They both maintained the street code that urchins must always stick together, no matter how old they were. But by Nikkos's tenth-form year, he'd had enough and found ties within the darker side of the Trevel trade world that took him to Upland Venice, where he lived his life as a Trevel ambassador and Bacht mechanic.

Holly, too, surprised everyone by completing only four years at ANA. She graduated with her Level One Certificate and found her heart too heavy to go on and complete the final two years of the Level Two Certificate and higher-learning graduation.

She accepted Gash Arabol's offer and retreated to the Blue Castle near her beloved Latoona. There she studied the art of flora transformations with a single-minded dedication, desperate to unravel the mystery of deadwood.

Holly also discovered a new lightheartedness in the company of the awkward chemist. She found solace in him and agreed to be his wife. They found much love and true companionship in their quiet life together.

Midway through Tanya's last two years of her Level 2 Certificate, Mitch received his final Freedom Points Tattoo and was released a free Bacht to find his own fortune in the Trevel world.

With a surprising grant from an anonymous and much-missed donor (for Marin Tambeaux had disappeared into the northern wilds of the Independent Trevel Nation of Kentari in Under Olland)

Mitchell Tambeaux opened up a Laray sporting store and trained young Trevel techies in the art of the Laray obstacle course manufacture and manipulation.

He also opened a youth hostel and took in a number of homeless Trevel urchins and taught them self-discipline through the Bacht martial arts. He was on his way to earning great respect among the Trevel when he made a grave mistake and fatal life decision.

Upon her final graduation, Tanya achieved great recognition as Valedictorian of Atlantis National Academy. But she threw it all away when she accepted Mitch's proposal of marriage. Such a mis-coupling would never be accepted in any society of Trevellia.

The Pact Continues

Marina's Return

Epilogue

The Pact Continues

Mitch and Tanya were married in a private ceremony in the blue-tinted courtyard of Gash and Holly Arabol's under-river castle. Hal and Salla were proudly in attendance, and the father of the bride gripped her fingers tightly as he walked her, teary-eyed, down the aisle.

Also in attendance were Roland and Katiel Rote with their beautiful fat baby girl, who was the very heartbeat of her daddy's life.

Nikkos Botticelli took time out from his busy Venetian mechanics shop, and all the ladies of every nation that hounded him for attention, to be by Mitch's side. He even arranged an all-male bachelor hunting party to go on a drunken camping trek in search of the famous, well-hidden dragons of Latoona.

The dragons watched the men's campfire antics with delight and had to stifle many a laugh so as to not actually be discovered.

Joshun and Misty not only attended but dressed the bride, and her wedding gown, despite being tainted by such a horrendous association, soon became the toast of Trevel fashion.

Breezer took time off and casually re-entered her friends' social circle as a much revered Royal Legions Champion

Commander. To the company at hand, however, she was still the ditzy air-head that didn't always get the joke.

Lexa sent her apologies and a crystal vase, to which, upon opening it, Mitch smiled and said,

"Well, that's much better."

There was one surprise attendee.

As the party wrapped up and the two sisters stepped aside into a private room for a final farewell, they were greeted by a long-forgotten companion who hailed them from their reflection in the mirror.

Colonah smiled at them as she sang.

Holly and Tanya held each other as they stood listening to a familiar song they were not sure they'd ever heard before. Colonah then bowed and spoke her piece to them.

"I bring you grave tidings on this celebration day. There is a storm still brewing in a teapot of long ago. A song is yet to be completed, as the discord was not discarded as it appeared to be."

Holly and Tanya looked fearful and questioned both the Dragon Mother and each other in silent concern. Before she faded from sight, Colonah continued with finality,

"He lives."

Marina's Return

Deep in the mines of Hanain, tests were being conducted and weapons were being forged. The mighty form of Lord Deagan prowled through the deep tunnels on his lion-drawn chariot and inspected the ranks that bred in the dark.

King Darsaldain had constructed a vague truce with Hanain, and the mines continued to feed the High Set with their beloved rare and precious diamonds.

Jaack Mining continued to operate under the scientific overseeing of Professor Mawkes. In fact, the Jaack Mining Company became well known for a special brand of clarity in its diamonds, unseen in other specimens.

The company also continued to ship glitter to Tanya and Mitch while they were at ANA, and the Shifter training grounds held quite the stockpile. Some of this found its way to Upland Venice and some into the outer regions of Kentari. All in all, the smugglers continued to stockpile in secret with hope of some closure sometime in the future.

Few of them kept in much contact with Lord Deagan himself due to the national misrepresentation of that fatal night of the Laray championship game. Lord Deagan preferred it that way and only maintained constant relations with his friend Gash Arabol.

The Shifter Lord contemplated his tenuous present, comparing it to the preparations for his future. He sighed as he wandered through the halls of his palace in the quiet evening hours.

As he only wore his Viking helm when he was about Strategist business, he now wore just his leather pants, wandering through the too-quiet rooms. Distracted, he absent-mindedly walked toward her abandoned quarters, still guarded by the birdcage.

As the Lorikeet whistled his approach, Lord Deagan's heart pulled in his chest. He thought he heard her voice on the wind.

"Come in."

He laid his great hand on the lintel of her doorway and bowed his head, momentarily lost in his memories. He heard it again.

"I am at leisure, if my lord should care to enter."

But this time, her voice was not on the wind. It was clear, and the strength of it made his heart beat hard. Lord Deagan entered her chambers as an untrained knight might enter a dragon lair. His palms were wet and his breath quite ragged.

She stood in the open window as if just alighted from a cloud. Her smile was genuine and she moved to him with grace and ease.

"Are you thirsty, my lord?" She placed her hand on a decanter of wine that had long waited for her return.

Lord Deagan blinked.

"How can this be?"

She smiled and explained,

"Your master is not so strong as to be able to imprison love in his grasp. Indeed, it would seem the more he tries to grasp it to himself, the more it slips through his fingers."

The Minotaur shook his head and strained to speak. "I cannot have you know and remain."

Marina walked nearer.

"But I do know, and am returned to you."

He was adamant.

"You cannot stay."

Marina placed her pale hand upon his red fury cheek.

"That is not your decision to make. I am here of my own will. I am here to be yours, and you don't get to claim or not claim what is given freely."

Lord Deagan could only raise his hand and lay it on hers at his cheek.

Marina whispered,

"I want to see you."

He paused a moment, then shivered out of form and stood bare chested before her, his black curls falling across his dark eyes and long slender nose.

She leaned in to kiss him and he embraced her with great passion.

Finis

Dragon Song Lullaby

from "Chronicles of Trevel; Dragon Tears"

Gregga J. Johnn
Lyndee Coleman

Review Requested:

As a reader, welcome to my family!

If you loved this book, would you please, kindly provide a review at Amazon.com?

Your input is appreciated, so if you have any concerns regarding this book, please contact me personally at greggajjohnn@gmail.com

If you didn't like this book at all, because stranger things have happened, feel free to find another book to read.

My blessings go with you

Peace and Goodwill to you all!

ABOUT THE AUTHOR

Gregga J. Johnn is a transient writer and performer. She has traveled around Australia performing in schools with poetry and puppets, and has over twenty years of experience on stage and small screens, in Australia and the USA; acting, directing and writing.

Currently, she lives on the spirit-filled, Springhill Farm outside Cedar Rapids, Iowa. There she builds her creative business, "Story-in-the-Wings," writing, performing, creating art, and directing. She is often seen as Artist in Residence at Usher's Ferry Historic Village creating seasonal events and Parlor Theatre presentations.

Gregga's published stories are available through Createspace, Amazon, and Kindle. She specializes in Fantasy/Sci-fi and allegory. All that she is doing can be explored on her website;

> greggajjohnn.wix.com/writer-performer

Passing on the Story of Life is her greatest passion. She believes everyone has a story to tell and cannot wait to hear yours.

END NOTE

(Rating is the author's suggestion only)

The Trevel Story-verse: (in chronological order)

"Bacht, welcome to the world of the Trevel."

The Forgotten Mermaid, *novella [M15+ rating, for mild horror and sensuality]*

Diamonds, Beetles, and Lucky at War, *booklet [M15+ rating, for bawdy profanity]*

The Last Poinsettia, *booklet [G+ rating, a Family Christmas Tale]*

The Tales of the Trevel, *collection of short stories [M15+ rating, for bawdy jokes]*

The Chronicles of Trevel; Dragon Tears, *novel [PG-13+ rating, YA+]*

The Chronicles of Trevel; Dragon Sweat, *novel [PG-13+ rating, YA+]* (TBA)

The Chronicles of Trevel; Dragon Blood, *novel [PG-13+ rating, YA+]* (TBA)

More books by Gregga J. Johnn from outside the Trevel Story-verse:

Seven Stories for Seven Sons, *Bedtime stories for Imagineers of all Ages.* [Family rating]

The Magical, Fantastical World of Springhill Farm, *novella* [PG-13+ rating, YA+]

How I Saved Myselves; an expose on the inner healing of a "crazy" mind, *Inspirational booklet* [M15+ Real World Issues]

Save Our Souls, *a play with a short pre-show play,* "Thumbs Up, A.OK" [Mental Illness M15+ Real World Issues]

Collecting Thoughts and Dreams, *an anthology of short stories and poems.* (TBA)

Intimate Meditations, *a prayer and meditation devotional* (TBA)

Transforming Weakness into Well Living, *a prayer and meditation devotional* (TBA)

Perception, *an allegorical novel* (TBA)

Check out Gregga's website at:

greggajjohnn.wix.com/writer-performer

All books in print are available through Createspace, Amazon, and Kindle.

For special discounts on bulk purchases, contact Gregga at **greggajjohnn@gmail.com**

Made in the USA
Charleston, SC
09 March 2016